FORBIDDEN PASSION

How many other women had he seduced so effortlessly with his male magnetism? she wondered. How had such a half-breed acquired such sophisticated talents? And what was she doing in his arms, responding to him with an eagerness that shocked her?

"Don't," Shannon gasped. She was shaking from head to toe as she pushed herself from Blade's arms.

My God! Blade thought, nearly as shaken as Shannon. If he continued like this he'd be bedding her on the hard ground in another moment. "This is what you wanted, isn't it?" he taunted. It took considerable effort to make his voice deliberately cruel and cynical.

"Are you trying to humiliate me?" Shannon struggled for breath, his cruel words fueling her anger.

"Is this why you came out here?" Blade replied with sly innuendo. "Does a half-breed kiss any differently from a white man? Or did you pick me to experiment on because I'm only half tame and the thought excited you?"

BEYOND THE HORIZON

CONNIE MASON

LOVE SPELL BOOKS NEW YORK CITY

LOVE SPELL®

April 1999

Published by

Dorchester Publishing Co., Inc.
276 Fifth Avenue
New York, NY 10001

ISBN 0-505-52306-X

Prologue

"Damn Yankee," *Shannon Branigan whispered,* hating the sight of Harlan Simmons lounging insolently on the elegant veranda as she twisted her head for one last look at her beloved home and family. Then she tightened her grip on the buggy reins and clucked the horse into a quicker trot down the long lane. Nothing remained for the Branigans now in Georgia, Shannon thought sadly as she dashed a tear from the corner of her eye. The old life was gone. Twin Willows belonged to that yellow-bellied carpetbagger now; her father was dead by his own hand, driven to the deed by the Yankees; and her brother Grady had been slain on the battlefield, sacrificing his youth for a lost cause.

"Are you all right, dear?"

Shannon turned her head and attempted a smile at her great aunt seated next to her in the buggy. Though Shannon had volunteered willingly to remain behind in Atlanta with Great Aunt Eugenia while the rest of the Branigans left to make a new life in Idaho, separation from her close-knit family was tearing her apart. It all seemed so final.

"I'm fine, Aunt Eugenia, truly."

But was she fine? Vividly she recalled her brother Tucker's parting words.

"We'll write as soon as we reach Boise," Tucker had said.

"Don't worry about me, Tuck," she had answered. "Aunt Eugenia and I are going to be fine. The Yankees haven't beaten the Branigans. They just think they have." But her brave words had fooled no one, least of all herself. How long would it be before she could rejoin her family in Idaho?

Shannon wasn't the only family member to remain behind. Seventeen-year-old Devlin had been arguing with Tucker for days about Devlin's refusal to run from the Yankees with his tail tucked between his legs, as he so aptly put it. He insisted on remaining behind to accomplish Lord only knew what. Shannon could sympathize with Dev. Both she and Dev were famous for their tempers and were known as the hotheads of the family.

Though Eugenia's watery blue eyes were dimmed by age, her agile mind grasped and understood perfectly her great-niece's anguish. A tremendous outpouring of love and compassion encompassed this special girl who had given up so much for an old lady unlikely to see the year through.

"You should be going with your family," Aunt Eugenia said in a dry whisper that spoke eloquently of her frailness, her inability to make the monumental journey the other Branigans were undertaking.

"You're my family, too," Shannon reminded her gently. "I'm here because I want to be, Aunt Eugenia. We'll show those damn Yankees they can't run us out."

* * *

Washington, D.C.—April 1867

"The President will see you now, Captain Stryker."

The man who walked through the door to the president's office wore the blue uniform of the Union Army, but that wasn't what set him apart from other young men his age. There was an indescribable power about him, as well as something profoundly mysterious.

"Come in and sit down, Captain Stryker," President Johnson invited. "As you can see, Major Vance is already here."

With a nod and a smile, Blade Stryker acknowledged his commanding officer and friend of many years. Then he directed his undivided attention back to the president. It was the first time he had met President Johnson, and he thought him a rather stern, unprepossessing sort of man.

"I suppose you're wondering why I sent for you," the president began, "but Major Vance assures me you are exactly the man I am looking for."

Blade raised a black eyebrow, slanting Major Vance a quizzical glance.

"I don't know what Major Vance told you, but I hope he mentioned I'm mustering out of the army and returning home."

"Just where is home?"

"Wyoming Territory—mostly," Blade replied somewhat mysteriously.

"Major Vance apprised me of your history, Captain, so there's no need for pretense here."

"I hope you don't think I was betraying a confidence, Blade," Major Vance interjected, "but I knew immediately you were the right man for the job."

"Then you know I am a half-breed, sir," Blade said with quiet dignity, addressing the president.

"I know you are a fine officer and a credit to the

army. I am curious, though, as to how and why you joined the war."

"My mother is full-blooded Ogallala Sioux, another name for the powerful Dakotas. My father was a French trapper. He fell in love with my mother and married her according to Indian rites. I was raised by the Sioux until my seventeenth year, when Father decided I needed to learn about the white man's world. He sent me east to school.

"When the war between the North and South began, I knew I must fight on the side of freedom for all races. Few knew of my mixed blood, so it was easy to join the Union Army."

"An interesting story, Captain Stryker. May I call you Blade?" Blade nodded. "I am convinced you are just the man I need. Will you listen to what I have to say, son?"

"Of course, sir, but it won't change my mind about leaving the army."

"There has been increasing unrest on the plains," President Johnson explained. "The great Indian tribes are unhappy with the treaty of '57 dividing the plains into territories and giving the Indians boundaries. Not only are the different tribes encroaching upon each other's hunting lands but they are openly warring with whites. They are attacking wagon trains and emigrants traveling the Oregon Trail, disrupting communications, and preventing the railroad from meeting its deadline.

"These atrocities must stop, Blade. People are dying every day, not only whites but Indians. But as long as guns are being smuggled to the Indians these unprovoked attacks will continue."

"Excuse me, Mr. President, but haven't the Indians been complaining for years about being cheated, of Washington not living up to the treaty agreement? What about dishonest agents who deliberately lie and cheat Indians out of provisions due them?" Blade challenged boldly.

"Blade, we don't know the Indians are being

cheated," Major Vance injected in an effort to disarm Blade's criticism.

"I won't deny there are dishonest men out there, but that is not the point. Guns are what I'm talking about," President Johnson continued. "Illegal weapons delivered into the hands of hot-blooded young men of the tribes who use them to raid and kill indiscriminately."

"I don't see how I can be of help," Blade said carefully.

"We think someone at Fort Laramie in Wyoming is arranging for the guns to be brought west by wagon train. Whoever this man is takes delivery, then sells the weapons to renegade Indians."

"You suspect an army man?" Blade asked.

"Not necessarily. It could be one of the townspeople, but all the information we have thus far indicates the involvement of someone directly connected to the army."

"And you want me to find out who that man is," Blade surmised. "I've already turned in my resignation."

"All the better," President Johnson replied. "We've already lost one man, a special agent sent to Fort Laramie to investigate, who was never heard from again. What I'd like you to do is carry out an investigation as an Indian, someone least likely to be suspect. Go back to your tribe. You're bound to learn who is dealing in guns from the young braves of the tribe. They are the ones to watch. But it is vitally important, Blade, that no one, absolutely no one, knows you are a special agent or connected to the army or office of the president. I've enough trouble on the homefront without answering to charges of concentrating on far-flung frontiers."

"I understand, sir. If I decide to accept, is there some special way I'm to travel to Fort Laramie?"

"Major Vance has made arrangements for you to travel with a wagon train as guide. You'll take them as far as Fort Laramie, where they will pick up a new guide and continue on to Oregon."

"The train captain is a man named Clive Bailey," said Major Vance. "He runs the trading post at Fort Laramie. We think he is one of those transporting illegal guns across the plains. Your first priority will be to learn if our suspicions are correct. This Bailey could very well be the man we're after.

"I know you are familiar with the territory," Vance continued, "and it would be essential for you to rely on your Indian instincts. The train captain will be informed you are a half-breed."

"I see," Blade acknowledged stiffly. "A half-breed who is considered barely human; a half-savage whom people fear and despise." He couldn't keep the note of bitterness from creeping into his voice.

"It is the only way, Blade," President Johnson said by way of apology. "Life as you know it will cease to exist if you accept this assignment. Your only contact will be Major Vance, who is being sent to Fort Laramie as second in command under Colonel Greer. Do you have an Indian name?"

"Among the Sioux I am known as Swift Blade."

"When you reach Independence you will become Swift Blade. All your Indian upbringing must be utilized if you are to survive. Forget the ten years you've lived as a white man and rely solely on your Indian instincts. Will you accept the assignment? A reward goes along with the capture of our man."

Blade looked at Wade Vance for guidance. They had been friends for a long time and he respected the major's views. Besides, Blade wasn't a rich man and the reward would come in handy. "You would be doing the country a great service, Blade," Major Vance reminded him.

It was enough.

"I'll do it, sir," Blade replied, answering the president's question.

Chapter One

*G*olden daffodils bloomed on the hillside and the gentle breeze was fragrant with the promise of spring, yet Shannon saw nothing but the fresh mound of earth at her feet where Great Aunt Eugenia had just been laid to rest. Who would have thought a little over a month ago when the rest of the Branigan family left for Idaho that Eugenia would die so abruptly of heart seizure? Though she had been too frail to survive the long overland trip by wagon train to Idaho, Eugenia wasn't in ill health when one considered her great age of eighty-nine.

Not once did Shannon consider herself exceptional for selflessly volunteering to remain behind in Atlanta with Aunt Eugenia instead of joining her family on their trek West. To Shannon it was an act of love, for she cared deeply about the old woman. Sense of family was strong in the Branigan clan and Shannon had inherited more than her share. She had planned sometime in the future to join the rest of the

Branigans in Idaho, traveling by train, for it was only a matter of a year or two before the railroad would stretch from coast to coast.

But Eugenia's sudden death had changed everything. There was still a possibility, albeit a slim one, that Tuck, Mama, and the little ones hadn't left Independence yet. It was that small chance that had provoked Shannon into selling Aunt Eugenia's house to a despised Yankee and using some of the money to purchase a train ticket to Independence, hoping to catch up to her family before they started West with the wagon train.

"Come on, Shannon. Standing here staring at Aunt Eugenia's grave won't bring her back."

Venturing a watery smile, Shannon turned and followed her brother Devlin from the cemetery. He was right; Aunt Eugenia wouldn't want her to grieve. Thank God Dev had heard about Eugenia's death. He'd arrived just in time to lend Shannon the support she needed. Dev had a penchant for turning up at the right moment. Hard telling where he'd be a week from now, but at least he was here to help her with the funeral and her travel arrangements.

"Are you certain you won't come with me, Dev?" Shannon asked hopefully. "There is still a good chance we can catch up with the family."

"Positive, Shannon. I've already had it out with Tuck, so don't you try to persuade me when my mind is made up. I wish you all well, but I'm taking charge of my own future."

The funeral had been a large one, for Aunt Eugenia had been well loved in life. But sadly, nothing Shannon could do or say stopped Devlin from leaving shortly afterwards. He hugged her fiercely, wished her well, and departed. Her aunt's passing and Devlin's leaving created a void in Shannon's heart that nearly defeated her. But Shannon knew Eugenia's philosophy wouldn't have allowed for maudlin sentiments. She recalled their last conversation.

"Once I'm gone, get on with your life, Shannon,"

the astute old woman had advised. "Don't let the horrors of war and the loss of loved ones stunt you emotionally. You're an exceptionally strong young woman with beauty and brains to match. Love will come one day when you least expect it, and I suspect you will embrace it with the same courage and selflessness that made you volunteer to remain in Atlanta with me."

Those were the last words Eugenia had spoken, for that night she had suffered a seizure and died. They were words Shannon would have cause to remember time and again.

Before Shannon left Atlanta she posted a letter to her mother in care of her cousin, Keegan Branigan, who lived in Idaho City and had urged the family to settle in the West. If she wasn't able to catch up to her family, the letter would reach them shortly after their arrival.

Dear Mama,

I'm on my way to Idaho! I'm sorry to report Aunt Eugenia died peacefully a short time after you left Atlanta. I'm leaving for Independence tomorrow in hopes of catching up to you, but if I don't, this letter will reach you soon after you arrive in Boise.

Devlin came to the funeral, and I tried to persuade him to come west with me, but as usual he was being obstinate. The Yankees are making Atlanta a living hell, and I'm glad to get out of here. I can't imagine why Dev refuses to leave. One day he'll show up when we least expect it.

I'll see you soon, Mama. Give my love to Tuck and the little ones.

Your devoted daughter,
Shannon

* * *

Independence, Missouri—June 1867

"I'm sorry, lady, the Branigan party left Independence over two months ago. By now they are well on their way along the Oregon Trail."

Weariness etched deep lines across Shannon's brow and profound disappointment dulled the sparkle of her deep blue eyes. With a toss of her rich chestnut curls she quelled the urge to vent her famous temper at God for allowing this to happen. Still, it wasn't the end of the world, Shannon thought, squaring her narrow shoulders.

"Two months!" she mused aloud. "I haven't enough money left for the stage coach. But if I join another wagon train I'll be able to meet my family in Idaho."

"Beggin' yer pardon, lady," the man said, "but it's gettin' a mite late in the year. Most wagon trains have already begun their journey."

A look of absolute horror crossed Shannon's lovely features. "You mean I'm stranded in Independence until next spring?"

The man she spoke with owned the outfitting store which, sooner or later, most emigrants found cause to visit while in Independence. He seemed to know everything and everyone.

"Well now," he said, scratching his whiskered chin, "might be yer in luck. There's a wagon train formin' outside town fer latecomers."

"Who do I talk to?" Shannon asked, heartened. Perhaps God hadn't abandoned her after all.

"Have yer man talk to Clive Bailey, he's the train captain and organizer. He owns the trading post at Fort Laramie and is carrying supplies to sell in his store. If you can't find him, ask for a man who calls himself Blade."

My man? Shannon thought dully. But before she could give voice to the question teasing the tip of her tongue a deep male voice asked, "Did someone mention my name?"

He stood like a tall shadow in the doorway of the store with the sun at his back blotting out his features. The breadth of his shoulders touched the jamb on either side and the magnificent expanse of torso and slim hips was supported by legs as sturdy as oaks. Shannon shuddered, feeling oddly threatened as he moved toward her with the rolling gait of a stalking panther, his pelvis pivoting in a manner so blatantly masculine that Shannon felt a dull red crawl up her neck.

"This young woman was ask'n 'bout joining yer wagon train, Blade," the storekeeper explained as he turned away to help another customer. "I'll leave you two to make arrangements."

Blade turned the full magnetic power of his penetrating black eyes on the young woman—he judged her to be under twenty—staring at him with unrestrained curiosity. She was a fetching little thing, he reflected, with chestnut hair neither red nor brown but rich and glowing with golden highlights. Her pert nose sported a sprinkling of tawny freckles and her full lower lip was caught between small white teeth. Deep blue eyes, wide and intelligent, sloped upward at their corners. A thrill of anticipation caught Blade by the scruff of his neck and refused to let go as Shannon fearlessly met his gaze, her eyes narrowing when she belatedly perceived what made this man so different from any others she had met.

He was an Indian!

Not only was he a member of a race feared and despised by good people everywhere for their cruelty and heathenish ways, but he wore the tattered jacket of a Union army soldier, thereby adding insult to injury. He looked ruthless, dangerous, and quite capable of violence.

"If you and your husband want to join the wagon train you have little time left in which to outfit a wagon. Clive Bailey is the captain and organizer. He'll advise you if you need help," Blade said, a brash smile hanging on the corner of his mouth. The young woman's reaction when she recognized his heritage had amused him.

It was puzzling, Blade thought in a burst of insight, that impeccably turned out in his army uniform, his hair cut to a respectable length and his face pale from Eastern winters, no one suspected he was Sioux. Yet now, dressed in buckskins, his shoulder-length hair held back by a rawhide headband, his skin burnt a deep bronze, he was unmistakably identified as a half-breed "savage."

"I—have no husband," Shannon stuttered, momentarily stunned by Blade's blatant sexuality.

His eyes were the dark black of night, mysterious and unrelenting, framed by thick, spiky lashes. His brows, finely drawn and faintly slanting, were velvet black. His mouth was wide and sensual, one corner tilted just enough to reveal the sardonic wit that doubtless lay behind his ruggedly handsome features. And there was no denying, Shannon admitted with brutal honesty, that the Indian was handsome. His features spoke eloquently of a bold nature, and those large, strong hands suggested a power and strength she could only guess at.

"You're not married?" Blade repeated sharply. "Single women aren't welcome on this wagon train unless they are traveling with family. How old are you Miss—?"

"Branigan. Shannon Branigan. I'm twenty, old enough to take care of myself."

"Hardly old enough to undertake a hazardous journey on your own. It is out of the question, Miss Branigan. Go back home where you belong."

Shannon bristled indignantly. No Indian, no matter how imposing or intimidating, was going to dictate to her. "Perhaps Mr. Bailey will have something to say about it."

"Clive Bailey might be train captain, but I'm wagon master and guide. Without me the wagon train can't leave Independence. I say you're not going. Furthermore," Blade stated, "I know of no other wagon train willing to take on an unattached woman as young and pretty as you. I suggest you find yourself a husband, Miss Branigan, if you want to travel West."

His dark face was stern and unrelenting, but undaunted, Shannon pressed on, forced to resort to the feminine wiles she abhorred. But desperate times called for desperate measures.

"I have no home, Mr.—Blade, that is your name, isn't it?"

Blade nodded warily. "I am known as Swift Blade among the Sioux, but Blade will do."

"My family left two months ago for Idaho. I remained in Atlanta to care for an elderly aunt who died unexpectedly and left me all alone in the world." She batted feathery eyelashes, managing to squeeze out a tear from the corners of her eyes.

"So you can see how desperate I am to leave." Her voice assumed a tremulous quality few men could resist. But Shannon had already guessed that Blade was not like most men. "If I joined your wagon train, I'll be able to meet my family in Idaho."

"Spare me your tears, Miss Branigan," Blade said, unmoved. "A beautiful young woman like you on a wagon train would only cause trouble. Big trouble. My answer is still no. Now if you'll excuse me, I've some last minute purchases to make."

Blade's refusal unleashed Shannon's famous Irish temper and she lashed out viciously at the handsome half-breed whose language sounded far too refined for an Indian, even while his bold, dark features spoke eloquently of his savage ancestry.

"Somehow I doubt you have the final say on this wagon train, Mr.—er, Blade," Shannon observed, her lip curling derisively. "What civilized man would trust his life to a wild Indian? You might speak like a white man, but you are pure savage. What poor soldier did you steal that jacket from? Let's hope he still has his scalp."

Stunned by her scathing insult, Blade stood stiffly aside as Shannon pushed past him and out the door, her skirts swaying in angry motion around her shapely ankles. It was the first time he could remember being rendered absolutely speechless by a female!

"Damn infuriating woman," Blade muttered beneath his breath as he approached the counter to make his purchases. When he passed a woman customer lingering nearby, she deliberately swept her skirts aside, her face a mask of disgust and fear. With Sioux uprisings now threatening the frontier, few if any decent citizens had any truck with savages.

Outwardly, Blade exhibited no reaction to the woman's insult, but inwardly he seethed with impotent rage. How ironic that he was good enough to fight for equality for all men, yet was treated like an outcast for the very reasons that persuaded him to join the war. Having lived as a white man for so many years had spoiled him; he had grown unaccustomed to being openly shunned and ridiculed. He felt shamed, for he had nearly forgotten his proud heritage and the noble people whose features he bore.

As Blade Stryker, handsome, mysterious army officer, women were drawn to him like bees to honey. He was sought most diligently by some of the loveliest ladies in Washington. But his transformation from army captain Blade Stryker to Sioux half-breed Swift Blade changed him overnight into a loathsome creature unworthy of respect. Even Clive Bailey, who needed his expertise on the trail, treated him with barely concealed contempt.

Blade had been in Independence nearly a month, snooping and secretly searching each wagon train for hidden weapons as they formed outside the city. Thus far he had found nothing incriminating, which was why he had narrowed his sights on the wagon train Clive Bailey had organized. Blade thought Bailey a

wily scoundrel. He was damn slick—a dishonest type
who probably cared little that providing guns to
Indians could result in the loss of countless lives to
both whites and Indians. If the man was a gun
smuggler, Blade intended to find out. As special agent
to the president, he took his duty seriously. No
woman, no matter how beautiful, was going to interfere with his assignment. And intuitively Blade knew
Miss Shannon Branigan represented more trouble
than he needed.

"I'm looking for Clive Bailey."

Clive Bailey peered over his shoulder at the striking,
chestnut-haired woman addressing him. She was a
looker all right, Clive decided, raking her tantalizing
face and form with slow relish.

"I'm Clive Bailey. What can I do for you, miss?"

Shannon had rented a buggy and driven herself
outside town to where the wagon train was forming so
that she might speak to Clive Bailey personally.
Fortunately, the Indian wagon master was nowhere in
sight and Shannon visibly relaxed. That man was far
too intimidating for her liking. "I'm Shannon
Branigan and I understand you are the man to talk to
about joining your wagon train."

"Do you and your husband have a wagon, Mrs.
Branigan?" Clive asked, disappointed that the little
beauty was already spoken for.

"I'm not married," Shannon said, lifting her chin
defiantly. "Does it matter?"

"You're going West alone? What about your family?" Clive was impressed by Shannon's willingness to
undertake the hazardous journey alone and unprotected.

"To make a long story short, my family left for
Idaho two months ago with an earlier wagon train. I
want to join them and yours is the last wagon train
forming this spring."

"It's more or less an unwritten law that young
women travel only in the protection of family or

husband. I'm sorry, Miss Branigan, but I don't think—"

"Please, Mr. Bailey, can't you make an exception?" Shannon implored. "Isn't there some family I could travel with? I'd work hard, and I could pay something for my passage West. I just don't have enough money to stay in Independence till spring."

"You are far too young and beautiful to be traveling alone, Miss Branigan, and there are too many unattached males along for me to believe your presence would go unnoticed or unappreciated. But perhaps this one time . . . ." he relented, never one to turn down an opportunity when one presented itself. Shannon Branigan looked ripe for the plucking, and he was a man who relished tender ripe fruit.

The fiery glow in Clive's pale eyes should have alerted Shannon, but she was too excited to notice.

"It's out of the question. Miss Branigan has no place on this wagon train."

Shannon raised startled eyes to meet Blade's determined gaze.

"You've met Miss Branigan?" Clive asked, furious that a half-breed savage had the audacity to address a lady.

He had employed Blade as wagon master and guide because Blade had been highly recommended and Clive needed him. This late in the year most qualified guides had already been hired. It grated on Clive's nerves to see Blade put on airs, as if he were as good as a white man. But at this late date Clive was grateful to find a competent man to lead them to Fort Laramie. Clive had too much at stake to wait around until next year, his cargo too precious for lengthy delays. If Clive hadn't had problems obtaining his goods, he would have left weeks ago.

"We've met," Blade said tersely, favoring Shannon with a brief nod. "And I won't have her disrupting my wagon train."

"You seem to forget you work for me," Clive said

bluntly. "I can always find another guide."

Blade's anger simmered as he struggled to keep from boiling out of control. Orders from Washington were to investigate Clive Bailey, and the only way he could do that was by remaining with the outfit. However, he felt obliged to point out the dangers involved in accepting an unattached female. Especially one as lovely as Shannon Branigan.

"Who will protect her when every randy buck on the wagon train starts fighting over her?"

"I can take care of myself!" Shannon shot back, angered over the way the two men talked over her but not at her, as if she weren't capable of making her own decisions.

"The hell you can!" Blade blasted, his hot temper erupting. Then realizing how he sounded, his voice softened. "Look, Miss Branigan, I have nothing against you personally, I just don't want to see you hurt."

"Strange words from a savage," Shannon snorted, tossing her tangle of chestnut curls.

Clive roared with laughter, delighting in Shannon's show of spirit. If the intimidating half-breed wasn't built like a bull and didn't look tougher than a two-bit steak, he would have put him in his place himself. "The lady is no cream puff, Blade. I think she will manage just fine. I'll see that no harm comes to her." And bed her in the process, he thought.

Blade's full lips tautened, stung by the smug expression on Shannon's face. He didn't like the way things were going one damn bit, but he had little power to change them. The strange light in Bailey's eyes told Blade exactly what plans the man had in mind for the unsuspecting Shannon Branigan. Still, he might be able to salvage something out of this, find a way to thwart Bailey's devious intentions for the young woman. She was too innocent to realize what Bailey intended for her and determined enough to make her way West some other way if she didn't travel with them. If she had to go, at least she would be where he could keep an eye on her, Blade reflected, though why it should matter to him totally escaped him.

"All right, it's your decision," Blade finally agreed.

His decided lack of enthusiasm did little to bolster Shannon's shaky conviction that she was doing the right thing by traveling alone. She wasn't ignorant of the dangers involved, just determined to catch up with her family. Tucker always said she was too stubborn and impulsive for her own good. "But I insist on finding Miss Branigan a place on the wagon train myself," Blade added.

"See to it, Blade," Clive ordered, sending Blade off with a careless wave of his hand.

Try though she might, Shannon couldn't take her eyes off Blade's loose-limbed gait as he strode off, his spine stiff and proudly defiant. His moccasined feet made silent footsteps on the dusty ground and his taut buttocks, tightly encased in fringed buckskin trousers, moved with sinuous grace. His shoulders beneath the offensive blue jacket were wide and impressive. Then, incredibly, her imagination took her on a forbidden path, for she could almost feel the smooth bronze skin of his torso beneath her fingertips.

Mercifully, Clive Bailey interrupted her dangerous mental journey.

"Miss Branigan—Shannon. May I call you Shannon?" When she nodded, Clive continued smoothly, "A word of caution about the half-breed. He comes highly recommended, but as you just saw he has lost none of his savage ways. It is unwise to trust him. I strongly urge you to steer clear of Swift Blade. Well-bred young ladies don't consort with Indians."

"I appreciate your advice, Mr. Bailey, and I assure you that Blade is not someone I'd care to associate with." Shannon had thought Blade full Indian but felt little comfort in learning he was a half-breed.

"It's just as well, Shannon—and please call me Clive. Everyone else on the wagon train does. It will be a wonderful experience, you'll see," he predicted. Especially for me, he added silently.

Chapter Two

Shannon hung on for dear life as the awkward prairie schooner, pulled by eight lumbering oxen, jerked into motion. Beside her on the unsprung bench sat the very pregnant Callie Johnson and her young husband Howie, who wielded the whip above the oxen's sturdy backs with amazing dexterity for an Ohio farmer.

Shannon was more than happy to be sharing the Johnsons' wagon rather than buying her own and hiring a driver. The cost of purchasing her own equipment would have been more than double what she paid the Johnsons for her passage. She hated to give Blade credit for the idea, but it was working out well. Callie was grateful for the company and someone with whom to share the chores, for her pregnancy hadn't been an easy one. Howie was also agreeable, concern for his young wife reason enough to share their wagon with a virtual stranger. Another pair of hands was always welcome on so arduous a journey.

From the corner of her eye Shannon saw Blade working his way down the line, speaking with each driver, offering encouragement where needed. Less than a week ago she had been introduced to the Johnsons, each sizing the other up as potential traveling companions. After a few hours spent in their company, Shannon felt right at home with the young couple, impressed by their courage and determination in seeking a new life despite their parents' objections to their marriage.

Callie's parents were wealthy tradesmen, while Howie's were poor dirt farmers. Despite countless obstacles and against all odds, the unlikely couple fell deeply in love, meeting in secret. When Callie became pregnant, they fled Ohio, fearing reprisals. Oregon and a new life beckoned and nearly all their savings were used to purchase a wagon, oxen, and the supplies necessary for the trip. They were married in Independence just a few days ago. Callie's condition was the only drawback to the great adventure they had undertaken.

"Everything all right, Howie?"

Blade's deep voice brought instant awareness and a tenseness to Shannon's body. For an electrifying eternity, black eyes burned deeply into blue ones, and Shannon was aware of nothing but his overwhelming presence. The very arrogance of this half-breed seared her, confused her, scattered her wits.

"Everything's just fine, Blade," Howie grinned with boyish enthusiasm.

"We'll keep to the old emigrant trail along the Blue Ridge Road," Blade informed him, finding it difficult to concentrate on anything but the play of sunlight on Shannon's chestnut curls. "I'll see you at the nooning."

With a curt nod, he rode off on his rangy gray pony. He looked every bit the savage with a battered felt hat covering his shoulder-length black hair. His superbly conditioned body was clad in deerskin trousers, with rows of long fringe along the seams, the same disreputable army jacket he constantly wore, and moccasins on his feet. The long knife attached to his belt looked dangerous and lethal. Once Blade disappeared from sight Shannon slipped back into her mental musings.

Her trip to Independence from Atlanta had been tedious and uneventful. She had taken a train from Atlanta to St. Louis, then traveled by riverboat on the Mississippi River to Independence. Thank heavens she had arrived in time to join Clive Bailey's wagon train for it was the last of the season. Composed mostly of latecomers and stragglers, the wagon train was small compared to others, which sometimes numbered two hundred wagons. Clive Bailey's outfit consisted of fifty-six wagons and two hundred people, including emigrants and outriders. They were accompanied by a herd of five hundred cattle and other diverse livestock owned by the emigrants.

They had left Independence just as the sun broke out of a bank of gray clouds. With slow precision the wagons rolled forward, each taking a previously assigned position in line. At the wagon master's signal, outriders galloped far ahead of the line with a whoop and a holler, working off some of their pent-up impatience. The prairie schooners then lumbered across the Missouri border and into the prairie.

At first the track was narrow, checkered with sunshine and shadowy woods, until, over an intervening belt of bushes, a green oceanlike expanse of prairie stretched to the horizon. For Shannon it was a moment of high excitement as well as one of nostalgia, for never again would her life be the same, never again would she see her beloved Atlanta and Twin Willows. She imagined how Tucker and her mother must have felt when they left on their own journey West.

After an hour or two, both Shannon and Callie joined most of the other women and children who made the going easier by walking beside the swaying, lumbering wagons. Mile upon mile of black-eyed susans grew in abundance amidst the tall prairie grass, and Shannon soon found herself stopping frequently along the way to gather up huge bouquets of the beautiful flowers.

"Don't lag too far behind, Miss Branigan."

Startled, Shannon glanced up to find Blade staring down at her from atop his gray pony, his dark eyes regarding her with penetrating thoroughness. Realizing how she must look with her sweat-soaked dress clinging to her body in a revealing manner—she had long since shed her petticoats—Shannon gathered the armful of flowers to her bosom, unaware of how wonderfully the yellow flowers complemented the golden tones of her skin.

Shannon didn't realize she had lagged so far behind until Blade rode up to remind her. Callie had gone inside the wagon to nap, and Shannon couldn't resist the urge to stop and pick wildflowers. Belatedly she noted the last of the wagons had left her far behind.

"I—didn't realize," Shannon stammered. "It won't happen again." The last thing she wanted was to draw attention to herself.

"Be certain it doesn't," Blade warned sternly. "We can't afford delay. It is too late in the year to accommodate daydreamers who become lost on the prairie and slow us down."

"I said I was sorry!" Shannon snapped, wondering why Blade was making so large an issue out of a small lapse. "I promise to be more careful."

Then, before Shannon knew what he intended, Blade swooped down and lifted her into the saddle in front of him. "What are you doing?"

"Taking you back to the wagon."

"I can walk."

"Look ahead. At the rate you're going you won't catch them until nightfall. I'm responsible for every person on this wagon train, including you."

Blade's hand was a hot brand against her ribs as he held Shannon firmly against the hardness of his body. The contact was electrifying, and far too stimulating for Shannon's liking. Why should a man like Blade affect her in such a strange manner when dozens of beaux back in Atlanta had failed to move her? She had reached the ripe age of twenty with her heart untouched and her emotions intact and no savage was going to change that! One day she hoped to meet a man she could love and marry, but only with the approval of her family. Nowhere in her life was there room for a half-breed who wore a Yankee jacket with a confidence and pride that irritated her.

Every place that Shannon touched, Blade burned. The little minx had no idea what she did to him. He was more than a little confused at the power exerted over him by a spoiled Southern belle he'd met mere days ago. From the moment he saw her he knew she was someone special, someone who could mean something to him if he allowed it. It was for that reason that he rebelled against the crazy attraction that sprang to life the moment they came into contact with each other. Shannon Branigan represented a dangerous distraction he could ill afford to indulge. The assignment he had accepted required all his wits about him. The only way he could function properly, Blade decided, was to make Shannon hate him, and from all indications he was succeeding only too well, for the fiery Irish lass couldn't wait to be rid of his annoying company.

Just being a half-breed earned Shannon's contempt, Blade reasoned. Most respectable women steered clear of Indians, though Blade had to admit that some of the females on the wagon train appeared eager to claim his attention. But not Shannon Branigan, which was probably good considering his unaccountable attraction to her. But Lord, she smelled delicious, like the sweet-scented wildflowers she still clutched to her breast. And she felt so soft, so damn soft, causing his hand to tighten almost painfully against her ribs. With a will of its own his thumb separated from his palm and grazed the curved underside of her breast.

The light brushing stroke was so fleeting, Shannon thought she had imagined it. But she didn't have long to dwell on it, for Blade was already lowering her to the ground beside the Johnson wagon.

"See that you don't stray again," he warned. Then he rode off toward the head of the long line of wagons, leaving Shannon flushed and confused.

"My, he's handsome," sighed Callie, an incurable romantic. After her nap she had climbed into the seat beside Howie. Now she descended to join Shannon.

Shannon snorted, an explosive, unladylike sound. "He's a half-breed." Her tone indicated no other explanation was necessary.

"I don't think I've ever seen a more compelling man, red or white. He's so powerful and outrageously virile that just looking at him frightens me." Callie shivered delicately. "It's no wonder he has all the young women on the wagon train agog over him."

"Not me," Shannon denied, blue eyes snapping. "The other girls are welcome to him."

"Nancy Wilson will be glad to hear that," Callie teased. "She was a mite worried when you joined the wagon train. Until you arrived, she was considered the prettiest single girl of the group. I know she hoped to be noticed by Blade."

"I have no desire to compete with Nancy Wilson," sniffed Shannon, recalling the brown-eyed blond beauty who looked to be her own age. She traveled with her parents, three younger siblings, and an older brother. Shannon remembered Todd Wilson vividly, for he spent a great deal of his free time making cow eyes at her.

After the first easy day, the emigrants camped that night beside a creek where water and firewood were plentiful. Blade had made the decision to ford the relatively placid water the next morning. Shannon saw little of Blade. He spent the evening going from wagon to wagon offering advice and words of encouragement. She noted that he ate with the Wilsons, having been invited by Nancy who, Shannon noted with a hint of disgust, hung onto his every word with breathless awe. Instinctively Shannon knew that these very people who depended on him for their lives would shun him like poison once the journey was over and they no longer needed him. She felt certain Blade knew it too.

After supper was cleared away and the dishes washed and stashed in their places, Callie retired inside the wagon while Howie bedded down underneath. Previous arrangements called for Shannon to share the wagon with Callie, but she felt so guilty about separating the young couple that after she had donned her voluminous gown and robe, she sent Howie inside with his wife, insisting she'd rather sleep outside on such a warm night. But Shannon soon found she was too keyed up to sleep. Seeking a place she might be alone, she wandered to the outer perimeter of the camp and sat down on a rock, staring at the star-studded sky.

"It's a lovely night."

"Oh!" Startled, Shannon leaped to her feet, relieved to see Clive Bailey looming beside her instead of the intimidating half-breed. "You frightened me."

"Sorry," Clive mumbled, his tone far from contrite. "How are you getting on with the Johnsons?"

"Just fine. I'm positive it will work out well for all of us."

"Glad to hear it." He paused, choosing his words carefully. "But if for some reason things don't go as they should, I'd be more than happy to offer my own wagon for your use. I refrained from doing so in front of the half-breed, but please keep in mind what I have offered. You are a lovely creature, Shannon Branigan," he added, his voice low and insinuating.

Shannon felt the first prickling of alarm when Clive sidled closer, replaced by panic when his words and their barely disguised meaning left his lips.

"Mr. Bailey, I'm not certain what you are suggesting, but I have no intention of leaving the Johnsons' wagon—for any reason. Now if you will excuse me, it is time I returned to the wagon."

She turned to leave, but found her way blocked by

the hard wall of Clive's chest. Short and stocky, Clive was an immovable force before Shannon's meager strength. "Are you trying to frighten me, Mr. Bailey?"

"The name is Clive and the last thing I want is to frighten you, Shannon. I just want us to be friends— good friends," he hinted. He raised a thick hand and stroked her shoulder in an awkward attempt to smooth her ruffled feathers. Evidently he had gone about this all wrong, he reflected wryly. The girl was as skittish as a young colt and required patience and gentling if he intended to seduce her.

"Then I bid you good-night, Mr.—Clive," Shannon said coolly, shrugging off his offending hand. Before he could stop her she whirled and fled to the safety of the shadows.

Shannon was panting when she reached the line of wagons, not only from being out of breath but from incredible anger. How could she have thought Clive Bailey a nice man? she wondered bleakly. What made him think he could insult her in such a vile manner? She prided herself on her ability to judge character, but this time she'd been wrong. Clive Bailey was a slimy worm and she vowed to steer clear of him in the future.

Just before she reached the Johnson wagon, Shannon felt a hand curl around her waist and froze, preparing to vent her Irish temper at Clive Bailey, certain he had followed her. She found herself staring into Blade's stormy features. "What do you want?" she spat, suddenly weary of confrontations. Clive Bailey had been more than enough to deal with for one night.

"Stay away from that man," Blade warned, his tone implacable. "You are too young and inexperienced to know what he's after. Set your sights elsewhere."

"If you are referring to Mr. Bailey, I assure you I have no designs on his person."

"Then quit enticing him," Blade advised bluntly.

"Entice him. Entice him!" she repeated, numb with disbelief. "Whyever would I do that?"

"Don't try to deny you lured Bailey out here tonight to meet you. You are even dressed for a midnight tryst," Blade observed dryly.

Shannon sucked her breath in sharply, stunned by Blade's cruel taunts. She didn't deserve his contempt, nor would she stand for it. "You were spying on me! How dare you!" she exploded.

Shannon raised her hand to strike him, but to her dismay she found her wrist suspended behind her in a viselike grip as Blade caught her to him, molding her unfettered body to his. He shuddered in suppressed delight when the firm peaks of her breasts stabbed into the muscular wall of his chest. Something inside Blade erupted, and before he knew it he was kissing Shannon, discovering the soft shape of her lips, tasting the sweet essence of her. She gasped in shock, affording him the opportunity to slip his tongue into her open mouth.

Blade's superior strength easily conquered Shannon's valiant struggles as shock rendered her nearly witless. At first Blade meant only to teach Shannon a lesson, to demonstrate what could happen to innocents who became involved with men they couldn't handle or things they didn't understand. But to his everlasting regret, what he accomplished instead was to prove to himself how susceptible he was to the Southern belle's fatal charm.

The kiss went on—and on—driving the breath from Shannon's lungs and turning her legs to jelly. Never had she been kissed in such a manner—or felt so utterly transported by an act she felt certain was meant to degrade.

Perhaps punishment had been Blade's original intent, but it was soon forgotten as the sweetness of Shannon's first timid response warmed his heart. It was that tentative stirring of passion that jolted Blade abruptly to his senses. What in the hell was he doing?

Just as Shannon felt herself on the brink of a great discovery, Blade broke off the kiss, steadying her as he backed away. "Play with fire and you are likely to get burned, Miss Branigan," he said pointedly, his voice deliberately harsh. "Enticing men can lead to trouble, as I've just demonstrated. I could have taken you right here on the ground in sight of all the wagons if I wanted you. Chivalry as you know it doesn't exist on the Western frontier. Keep away from Clive Bailey and the other men sniffing around you. But if you find you have an itch that needs scratching, I'd be more than happy to take care of it." Blade knew he was being deliberately cruel and insensitive but felt it necessary to impress upon Shannon the danger she faced on this journey.

That was the last straw! "You—you filthy, savage bastard! You're the one I need to beware of!"

Blade winced, the viciousness of her words scalding him, yet he had asked for it. He had meant to teach her a valuable lesson and succeeded, at the cost of his own pride. He didn't usually treat women with such casual disregard, but his assignment demanded nothing less than total concentration, and the only way he could do that was make Shannon hate him. It was in Shannon's best interests to think of him as a despicable savage, he told himself sadly. And it was neither the first nor the last time he'd be referred to that way.

The first weeks on the trail were easy, the wagons traveling northwest toward Nebraska and the Platte River. Small streams were forded without mishap. The climate was mild and the land bucolic. It provided the emigrants with a perfect time to learn to handle a prairie schooner, to shake down the routine and to become accustomed to the extraordinary adventure on which they were launched.

They spotted their first stray Indians, but were neither challenged nor molested by them. It amused Shannon to note that these initial few sightings produced a display of arms in the most approved warrior-like style. Actually, the Indians of Kansas were pitiful, defeated, ragged, starving creatures who often approached the emigrants begging for food.

Because the long summer days did not exhaust the travelers, evenings at the campsite were given over to children's games and to parties, music, and dancing by the elders. Shannon didn't lack for partners, being one of the more popular single women. Blade, she noted, kept to himself, neither invited to join the gaiety nor expecting to be asked. But that still didn't stop some of the young women, Nancy Wilson in particular, from shamelessly competing for his attention. Shannon tried to tell herself she didn't care how many women fawned over the half-breed. Yet the fact remained that the memory of his kiss still burned her lips and warmed her soul.

On Sundays the emigrants were left much to their own devices according to their beliefs and tastes. If a minister or missionary traveled with a wagon train, a service was offered. None, however, was listed among Shannon's traveling companions. Horseraces were often held and a general day of relaxation and rest was called for.

Under Blade's competent guidance, the wagon train arrived at the Big Blue, a tributary of the Kansas River. The Big Blue was a cantankerous, crotchety stream that demanded strict attention. It had rained the night before and word passed down that the travelers would camp on the bank until the water receded. Shannon welcomed the respite. It was one of the most idyllic campsites along the entire length of the trail, as well as one of the most romantic. It was called Alcove Springs, its name carved in rock at the site.

That night Callie was feeling uncomfortable and Shannon worried that delivery was imminent. Since there were still several weeks remaining before the expected delivery, Shannon's concern was very real. Knowing something about birthing and babies from her large family, she quietly prepared for a premature delivery. Mercifully, she was relieved of that duty when two women more experienced in such things offered their services. Somehow the news filtered down to Blade and he showed up unexpectedly at their campsite after weeks of ignoring Shannon. Howie was inside the wagon with Callie, leaving Shannon alone when Blade arrived.

He moved into the circle of firelight with loose-hipped grace, hunkering down beside Shannon where she sat close to the wagon. "How is Mrs. Johnson?"

"Hanging on," Shannon said tightly. "It's too early for her to deliver."

"These things happen." Blade shrugged philosophically. "Do you need help if the baby decides it's time?"

"Mrs. Wilson and Mrs. Cormac have already volunteered."

"They are both capable women, and Mrs. Johnson is young and healthy. There's no need for you to worry."

If Blade's words were meant to reassure her, Shannon reflected, they failed miserably. She lowered her head, trying to overcome her apprehension. Suddenly her head jerked up, startled when she felt Blade place his hands over hers in a gesture that struck Shannon as very intimate.

The flickering campfire softened the hard planes of his face and the expression in his dark eyes was one of warm regard instead of the usual stern disapproval he exhibited toward her. For a brief moment Blade had lowered his guard, allowing Shannon an unintentional glimpse of the sensitive man beneath his austere facade. He looked—my God, Shannon thought, thunderstruck—he looked like any other man burdened with responsibilities and worries!

Then, just as swiftly as he had appeared, the man Shannon thought she had discovered vanished, replaced by the half-breed, Swift Blade. When the warmth of his hands left hers, Shannon felt strangely deprived, yet vastly relieved.

"Don't fret, Shannon," Blade said softly. "Callie will be just fine. I suspect the baby is large enough to survive should she deliver early."

Then he was gone. One moment he was there beside her, the next he was gone, nearly convincing Shannon that she had imagined the whole thing.

Chapter Three

*L*ate that night Callie went into premature labor. Mrs. Wilson and Mrs. Cormac were hastily summoned and Shannon was shooed outside to placate Howie who was on the verge of panic. The poor man was beside himself with worry, and with good cause. At dawn Callie appeared to be no closer to delivery than she was at midnight. By noon the entire wagon train was aware of Callie's travail and her difficulty in delivering. As dusk approached both Mrs. Wilson and Mrs. Cormac came out of the wagon to announce that Callie was growing visibly weaker and they feared for her life. Both good women looked exhausted and Shannon immediately offered her assistance.

"There is nothing you can do, honey," Mrs. Wilson said, patting her hand consolingly.

Those words seemed to send Howie, already prostrate with grief, over the edge. "Please do something," he begged, tears rolling down his cheeks. "Don't let Callie die."

"Perhaps I can help."

All eyes turned to Blade. His silent approach never failed to amaze Shannon. Obviously he had heard both Mrs. Wilson's words and Howie's impassioned plea.

"What seems to be the trouble?"

Mrs. Wilson flushed, unaccustomed to discussing intimate details of childbirth with a man. Blade sensed her reticence and resisted the urge to rail at her misplaced modesty. Didn't she realize that a woman's life was at stake?

"How can I help if I don't know what the trouble is?"

Mrs. Wilson glanced at Howie and, when he voiced no objection, explained, "The baby won't come. We think it's turned wrong."

Grasping the situation instantly, Blade turned to Howie. "Do you trust me, Howie? Do you trust me enough to let me help your wife?"

At first Howie seemed disturbed by the thought of another man touching his wife. But contemplating her death was even more abhorrent. If Blade could help Callie, what did it matter that he was a man—or an Indian? Howie reasoned sensibly. "I'd be grateful if you could help Callie," he said evenly, realizing by the shocked faces around him that his fellow travelers thought he had lost his mind. What did a half-breed know about birthing?

"I'll assist you," Mrs. Wilson offered, her lips pressed tight in disapproval.

"You're exhausted, Mrs. Wilson, and so are you, Mrs. Cormac," Blade said dismissively.

Blade glanced around the circle of people gathered around the Johnson wagon, aware that propriety demanded another woman be present during the birth. He scanned the faces staring at him, some with awe, others with outright distrust, and settled on one. "Miss Branigan is close to Mrs. Johnson. She'll do just fine."

Surprised, Shannon stepped forward, more than eager to do whatever was necessary to help Callie.

"But Miss Branigan is unwed," Mrs. Cormac complained, shocked to the core. "It's not proper."

"I have several younger brothers and sisters, and childbirth is no mystery to me," Shannon declared stoutly. Turning on her heel she climbed into the wagon, followed closely by Blade.

Shannon knelt beside Callie, who lay moaning softly on a sweat-soaked pallet. Deep purple shadows marred the delicate skin beneath her eyes and it was obvious her strength was swiftly ebbing.

"Callie, can you hear me? It's Shannon."

Callie opened her eyes, grasping desperately for Shannon's hand. "Am I going to die?" Her fear was stark and real.

Shannon and Blade exchanged worried glances. "No, of course not. Blade has come to help you."

"Blade?" Callie asked, confused.

"I can help you, Mrs. Johnson—Callie—if you let me," Blade said. "Do you trust me?"

Callie shifted her gaze from Blade to Shannon, then back to Blade. She wanted her baby, wanted to live, and found only one answer. "I trust you, Blade."

Flashing a reassuring smile, Blade stuck his head through the wagon flap, issuing crisp orders. "Hot water and strong lye soap."

When they arrived he told Shannon to sit beside Callie and hold her hand. Shannon complied without question while Blade thoroughly washed his hands and arms. When he was ready he began talking to Callie in low soothing tones, telling her what he was going to do and not to be afraid.

Shannon held her breath as Blade carefully inserted his hand into Callie's body, examining the position of the baby. He grunted in satisfaction when he discovered the problem and then proceeded to turn the infant into the right position for birthing. Callie screamed once, twice, panting from the pain. From that point things moved along swiftly and shortly afterwards the baby slid effortlessly into Blade's big hands.

"It's a boy," he said, handing the child to Shannon. Then Blade climbed out of the wagon, satisfied to let the women take over. Within seconds he had disappeared into the encroaching darkness.

Later that night Shannon sought out Blade. No matter what she thought about him personally, the man had saved Callie's life and received little thanks for his efforts. Having learned he was on guard duty that night, she found him leaning against a tree some distance from the perimeter of the camp.

He looked as if he were totally relaxed, but Shannon detected a constant alertness in his gaze and stance. He seemed aware of every noise and movement, knowing the precise moment Shannon neared.

"What are you doing roaming about this time of night?" Blade asked, frowning.

It was as if he had conjured her up, for he had been thinking of her and how she hadn't turned squeamish or appeared shocked when he did what he had to do to save Callie and her child.

"I—I want to thank you. For what you did for the Johnsons. Callie would have died if you hadn't offered to help and known what to do."

"I told you before, I'm responsible for every person on the wagon train. I do what I have to do."

"How did you know *what* to do?" She hadn't meant to be so nosy, but curiosity got the best of her.

"Indians know many things," he replied. His cryptic words told her little.

What he couldn't say was that as a young army lieutenant he was once called upon to assist the company doctor in just such a delivery. During a march, their outfit had sought lodging at a remote plantation and they couldn't have arrived at a more convenient time. The young mistress, alone but for a single male slave, was giving birth. The doctor promptly offered his services and Blade volunteered to assist. As it was with Callie, the baby was turned wrong and the mother and child would have perished if the good doctor hadn't known what to do.

Shannon searched Blade's face, wondering how so compassionate a man could look so big and dangerous. This was a side of him he rarely showed. It was also a mystery to her why he seemed to dislike her.

"Why don't you like me?" she asked bluntly.

"Is that what you think?"

"It's obvious my presence on this wagon train offends you."

"Nothing about you offends me, Shannon," Blade muttered beneath his breath, "except what you do to me."

"What?" Surely she hadn't heard him right.

"I said you don't offend me and I don't dislike you. It's more like I offend you for being what I am." Blade hadn't meant to say so much, but somehow this exasperating female put words in his mouth.

Shannon flushed. A few weeks ago that might have been true, but as the days slid by she had come to regard Blade as a man, not as a half-breed Sioux.

"Is it true, Shannon? Do you think of me as less than human?" His voice was soft and low and utterly beguiling, turning Shannon's legs to water. She couldn't have spoken had she known what to say.

He was so close that she could smell his musky masculine odor, feel the tenseness in his body. With rising panic she studied the shape of his lips as they hovered dangerously close to hers, mesmerized by their rich, full contours. Vividly she recalled their softness, the unique taste when his tongue explored her mouth.

"Shannon." Her name was a groan on his lips, softly uttered, barely heard, swept away on the warm summer breeze.

Without realizing exactly how it happened, their lips meshed, clinging, tasting. A shudder passed through Blade as his tongue outlined the generous contours of her lips, lingering at their moist corners, savoring their sweetness. He knew he had no business kissing Shannon, it could only lead to problems for both of them. But a compelling force inside him blanked out all reason and bid him take this small pleasure and savor it. Seeking a deeper intimacy, he meshed their bodies, his desire rising between them like a hot brand. Blade's strangled moan seemed to bring a semblance of order to Shannon's scrambled wits as she came abruptly to her senses.

What was she thinking, to allow a man she hardly knew such liberties? His mouth was demanding things she knew nothing about while his hands searched her body with practiced expertise. How many other women had he seduced so effortlessly with his male magnetism? she wondered. How had a half-breed acquired such sophisticated talents? And what was she doing in his arms, responding to him with an eagerness that shocked her?

"Don't," Shannon gasped. She was shaking from head to toe as she pushed herself from Blade's arms.

My God! Blade thought, nearly as shaken as Shannon. If he continued like this he'd be bedding her on the hard ground in another moment. "This is what you wanted, isn't it?" he taunted. It took considerable effort to make his voice deliberately cruel and cynical.

"Are you trying to humiliate me?" Shannon struggled for breath, his cruel words fueling her anger.

"Isn't this why you came out here?" Blade replied with sly inuendo. "Does a half-breed kiss any differently than a white man? Did you pick me to experiment on because I'm only half-tame and the thought excited you?"

Shannon sucked her breath in sharply. Then she bombarded him with her Irish temper. "You conceited jackass! I don't understand you. One minute you're kissing me and the next you're accusing me of despicable things. But why should I expect gentle treatment from a half-civilized savage? You may have fooled some people on this wagon train, but you don't fool me!"

Abruptly she turned and stalked away, leaving Blade with a bad taste in his mouth. It was a helluva long way to Fort Laramie and Shannon Branigan wasn't going to make the trip an easy one!

The wagon train lingered another day on the bank of the Big Blue then crossed with relative ease, since the water was down. The oozy bottom looked threatening to Shannon but Blade seemed to know exactly where to cross.

Beyond the crossing the trail ran up into Nebraska to meet the Platte River, which emigrants described as bad to ford, destitute of fish, too dirty to bathe in, and too thick to drink.

There were many Indian sightings now, mostly Pawnee who had to be watched carefully, for they stole horses and cattle and pilfered food indiscriminately. The emigrants crossed trails of Pawnee leading from permanent winter villages to hunting grounds to the south. Blade appeared unconcerned over these sightings, which eased the emigrants' minds considerably.

The journey was tedious now, as they passed up the middle of a long, narrow sandy plain reaching like an outstretched belt nearly to the Rocky Mountains. Wood was practically nonexistent and the trail became littered with stoves, which were of no further use and too cumbersome to be of value. Following behind the wagons, the women and children now collected buffalo chips for fuel. They burned with surprisingly little smoke or odor, but it was an unending chore. As far as the eye could see, women and children carrying baskets or using their aprons bent to the task of picking up buffalo chips from the ground. Shannon didn't particularly like the job, but Callie was still recovering from childbirth and the disgusting chore fell to her.

Shannon found herself thinking of Blade on those long, hot days trekking behind the wagons. He was an enigma—a man who both attracted and repelled her. Would she ever understand the workings of his mind? Perhaps it was best if she didn't try.

Sweat trickled from beneath Shannon's sunbonnet and she whisked it off her forehead. She wrinkled her sunburned nose, the scent of her perspiration-soaked dress offensive even to her. But she took comfort from the fact that she was no different from the other women. In a day or two they would reach the Platte River, and Blade promised the women they would have the opportunity to bathe and wash clothes.

As though she'd conjured him up, Blade appeared beside her on his gray pony.

"Put your bonnet on. Do you want the prairie sun to fry your brains?"

"I just took it off for a moment," Shannon tried to explain.

"Your face is flushed and your nose is peeling. Your skin is too delicate to be exposed to the harsh rays of the sun."

Her skin delicate? Shannon was shocked he'd even noticed. Dutifully she clapped the bonnet on her head and tied the strings under her chin. It rankled her to think that the only time Blade spoke to her these days was to criticize. He seemed to find fault with everything she did.

"That's better." Without another word he spurred his horse and rode off.

What the devil had possessed him to stop and speak to Shannon? Blade asked himself, bewildered. When he saw her trudging behind the wagon, her single garment flapping about her shapely legs and her rich chestnut curls glistening in the sun, he just couldn't help himself. Because of the heat, most of the women had shed all unnecessary female fripperies like corsets and petticoats, sometimes even gathering their skirts between their legs and tucking them in at their waists. It created more sensible walking attire and was vastly more comfortable.

It amazed Blade that Shannon could still manage to look so beautiful with her face red from the sun and her nose sprinkled with tiny brown freckles. The sight was so tempting that something compelled him to stop, to experience again the full magnetism of those incredible blue eyes. On his way back to the head of the line of wagons he deliberately stopped beside the Wilson rig to flirt with Nancy, hoping her teasing would divert his thoughts from Shannon.

Shannon couldn't help but notice where Blade stopped, or how long he lingered, flirting with that Wilson hussy. That it should even matter shocked her. Blade had avoided her like poison these past few days and that was just fine with her. The part of him that was Indian made her mistrust him—yet his blatant masculinity transcended all notions of red or white. He was a man. Beautifully, incredibly male. But so damn arrogant she wanted to lash out at him every time she saw him. Was it any wonder Nancy Wilson found him so intriguing?

Clive Bailey watched the exchange between Shannon and Blade, a satisfied smirk lifting the corners of his mouth. Until now duties kept him from pursuing Shannon. But since they had adapted to a daily routine, he had more time to indulge his fantasies where Shannon Branigan was concerned. She had struck his fancy from the moment they met and he hadn't given up his dream of possessing her. At first Clive had thought Shannon was attracted to Blade, but with each passing day it became more apparent that they couldn't stand one another. Shannon was too much of a lady to allow a half-breed to sweet-talk her. A man like Blade deserved sluts like Nancy Wilson who spread their legs for anything in pants. Clive even had a taste of her himself a few days ago when she sneaked away to meet him in the middle of the night. But that hadn't slaked his lust for Shannon Branigan—not by a long shot.

A few days later they came upon the Platte River after traveling through two lines of hills flanking a narrow valley at a distance of a mile or two on the right and left. The level monotony of the plain was unbroken as far as the eye could see. The Platte ran through the valleys in a thin sheet of rapid, turbid water, half a mile wide and barely two feet deep. Its low banks, for the most part without bush or tree, were composed of loose sand. Only the islands sported cottonwood or willow trees, something Shannon thought most curious.

They followed the Platte for some distance. Because it was so late in the year, the river was extremely shallow. The bed was quicksand that sucked at boats and wagon wheels. It could not be ferried and was too dangerous to ford. For a distance of three miles on both sides of the Platte, the land rose in sandstone cliffs that grew higher and more broken as the trail moved west.

Shannon was amazed at the prairie wildlife— antelope, deer, coyotes, grizzlies, and black bears, buffalo, and prairie dogs. Prairie dog villages sometimes covered five hundred acres. Worst of all were the hordes of mosquitoes and gnats. Buffalo weren't as plentiful as they once were but they could be a nuisance. Sometimes potable stream water turned dark and redolent as herds wandered through it. At other times, emigrants' oxen and cows might stray off with the buffalo herd, never to be seen again.

Trouble with Indians was rare along this stretch, for the Platte valley lay in a kind of no man's land between the Pawnees to the north and the Cheyenne to the south. Though their meetings with Indians were peaceable affairs in which the tribesmen traded buffalo meat for tobacco, ironware, and the travelers' worn-out clothing, Blade insisted the wagons be drawn up into a corral at every campsite. This also served the practical purpose of enclosing some of the livestock overnight so they could graze. The corral was formed by interlocking wagons, with the tongue of one extending under the wagonbed of the other.

It was during the long tedious trek along the Platte that Clive Bailey began actively pursuing Shannon, much to Blade's consternation.

Shannon hugged little Johnny Blade Johnson to her breast, thinking how much she missed her own close-knit family. The little boy was precious to her, and she would miss him terribly when they parted. Callie's strength had slowly returned, and fortunately her milk was plentiful enough to keep her baby well fed and happy. As its youngest member, he soon became the darling of the wagon train.

Clive Bailey took to stopping by frequently to visit the baby, but the premise did not fool Shannon. She did her best to discourage Clive, but he remained insensitive to Shannon's coolness. When an impromptu dance was announced for their Sunday night entertainment, Clive plotted to get Shannon alone.

Blade rarely attended these festivities, nor was he invited. He usually stood on the sidelines to watch and listen, recalling with fondness some of the festive balls he had attended before and after the war. He had never lacked for partners then. But out here on the Western frontier, he was a misfit, a man neither white nor red, living on the fringes of society. Occasionally Nancy Wilson or one of the other young ladies insisted on a dance, but he usually declined, unwilling to flaunt custom or anger parents.

The dark, mysterious pools of Blade's eyes followed Shannon's lithe figure as she flitted from one man's arms to another's. His body reacted spontaneously to the memory of how she felt in his arms, all soft and warm and vibrantly female.

Spinning to the music of the fiddler, Shannon suddenly found herself dancing with Clive Bailey. She still hadn't forgiven him for behaving so despicably toward her and the smile faded from her lips.

"I've not had the opportunity to properly apologize for acting like a fool, Shannon," Clive said. His obsequious smile did little to ingratiate him with Shannon. "I meant no disrespect. I don't know what got into me. Can you ever forgive me?"

"It is over and done with," Shannon said with cool disdain. "I don't wish to speak of it. Perhaps my traveling alone gave you a false impression of me."

"If we can start over again, I promise to behave like a perfect gentleman."

Shannon doubted Clive Bailey's sincerity, but her generous nature prompted her to give a grudging consent. A sly smile curved Bailey's thin lips as he whirled Shannon around the circle of dancers.

Blade's eyes narrowed dangerously as he noted Clive's preoccupation with Shannon. Though he hated to leave Shannon in Bailey's clutches, Blade slipped stealthily into the shadows, melting like a wraith into the darkness. There were still several wagons he hadn't searched for hidden weapons and he couldn't have asked for a better time than the present to do it. The impromptu revelry had drawn everyone to the music and dancers. With the stealth of a cat Blade slipped into a wagon belonging to Fred Hankins and his family. Fred was a loud-mouthed braggart who abused his family shamefully. But no matter how badly Blade wanted to involve the man in gun smuggling, he found nothing to suggest his guilt.

He chose another wagon in the circle and again came away without a shred of incriminating evidence. Perhaps Washington was mistaken and the guns were already on their way to Fort Laramie concealed on another wagon train. The next wagon in line belonged to Clive Bailey, and as usual his driver, a big Swede named Olson, lounged nearby. Blade cursed his rotten luck. Time and again Blade had been prevented from searching Bailey's wagon because of Olson's annoying habit of spending his leisure hours leaning against the rear wheel whittling on a piece of wood. Somehow,

Blade reflected grimly, he'd have to devise a way to get Olson away from Bailey's wagon long enough for him to inspect it.

Excluding Bailey's wagon, Blade was left with two others to search, one of them belonging to the young Johnsons. Glancing toward the festivities, Blade noted that both Johnsons were occupied. Howie was with a group of men and Callie sat amidst a circle of women who were admiring the baby. Shannon was now dancing with young Todd Wilson. Blade's moccasined feet were noiseless as he eased through the rear opening of the Johnson wagon. He didn't actually suspect the Johnsons, but he felt duty-bound to search every wagon.

Determined to refuse the next dance so that she might catch her breath, Shannon strolled over to the group of women surrounding Callie and the baby. She was greeted warmly and would have joined in the conversation but for the sudden breeze that sent a chill down her spine. Callie felt it too, and when Shannon said she would return to the wagon for their shawls and a blanket for little Johnny, Callie thought it a prudent idea. Shannon left immediately.

It was dark at the outer perimeter of the campsite where the wagons formed a protective circle around the dancers, and Shannon slipped inside the wagon as silently as Blade had done only minutes before. The moment Shannon entered the dark interior she sensed immediately that she wasn't alone. A frisson of fear raced up her spine and she felt the hair rise at the back of her neck. She stood frozen in a sort of limbo, waiting, undecided whether to scream or issue a challenge. She chose the latter, marshaling her courage to ask, "Who's there?"

Silence.

"I know someone is in here. Who is it? I'll scream if you don't answer me."

Then suddenly Shannon knew! She recognized immediately the clean musky scent of him and the aroma of woods, smoke and leather that clung to him. She didn't need a light to identify Blade, for his nearness created a subtle awareness in her that was hard to define but easily recognized. "Blade? What are you doing in the Johnsons' wagon?"

He crawled out from behind some stacked boxes, the dim light from the campfire confirming his identity. How did Shannon know it was him? Blade wondered, mystified. Was she one of those fey Irish lasses who had the vision? Or was she as profoundly aware of him as he was of her?

"I hoped to be gone before anyone returned." Blade's cryptic words made little sense.

"What could you possibly want in here? The Johnsons have nothing of value to steal."

"You think I'd steal from the Johnsons?" His voice was harsh with reproach. It rankled to think she thought him a thief.

"I don't know what to think. Indians are notorious pilferers."

"What about that half of me that's white?"

"If you're not stealing, what *are* you doing?" Shannon wanted to give him the benefit of the doubt but it was difficult, having caught him red-handed.

"I can't tell you." The firm line of his mouth quirked downward. "And I'd strongly advise you to forget you saw me here tonight."

"Are—are you threatening me?" Shannon gasped. Disbelief colored her words.

"Perhaps," Blade hedged.

"I don't scare easily." Blade nearly laughed aloud when Shannon's firm little chin jutted out defiantly. He could snap her in two with little effort. "Convince me otherwise and I'll take your—request into consideration."

"I can't explain. You'll just have to trust me."

"Trust you! Is that the best you can do?" Shannon really did want to trust Blade, but she felt she deserved an explanation.

A spark caught fire and grew in Blade's dark eyes. "I

can do this," he said huskily, catching her in his arms and drawing her close. "And this." His mouth slanted across hers, searching for the sweetness he remembered with vivid clarity as he meshed their bodies together. Shannon felt the brazen thrust of his manhood between them as his tongue nudged her lips apart.

He pulled her closer still, his hands molding her buttocks, now clutching her waist, finally finding the soft mounds of her breasts. All restraint fled as Shannon moaned, her arms creeping around his neck with a will of their own, her fingers sliding upwards into the thick silk of his hair.

"You're an Irish witch, Shannon Branigan," Blade rasped. All reason fled as he slid downward with her to the wagonbed.

Blade's kiss was so potent that Shannon wasn't aware of her danger, or where her surrender was likely to lead. Nor did she feel his hands tugging at the buttons of her bodice. What she did feel was Blade's lips sliding down her neck, tasting the shell-like indent of her ear, his tongue teasing the swell of flesh rising above the neckline of her chemise.

"Shannon, are you in there? Callie grew worried when you failed to return."

Howie! A strangled curse flew from Blade's lips. "Tell him you'll be right out," he hissed when Shannon was slow to regain her wits. "Say nothing about me." His voice was ominously low and fraught with warning.

"Shannon!" Howie was close to the wagon—too close. Shannon perched on the horns of a dilemma. She could keep Blade's secret or she could tell the entire wagon train he was a thief. But try as she might, she really didn't believe that Blade was capable of theft.

Unbidden, her thoughts returned to the way Blade's mouth felt on hers, how her body burned everyplace he touched, and only one answer was possible. "I'm coming, Howie. I couldn't find my shawl."

Hastily buttoning her dress and gathering what she had come to the wagon for, Shannon appeared at the entrance. Howie was already holding back the flap and offering a hand to help her to the ground. She glanced over her shoulder only once as she walked away, aware that Blade was watching, wondering what he'd do if she decided to make his nighttime activities known. How many other wagons had he secretly invaded? Shannon wondered grimly. She found her answer later that evening when she returned early to the wagon and spied Blade slipping out of the Carpenter wagon.

At first Shannon thought it was just the Johnson wagon Blade was curious about, but he had disproved that theory by skulking inside other wagons as well. Her natural curiosity demanded an answer to the mystery.

Blade slipped from the Carpenter wagon with no more proof of gun smuggling than he had the day they began this journey. During these past weeks he had managed to search every wagon but the one belonging to Clive Bailey with no one the wiser until he had been confronted by Shannon. He turned, melting into the shadows, and from the corner of his eye spied Shannon watching him. He knew then that he must find a plausible excuse to allay her suspicions or he would find himself in deep trouble. But how in the hell was he supposed to do that when he couldn't even remember his own name whenever he got within two feet of Shannon Branigan?

The next morning Blade surprised Shannon when he asked her to ride ahead with him while he scouted the area. As usual he was mounted on his big gray pony, Warrior. Shannon and Callie were walking behind the wagon when he approached holding the leading reins of a gentle black mare.

"Can you ride?" he asked Shannon, nodding pleasantly at Callie.

"Of course." Did he think she possessed no skills at all? Shannon wondered.

"I thought you might enjoy riding along while I scouted ahead."

Shannon looked startled. "I prefer to walk."

"I suggest you think again," Blade persisted. There wasn't a place on her body that wasn't touched by his dark gaze.

Callie stared with interest at the two antagonists, wondering if there was something she had missed. She'd swear there was something deep and profound between Blade and Shannon; something that reeked of dark secrets and tension and had nothing to do with mere friendship.

"Go on, Shannon," Callie urged, "it will do you good to get away for a while."

Before she could protest, Blade dismounted and hoisted Shannon into the saddle, handing her the reins. "We'll ride west a few miles and meet you at nooning," he told Callie. Then he slapped the rump of Shannon's mare and led the way past the meandering line of wagons.

Shannon's cheeks bloomed with color not of the sun's doing as dozens of pairs of eyes followed their progress—especially those of Nancy Wilson and Clive Bailey.

Blade knew he wasn't helping Shannon's reputation by insisting that she ride with him, but it was no more than what some of the other young women had done from time to time these past weeks. Besides, there was no other way to get Shannon alone in order to convince her to remain silent about his suspicious behavior.

They rode without speaking for several miles, leaving the wagon train far behind. Finally Blade halted at a narrow offshoot of the Platte to water the horses. Shannon slid from the saddle and knelt beside the stream, using her hands to scoop up water to dampen her neck and face. Then she removed her bonnet, shaking out her tangled mass of chestnut curls. Mesmerized, Blade thought they looked like lustrous strands of burnished copper. No sooner had she refreshed herself than she turned to Blade, storm-clouds gathering in her blue eyes.

"What is this all about, Blade? Did you bring me here to explain why you've been rifling wagons? I saw you leaving the Carpenter wagon last night after you'd been prowling around in the Johnson wagon."

"Thank you for not giving me away. What I am doing will hurt no one."

"If it hurts no one, why can't you explain?"

"I know it doesn't make sense, Shannon, but what I'm doing is important."

"Important to whom? To what? Are you waiting for your people to arrive and attack the wagon train? Have you been searching for hidden wealth and possible loot?"

"I'd never betray the lives I was hired to protect." Blade said it with such heartfelt sincerity that Shannon was inclined to believe him. "I consider myself as much white as Indian. I'm as proud of my mother's Sioux blood as I am of my father's white heritage."

"Sioux!" Shannon gasped, the name instilling fear in her heart. The war-like Sioux were daring raiders who had resumed attacking wagon trains, railroads, and stage coach stations along the Oregon Trail after becoming increasingly dissatisfied with their treatment at the hands of the American government, the large number of emigrants moving across their hunting grounds, and the callous slaughter of their buffalo.

Immediately Blade sensed her fear. "My mother is Sioux. My father was a mountain man, a trapper adopted into Yellow Dog's tribe. He fell in love with and married my mother." Blade had no idea why he was telling Shannon all this except that he needed her trust and her silence.

"Are both your parents still living?"

"Only my mother. My father was killed by a grizzly bear a few months ago."

"I'm sorry. They must have been conscientious parents, for your education wasn't lacking."

"Father wanted me educated as a white man so that I could make my way in the white man's world if I so desired."

Shannon eyed Blade suspiciously, her gaze settling on the blue army jacket he wore with casual pride. "You were educated in the North? You're a Yankee?" She made it sound as if an Indian half-breed was several notches above a Yankee.

"You hate Yankees so much?"

Shannon's face twisted into a bitter grimace. "Yankees killed my brother. They were the cause of my father's death and the loss of my home. Did you fight for the North?"

Shannon's blunt question caught Blade off guard. President Johnson had advised him to tell no one that he was an army officer. Every aspect of his assignment was to remain secret. The answer he was forming never left his mouth as his eyes drifted past Shannon to a place above her head where the brown hills rose in an unbroken line.

Shannon felt his body tense, saw him look past her, and asked, "Blade, what is it?"

"I don't know, but every bone in my body tells me something isn't right."

"What do you see?"

"Nothing, it's just a feeling I have. Perhaps I was wrong. What were you saying?"

"I asked if you were a Yankee soldier."

"Would it matter if I were?"

"Actually, I don't care one way or another," Shannon sniffed haughtily.

Suddenly Blade went rigid, and she saw him look past her to a ridge rising behind her.

His voice was low and grating, his words terse. "Turn around and walk slowly to your horse. Don't panic and don't make any sudden moves. I'll follow and help you mount. Then ride hell-for-leather back to the wagon."

"Are we in danger?"

"Perhaps," Blade said slowly. "We're surrounded by Sioux."

Shannon paled. She wanted to turn and scan the hills, but didn't dare. Instead she did exactly as Blade suggested, walking on rubbery legs toward her horse.

"Stop!" Blade's voice was harsh, his body taut. "It's too late. Here they come."

Chapter Four

There was no longer a need for caution as Shannon whirled to face the danger descending on them. With pounding heart she watched twenty-five or thirty warriors ride down from the hills. They were dressed in full war regalia and gaudily painted. Shannon surmised that they were either returning from or on their way to a raid.

From what Shannon knew of the Sioux they were a fierce, war-like people, often referred to as the "terror of the mountains." As they drew near, Shannon could see they were also a handsome lot, more than the Pawnee or others she had seen. Like Blade, they were tall and strongly made, possessing firm features and light copper skin. They appeared clean and well-kept down to their shiny black hair. Shannon also knew that since 1860 the Sioux had become increasingly hostile toward travelers across their land. They tended to attack small wagon trains and stragglers, for attacks on well-armed wagon trains were dangerous and brought immediate retaliation from the United States army.

Blade's eyes narrowed into dark slits as the warriors surrounded them. His hands hung loosely at his sides, his body alert, wary but showing little outward emotion or alarm. To Shannon, Blade appeared thoughtful but watchful, and it struck her that he might have been expecting Indians to appear. Did it have anything to do with his searching the wagons? she wondered. Then all thought skidded to an abrupt halt as the Indians formed a circle around them and the leader nudged his horse forward.

Blade stood his ground. Shannon was amazed that he could appear so cool and emotionless at a time like this. Nothing in his expression gave Shannon a hint of his thoughts or what he intended. She would have been stunned had she been able to understand Blade's words as he addressed the formidable warrior in the Sioux language.

"It has been a long time, Mad Wolf."

Mad Wolf stared at Blade for several thoughtful minutes before a slow smile curved his lips, a smile that did not reach the black darkness of his eyes.

"Not nearly long enough, Swift Blade." Recognition came slowly but surely to Mad Wolf. "We thought the white man's ways claimed you long ago. Why do you return?"

"To see my mother and grandfather," Blade answered. "I have never abandoned my mother's people. Even while I fought in the war I knew I would return one day. What are you doing here? Are you making war on the white man?"

"White men kill our buffalo, they trample the prairie and despoil our hunting grounds," Mad Wolf spat angrily. "They tell us we must stay on the reservations and starve while they steal our lands. The old ones might be satisfied to sit in front of their tipis and dream of bygone days, but the young warriors band together to drive away the whites."

"You and the others face an impossible task," Blade

observed. "There are more white men than blades of grass on the prairie. They travel West in great numbers and you cannot stop that which is inevitable."

"Perhaps not, but I will die trying," Mad Wolf snarled. Fierce determination and hatred twisted his face into an ugly mask. "Soon, very soon," he added slyly, "we will fight the white man with his own weapons."

Blade's interest sharpened at the mention of weapons. Were the guns he was tracing intended for Mad Wolf and his band of renegades?

"How will you get weapons? It is against the law to sell guns to Indians." When it became obvious that Mad Wolf wasn't going to respond, Blade prodded, "You haven't answered my question. What are you doing so far from the village?"

"We go where we please," Mad Wolf said after a pause. "Yellow Dog is old and dreams of peace, but we know that day will never come."

"So you kill and raid indiscriminately," Blade charged. His contemptuous gaze settled on the scalps decorating Mad Wolf's lance. "You make war on helpless women and children."

"The soldiers take our women, use them, insult them, and then discard them. They kill our children and old people and destroy our villages. It is up to us, the young and strong, to defend our people. You have lived with the whites for many moons, ate their food, enjoyed their women. Have you also betrayed your mother's people? Are you a spy for the soldiers?"

Blade started violently. Mad Wolf was closer to the truth than he knew. Unfortunately, Shannon chose that moment to bring attention to herself by tugging at Blade's arm and asking, "What is it? What are you talking about?" She sensed the tension in Blade, felt the antagonism leap between the two men, and could hold her tongue no longer.

Mad Wolf's cold gaze slid to Shannon, raking her trim figure from head to toe, drawn hypnotically to the rich chestnut sheen of her hair. Noting the direction of Mad Wolf's gaze, Blade hissed, "Put on your bonnet!"

Shannon obeyed instantly, but it was too late. Mad Wolf's face had already assumed an anticipatory gleam and his hard, dark eyes blazed with an inner glow that Blade correctly identified as lust.

"Who is this woman? If she is yours, I will buy her from you." Mad Wolf's expression sent a chill down Shannon's spine. "She will give me fine sons and daughters."

"Little Firebird is not for sale." The moment they met, Blade had given Shannon the rather colorful Indian name, but this was the first time he had dared speak it aloud.

Shannon was frighteningly aware that the fierce warrior was talking about her. She didn't like the way his bold, black eyes impaled her. Unconsciously she stepped closer to Blade, seeking the protection of his comforting presence.

"What is he saying?"

"Mad Wolf wants to buy you." Blade's words were accompanied by a chuckle of amusement.

"Buy me? No one owns me!"

"I will give you ten ponies," Mad Wolf offered magnanimously. By Indian standards it was a generous offer.

"Little Firebird is not for sale," Blade repeated. This time there was no hint of amusement in his voice. "She is my woman and I intend to keep her."

Mad Wolf merely grunted as he continued to devour Shannon with an avid gaze that set her teeth on edge. Blade broke the tense silence by asking, "Are we free to go? Yellow Dog still wields enough power to demand retribution from the man who harms his grandson."

"Go back to the wagon train and the white man's ways, Swift Blade. You ceased being Sioux long ago. Take Little Firebird with you, but don't grow lax, for you haven't heard the last from me. I have been following the wagon train for many suns."

"You planned to attack the wagon train," Blade accused him.

"Perhaps." His words gave away nothing. "Then again, I might have been merely watching its progress."

"Why would you do that?"

"I owe you no explanation, Swift Blade. Take your woman and go before I forget you are Yellow Dog's grandson and Sioux blood flows through your veins."

He sent Shannon a burning look, then wheeled his pony and galloped off, his war cry loud enough to raise the dead. His followers were close on his heels, except for one warrior who lagged behind to issue a warning. Blade recognized him immediately as Big Crow, one of the young men with whom he had been friends when he lived in his mother's village.

"Beware of Mad Wolf, Swift Blade. He is determined and proud. He will find a way to get what he wants." He glanced meaningfully at Shannon.

"Why do you follow him, Big Crow? I remember Mad Wolf well. He is ruled by anger and resentment. He is not the kind of leader young men like you should emulate."

"I follow Mad Wolf because I believe as he does," Big Crow revealed. "The whites will destroy us if we do not fight back."

Without waiting for a reply, the young warrior raced off after Mad Wolf and his braves.

Shannon went limp with relief, sagging against Blade for support. "Will they come back?" Her voice shook and her legs trembled, as much from excitement as from terror.

"This is Sioux country." Blade's cryptic explanation did little to ease Shannon's mind. "Come, I'll help you mount. It's time we returned to the wagon train."

"Did you know those Indians? It seemed as if . . ." Her sentence trailed off, almost afraid of what she would learn.

"They are from my village," Blade admitted slowly.

"Mad Wolf and I were never great friends. He was too arrogant and hot-headed for my liking. He indicated that he has left the village and is now leader of a band of renegades."

"Will they attack the wagon train?" Shannon asked. She thought of the dozens of innocent women and children who would die in a raid.

"Perhaps, but I don't think so," Blade answered, hoisting Shannon into the saddle. "Something Mad Wolf said led me to believe he was merely observing our comings and goings."

A question formed in Shannon's mind but was never voiced as Blade leaped astride Warrior and set both mounts into motion with a slap of the reins. Whatever he wanted to discuss with Shannon was forgotten, pushed aside by more pressing matters.

News of the Indian sighting swept swiftly through the ranks of those traveling with the wagon train. Blade had called the men together shortly after he and Shannon returned and issued a warning. The fact that it had been a war party was taken seriously and immediate precautions were instigated to protect the emigrants should the Sioux reappear. Even the women were instructed in the art of loading and firing a gun and how best to protect themselves and their children. Blade warned against straggling behind and cautioned everyone to remain safely within the camp perimeter at night.

Of all those concerned, Clive Bailey remained strangely unaffected by the Indian sightings, openly scoffing at the danger and voicing his doubt concerning an attack. He appeared so unconcerned that Blade immediately became suspicious. He cursed his luck at being unable to search Clive Bailey's wagon, for he truly believed he'd find much more than goods and supplies. Did Mad Wolf know Clive Bailey? Were Mad Wolf and his renegades actually protecting the wagon train from other raiders, aware of what it held?

The guards were doubled that night and the camp

subdued. Shannon slept fitfully inside the wagon with Callie and the baby. A thunderstorm during the night drove Howie inside and Shannon relaxed somewhat, certain the Indians wouldn't attack in so violent a storm.

Storms were common on the prairie in the spring and summer, providing brilliant displays of lightning and claps of thunder that shook the wagons. However, when no rain fell for days, as was often the case, they had to contend with alkali dust that lay as deep as six inches on trails, churned into gritty, blinding clouds by wagon wheels and animal hooves.

When Shannon awoke the next morning she learned that some of the cattle had been spooked by the storm and much of the day was spent rounding up the strays. Blade led a group of men out at dawn, and both Shannon and Callie were on hand to watch their departure, for Howie was one of those joining Blade. Rather than wait for the men, the wagon train rolled down the trail under the guidance of Clive Bailey, who assumed the role of wagon master in Blade's absence.

The men still hadn't returned with the cattle after the nooning, when the band of Sioux rode down from the hills without warning. They approached the wagons, signing that they wished to talk. The wagons rolled to a stop and a group of armed emigrants joined Clive where he waited for the leader to speak his piece. Shannon recognized Mad Wolf immediately and walked to the edge of the crowd so she might better hear what was being said. She was shocked when Mad Wolf spoke to Clive in halting but clearly understandable English.

"We are not here to do you harm," Mad Wolf stated.

"I hope not," Clive replied, "this wagon train has valuable cargo bound for Fort Laramie." His gaze met Mad Wolf's in mutual understanding. "What do you want? We have trade goods you might be interested in."

Mad Wolf motioned to one of the warriors who

immediately rode forward leading a string of ponies. "A trade is what I had in mind. I offer ten ponies for Little Firebird."

"Little Firebird?" Clive repeated, mystified.

"Little Firebird will give me fine sons," Mad Wolf said. Now Clive really was confused.

But Shannon knew exactly what Mad Wolf meant and started backing away. The movement alerted Mad Wolf, who raised his arm and pointed directly at Shannon. "The woman with fire in her hair is Little Firebird. I wish to buy her. Ten ponies is a generous offer."

"No!" At the sound of her voice all eyes swung in Shannon's direction. "It's against the law to buy and sell human beings."

"The Sioux make their own laws," Mad Wolf proclaimed loudly.

"See here," Clive blustered, stalling for time, "Miss Branigan is not for sale at any price."

Mad Wolf looked unperturbed by Clive's words. "I can wait," he grunted. His words hinted at fierce determination and masculine arrogance. "Little Firebird belongs to me."

"What are you doing here, Mad Wolf? I already told you Little Firebird belongs to me and is not for sale."

While the emigrants were gathered around the Indians, Blade and the others rode in unnoticed. He approached Mad Wolf in time to hear his outrageous claim. Blade's words were spoken in precise Sioux; his face was stiff and unrelenting.

"Perhaps Little Firebird will prefer me," Mad Wolf hinted arrogantly.

"Shannon!" Blade barked in English. "Come here."

All eyes focused on Shannon as she walked on rubbery legs to stand beside Blade. Though her insides churned and her chin trembled, her eyes did not waver from the fierce warrior challenging Blade. Only Blade's staunch bulk and his hand on her shoulder lent her a measure of courage.

"Mad Wolf has offered ten ponies for you," he said in careful English so that the renegade would not misunderstand.

Shannon's nostrils flared and her eyes turned to pure blue flame. "I am not for sale." The defiant tilt of her chin only increased Mad Wolf's desire and his determination to have her.

"Among my people I am much admired," he bragged, puffing out his chest importantly. "You and the children you give me will be well provided for."

How dare he even suggest such an monstrous arrangement! Shannon raged silently. She was about to blast him with her Irish temper when Blade hissed in her ear, "Don't insult him, Shannon, he is serious about this."

Blade was quick to recognize Shannon's anger and his warning gave Shannon pause. She cast a cautious glance at Mad Wolf, realizing much depended on her answer. The emigrants knew it too, for their fear was openly displayed for all to see. Most realized Shannon's refusal meant instant reprisal. Even Mad Wolf's companions seemed aware that the outcome of their visit depended solely on Shannon's reply.

Weighing her words carefully, Shannon said, "I am honored by your offer, Mad Wolf, but I cannot accept."

Mad Wolf stiffened, his eyes narrowing dangerously as they settled thoughtfully on Blade. "Swift Blade has spoken the truth. You have made your choice. But I do not accept it."

Wheeling his mount, he signaled his companions and they all thundered off across the plains toward the surrounding hills, their blood-curdling war cries reverberating with chilling horror.

"Shannon, what was that all about?" Callie wanted to know. Breathless with awe, she eyed Shannon curiously. She wasn't the only one who wanted to know as the emigrants crowded around Shannon demanding an explanation.

"Mad Wolf has taken a fancy to Shannon." Blade's terse explanation saved Shannon from forming a reply.

"Will he return?" one of the men asked.

"I don't think so," Blade lied, "but it won't hurt to continue posting extra guards and remain alert." He didn't wish to alarm the emigrants but neither did he want them unprepared. He knew that if he wanted Shannon as badly as Mad Wolf obviously did, he'd let nothing keep him from her.

"Mad Wolf won't attack," Clive Bailey predicted calmly. "We outnumber those renegades four to one. They might try to steal our livestock but they're not stupid. Go back to your wagons, everyone, let's get rolling."

The crowd dispersed reluctantly, but Blade remained behind to speak with Clive. "What makes you so damn certain the Sioux won't attack?"

"I just know," Clive said cryptically.

"Have you met Mad Wolf before?"

"Just do the job you are getting paid for and don't question my judgment," Clive retaliated. "Come along, Shannon, I'll see you back to your wagon."

Blade looked as if he wanted to object, but when he did not Shannon shrugged and walked away. Blade's gaze followed the graceful sway of her hips, the proud tilt of her head, and the sudden, inexplicable urge swept over him to sweep Shannon up in his arms, carry her to a secluded spot and make love to her tenderly—endlessly. Something about Shannon Branigan moved him deeply despite the fact that she held him in contempt. She already knew he was a half-breed—what would she do if she discovered he'd fought with the Yankees? The haughty Southern belle had voiced her hatred more than once for Yankees.

Shannon flounced off with a toss of her chestnut curls, feeling quite pleased with herself for the way she had put that renegade Mad Wolf in his place. But for some reason Blade seemed remote and preoccupied. The scowl appeared permanently etched on his face, especially when Clive Bailey was nearby. Vaguely she wondered at Mad Wolf's puzzling words. What did Blade tell the truth about? The glance Mad Wolf leveled at Blade before he rode off spoke eloquently of jealousy and hatred. What had Blade told Mad Wolf to make him jealous? Sighing wearily, Shannon climbed aboard the wagon with Callie as Clive tipped his hat and walked away. There were so many contradictions surrounding Blade that it would take the rest of her life to sort through them.

Horrified, Shannon realized where her thoughts were leading and blanched. The rest of her life? With a half-breed? Ridiculous!

Chapter Five

The wagon train continued along the Platte River.
Mad Wolf did not reappear, much to Shannon's relief.
Twice mail wagons escorted by eight or ten cavalry-
men from Fort Laramie sped by with little more than
a wave and a holler.

At this point the riverbed stretched one half mile
wide and was scantily covered with water a foot and a
half deep. Shannon was surprised by the furniture,
relics, and treasures strewn along the trail by emigrants no longer in need of such fripperies. They
passed a small trading fort made of logs, then crossed
a rapid stream running into the Platte. Excitement
was high when they reached Plumb Creek Station, the
only stopping place between Fort Kearney and
Julesburg, which had once been a connecting chain
for stage lines and mail. They spent but one
night, recalling that in 1864 the dozen or so inhabi-
tants of the station were killed and scalped by renegade Sioux.

They continued on to Cottonwood Springs, a good

camping place eighty miles west of Fort Kearney. Having gotten this far without mishap was cause for celebration, and after supper the fiddlers gathered at the center of the camp and soon dancers were stomping and whirling about with gay abandon. Even those who didn't dance stomped their feet and clapped their hands to the music. Catching her breath between dances, Shannon glanced around and saw that Blade was suspiciously absent. Then she noted that Clive Bailey stood a short distance from his wagon, a sour look on his face. His driver, Olson, had been assigned to guard duty tonight and Clive seemed disinclined to stray far from his wagon, though he looked as if he'd much prefer to join the revelry.

Suddenly Shannon saw something that made her heart slam against her ribs. A dark crouching figure detached itself from the shadows and entered Clive's wagon. Within seconds the shadowy figure became a part of the dark interior.

His attention on the dancers, Clive appeared not to notice. Was she the only one who saw what was happening? Shannon wondered. She was certain that Blade was continuing his mysterious search of each wagon and was amazed at his daring.

She was about to turn away when she saw Clive assume a thoughtful expression, then pause before the back flap of his wagon as if undecided whether or not to enter. All Shannon's senses screamed in silent warning, strangely unwilling to let Clive learn of Blade's suspicious behavior. She had no idea what was going on, but of the two men she'd trust Blade before Clive. But if she didn't act fast Blade would be in big trouble. Something inside her made her act spontaneously and without conscious thought to the consequences.

"Clive, won't you dance with me?"

Clive turned, a slow smile curving his thin lips. He couldn't believe his luck when he saw Shannon approach and ask him for a dance.

Blade had just entered Clive Bailey's wagon, convinced he'd find weapons but needing sufficient proof. Fort Laramie lay mere days away and time was running out. Blade knew he was pressing his luck, but he had waited a long time for just such an opportunity. Clive Bailey was less vigilant than Olson, so Blade threw caution to the wind and entered the wagon while Bailey's mind was occupied elsewhere.

A surge of elation seized Blade when he discovered a false bottom in the wagon. But it was short-lived. Clive's shadow fell across the opening of the wagon and Blade froze, knowing full well what would happen if he was discovered skulking inside wagons, especially Clive Bailey's wagon. Being a half-breed placed him in a dangerous position. One misstep and he'd find himself dangling from the end of a rope. People had little use for breeds in this part of the country. Besides, Bailey would know exactly why Blade was searching his wagon and wouldn't let him live long enough to tell. Blade had nearly resigned himself to being discovered when a flirty voice diverted Bailey's attention.

"Clive, won't you dance with me?"

"Why of course, Shannon," Blade heard Clive reply. "How could I refuse so pretty a request?"

Diminishing footsteps crunched in the dirt and Blade allowed himself to breathe again. Shannon didn't know it, but she had probably saved his life. Was she aware of what she did or did she really want to dance with Clive Bailey? He banished that disturbing thought from his mind as he quickly resumed his examination of the false wagonbed. Hoping the fiddlers would drown out the noise, he pried up a board and inserted his hand into the opening. His breath slammed from his chest as his fingers brushed the barrel of a rifle, then another, and another. Evidently the entire wagonbed held a treasure trove of weapons. And he'd bet his right arm Mad Wolf knew it!

Carefully Blade replaced the board and left the wagon as silently as he entered.

"Thank you for the dance, Shannon," Clive said, edging toward his wagon. He'd much rather stay and hold the elusive Shannon in his arms, but he hated to leave his wagon unprotected. He didn't trust that half-breed—he was far too nosy for Clive's liking. Actually, he didn't trust anyone on the wagon train. Anyone, including the half-breed, could be a government agent and the weapons he was smuggling inside his wagon were worth a small fortune.

Shannon's heart raced furiously as Clive edged toward his wagon. Though she'd kept her eyes peeled she hadn't seen Blade leave Clive's wagon and instinctively she knew he was still inside searching for God knew what. She couldn't let Clive leave now and discover Blade at whatever dirty work he was up to.

"Must you go?" she asked, surprising Clive. "It's such a beautiful night and I'm in the mood for a stroll."

Clive couldn't believe his ears. He'd spent weeks trying to get close to Shannon Branigan and had been thwarted at every turn. He was smart enough to take advantage of the unexpected bounty offered him and answered with alacrity. "I'd be happy to walk with you, Shannon. With Indians about I wouldn't want you walking out alone."

Clive didn't actually think Indians still lurked in the area, but he reckoned it wouldn't hurt to frighten Shannon a bit. He offered her his arm and they strolled together just beyond the circle of wagons, careful to keep well within the area between the sentries and line of wagons. It was a dark night except for the twinkling stars, and Shannon began to doubt the wisdom of being out here alone with Clive Bailey. She was about to suggest they return when she felt Clive's arm snake around her waist.

"I'm glad you finally came to your senses," Clive said. His smug tone set Shannon's teeth on edge. "At first I thought you were sweet on that half-breed, but he's not good enough for you. I realize he's a handsome brute, but he's a savage nevertheless."

Shannon froze, realizing she had made a serious error in judgment. "Take your hands off me."

"What's the matter, honey? Don't be bashful, you're the one who lured me out here. We're alone. Everyone is busy dancing and having a good time. Besides, the tall grass will hide us well enough." He began pulling her down to the ground with him, pinning her beneath him.

"Clive, no!" Shannon fought valiantly to resist. "I'll scream!"

Clive seemed confused. Isn't this what Shannon wanted? Acting spontaneously, he placed a hand over her mouth. "What kind of game are you playing?" he hissed in her ear. "Why did you invite me out here if it wasn't for a romp in the hay? Lay still, you little tease, and I'll try to make it good for you. But if you aggravate me, I'll take my pleasure and forget about yours."

Shannon could do little more than make desperate noises in her throat and shake her head frantically from side to side. What had once seemed like a good idea had swiftly disintegrated into a horrible nightmare. Why hadn't she left Blade to his own devices? she wondered grimly as she struggled with Clive. Having embarked on a dangerous path, Blade should have been prepared to accept the consequences. Why, oh why did she think she could help him?

Suddenly the pressure on her mouth eased and Shannon drew in great gulps of air. Though she couldn't see him, she knew Blade had found her in time to rescue her from Clive; it was the second time since the wagon train left Independence.

She was wrong—dead wrong.

It was true Clive no longer pressed her down onto the ground, but someone definitely more menacing had taken his place. A grotesque mask floated above her, its face streaked with paint, teeth white against the rich hue of copper skin. With recognition came fear, and Shannon opened her mouth to scream, only to find herself effectively muzzled by Mad Wolf's thick hand. She had replaced one devil with another!

Mad Wolf spoke not a word, grinning delightedly at having found Shannon so easily. He had expected difficulty in stealing Swift Blade's woman from under his nose, but Wakan Takan, the Grandfather spirit, must surely favor him to bring Little Firebird out to meet him. He moved with agile grace through the tall grass, dragging Shannon behind him, his hand still covering her mouth. He spared but one contemptuous glance at Clive Bailey's prone form. He hadn't clubbed him hard enough to kill him, but he would have had it been anyone else out here with the woman he desired for his own.

Shannon's struggles were like nothing to the powerful Sioux warrior. From the corner of her eye she caught a glimpse of Clive Bailey stretched out on the ground. She knew he wasn't dead, for he was moaning and thrashing around. Vaguely she wondered why the guard gave no warning—and then she knew. Olson lay near his post in a pool of blood, a tomahawk protruding from his back.

Beyond the outer perimeter of the camp, Mad Wolf's companions waited with horses. Flinging Shannon onto his pony, he leaped up behind her and whipped the animal into a gallop before Shannon had regained her breath. Her scream came too late, lost to the wind and the screech of an owl.

Blade casually rejoined the emigrants at the center of the camp. A deep frown worried his brow when he saw no sign of either Clive Bailey or Shannon. He would have left immediately to search for them if Nancy Wilson hadn't sidled up beside him and engaged him in conversation. When he was finally able to extract himself, Shannon still hadn't reappeared, and a terrible premonition seized him.

Blade made a thorough search of the camp once he escaped from Nancy Wilson, who seemed unwilling to let him go. Her eyes spoke eloquently of secret pleasures, and her voluptuous curves were tempting. But

Blade had other things on his mind. Shannon and
Clive were nowhere in camp, of that he was certain.
Had the little vixen lured Clive out on the prairie for a
reason? he wondered distractedly. Didn't she know
how dangerous the man was? She had barely escaped
Clive's attentions once—why did she deliberately
flout fate by tempting him again?

Just then someone screamed, followed by a commotion and general rush of people toward the wagons.
Setting his long legs into motion, Blade pushed his
way through the crowd, his heart leaping into his
mouth when he saw Clive Bailey stagger from between
two wagons.

"Injuns!" Clive gasped, falling to his knees.

That dreaded word sent the emigrants scrambling
to their wagons in search of weapons. Blade quickly
sized up the situation and took charge, dispatching
men to the guardposts and barking orders to those
remaining. Then he turned to Clive, his face a mask of
fury.

"Was Shannon with you?"

"Didn't she come back?" Clive asked groggily.

He swiped at the blood trickling from a minor head
wound and considered himself lucky to be alive. Truth
to tell, he hadn't given a passing thought to Shannon.
Moreover, he thought them safe from Indian attack
because of his alliance with Mad Wolf. If he learned
Mad Wolf was behind this, that scoundrel would pay
more dearly than he expected for the contraband
guns.

"Mad Wolf!" Blade spat, bombarding Clive with his
terrible anger. "You bastard! You let Mad Wolf take
Shannon! You know Mad Wolf wanted her—why did
you take her beyond camp?"

"Shannon wanted to take a stroll," Clive tried to
explain, backing away from Blade's implacable fury.
"I was only obliging her. Besides, we don't know Mad
Wolf has Shannon."

"Olson is dead!"

A foul oath leapt past Blade's lips.

One of the men had just returned from a search of the area with the grim announcement of Olson's death. The news sent the emigrants into a panic.

"What else did you find, Joe?" Blade asked, his voice low and strident.

"Nothing, all was quiet."

"Any sign of renegades?"

"If they were here, they're gone now," Joe revealed importantly. "We did find an area of tramped-down grass. Could have been made by Indians."

"Blade, I can't find Shannon!" Callie was beside herself with worry. She had looked for Shannon but could find her nowhere. "Where can she be?"

Distress turned Blade's black eyes bleak, his mouth a line of grim forboding. "I fear Mad Wolf has her."

"Oh, God!" Callie sobbed, clutching at Blade's arm. "What will he do to her?"

"We know he wants Shannon. The worst he can do is force her to become his—wife. My guess is that he won't harm her," Blade predicted, deliberately concealing his own fear. He knew Mad Wolf, knew what he was capable of. He also knew Shannon and her fiery temper and how easily she could rile Mad Wolf. He prayed he'd find her before it was too late.

"Oh, Blade, can't you do something?" Callie wailed. She desperately needed to be reassured.

"Of course I'm going to do something," Blade said tightly. "As soon as I speak to the men, I'm going after Shannon."

"What about the wagon train?" Clive charged. "You were paid to take us to Fort Laramie."

"You are close enough now to get yourselves to Fort Laramie," Blade returned shortly. "Dock my pay if you want, but nothing or no one will prevent me from going after Shannon Branigan." He turned to leave.

"Thank you, Blade," Callie called after him. "I know you'll find her."

Mounted before Mad Wolf, Shannon had a difficult time staying awake. They rode continuously through the night, stopping for nothing. If Mad Wolf's bronze arm hadn't held her on the horse's back, Shannon was certain she would have fallen off. Would Blade organize a search party and come after her? she wondered. Would they be able to find her? They should have discovered her absence by now. Clive will have told them after he returned to camp. What did Mad Wolf intend for her?

It was mid-morning and Shannon dozed fitfully against Mad Wolf's chest despite the fact that she tried desperately to remain alert. With a jolt of awareness she realized she was no longer in motion. Mad Wolf had reined his pony to a halt and Shannon's eyes jerked open to find dozens of Indians surrounding her. With a start, she realized that Mad Wolf had brought her to his village. Her spirits plummeted. How could she ever hope to be rescued from an entire village full of savages?

"Get down!" Mad Wolf snarled, shoving her from the pony's back. Shannon dropped with a thud, then slowly picked herself up from the ground.

Those watching the spectacle showed little emotion as Mad Wolf grabbed her long hair, dragging her toward one of the tipis scattered about the clearing. They had gotten no farther than a brightly painted tipi when an elderly man stepped out, raising his hand in greeting. Though the old Indian's face was deeply etched with fine lines, he wore his chief's regalia with pride. Nor had age dimmed his eyes, which were alive and quickly intelligent.

Mad Wolf ground to a halt just as a woman emerged from the tipi behind the chief. Younger than the chief, she possessed a mature beauty that was ageless. Wings of gray at her temples relieved the midnight of her hair, and her eyes were softly dark with compassion. The chief addressed Mad Wolf in the Sioux language.

"We have not seen you in many moons, Mad Wolf." For some reason the chief was not yet ready to acknowledge Shannon. "The young men of the village are greatly missed."

Several of Mad Wolf's band of renegades ducked their heads guiltily, aware that they should be spending their days hunting and providing for their families instead of raiding and killing.

"Someone must drive the White Eyes from our land, Yellow Dog," Mad Wolf answered rudely. "The old ones had their chance, and now it is left to the young warriors to save the people. The time swiftly approaches for new leadership. None can dispute my ability. My prowess and courage makes me the logical choice."

His bold words angered the lovely woman standing beside Yellow Dog. She would have lashed out if Yellow Dog hadn't motioned her to silence.

"One day your pride will be your downfall, Mad Wolf," Yellow Dog predicted. "I pray that when the time comes our people will chose a wise leader who realizes our future depends on our ability to live in peace with the white man. When my grandson returns, he will tell you what I say is true."

"Swift Blade has betrayed his heritage. He lives by the white man's laws. He fought in the white man's war." Mad Wolf's words dripped with venom.

"Don't speak so of my son!"

Shannon watched in consternation as the lovely Indian woman stepped forward, no longer able to hold her tongue. Shannon wondered what Mad Wolf said to make her so angry.

"Do not let Mad Wolf's words anger you, Singing Rain," Yellow Dog said, placing a restraining hand on her arm. "The young are hot-blooded and swift to accuse."

Then Yellow Dog's attention strayed to Shannon, who had astutely remained mute but watchful. She did not quail before the old chief's scrutiny; her candid blue eyes regarded him with curiosity and awe.

"The woman is my prisoner," Mad Wolf revealed, answering Yellow Dog's silent question.

"Is that wise?" Yellow Dog asked. "Where does she come from? I fear your rash impulses will one day bring trouble to our village."

"Little Firebird comes from one of the wagon trains invading our land," Mad Wolf stated. His lips curled into a snarl when he thought how easily he had captured her.

"Does Little Firebird have a husband?" Singing Rain interjected, her soft heart going out to the unfortunate young woman.

"I will be Little Firebird's husband." Mad Wolf emphasized his words by pounding a fist against his broad chest. "Tonight she will cradle me between her white thighs and I will give her a son."

Had Shannon understood his words she would have vented more than her anger on him.

Aware that he held little authority over the impetuous young warriors who thirsted for white man's blood, Yellow Dog did not object when Mad Wolf began dragging Shannon away. But Shannon objected violently.

"No! What do you want with me?" She screeched at the top of her lungs, digging her heels in the dusty ground. "Don't let him take me," Shannon begged, aiming her words toward Singing Rain. There was no one else to appeal to except the lovely woman with sympathetic eyes.

A frown marred Singing Rain's wide brow. She had no right to interfere with Mad Wolf, nor did Yellow Dog. Sioux law made Little Firebird Mad Wolf's property to do with as he pleased. Mad Wolf had every right to claim the captive and mate with her. Perhaps Little Firebird did not realize it was to her advantage to be Mad Wolf's wife rather than his slave. Boldly she stepped before Mad Wolf, risking his rage by stopping him in his tracks.

"Out of my way, Singing Rain."

"I would speak with the girl," Singing Rain demanded.

"Why?"

"She is frightened. Perhaps I can help."

"Pah! You and your half-breed son are too sympathetic toward the white man whose soldiers massacre our woman and children, kill our buffalo, and trample our sacred grounds."

"Little Firebird has done none of these things you speak of," Singing Rain defended. She had no idea why she felt such empathy for this particular young woman, but something about her moved her deeply.

"Speak then," Mad Wolf permitted grudgingly. He stood mutely aside, arms folded against his massive chest as Singing Rain approached Shannon.

Singing Rain's interference sent Shannon's hopes soaring and she lifted pleading eyes to the Indian woman. "Let me go back to my people," she choked out, certain the woman understood. "My name is Shannon Branigan and I'm on my way to join my family in Idaho. I've done you no harm."

"I am called Singing Rain."

"Thank God you speak English. Can you help me?"

"I am powerless to help you return to your people," Singing Rain said sadly. "I can only ease your mind about Mad Wolf's intentions. If you obey Mad Wolf, you will not be harmed."

Mad Wolf grunted his approval. Singing Rain interpreted it as permission to continue. "Mad Wolf is a mighty warrior. You and your children will be amply provided for."

"Children! I—I don't understand." Deep in her heart she knew exactly what Mad Wolf wanted from her, but she had deliberately blanked it from her mind.

"Mad Wolf isn't required to mate with you," Singing Rain tried to impress upon Shannon. "He could use you himself or give you to the other men to use as they please. He does you honor by taking you to wife. You must accept your new life."

"Never!" denied Shannon, her blue eyes wide with horror. "I won't be a wife to a—a red savage!"

"Enough!" Mad Wolf barked. "I will tell Little Firebird all she needs to know." Grasping her wrist he pulled her along behind him.

"Singing Rain! Don't let him take me away!" Shannon beseeched.

"Quiet!" Mad Wolf admonished. Harsh disapproval made him unnecessarily rough as he jerked her forward.

Abruptly he halted before a tipi, threw open the flap, and flung Shannon inside. "What are you going to do?" she asked, looking around furtively for a way to escape.

"I will send Crow Woman to you," Mad Wolf said, unable to disguise the flare of desire turning his body to granite hardness. Never had he wanted a woman as badly as he did Little Firebird. His nostrils flared and his mouth quivered with a need that no other woman could assuage.

"Who is Crow Woman?" Shannon demanded to know, "and why are you sending her to me?"

Mad Wolf's lips curled in a curiously smug smile. "Crow Woman is my wife. You will obey her."

"Your wife! Why do you want me if you already have a wife?"

"It is our way," Mad Wolf said tersely. "Tonight you will mate with me and share the chores with Crow Woman." Having said all he intended, Mad Wolf turned to leave.

"I won't do it!" Shannon defied, eyes ablaze, her body tense. Mad Wolf merely smiled with chilling effect as he left the tipi.

Shannon rushed to the entrance, lifting the flap and peering out—only to find one of Mad Wolf's followers stationed outside. Whirling, she calmed down long enough to examine the interior of the tipi, hoping to find another way of escape.

The tipi was surprisingly spacious. Four long poles held the buffalo hide in place with an adjustable flap at the top to either retain heat or provide ventilation. Wooden lodge pins held the skins in place and were easily removable so the tent could be folded for traveling. A firepit had been dug at its center for cooking; a tripod and buffalo-pouch cooking pot stood nearby. In addition to rolled buffalo-skin bedding, a backrest leaned against one of the poles. Several parfleches, used primarily for storage, hung from the walls, as did a medicine bag holding sacred items. A wooden bow and quiver with arrows also hung from the tent's interior, but Shannon realized they'd be useless in her unskilled hands.

Shannon was about to search the parfleches when the tent flap was flung aside and a woman, somewhere near her own age, entered. She was possessed of a striking handsomeness, but she was not pretty in a strictly feminine sense. She was tall; her figure was good but not extraordinary. Her coal-black eyes blazed at Shannon with implacable fury.

"Who are you?" Shannon asked, backing away. The Indian woman was several inches taller and many pounds heavier than she. Shannon's question was met with bared teeth and a snarl. "Are you Crow Woman?"

"Crow Woman speaks no English." Mad Wolf had entered behind Crow Woman. "Do not anger her. She is here at my bidding." Then he turned abruptly and left the tent.

Crow Woman advanced on Shannon, an unholy glint in her black eyes. Obviously the woman was less than pleased with the prospect of her husband's taking another wife. Shannon wasn't happy about that herself. Then Crow Woman began tearing at Shannon's clothes. Shannon protested vigorously, for all the good it did her. The woman's strength was awesome, and soon Shannon stood gloriously nude before Crow Woman's appraising glare. Shannon was stunned when the woman turned and left with every stitch of her clothes clutched in her hands.

"Wait! My clothes!" Shannon's temper flared as she raged at God for letting this happen. Surely this wasn't in his plan for her. She knew she wasn't always as good a person as her mother would like her to be, but she had a deep and abiding faith in God that did not waver despite her predilection for getting herself

into trouble and expecting God to rescue her. This
time she'd really done it!

By the time Crow Woman returned with a pouch of
water, Shannon had found a blanket to cover her
nakedness. Crow Woman snorted in disgust and indicated that Shannon was to use the water for bathing.
Shannon wanted to resist, but then relented, deciding
she could indeed benefit from a bath. Using the
blanket as a shield she washed hurriedly under Crow
Woman's menacing glare. When she finished, Crow
Woman removed a soft doeskin dress from a basket
and tossed it at Shannon. Grateful for any decent
covering, Shannon shrugged into the single garment.

The doeskin dress felt soft and exquisitely comfortable against her skin. A dull tan color and richly
embroidered and fringed, it skimmed her body, falling in graceful lines to midcalf. Moccasins laced to her
knees were provided somewhat grudgingly by Crow
Woman. When Shannon was dressed Crow Woman
pushed her outside, pinching her painfully when she
failed to move fast enough. She set Shannon to the
task of grinding dried corn into fine meal. Mad Wolf
came by once, stared at her with expressionless eyes,
then left. No one else seemed to pay her any heed
except for Crow Woman, who observed Shannon with
bitter resentment.

The chore Shannon performed left sufficient time to
ponder her fate and what was likely to happen to her
tonight. She hadn't entirely abandoned hope that God
would somehow perform a miracle and arrange a
rescue from this terrible situation. But with each
passing hour she grew more doubtful. Shannon knew
that when darkness arrived Mad Wolf would rape her,
proving his mastery over her in the most basic way.

Time and again her mind turned to Blade and how
his kisses made her feel, the way his hands turned her
flesh to liquid fire. What would have happened if she
had succumbed to Blade's desire and her own? she
wondered wistfully. At least she would have known
what to expect tonight. Without being told, Shannon

knew Blade would have made her first time memorable.

Then Shannon thought of her family—how much she loved them, how she longed to see them again—and resolve stiffened her spine. She *would* see them again. Stubborn to a fault, courageous, fiercely proud —just like all the Branigans—Shannon had already decided she wouldn't submit easily to Mad Wolf. She might earn herself a beating, or worse, but she'd resist to her dying breath. Mama didn't raise any timid girls, Shannon reflected, but if she ever needed the Branigan courage, it was now.

Chapter Six

Dusk brought a flurry of activity to the village as the women prepared supper. Shannon, instructed by Crow Woman, prepared a sort of fried bread made out of the cornmeal she had ground earlier. When the meal was prepared, Mad Wolf returned to the tipi, sitting in stoic contemplation while Shannon served him. Shannon felt his dark eyes follow her—probing, unfathomable, stark in their intensity—and she shuddered. Revulsion rose stark and black in her breast and panic nearly paralyzed her.

Mad Wolf was so immersed in his fantasies of Shannon and how he would subdue and possess her that he failed to hear the commotion outside the tipi or the sound of voices raised in excitement. Even Crow Woman seemed unaware of the disturbance, her jealousy making her oblivious to all but Mad Wolf's obsession with the white woman.

"Leave us!" Mad Wolf snarled at Crow Woman, making a chopping motion toward the door. Slanting

Shannon a malevolent glare, Crow Woman turned abruptly and left the tipi.

"No! Don't go!" Shannon cried, stiff with terror. She didn't understand what Mad Wolf said but when Crow Woman left, she knew. Oh yes, she knew, but she wasn't going to submit meekly.

Eyeing the entrance of the tent in a speculative manner, Shannon came to a sudden decision. Gathering her courage, she bolted from the tipi, not caring where she went as long as it was far away from Mad Wolf. In her heart she knew she hadn't a prayer of escaping Mad Wolf or leaving the village alive, yet Shannon ran—and ran—and ran straight into a massive bronze chest and a pair of arms that trapped her as effectively as steel bands. A ragged scream ripped from her throat.

Blade rode into the village a few hours behind Mad Wolf and Shannon. He knew exactly where Mad Wolf was headed. Having spent many happy years there with his mother and father, he knew the precise location of the village. The last rays of the waning sun reflected off the broad expanse of his pale bronze chest and his buckskin clad legs clung firmly to the back of his saddleless gray pony. His face was set in grim lines, his eyes dark and potent with determination.

The people watched curiously as Blade rode through the village, some hostile but most merely inquisitive. It had been ten years since anyone in the village had seen Swift Blade, and during those years his youthful form, though strong and powerful even then had matured into a finely tuned machine of muscle and brawn. He rode with the superb horsemanship of the Sioux, his body a part of the animal, his movements fluid and graceful. His carriage was proud, yet that part of him that was white was easily discernible in the light hue of his skin and slight wave to his thick black hair.

Suddenly a tall young man burst forth from the

throng of people, his face wreathed in smiles. "Swift Blade!"

A wide grin parted Blade's full lips as he brought one long leg over Warrior's neck and slid from his broad back. Immediately one of the children sprinted forward to take the reins and lead the big gray away.

"It is good to see you again, Jumping Buffalo," Blade greeted warmly. "It has been many moons." The two men embraced, clasping forearms and pounding each other on the back.

"Your mother and grandfather have awaited your return."

"How are they?"

Jumping Buffalo beamed. "Judge for yourself, they approach now."

Leaving Chief Yellow Dog behind, Singing Rain's face was radiantly alive and happy as she rushed toward her tall son. She had prayed daily to Wakan Takan for his safe return, and at long last her prayers had been answered. Blade held out his arms and Singing Rain was swept into her son's brawny embrace.

"Mother," he said with quiet dignity. "I am sorry about Father."

With stoic Indian fatalism, Singing Rain said, "He died bravely, my son. He killed the grizzly, but his wounds proved fatal. He survived but a few hours."

Yellow Dog reached Blade now, his faded eyes alight with fierce pride. "Welcome home, my grandson."

"Thank you, Grandfather," Blade answered with warm regard. He loved this wise old man dearly.

"Have you come home to stay?"

"Is Mad Wolf here?" Blade asked, deliberately disregarding Yellow Dog's question.

Yellow Dog and Singing Rain exchanged worried looks. "Why do you seek Mad Wolf?" Singing Rain asked cautiously.

"Mad Wolf has stolen my woman."

"Your woman!" Singing Rain repeated, stunned.

"Mad Wolf told us he stole Little Firebird from a wagon train."

"He did," Blade said tightly. "Like a coward, he stole Shannon Branigan after I told him he couldn't buy her. Like thieves in the night they came and took what was mine." He turned and looked pointedly at Jumping Buffalo, his eyes accusing.

Jumping Buffalo stepped forward, his expression indignant, his head held high. "I do not ride with those hot-bloods. I follow the rules set forth by Yellow Dog and the council."

"I am happy to hear it." Then he turned to Yellow Dog. "Where has Mad Wolf taken my woman?" His eyes were hard, his tone implacable.

He hoped Shannon would play along with him on this. The only hope he had of wresting her from Mad Wolf's grasp was by claiming her himself. He prayed Mad Wolf hadn't already taken Shannon by force. Not only would it make his job more difficult, but he worried about what it might do to Shannon's spirit. It was one of the traits he admired so much in her.

Yellow Dog pointed to Mad Wolf's tipi just as Crow Woman stomped out of it in angry defiance. Blade looked to Yellow Dog for confirmation. The old chief nodded and Blade set his long legs in motion. He had taken just a few steps when Shannon burst from the tipi, her eyes wild, her face masked in terror. Mad Wolf followed in hot pursuit. A ragged scream ripped from Shannon's throat when Blade snatched her up in his arms, pulling her against his bare chest. His arms enclosed her like bands of tempered steel as he held her soft body, a pang of something deep and profoundly moving jolting through him.

"Shannon," he said. "Little Firebird," he repeated, attempting to calm her without adding to her fright. Mad Wolf had already done an admirable job of that. "Stop fighting me."

The voice hardly registered as Shannon struggled against the restraining arms holding her prisoner. His strength was awesome, his powerful, bulging muscles effectively quelling Shannon's struggles.

"Shannon," Blade repeated once more.

Shannon froze. Blade! Blade had come to help her. She went limp, profound relief turning her muscles to jelly. Then she realized that nothing had changed when Mad Wolf, following close behind, pulled her rudely from Blade's arms. He was determined to have Shannon at any cost.

Blade knew the moment Shannon recognized him, for she went limp in his arms. He wanted to tell her everything was going to be all right, longed to ask her if Mad Wolf had hurt her—but there wasn't time. Hard on Shannon's heels, Mad Wolf yanked her from Blade's arms, his mouth curved in a snarl.

"Little Firebird is mine," Mad Wolf rasped menacingly.

"You have no right," Blade challenged. "Little Firebird is my woman." Addressing Shannon, he asked, "Has Mad Wolf hurt you, Shannon?"

"N-no," Shannon stammered. Try as she might, she found it difficult to believe that Blade had arrived so quickly.

Blade drew in a ragged breath. "Thank God."

"Blade, don't let him take me," Shannon implored, aware that Blade and Mad Wolf were arguing over her. "Tell me what is going on?" Not knowing what was happening made the situation seem even more desperate.

"It's all right, Shannon," Blade explained, slipping easily into English. "I told them you belonged to me, that Mad Wolf couldn't have you."

Shannon mulled over Blade's words; the intensity of his gaze begged—nay, demanded—her compliance. In her mind she knew he was trying to convey something—something vital to her survival. If she expected to walk away from this intolerable situation she had to place her trust in Blade. For some unexplained reason, it seemed imperative that she proclaim herself Blade's woman.

Wise from the weight of many years, Yellow Dog

intuitively sensed Shannon's confusion. In halting English, he asked, "Does my grandson speak the truth? Are you his woman?"

"Grandson! Is Blade your grandson?" Shannon asked, stunned.

"And my son," Singing Rain claimed, stepping forward. Maternal pride brought a softness to her voice and a special brightness to her eyes.

"Answer Grandfather's question, Shannon," Blade prodded. He spoke in low urgent tones that demanded total submission to his will.

Shannon hesitated a brief instant before responding. "Blade does not lie, I am his woman." She nearly choked on the words.

"She lies!" Mad Wolf blasted, increasing his grip on Shannon's arm. "I watched the wagon train for many suns, and not once did Swift Blade share a mat with Little Firebird. She travels with another man, his mate and their papoose. She sleeps alone each night." He slanted Blade a fulminating look. "Do you truly believe a virile man like Swift Blade would allow his woman to sleep alone?"

"You do not understand the white man's ways," Blade replied, unperturbed. "Little Firebird is my woman, but if her people suspected they would despise and shun her. White women do not bed half-breeds."

Mad Wolf looked confused and Blade used his confusion to press on. "I will take Little Firebird back to her people." With determined force he claimed Shannon's arm from Mad Wolf's grasp.

Mad Wolf exploded in angry frustration. "No! Little Firebird is mine. Together we will produce strong sons."

"Perhaps she is already carrying mine," Blade hinted.

The two men appeared ready to tear each other apart—and would have if Yellow Dog hadn't interceded.

"Cease! The council of elders will decide who will

claim Little Firebird. Mad Wolf must adhere to tribal law as long as he remains in our village. It is the same with you, Swift Blade. No man is above our law."

The Sioux nation was divided into several independent bands, united under no central government. They rarely united, even in war, though they spoke the same language and had the same usages and superstitions. Each band was divided into villages; each village ruled by a chief who was honored and respected only so long as his personal qualities commanded respect and fear. Sometimes the chief's authority was absolute, and often a council of elders influenced his decisions. Because this decision involved his grandson, Yellow Dog wisely elected to call a council meeting to help him reach a fair conclusion. It was due to his just judgment, courage, and sense of fairness that the aging chief still ruled his village. Among the Sioux, who wandered incessantly winter and summer, he was well loved and obeyed by all, but for men like Mad Wolf who sought to usurp his power.

"Take Little Firebird to your tipi, my daughter," Yellow Dog directed. Singing Rain moved to obey. "The council will decide this issue when they meet tomorrow."

Singing Rain took Shannon gently by the arm. "Come."

"Where are you taking me?" Shannon asked, aiming a silent plea in Blade's direction.

"Go with Singing Rain, Shannon," Blade encouraged. "My mother will see that no harm comes to you while your fate is being decided by the council."

"There is nothing to decide," Shannon vowed staunchly. "I want to leave."

"It's not that simple," Blade tried to explain.

"The council will decide in my favor," Mad Wolf loudly proclaimed. His arrogant tone and smug confidence left a bad taste in Blade's mouth. "You cannot claim a woman you have never bedded." Mad Wolf pressed on. "I am the one who will lie between her white thighs and pillow my head on her soft breast."

Whirling on his heel, he stomped away.

Mad Wolf's audacious words brought a sputter of outrage from Blade's lips. He was well aware that the decision could go in Mad Wolf's favor if Shannon was asked point-blank whether Blade had bedded her, and she either faltered or was slow to reply. Intuitively Blade knew Shannon would be an inept liar, and that the council of elders were wise enough to recognize the difference between a lie and the truth.

"Wait for my return, my son. We have much to discuss," Singing Rain said as she led Shannon away.

Blade nodded, his eyes following Shannon's trim back as she walked reluctantly beside Singing Rain. She looked back once with such pleading in her eyes that it nearly broke Blade's heart.

He had been so engrossed in his confrontation with Mad Wolf that he hadn't noticed how enchanting Shannon looked dressed in Indian garb. Every line and curve of her supple form moved with fluid grace beneath the single garment. He thanked God that he had arrived in time to save Shannon from being raped by Mad Wolf.

Blade felt a compelling need to protect and comfort Shannon. Twice he had come close to making love to her and gained his senses in the nick of time. She didn't need a half-breed complicating her life, yet the hungry yearning to possess her was a constant ache in his loins. Not only did he crave to taste her innocent sweetness, but he wanted almost as much to comfort her and appease her every wish. My God! Blade thought, astounded at the direction of his thoughts. He was waxing sentimental in his old age.

"What will happen to me?" Shannon asked Singing Rain as she settled herself on the mat inside the Indian woman's tipi.

It had grown dark, and Singing Rain busied herself lighting a fire. Once that task was completed she crouched down beside Shannon and spoke in low, soothing tones.

"The council of elders will meet tomorrow and decide your fate. Try not to worry. I'm sure they will decide in Swift Blade's favor."

"Try not to worry!" Shannon repeated numbly. "They could give me to Mad Wolf. Where is Blade? Why can't I see him?"

Singing Rain smiled a secret smile. She had always hoped her handsome son would find a woman to match him in strength and courage, and she was pleased he had chosen the woman called Shannon.

"It grows late, Little Firebird. Lie down and sleep. We must trust the elders to make the right decision. Before they pronounce judgement you will be called upon to answer a few simple questions. It is important that you answer them honestly, for the elders are wise men who can easily distinguish lies from the truth."

"What kind of questions? What should I say?"

"You must speak what is in your heart," Singing Rain advised. Her ambiguous answer did little to appease Shannon's fear. "I must go now and speak with my son."

"No! Don't go!"

"No harm will come to you here. It has been ten long years since I have seen Swift Blade."

"Oh," Shannon said in a small voice. How selfish of her to monopolize Singing Rain when she longed to speak privately with her son.

After Singing Rain left, Shannon stretched out on the mat, grateful for her reprieve, no matter how short-lived. It wasn't long before her lids dropped; the day had been long and arduous and she'd had blessed little sleep in the past forty-eight hours. All she managed before falling asleep was a short prayer thanking God for sending Blade and asking His forgiveness for doubting Him.

Singing Rain smiled up at her tall son with fierce pride. He had left as a youth and returned a powerful warrior, handsome, virile, strong. Timidly she touched his face, her soft brown eyes conveying her love without having to say the words.

"You've changed, my son."

"I am a grown man, mother. These past ten years I have learned the white man's ways to please my father."

"He would have been proud of you, just as I am," Singing Rain said. Profound sadness colored her words. "He was content with your decision to join the white man's war. Slavery was not his belief. Will you stay?"

"I cannot stay, Mother. I am on an important mission for the Great Father in Washington," Blade explained cautiously. "Many lives depend on my success. I cannot tell you more than that, and you must not speak of what I have just revealed."

"I will say nothing, my son," Singing Rain promised. "Are you in danger?" Blade hesitated a moment too long, his silence answer enough. "Please be careful, Swift Blade."

"I've lost none of my Sioux cunning, Mother," Blade smiled crookedly.

"What about the girl? Mad Wolf is determined to have her."

"I know," Blade acknowledged grimly. "I am hoping the council will decide in my favor."

"Is Little Firebird truly your woman?"

"I have said it, haven't I?"

"Swift Blade, you know what I mean," Singing Rain chided gently. "She must speak truthfully when she is asked if you have taken her to your mat. I fear that you have said it only to save her from Mad Wolf." She leveled Blade a measuring look. "Only if you speak the truth will you be allowed to claim her. But if her answer is no or the council thinks she is lying . . ." Her sentence trailed off, leaving much unsaid. "Can you be absolutely certain the council will believe her if her answer is yes?"

Blade remained silent, chewing on Singing Rain's ominous words. Her meaning did not escape him. The message she tried to convey was that Shannon would only be believed if Blade had actually bedded her. The elders would recognize the truth when they heard it. My God! Did he dare? Did he actually dare so brazen a thing? His body grew hard just thinking about it. Would Shannon hate him for even suggesting something so outrageous? With a twinge of regret he decided his way was the only method he could think of to keep Mad Wolf from having her.

"Your point is well taken, Mother," Blade acknowledged.

Beads of sweat broke out on his forehead and his mouth turned dry. He knew what he had to do was wrong, but he had no other choice.

Singing Rain searched Blade's face and saw that he understood clearly what must be done. She was satisfied that she had done her duty. It was up to Blade now to find the will and the way. It was not what she would have wished for Little Firebird, but her fate depended solely on Blade.

"Go now, my son. We will talk tomorrow." Her soft brown eyes searched Blade's face, conveying a silent message. "I will sleep in Yellow Dog's tipi tonight."

Singing Rain's departing words reverberated like thunder in Blade's brain. Shannon would be alone tonight!

The village was quiet. Even the dogs had settled down for the night. Everyone slept—everyone but Blade. He approached the tipi where Shannon slumbered as silent as a wraith. Pushing aside the tent flap, he slipped inside. Glowing embers still burned in the shallow firepit, and Blade could see Shannon clearly. She lay on her side, the rise of her hip and slender curve of her waist titillating his senses. Long lustrous strands of chestnut hair fell across her face in glorious disarray and Blade stood mesmerized by the utterly enchanting picture she made. Then the look on his face changed abruptly to one of grim determination. Hunkering down beside her, he gently shook her shoulder.

Shannon awoke with a start; her dreams had been filled with terrible visions and premonitions. She never would have allowed herself to sleep tonight if Singing Rain hadn't promised her she wouldn't be disturbed. She trusted Blade's mother but wondered at her wisdom when she was rudely awakened and found someone crouching over her. Her first inclination was to scream. Then she recognized Blade.

"Blade, you frightened me! What are you doing here?"

"Shannon," Blade said with gentle persuasion, "you want to leave here, don't you?"

"Of course. What kind of question is that?"

"An important one," Blade said urgently. "Mad Wolf wants you, and there is only one way I can save you."

"My God, don't play games with me! I know you came here for me. Why can't we just leave?"

"It is not that simple, Shannon. Because my grandfather is chief, I feel obligated to obey tribal customs. But there is a way. In order for it to work, you must do exactly as I say. I told Yellow Dog and the council that you were my woman. It is up to you now to convince them that I speak the truth. You will be required to appear before them tomorrow and answer their questions."

"Tell me what to say," Shannon said eagerly. "I already admitted I was your woman—what more can I tell them?"

"What I tell you now may make you angry but it can't be helped," Blade said slowly. "You will be asked if I have bedded you. Only an affirmative answer will save you from Mad Wolf."

Shannon went numb with shock. How could anyone ask such a question of her? "No, I won't do it! Besides, I—I'm a terrible liar. They will know immediately that it's not true. I've never heard of such a thing."

"Indians don't follow white man's laws," Blade said pointedly. "The council consists of old and wise men trained to recognize lies and deception. You can tell them we are lovers, but if we are not they will read the truth in your eyes. Unless . . ." His sentence dangled in the air, waiting for Shannon to grasp his meaning.

A dull red crept up Shannon's neck and face. "Unless . . ." The word was a mere whisper.

". . . unless it is true," Blade said, expelling his breath sharply.

"Blade, you can't mean . . . You don't expect to . . . No! I won't let you!" Comprehension slammed into her like a bolt of lightning.

"Is making love with a savage so unthinkable? Would you rather take your chances with Mad Wolf?" Blade's blunt questions made more sense than Shannon cared to admit. It was just that she always thought making love was something one did only if love was present. Blade would be taking her virginity for the wrong reasons. But was there any other choice?

"Is there no other way?"

"I'm afraid not," Blade responded, captivated by the play of emotions on Shannon's lovely features. "You've never made love with a man before, have you?"

"Of course not!" Shannon spouted indignantly. "That right belongs to my husband."

Shannon hated to admit to Blade that making love with him didn't frighten her—far from it. If anything, the thought brought a shiver of wild anticipation. It was allowing so intimate an act to a man not her husband that concerned her. It was clearly something that was never even discussed in her family, for her strict upbringing forbade intimacy without the benefit of marriage for any reason.

"I'm sorry, Little Firebird, but it has to be this way. I'm not unskilled; I won't hurt you. You may even enjoy it," Blade added with a mischievous chuckle. He slid his lean length down beside her on the buffalo robe.

"No! I can't," Shannon cried, scooting backwards. "It seems such a cold thing to do. It's not right!"

"No, not cold, Little Firebird," Blade whispered

huskily. "I've thought about this from the first moment I saw you. If my kisses didn't repel you, why should my lovemaking? Forget I'm an Indian and think of me as a man—a man who wants you not merely to keep Mad Wolf from having you but because you are a beautiful, sensual woman ripe for love."

He kissed her eyes, her nose, each tiny ear before sliding his mouth down her neck and then slowly up again to claim her lips.

Shannon wanted to resist, wanted to deny that his words affected her in any way, but she could not. She couldn't count the times she had thought about his kisses, dreamed about lying like this in his arms, knowing all the time it was impossible. It was wrong —wrong—wrong.

But if that were true, how could anything that felt so wonderful be sinful? Even as her body responded, her mind rejected utterly what Blade was doing, what was going to happen, and she stiffened. Though her head might be whirling in confusion, she couldn't accept this without offering resistence.

"Don't do this, Blade."

"You know I must."

"I realize you think this is necessary, but I'll hate you afterwards."

"I accept that. Understand this, Little Firebird, I'll do anything to save you from Mad Wolf, even live with your hatred."

"It changes nothing."

Blade winced but continued as if she hadn't spoken. "Lift your arms, I'll help you remove your dress."

"Must you?"

"Please, Shannon, trust me. I don't want you to go through life fearing men or marriage because of what I must do. I don't want to leave scars for an act that should bring pleasure. Let me do this right and I promise that when you join your family, the physical side of marriage will hold no more fears for you. Hate me if it will ease your conscience, but don't fight me."

Shannon swallowed convulsively. She searched Blade's dark face for the space of a heartbeat before obediently lifting her arms so he could slide her dress over her head. Blade's hands shook as he slowly bared Shannon's body. He'd dreamed often of what she would look like naked, fantasized holding her in his arms, loving her, burying himself in the tight, hot folds of her woman's flesh. He knew it was forbidden him, tried not to think about it. But now that it was about to become a reality he felt stimulated, aroused and so excited he couldn't stop shaking.

"My God, you're incredible!" Blade said reverently. The satiny expanse of milky white flesh he had just exposed left him speechless. Blade had seen more than his share of nude women, but none so lovely as Shannon. Her breasts were high, the nipples full and rosy, as ripe as summer's first fruit, as sweetly tempting. Her legs were long and supple; her body expressly made for loving, for countless hours of leisurely exploration.

With more tenderness than he thought possible, Blade cradled her breast with his palm, eliciting a gasp from Shannon. Her breath came with ragged quickness that only increased when his thumb played lightly over her pink-hewed nipple. They rose impudently, causing Blade to grin with easy arrogance.

"You like that?" he asked. His arms slid tightly around her and his mouth replaced his hand on her breast. Her body went rigid and hot, and soon she was certain her flesh was melting as he sucked her nipples, first one then the other.

"Y . . . yes," Shannon admitted with a pang of guilt. "Oh God, yes!"

His mouth left her breast, his tongue slid up her neck to her ear, leisurely exploring each curve and crevice, making her thoughts fly off in tattered confusion while his hands shifted up and down her back. Then he found her mouth and the briefest of seconds passed as his gaze locked with hers. All her senses seemed to freeze until she was overwhelmed with sensation.

The tip of Blade's tongue moistened the corners of her mouth, urging her lips apart, but Shannon did not understand. "Open your mouth, Little Firebird," Blade whispered against her lips. Then his tongue intruded into the sweet dampness of her mouth. His kiss was fiercely demanding, yet so tender Shannon scarcely realized she was kissing him back; his arms were iron and stone, yet so gentle she welcomed the pressure.

Shannon felt his hands on her breasts, caressing the naked flesh, his palms rough and painfully exciting against the hardened nubs. His kiss was like nothing she had ever experienced; his previous kisses mere child's play compared to this invasion of her senses. Overwhelmed and frightened by the sensations and feelings scattering her wits and stealing her will, Shannon made a valiant effort to control the course her life was taking.

"Blade, no, I'm frightened!"

"Relax, Little Firebird, you're doing beautifully," Blade crooned in her ear. "Don't think, let your body speak for you. It tells me what you like, see?" he said, taking her hand and placing it between her legs. "Feel how wet you've become? It tells me you are nearly ready."

Then he was kissing her again, dragging her down into the pit of swirling passion. When she tore her mouth from his, he groaned with disappointment, thinking he had frightened her with his unbridled lust. "Shannon," he groaned, "let me, let me . . ."

His fingers dug into her hair, pulling her lips back to his. If anyone had told Blade that making love to Shannon would be such exquisite delight he wouldn't have believed it. His body straining for desperate relief, Blade dragged his lips from hers, waiting for his passion to subside so he could continue. He'd promised Shannon pleasure, and he was a man of his word.

He used the brief respite to shed his trousers, and when he came back to Shannon she felt the hard thrust of his manhood against her stomach. Overcoming her shyness, she dared to glance down, not too frightened to satisfy her curiosity.

"Look to your heart's content, Little Firebird," Blade said. His voice shook with wry amusement and he gave her a grin so wicked she felt a shiver of excitement run up her spine. "I want you to know what is going to give you pleasure."

With a desperation Shannon refused to question, she pulled Blade down atop her. She felt herself go hot and liquid at the feel of her distended nipples against his own hard male nubs. And then his hand was between her legs, against her soft woman's flesh, stroking, probing with bold command and tender concern. The heat of his touch swirled over her in searing, liquid fire. He caressed her boldly, deeply, setting up a rhythm that seared her; the pad of his thumb against her tender flesh left her weak and gasping and she pushed against him when the sensation became sweet agony.

"Yes, Little Firebird," Blade rasped raggedly, no longer able to contain his rampaging desire. He couldn't remember when a woman had affected him as profoundly as Shannon. What made this feisty Southern belle different from any of the other women he'd bedded? Blade wondered. "Open your legs, Shannon."

Shannon froze as his huge hot shaft probed between her legs. How could she go through with this? she asked herself in a brief moment of sanity. She couldn't. "No!" she cried, shaking her head from side to side. She jerked backwards, trying to escape his relentless prodding, but it was too late . . . too late . . .

"Yes," Blade answered, having come too far to turn back now.

He moved gently, slowly, deeply into her. She felt

herself fill and stretch with the hugeness of him. A sharp pain between her legs brought Shannon surging against him in an effort to dislodge him. Nobody warned her it would hurt so much! A gasp of agony left her mouth.

"Blade, I can't bear it!"

He covered her mouth with a searing kiss, waiting for the pain to ebb to a slow burning. He hated hurting her, but it couldn't be helped. No amount of gentleness could erase the pain a girl felt when she was led into womanhood.

A low, rough moan burst from Blade's throat as her hot, moist flesh closed tightly around him. He entered fully now, one quick thrust that made her his, sliding slowly in and out, deeply, sweetly, using all his strength to delay his own release until Shannon found hers.

"You're mine, mine, mine," he whispered savagely.

Once the pain subsided, Shannon experienced a pleasure so intense that she had to bite her lips to hold back a scream. She never counted on anything like this, never realized such feelings existed or were even possible. Then her wits scattered as Blade suckled and licked her nipples, every stroke of his tongue sending fire running wildly along her nerves to that place where he rocked within her. The feeling Blade was creating drove her inexorably toward something . . . something . . . .

"Blade, what's happening to me?" With desperate yearning she clutched at the firm bronze flesh of his shoulders.

"I feel it, too, Little Firebird," Blade groaned. Incredible awe tinged his words. "Concentrate. Think of nothing but what I am doing to you, of how I feel pushing inside you. God, you're magnificent! So tight and hot and—and—sweet. Sing for me, Little Firebird, croon your song of love."

His words, so erotic, so arousing, propelled Shannon deeper into ecstasy, her soft moans swallowed by

Blade's mouth. "Hurry," he whispered urgently against her lips. "Oh, Shannon, I don't know if I can wait."

Lost in the maze of her fragmented thoughts, Shannon heard Blade's words but didn't know what they meant. Yet her body strained toward a goal, a place where she had never been before. Then, amazingly, just when she despaired of ever finding it, she was there. Her body shook with the effort, her limbs trembled and she arched against him, driving Blade over the edge. He shouted in exultant ecstasy as he plunged deeper inside her and gave up his seed.

"Mine, Little Firebird, mine," Blade repeated as he collapsed against her in perfect contentment.

Chapter Seven

*B*lade fell asleep instantly, but Shannon had too much to think about to allow sleep to claim her. She had just experienced something so incredibly profound she was confused and excited at the same time. How could a half-breed savage bring her such extraordinary pleasure? she wondered. Was it possible with any other man? Somehow she doubted it. At first the sinfulness of the act had overwhelmed her. Was claiming her virginity really necessary to save her from Mad Wolf and captivity, or had Blade seduced her with his erotic words and blazing passion in order to satisfy his lust? Well, thanks to Blade she was no longer a virgin, but now she was free to leave Yellow Dog's village and get on with her life. She could forget about Blade and what he did to her. She need explain her loss to no one but her husband, once she found one.

Utterly exhausted, Shannon closed her eyes, taunt-ingly aware of Blade's naked warmth pressed intimately against her own nude body. She tried to hate him, needed desperately to salve her enormous guilt over her wanton behavior. But somehow she couldn't hate a man who might possibly have saved her from a fate worse than death. Then Blade stirred and reached for her again.

"Why aren't you sleeping?" he asked. His lazily, knowing smile infuriated Shannon. "You should be tired."

Shannon flushed, his words reminding her of the wild abandon she found in his arms. "I—I'll be able to sleep once you leave," she replied, stumbling over the words.

"I want to love you again."

Shannon's blue eyes grew wide with alarm. "It's not necessary. You've accomplished what you set out to do. Thanks to you I won't be required to lie to Yellow Dog and the council. Please leave."

"What I did was for your sake, though I admit I don't know when I've enjoyed anything more. You've put a spell on me, Little Firebird, with your siren's song and sweet surrender."

"I did no such thing!" Shannon hissed, his words provoking her to anger. She had no intention of repeating her grievous sin. "Why do you call me Little Firebird?"

"Don't you like the name?"

Shannon looked confused. "I—I don't know."

"It fits, you know. I've thought of you as Little Firebird for a long time. There is a fire in you that beckons to me; I can't resist the flame that burns within you. Now that I have been scorched by it, I can't seem to put out the blaze."

Abruptly Blade rolled over and kissed her, his mouth stifling her angry tirade. When she was sufficiently quiet his lips strayed from her in ragged passion to fall against the arch of her throat and downward, his mouth now encircling her breast, his tongue sweeping against it, bringing a startled, anguished cry from her lips. He did not demand a response, but instead drew it forth so expertly that Shannon found it impossible to cling to her resolve to deny him the surrender he craved.

She felt his masterful nudge between her long legs as he rolled atop her, and the deep sliding push of full possession. Then Shannon was lost to the magic he wove around her senses.

Afterwards she lay still, a flood of hot tears slipping from between her closed eyes. The first time Blade made love to her had been for necessity's sake, but this—there was no excuse for this except pure lust. If she didn't hate Blade before, she certainly had reason to now. She felt used and degraded. She was angry, damn angry. She opened her eyes and glared at him, fire glittering in their stormy depths.

"Get out of here! Haven't you done enough to humiliate me? You're loathsome—an animal, a—a—savage!"

Blade's eyes blazed like shards of black glass, sharp and piercing. "You enjoyed that as much as I did. Don't expect me to apologize for something that gave us both pleasure."

"I forgave you for the first time, Blade, but when you did it again you passed the bounds of decency. Granted you may have saved me from Mad Wolf, but I could only give my virginity once."

"It is much too late for recriminations," Blade said tightly.

Realizing that there was no placating Shannon in her present mood, Blade uncoiled his lean length and rolled to his feet. Granted, he shouldn't have made love to Shannon a second time, but he couldn't help himself. He'd do it again if he didn't get out of here fast.

The sight of Blade clothed in glorious nudity nearly took Shannon's breath away. She tried, but couldn't take her eyes from his thickly muscled torso and taut buttocks as he pulled his buckskin trousers up his long sinewy legs. She closed her eyes, and when she opened them he was standing beside her. His skin was like oiled bronze, mellowed by the soft glow of firelight; the heavy muscles in his arms, shoulders and thighs rippled with repressed power.

"What are you waiting for?" Shannon hissed. She desperately needed to banish Blade from her sight in order to erase him from her mind. "Go!"

"Shannon, I—" His hand reached out, then dropped helplessly to his side. "Try to understand. We'll talk tomorrow."

It was amazing how her legs shook and yet were able to hold her up, Shannon reflected. At first light, Singing Rain had appeared to tell her she had been requested to appear before the council at high noon. It was a request she didn't dare disobey. When the time came, Singing Rain accompanied her, bolstering her courage when she needed it most. Blade's solid presence beside her helped, but not enough to stop her from trembling.

Dressed in ceremonial robes, six elderly men, including Yellow Dog, sat in a circle smoking and talking. Silence fell when Shannon stepped forward. As if on cue, Mad Wolf took his place on one side of her while Blade stood on the other. She felt her knees buckle. Sensing her terror, Blade reached out to steady her.

"There is nothing to fear," Blade encouraged, squeezing her arm.

His words lent Shannon courage, but more than that it made her realize she was acting like a coward. Stiffening her spine, she held her head high, commanding herself not to flinch as the Indians stared at her in silent contemplation. After what seemed like hours, Yellow Dog began speaking in halting English so that Shannon would clearly understand his words.

"The council of elders has considered both Mad Wolf and Swift Blade's petitions. They are still uncertain in their minds which man has the right to claim you, Little Firebird. Only you can tell us the truth.

They wish to know if Swift Blade has taken you to his mat as he claims. You must answer honestly. The council will base their decision on your reply. But keep in mind," he warned ominously, "that lies will only hurt you."

Bright red crept up Shannon's neck clear to her hairline. To confess to something so sinful, so immoral, was devastating to her. She opened her mouth but nothing came out.

"Speak freely and truthfully," Blade urged in a low voice.

"Heed my grandson, Little Firebird," Yellow Dog advised.

"I—yes, it is true," Shannon admitted shamefully. "Blade and I have—he has—we've been . . . " The words were dragged from her.

Yellow Dog translated. A hush fell over the council and those who had come to watch.

"No! She lies!" Mad Wolf cried, unwilling to admit defeat.

Yellow Dog's eyes raked Mad Wolf contemptuously before turning aside to confer with the council. Six pairs of penetrating black eyes lifted to regard Shannon in silent contemplation. She was ready to scream with frustration when Yellow Dog grunted and rose to his feet. He walked over to Blade, placed a hand on his shoulder and said, "The council has reached a decision. Little Firebird belongs to Swift Blade to do with as he pleases."

Shannon stiffened. She wanted to cry out that no man owned her, that she belonged to herself, but she was astute enough to hold her tongue. Once they were away from this horrid place she'd give Blade the tongue-lashing he so richly deserved.

Standing tall and proud beside Shannon, Blade felt a great weight lift from his shoulders. He might have earned her hate, but he felt no guilt over what he did since it ultimately gained her freedom. With a pang of regret he realized that a girl with Shannon's high standards could never forgive him for making love to her. Then he had compounded his sin by making love to her a second time when once would have been enough. She might have forgiven that first time, since it was to save her from Mad Wolf, but he went beyond the bounds of decency when he deliberately seduced her a second time. Truth to tell, he had wanted Shannon too fiercely to stop and consider the consequences. He had no recourse now but to accept them along with Shannon's contempt. He knew that making love with a half-breed and enjoying it must offend and sicken her.

His face a mask of cold fury, Mad Wolf did not accept the council's decision with good grace. His eyes blazed with hatred, for he had never liked Swift Blade, not even when they were children. Blade had always been faster, more clever and stronger. Praise and glory were heaped upon Blade, while Mad Wolf's feats of strength and bravery went largely unheralded and unappreciated.

"You may have won this time, Swift Blade, but my day will come. You have shown yourself more white than Indian, and I shall destroy you along with the other White Eyes."

Whirling on his heel, he leaped onto his pony, whipping him into a gallop with a blood-chilling whoop. One day soon, the people would come to appreciate him for his cunning and bravery and look to him for leadership. Yellow Dog was old, Mad Wolf consoled himself, and he was the logical choice to replace the aging chief. The people would realize this when he made a triumphant return to the village with guns and ammunition. Then all the praise and glory would be his. The people would realize he was the only man brave enough to defy the Great Father in Washington and free their land.

"What's happening?" Shannon asked. With trepidation she watched Mad Wolf and his renegades ride off.

"Mad Wolf is angered by the council's decision," Blade explained. "Ignore him. He can't hurt you as long as you are with me."

"Where did he go?"

Blade had a damn good idea where Mad Wolf and his hotheads were going. It concerned the hidden stash of weapons in Clive Bailey's wagon, but he couldn't divulge that information to Shannon.

"He probably has a camp somewhere in the hills, away from the village and the council's jurisdiction."

"Are you saying the majority of your people don't adhere to Mad Wolf's warlike ideals? That your people are peaceful?"

"Some are," Blade said slowly, "while others think Mad Wolf is right to raid and kill. It is the same with the whites. There are bad ones as well as good."

"What is your belief?" Shannon asked, startling him.

Blade chose his words carefully. "I love and respect my mother's people. I will never forget that I am half Sioux nor lose pride in my Indian heritage. But I've lived too long among the whites to doubt their ultimate victory over the Indians. The day when the Indians roamed freely over the plains is swiftly coming to the end. I fought in the war between the states because I believed in man's freedom, and I will do all in my power to prevent further bloodshed."

Shannon blanched, her eyes wide with shock. "I should have known! Not only are you a savage, but a damn Yankee! I thought you had stolen that blue coat you're so fond of wearing."

"I served in the Union Army, proudly. But I should have never told you. I must insist you tell no one what I have just divulged. Lives depend on your silence. If you are wise, you will forget what you have goaded me into admitting."

"You expect me to forget that you fought with an army that killed my brother and caused my father to take his own life? Never!"

Blade cursed his stupidity for telling Shannon things she had no business knowing. But she confused him so that at times he didn't even know his own name. "I'm sorry about your family, Little Firebird. But you owe me your silence. I could have let Mad Wolf have you instead of coming after you. I could have continued on with the wagon train and forgotten you even existed."

Shannon couldn't argue with his reasoning. She owed Blade a large debt. She had no intention of thanking him for taking her innocence, but she could keep his secret—though why it should matter remained a mystery.

"Does keeping your secret have anything to do with your searching those wagons?" Shannon asked suddenly.

"Dammit, Shannon, you're too inquisitive for your own good. We can't talk here." Grasping her arm he dragged her toward his mother's tipi, pushing her rudely inside. He stood facing her, glaring, hands on hips, his face implacable.

"You don't have to be so rough," Shannon said reproachfully. She rubbed the place where his fingers left marks on her soft flesh.

"I've warned you before to forget that you saw me inside those wagons. It doesn't concern you. No one was hurt by my snooping and it may save lives. Furthermore, once you head north into Idaho with the wagon train, it will make little difference whether I fought for the North or South."

"But . . ."

"You want to leave here, don't you?" Blade asked with quiet menace. "I can still give you to Mad Wolf if it pleases me. You are mine to do with as I please."

"Nobody owns me!" Shannon charged hotly. Unfortunately her words bounced off him like pebbles.

"I'll have your promise, Shannon. And in return you have my word that what I did will bring no harm to you or your friends."

"Never did trust the word of a Yankee," Shannon muttered crossly.

"Shannon—" It sounded as if her name was forced through gritted teeth and Shannon knew when to relent.

"Oh, very well, I promise. But if I learn you're involved in dirty dealings, I'll report you to the army."

"Fair enough." Though Blade was somewhat reluctant to trust her, he had no alternative.

"Can we leave now?"

"I planned to stay a day or two and visit with Singing Rain and Yellow Dog. I've had little opportunity to talk with them."

"Please, Blade, I don't feel comfortable here. What if Mad Wolf returns? Or the council changes their minds?"

"You're safe now, Little Firebird. No one will harm you."

"Don't call me that!" It reminded Shannon too much of last night when Blade murmured the name repeatedly as he made love to her.

Shannon wanted to forget that embarrassing episode forever. She needed no reminders of the shameful ways Blade made her body respond to his touch. Amazingly, it hadn't seemed all that shameful at the time Blade was working his magic on her, or bringing her body to exquisite pleasure. It was degrading, thrilling, humiliating. Wonderful.

Blade sighed. He was in no mood for arguments. In his mind it was settled. He saw no harm in remaining a day or two longer in the village. "Singing Rain will see to your needs while you're here."

Somewhat mollified, Shannon gave grudging consent. She liked Blade's gentle mother and no longer feared Yellow Dog, but being in an Indian village made her nervous. She had heard too many tales of atrocities to simply ignore them. But an even greater threat to her peace of mind was Blade. He had but to touch her and she knew the promise of both heaven and hell.

"I like your woman, my son," Singing Rain said shyly. "She is strong. Little Firebird will give you fine sons and daughters. I hope I live to see them."

Mother, son, and grandfather sat in Yellow Dog's tipi. The men shared a pipe while Singing Rain merely sat admiring her tall, handsome son. She had begun to decline after her husband's death, but Blade's return brought her renewed vigor. She no longer felt at the end of her life.

"You have many years left, Mother," Blade predicted. "The message sent to me by Pierre Labeau not only told of my father's death, but hinted that you were in ill health."

"That all changed the day you returned to our village, my son." Her dark eyes lavished him with love and pride.

She had aged in the past ten years, Blade saw, yet had lost none of her gentleness. It was one of the qualities his father admired so much in her. Blade thought the fine lines around her mouth and eyes detracted nothing from her beauty.

"Why must you leave so soon?" Singing Rain lamented sadly. "I would like to see you and Little Firebird joined according to our customs. We will hold a ceremony followed by a feast and dancing. There has been too much sadness lately. A celebration will bring our people much joy."

"I'm sorry, Mother, there is no time. I must rejoin the wagon train and fulfill my obligation to lead them to Fort Laramie. Besides, if and when I marry Shannon Branigan it will be in a white man's ceremony," he hedged, unwilling to divulge that he and Shannon would soon part and in all likelihood never see one another again. "But I promise to visit often. Fort Laramie is not so far that I can't find time to spend with you and Grandfather."

"You will stay at Fort Laramie?"

"Yes, I have a job to do."

"And afterwards? Will you come back to your people?"

"Perhaps," Blade temporized.

Truthfully, he had no idea what course his life would take once he found the gun smugglers and turned them over to the army.

Shannon waited as long as she could for Singing Rain to return to the tipi that night, but exhaustion finally claimed her. It was very late when she awoke abruptly to the sound of rustling clothes.

"Singing Rain?"

The deep male voice that answered jolted her instantly awake. "No, Little Firebird, Singing Rain sleeps tonight in Grandfather's lodge."

"Get out of here!" Shannon hissed, pulling the buffalo robe up to her chin.

Blade sighed wearily. He could hardly blame Shannon for wanting him gone. He had certainly acted more like the savage she thought him than an officer and a gentleman. "Relax, Shannon, you're safe from me tonight. I only want to sleep."

"Sleep elsewhere."

"Don't you think it would look odd for me to sleep elsewhere after declaring before the entire village that you are my woman?" Calmly he unrolled another bedroll he found nearby and lay down close to Shannon.

Shannon froze. Blade hadn't even touched her, yet her flesh tingled and burned all over. What was wrong with her? How could a half-breed savage affect her that way? What would she do if he reached out to her? The question was moot, for the steady cadence of his breathing told her Blade was already asleep.

They spent one more day and night in Yellow's Dog's village. Most of that time Shannon stayed close to Singing Rain while Blade renewed old acquaintences with his friend Jumping Buffalo and other young braves.

Blade had a reason for courting the young men's friendship. He felt they were the ones who could tell him what Mad Wolf was up to. Thus far he had learned precious little except that Mad Wolf and his renegades were responsible for many raids on settlers, wagon trains, and railroads. According to Jumping Buffalo, Mad Wolf bragged that when he returned to the village, it would be in triumph. The people would hail him as a hero instead of treating him like an outcast.

The next day Shannon and Blade rode away from the village. The skies were overcast and thunder rolled ominously in the distance, but Shannon had few regrets about leaving. Though she had become fond of Singing Rain, Shannon lived in fear that Mad Wolf would return for her despite the council's decision. Mad Wolf didn't strike her as one who would let a few old men stop him from getting what he wanted.

Grateful for the loan of a horse and blanket, Shannon rode most of the day beside Blade. Difficult though it was, she tried to ignore his awesome presence and the aura of sensuality that leaped out and overwhelmed her. She hated the man, she tried to tell herself, yet at the same time she was aware of the large debt of gratitude she owed him. Everything about Blade was a contradiction. Nor was there any logic in the way she felt about him.

Blade seemed unaware of Shannon's rapt perusal. He appeared inordinately interested in the lowering sky and strange bluish-green clouds that swirled overhead. His eyes strayed so often to the unusual phenomenon that Shannon soon noticed his preoccupation with the elements. She thought the abnormal hush that abruptly fell over the land strange, and turned to question Blade about it. The words never left her lips. Suddenly rain began to fall in a great rush of wind-driven sheets, pelting them like a thousand needles.

"Ride! Ride for your life!" Blade shouted above the roar.

"What is it?"

"Tornado!"

The word struck fear in Shannon's heart. Though she had never experienced one, she'd seen the aftermath of death and destruction wrought by nature's fury. What would a tornado do out here on the prairie? she wondered as she whipped her pony into a froth. Where does one seek shelter with nothing in sight but grass plains and low hills?

Shannon could see the twisting, churning monster now, spiraling down from the roiling clouds like a devouring snake. Panic seized her as she realized there was no place to hide, no time to escape. "Blade—"

"Up there!" Blade pointed toward a line of low-slung hills rising in the near distance.

The dun-colored hills were nearly obscured by the combination of pouring rain and flying debris, but offered their only hope of finding shelter. If luck was with them there would be a gully or crevice to protect them from the tornado's onslaught. Blade prayed there would be enough time. He didn't relish the thought of both of them being swept away in the maelstrom.

The horses were jittery, nearly out of control as Blade and Shannon plunged up the hill. Time was running out. The roaring, swirling monster made talk impossible now. The rough ground beneath them offered nothing but tufts of rain-beaten stubble and brush. No gully, no crevice, no place to escape the tornado's inevitable and fatal outcome.

"Blade, look!"

Shannon saw it first. Just below them, where years of winter runoff had eroded the earth. The gully wasn't deep, but it was better than nothing. Reining to a halt, Blade flung himself off Warrior, then reached for Shannon. She scrambled into the gully the moment she hit the ground, flattening herself against the wet earth. Blade had the presence of mind to snatch their bedrolls, canteens and rifle and toss them after her. The minute he loosed the reins the ponies reared in terror and galloped off. The tornado was already roaring down on them when Blade hurled himself atop Shannon, knocking the breath from her lungs. Then the murky dimness changed abruptly to black midnight, and a terrible explosion of noise filled the void around them.

Chapter Eight

A terrible stillness settled around Shannon. It was as if she existed in a void. Was she dead? The inescapable weight pressing her down into the soft earth sent that thought flying from her brain. The rain had stopped—she was certain of that—and it was dusk. But the greatest miracle of all was that she was alive.

"Blade, you can get up now," she said, gasping for breath.

No answer.

"Blade."

Still no answer.

"Blade, what's wrong?"

Growing frantic, Shannon twisted around but could see little except the outline of Blade's face.

With great difficulty Shannon squirmed from beneath Blade, sitting beside him a few minutes to catch her breath. She was soaking wet and shivering in the cool night air. Gingerly she turned Blade over, wondering what could have rendered him unconscious. Her hands moved quickly, impersonally over his body, finding nothing amiss. When she reached the back of his head her hand came away sticky. Blood! Had he been injured by flying debris? Remembering the canteens Blade had rescued, she tore off a piece of his shirt, moistened it with water and pressed it against the injury in an effort to stop the bleeding. Blade moaned but did not awaken.

There was nothing more Shannon could do. After covering Blade with the blankets he had the foresight to provide, she sat back on her heels and waited for him to come out of his stupor. When she grew tired, she settled down beside him in order to share his body heat and fell asleep, her arms circling his lean middle.

The relentless stab of sunlight against his lids awakened Blade. His mouth was dry, his head throbbed painfully, and his limbs felt leaden and useless. Then he remembered the tornado and their close brush with death.

"Shannon!"

A weight on his chest made him glance down. Shannon's bright head was resting on his chest. A wave of something so unspeakably tender shuddered through him that he couldn't resist the urge to rest his hand protectively on that tangled mass of chestnut curls. The thought that she might be injured—or worse—sent his emotions spinning crazily.

"Blade?"

Shannon stirred, raising her head to find Blade staring back at her with a strange look on his face.

"Thank God you're all right." The prayer was a breathless sigh that moved Blade profoundly.

"Are you hurt, Little Firebird?"

"No, I'm fine. I must have fallen asleep. How is your head?"

"Hurts like hell," Blade complained. "What happened?"

"You must have been struck by something churned up by the tornado. You were out for hours."

Blade tried to rise, groaned, and braced his hands on the ground.

"Blade, what's wrong?"

"Dizzy."

"Is your injury serious?"

"I don't think so. Concussion, I suspect."

"Perhaps you should lie back down."

"Do you see the horses nearby?"

Shannon scanned the prairie and surrounding hills in all directions. The air was crisp and clear, the sun a bright ball in the sky. What they had gone through the day before seemed incredible in the golden daylight. "I don't see anything. Either the horses have run off or they are dead."

"Damnation!" Blade cursed, wincing from pain. "Looks like we have a long walk ahead of us."

The sun blazed down with relentless fury. The prairie was endless, and the tall grass reached nearly to Shannon's waist, making walking difficult. For the first few miles Blade was unsteady on his feet, stopping often when dizziness made his head whirl. In addition to his rifle, Blade carried his blanket and canteen, leaving another blanket and canteen for Shannon to tote. As the day progressed, Blade's strength returned while Shannon drooped from exhaustion and hunger. They'd had nothing to eat that day except for berries they found growing beside a stream, and wild onions.

It was nearly dusk when Blade called a halt beside a creek feeding into the North Platte River. If not for last night's deluge, its bed would have been bone dry, but now a few feet of water lapped at the bank. Having traveled north from Ogallala, they were now following the south bank of the North Platte.

"Rest here, Shannon, while I hunt us up something to eat," Blade said after refreshing himself in the stream.

Once Blade left, Shannon removed her doeskin dress and washed thoroughly in the stream. If she had had a piece of soap she would have washed her hair, but she made do with drenching her long tresses, then running her fingers through them to smooth out the tangles. Then she plaited them into a long braid. Next she turned her attention to her dress. She shook it out and brushed it with her hands to rid it of splattered mud and sand.

Blade returned a short time later, grinning and holding a rabbit aloft in each hand. He quickly skinned and gutted the animals, built a fire and arranged them on a spit while Shannon watched, her stomach growling hungrily. Then, slanting Shannon an oblique look, Blade proceeded to strip.

"What are you doing?" Her eyes grew wide with alarm.

"I'm going to bathe," Blade said, "do you mind?"

"Oh." Shannon said in a small voice.

She promptly turned her head, pretending great interest in the cooking rabbits. Yet despite her best efforts, she couldn't keep her eyes from straying to the perfect symmetry from his impossibly wide shoulders to his slim hips and long legs. Her cheeks burned when she recalled that powerful body poised above her, claiming her in the most intimate way. He had transported her to heights she never knew existed.

Unabashed, Blade waded naked into the shallow stream, aware that Shannon wasn't nearly as disinterested as she pretended. He wondered if he affected her in the same way she affected him. He'd bedded many women in the past, some beautiful, some intelligent, some both, but none as spellbinding as Shannon Branigan. It occurred to him that she was too good for him, but that didn't stop him from wanting her again—and again—until he was sated with the taste and sweetness of her. Though he seriously doubted such a state could be achieved.

When the rabbit was cooked, they ate in silence, savoring the tasty feast Blade had provided. Blade watched, mesmerized, as Shannon licked every bit of grease from her fingers, the sight of her tongue gliding over her flesh producing powerful erotic fantasies that nearly unmanned him.

"I don't know when I've eaten anything that tasted so good," Shannon sighed, replete.

Blade wanted to say that her sweet flesh was a tastier feast, but didn't dare. "Nor I," he agreed.

Rising nearly in unison, they walked to the stream and washed their hands and faces, then returned to the fire. An awkward silence ensued, until Blade fetched the blankets and spread them out.

"Its time we bedded down. We've a long walk ahead of us."

"Do you think we'll find the horses?"

"I doubt it." Blade said slowly, unwilling to give hope where none existed. "We're fortunate Fort Laramie isn't too far away." He stretched out on the blanket, wrapping it around himself like a cocoon.

Shannon did the same, tired enough to sleep but too aware of Blade's daunting presence to close her eyes. After listening to her tossing restlessly for some minutes, Blade dared to ask, "Can't you sleep either?"

"N-no," Shannon stammered. She had no idea that she had disturbed him. "I can't seem to relax."

"I know of a way to relax you," Blade said. Shannon could hear the smile in his voice and tried to ignore his blatant hint. "Perhaps I could show you."

"That won't be necessary."

"Let me make love to you, Little Firebird."

"I'll not let you seduce me again, Blade," Shannon declared. "You have my gratitude for getting me out of a terrible situation, but that's as far as I'm prepared to go."

"Don't tell me you didn't enjoy it, for I'm experienced enough to know better."

"That's beside the point," Shannon argued. "Suffice it to say it will never happen again. Go to sleep. You're still recovering from your head injury."

"Your reluctance wouldn't have anything to do with my being a half-breed, would it?" Blade asked tightly.

Shannon deliberately withheld her answer, unwilling to give Blade the satisfaction of knowing his heritage had nothing to do with her decision. What

she couldn't tolerate was the shameful way he made
her feel. Her upbringing forbade what was happening
between them. Such intense feelings were reserved for
married couples who loved one another. She blamed
inexperience and lust on the wanton way she had
responded to Blade's expert caresses and erotic seduc-
tion. Just thinking about it made her tremble with
repressed longing. She'd give her soul to feel his arms
around her, his mouth exploring her body, thrusting
into her until she cried out in wild abandon.

"I thought so," Blade said, disgust making his voice
harsh. When Shannon failed to reply he assumed her
silence meant she agreed with his reasoning. "Relax, I
won't ask you to dirty yourself with an Indian.
Good-night, Miss Branigan."

Shannon winced, his words cutting her deeply.
She'd always prided herself on her ability to judge a
man on his merit, but Blade was a man like none
other. He might be an Indian, but he was more man
than any she'd ever known. Unfortunately she
couldn't tell him how she felt. It was best for all
concerned to let him think she despised him for what
he was rather than let him know how deeply and
quickly he had gotten under her skin. Besides, he was
much too arrogant for her taste.

The next day was a repeat of the first. They walked
until their legs gave out, rested, then walked some
more. They spoke sparingly, saving their energy to
propel them forward, one step at a time. The sun
became their enemy, blazing down on them with
relentless fury. Shannon had lost her sunbonnet, and
her face and arms turned a dull red. The freckles
across the bridge of her nose stood out in stark relief,
which privately Blade thought endearing. They
stopped frequently to pick berries, then trudged on.

"How much farther, Blade?" Shannon asked,
breaking the long silence. She couldn't bear their not
speaking when they were the only humans around for
miles.

Blade started violently, Shannon's lilting voice a welcome relief from the profound stillness surrounding them. "Two, three more days," he estimated, squinting toward the western horizon. "See that tall limestone shaft in the distance? That's Chimney Rock. Beyond that's Scott's Bluff. Fort Laramie lies a short distance from Scott's Bluff."

"Do you think the wagon train is still at Fort Laramie?"

"I doubt it," Blade said thoughtfully. "My guess is that they wasted little time at the fort once they bought supplies and necessities. They have a long way to go yet to reach Oregon and can't afford to delay. Snow comes early to mountain passes."

"How will I get to Boise if the wagon train is gone?" Shannon wailed despairingly. "Will I be able to join another train?"

"Not until next spring." Blade's answer stunned her.

"Next spring! What will I do till then?"

"I'm sure quarters can be found for you with a family at the fort," Blade assured her. "That's the usual procedure. The commander . . . " Suddenly his words trailed off, and his face assumed a watchful look.

"Blade, what is it?"

"Riders," Blade said tersely.

"What! I don't hear anything."

"You will." He crouched low, placing his ear to the ground.

"What can we do?"

"Nothing. The horses are shod. They aren't Indians."

Shannon's mouth flew open, amazed at Blade's perception and incredible ability to hear things no one else could. Several suspenseful minutes passed before the horsemen came into view. They formed a double line as they galloped across the rolling prairie.

"Cavalry," Blade said. His voice was utterly devoid of emotion, his face unreadable.

"Thank God. Perhaps I can still reach Fort Laramie before the wagon train departs."

They watched in silent contemplation as the column approached. Deep in his heart Blade knew that reaching Fort Laramie meant the end of all contact between him and Shannon. Her reputation had already been damaged beyond repair by the very fact that she had been kidnapped by Indians and spent time alone in the company of a half-breed. Many would be quick to condemn her for something she had no control over. Women kidnapped by Indians usually were raped. Shannon could truthfully deny that charge despite the fact that what he had done could be construed by some as rape. For Shannon's own good, Blade had already decided to break all contact with her once they reached the fort.

A pang of some unexplainable emotion smote Shannon at the thought that Blade would become a virtual stranger to her once they reached Fort Laramie. Instinctively she knew it wouldn't be proper to continue a friendship with a half-breed.

Since when did you worry about what was proper? a small voice inside Shannon asked. Hadn't Mama always said she was a hoyden and despaired of her conduct?

"Here they come, Shannon," Blade said, distracting her from her thoughts. His warning was unnecessary. The lieutenant in charge was already signaling the column to a halt.

The lieutenant dismounted and approached Shannon, executed a precise bow and asked, "Miss Branigan, I presume?"

Despite her weariness, Shannon's cracked lips opened in a smile. "In the flesh, Lieutenant."

"And lovely flesh it is, Miss Branigan," he complimented her gallantly. "I'm Lieutenant Ronald Goodman. We've been sent out from Fort Laramie to rescue you."

"You have?" Shannon asked, surprised.

"Your friends from the wagon train reported that

you had been kidnapped by Mad Wolf and his band of renegades. They were quite adamant about our finding you, particularly the young Johnsons."

"Are they still at Fort Laramie?" Shannon asked hopefully.

"They were to leave this morning," Lieutenant Goodman revealed, dashing her hopes. "The new guide was waiting for them at the fort and they pushed on to Oregon. Except for Clive Bailey, of course, who runs the trading post at the fort."

Suddenly Goodman seemed to notice Blade, who stood quietly beside Shannon, a bemused smile on his face. "Are you the half-breed they call Blade?" His lip curled in derision as he raked Blade with barely concealed contempt. Obvious he had little liking for savages and didn't care who knew it.

"I am Swift Blade."

"Why are you afoot? Did you encounter trouble with Mad Wolf? We were prepared to help, but I see you managed just fine on your own."

"It is a long story, Lieutenant, one which I'll be more than happy to relate at a later time. Right now I suggest you get Miss Branigan back to the fort. She's been through a harrowing experience."

Lieutenant Goodman's mouth tightened with displeasure. "I don't need a half-breed telling me my job." he said sourly. He turned to Shannon. "Forgive me, Miss Branigan, I'm not usually so thoughtless. You can ride with me, and there's an extra horse for the breed."

Shannon slanted Blade a searching glance, but his stoic expression told her nothing. If he felt anger at Goodman's disparaging remarks he kept it well hidden. Then, in an unguarded moment, Shannon saw the cold fury in his eyes and knew he wasn't as unaffected as he appeared. As for Shannon, she was furious, though she had no idea why except that it didn't seem right to classify Blade with all savages when he was half white. Nor was she so certain anymore that all Indians were bad. She greatly admired Singing Rain, and had learned to respect Yellow Dog. It was Mad Wolf and those like him she feared and hated.

Blade's tightly clenched fists were all of his temper he allowed to show. His job was to find the man or men responsible for selling illegal weapons to Indians, not to fight prejudice. He knew when he accepted this assignment that he'd face a certain amount of prejudice. It was inevitable. Men like Lieutenant Goodman were no better than Mad Wolf and his renegades. They hated indiscriminately.

Lieutenant Goodman boosted Shannon aboard his horse's broad back and mounted smoothly behind her. Shannon felt his arm brush her breasts when he reached around to grasp the reins, and frowned. She cared little for the way the arrogant lieutenant spoke to Blade, nor did she appreciate his brazen familiarity.

"I didn't want to say anything in front of the men, Miss Branigan, but are you all right? The Indians didn't—er—hurt you, did they?"

The inflection in his voice told Shannon exactly what he thought the Indians did to her.

"I'm fine, Lieutenant," Shannon assured him. "I wasn't harmed in any way." She stressed the words, wanting him to know in no uncertain terms that she hadn't been ravished.

"What about the breed? Experience has proven they can't be trusted. I hope he didn't try to—that is—"

"Lieutenant Goodman," Shannon said testily, "Blade saved me from Mad Wolf and a terrible fate. I owe him a debt of gratitude I'll never be able to repay. Please don't speak of him in so disparaging a manner."

Stunned, Goodman was rendered nearly speechless. It sounded as if the luscious redhead preferred a savage Sioux half-breed to a refined gentleman like himself. Idly he wondered if she had already been seduced by the Injun. Or had she been forced by him and was too ashamed to admit it? He seriously doubted the Irish miss was as innocent as she pretended. She'd been in the company of Indians far too long to remain a virgin. Since her reputation was already in question, Goodman reflected gleefully, she might be persuaded to share her favors with him.

A handsome man with sandy brown hair, pale blue eyes, and a slim mustache that might be called dapper, Goodman was in his early thirties. Tall and slim, he cut a dashing figure in uniform and knew it.

They rode steadily west, stopping only to rest the horses and eat. Soon they came to Chimney Rock. It stood out in the absolute emptiness of earth and sky, the cactus-studded grassland rising to meet it. They continued on, making camp that night at Scott's Bluff, a gloriously beautiful semi-circular ridge of rocky knobs tinted with delicate shades of ochre and soft pink.

Shannon saw little of Blade except from a distance. He kept more or less to himself, carefully avoiding her. With a pang of regret Shannon realized that it probably was for the best. Yet she couldn't help following him with her eyes, remembering, remembering . . . .

They broke camp again at first light. Shannon felt well rested after passing the night in comparative comfort in Lieutenant Goodman's small tent. Since the weather was warm and dry, he and his men slept under the stars. According to Goodman they would reach Fort Laramie sometime later in the day.

A rapid stream appeared at the foot of barren hills, running into the Platte River. Beyond was a green meadow dotted with bushes, and in the midst of these, at the point where the Platte joined the Laramie River, lay the sprawling compound of Fort Laramie. An American flag waving atop a tall pole crowned an eminence on the left beyond the stream. Behind stretched a line of arid and desolate ridges. They forded Laramie Creek, its flow greatly diminished this late in the summer. Shannon noted with interest that a bridge was being constructed but was not yet finished.

The column crossed a little plain, descended a hollow and rode up a steep bank and approached the fort.

Originally Fort Laramie had been established by the American Fur Company. In 1849 it was purchased and garrisoned by the army for the purpose of protecting emigrants from Indians who were becoming increasingly hostile after a period of relative peace. Fort Laramie did not fit the commonly held image of a fort with palisades. Initial plans had called for a log or stone wall with blockhouses, but since Indian threat at that time was small, funding was not forthcoming, and Fort Laramie was built without walls. Houses, quarters, and buildings constructed of adobe and clay were built around a yard, or parade ground, about one hundred and thirty feet square. Every apartment and building faced the parade ground.

The cavalry and infantry barracks stood by themselves, each company with its own mess hall and kitchen in the rear. Officers' Row faced the square, as did the sutler's building, post trader's store, guardhouse, bachelor's officers' quarters, surgeon's quarters, and the two-story clubhouse called "Old Bedlam." Shannon would learn later that many gay parties and dances were held in "Old Bedlam," for strange as it might seem, in its entire history the fort had never been attacked by Indians.

On the banks of the Laramie River sat General Sink, the latrine that served four companies. Sewage was channeled from there to the river.

A monthly mail service originated at the fort, which also served as a trading post for Indians and emigrants.

As the column passed into the busy square, Shannon was amazed to see tall Indians wrapped in colorful blankets striding across the area or reclining on porches and in the doorways of apartments. Gaily bedizened squaws stood in pairs gossiping among themselves, their bright garb highly visible amidst the army blue.

The column halted in the dusty yard. Lieutenant Goodman dismounted, then lifted Shannon from the saddle as if she were weightless. Almost immediately, an older man with steel gray hair and bushy eyebrows emerged from one of the buildings emblazoned with the words, "Post Headquarters."

In several long-legged strides he was beside Shannon, his hand held out in genuine welcome.

"Welcome back to civilization, Miss Branigan, I'm Colonel Greer," he said, smiling warmly. "You don't know how glad we are to see you safe and sound. I'm sure it must have been a harrowing experience for you, but you can put all that behind you now."

He turned to Lieutenant Goodman. "Good work, Lieutenant, you'll earn a commendation for this. You can give your report later in my office. Dismiss your troops."

"Yes sir." Lieutenant Goodman snapped off a salute, delighted with the colonel's praise.

"Come along, Miss Branigan, you can stay with my family until quarters are found for you. I have a daughter just about your age and a wife who will no doubt pamper you just as she does our Claire."

"Wait," Shannon balked. "What about Blade?"

"Who in the devil is Blade?" Greer asked, perplexed.

"Swift Blade," Shannon elaborated. "He's the man who rescued me from Mad Wolf. Lieutenant Goodman and his men found us only two days ago after we lost our horses."

Colonel Greer flicked a glance at Blade, who stood leaning against his mount in lazy contemplation. His lip was curled in an expression of utter boredom—or was it amusement? Greer promptly dismissed the darkly handsome half-breed with a careless gesture.

"The breed will be suitably rewarded. Don't concern yourself with him."

Taking her firmly in hand, he led Shannon off, allowing her no time for a private word with Blade. Nor did Blade offer a word or gesture of his own. He merely regarded Shannon with his dark, piercing eyes, eyes as profound and mysterious as the midnight sky.

Chapter Nine

"**M**y dear, what a terrible ordeal for you," Molly Greer sympathized.

A kindly matron of middle years, Molly clucked her tongue in motherly distress as she helped Shannon into the tub of steaming water. Her daughter Claire, a stunning, violet-eyed brunette who resembled neither of her parents, stood nearby, a calculating look on her lovely features.

"What did the Indians do to you?" Claire asked bluntly. "Did they rape you? How many of them—"

"Claire!" Molly gasped, horrified by her daughter's indelicate questions and crude suppositions. "Don't badger Miss Branigan. Where are your manners? She's a guest in our home, and if she wants us to know what happened she will tell us."

"Nothing happened, really," Shannon hastened to add. "And please call me Shannon."

Would everyone assume she'd been raped by the Indians? Lord, what a fine mess!

"Of course not, dear," Molly commiserated. Her tone suggested she was not really convinced by Shannon's denial. "You must call us Molly and Claire. And please pay no heed to Claire, she's much too forward. You take your time bathing while I see to supper. Claire can keep you company if she minds her manners. When you're finished, you'll find your clothes in those trunks against the wall. Your friends left them for you. That's how certain they were that you'd be found and delivered safely by that half-breed they hired as wagon master."

Claire waited until Molly left the room before sidling closer and saying, "I envy you being alone with the half-breed." She shivered delicately. "I saw him walking across the parade grounds. He might be half savage, but he is the handsomest man I've ever seen. He looks so strong and fierce, just thinking about him frightens me."

"If you're talking about Blade, he saved me from Mad Wolf. I'm not frightened of him at all."

"Blade, is that his name? Somehow it fits." She snickered at the picture his name evoked. "Did he force you? Was he a savage lover?" She licked her lips in eager anticipation of Shannon's reply.

"Really, Claire," Shannon chided reproachfully. "Nothing happened. It's due entirely to Blade's timely intervention that I returned unscathed. That's all I'm going to say on the subject."

"I was merely curious," Claire said peevishly.

Miffed, she walked to the window, pretending interest in the comings and goings outside while Shannon finished her bath.

"There he is now, going into Papa's office."

It was difficult to pretend indifference in the face of Claire's barrage of explicit questions and avid curiosity. It was a good thing the pretty brunette couldn't hear the wild thumping of Shannon's heart. Would Blade relate all the intimate details of her rescue? Or would he be discreet and not mention exactly how he managed to bring Shannon out of Yellow Dog's village with so little difficulty? She couldn't help but fret, for it took little imagination to know how she'd be treated if people suspected she'd bedded an Indian.

Blade approached Colonel Greer's office, having been summoned only moments before. He realized he'd be questioned closely by the post commander and hoped his answers would prove satisfactory. He hadn't had time yet to call on Clive Bailey, but he intended to do so the moment he left Colonel Greer's office. He'd been delayed so long getting Shannon to the fort that Blade feared Bailey had already disposed of the contraband weapons. He also wondered if Wade Vance, Blade's contact, had arrived yet. His question was answered when he was ushered into Colonel Greer's office and saw that the colonel was not alone. Major Vance had indeed arrived and was seated in a chair across the desk from Colonel Greer. Lieutenant Goodman was also present, standing at ease before his superiors.

"Ah, Swift Blade, come in," Colonel Greer said, motioning Blade forward. "You know the lieutenant, and this other gentleman is Major Vance. He has been newly assigned to Fort Laramie and is my second in command."

Blade acknowledged both men with a nod, his face carefully composed to display no recognition for the major he had known and respected for many years.

"Lieutenant Goodman tells me his patrol came across you and Miss Branigan about thirty miles east of the fort. We know you followed the young lady after she was kidnapped by Sioux renegades, but what happened? Was it difficult retrieving her from Mad Wolf?"

"Miss Branigan was taken to a Sioux village by Mad Wolf, who wanted her for his wife," Blade explained. He carefully refrained from using Shannon's first name. No Indian would be granted such outrageous familiarity. "Fortunately I reached the village in time to stop Mad Wolf's plans for the young lady."

"Just how did you accomplish so amazing a feat?" Goodman asked, openly skeptical. "From what we know of Mad Wolf, he is a hot-headed renegade who makes his own rules."

"Since he had taken Miss Branigan to Yellow Dog's village, he was obliged to adhere to council rulings. I petitioned Yellow Dog and the council for Miss Branigan's release and they ruled in my favor."

It was a fairly uncomplicated explanation, but Blade had no intention of delving into the details regarding Shannon's release.

"Why would they do that?" Colonel Greer asked curiously. "Do you know Yellow Dog personally? Are you from Yellow Dog's village? Why haven't we seen you around the fort before?"

"I lived with my father, who was a trapper," Blade said, telling half-truths. "When he died, I scouted for a while with the army at Fort Kearney, then went to St. Louis where I hired on as guide for a wagon train."

"That still doesn't explain why the council decided in your favor," Goodman objected, convinced that Blade was lying.

"Give him a chance," Major Vance, entering the conversation for the first time. "The young man did a brave thing by rescuing Miss Branigan. Few men would challenge Mad Wolf's authority."

"Well?" Goodman prodded, leveling Blade an austere glance. "Tell us how you performed this miracle."

"I spent my early childhood in Yellow Dog's village," Blade confessed. "My mother was Sioux. Mad Wolf is not well liked in the village. He has his followers, but most are hotheads and outcasts like himself."

"Your mother is dead?" Greer asked sharply.

"Yes," Blade lied, for some obscure reason unwilling to divulge his mother's whereabouts and reveal his relationship to Yellow Dog.

"We are grateful Miss Branigan has been returned safe and sound," Greer allowed.

"Whatever method of persuasion you used certainly earns our gratitude," Vance added with a hint of admiration.

Lieutenant Goodman slanted Blade a penetrating glance. "I sense you're not telling us everything."

Blade stiffened. "Are you calling me a liar?" His features hardened to stone, his mouth a thin slash in his swarthy face. He didn't like the cocky lieutenant, not one damn bit. There was something about him he didn't trust.

Goodman recognized the quiet menace in Blade's dark features and was too cowardly to tangle with the powerful half-breed, fearing he'd find himself on the receiving end of his implacable anger.

"I meant no harm by that remark, Swift Blade," he blustered. "No one is questioning your veracity. We just want the whole story."

Major Vance hid a smile behind his hand. He hadn't been at the fort long, but it did his heart good to see the brash lieutenant quail before Blade's steely-eyed glare. Goodman was the colonel's fair-haired boy who could do no wrong. Personally, Vance didn't like the man, and he was pleased to note that Blade shared his feelings. His judgment hadn't failed him yet.

"That is enough, gentlemen," Greer warned sternly. "I think you've told us all we need to know, Swift Blade. What are your plans now? The wagon train has already hired another guide, and there will be no others through till next spring."

Blade sent the colonel a searching look. "Are you offering me a job?"

"There is one available if you are interested," Greer said slowly. "Are you?"

"Depends on what you have in mind."

"We need a scout. Our last died from a rattlesnake bite. The job is yours if you want it."

Blade pretended to ponder the offer, glancing at Major Vance from beneath shuttered lids. The major's barely discernible nod provided him with an answer.

"I reckon I'll just take you up on the offer, Colonel Greer."

Blade smiled, offering his hand. Greer did not hesitate, accepting Blade's handshake to seal the bargain.

"See the quartermaster—he'll assign you quarters. If you need a horse, choose one from our stables."

Blade nodded curtly, turned, and left the room.

"I fear you've made a mistake," Goodman advised, frowning. "I don't trust the breed. The Sioux are a savage lot who don't easily adjust to civilization."

"Give the man a chance," Vance allowed. "He looks trustworthy to me. If there had been a problem, I'm certain Miss Branigan would have spoken up."

Colonel Greer nodded sagely and Lieutenant Goodman reluctantly dropped the subject, vowing to keep an eye on the breed, for something told him the man wasn't what he appeared.

Blade didn't complain when he was assigned a small room behind the blacksmith shop that obviously wasn't fit for either officer or ranking NCO. At least he'd be alone, with no one keeping track of his comings or goings.

But when Blade went to select a horse, he received the surprise of his life. There, munching contentedly on hay with the other animals, was Warrior. Placing two fingers in his mouth he let loose a shrill whistle. The gray's ears perked up, neighing in recognition as he trotted over to greet Blade. Blade scratched Warrior's head, speaking to him in a low voice.

"He seems to know ya, mister." Blade spun around as the stablemaster appeared at his side.

"He should, I've owned Warrior many years. We've traveled a long way together. How did he get here?"

"Wandered in a couple days ago. Figured someone would claim him sooner or later. I'm Sam Daniels."

"I'm called Swift Blade, but just Blade will do," Blade offered. "I just hired on as scout. Never thought I'd find Warrior. Was he alone?"

"Yep, and he made hisself right at home, almost as if he was waitin' on ya. Was he stole?"

"Lost him in a tornado a few days back. I assumed he was dead. Glad to see I'm wrong. I missed the old boy."

"You mean I'm stuck here for the winter?" Shannon lamented. "Whatever will I do? Are you certain no other wagon trains will come through this year?"

Shannon was seated at the supper table with the Greer family, enjoying an excellently prepared meal while Molly clucked over the small portions she selected. She had already been with the Greers several days and Colonel Greer had promised to look into the possibility of getting her to Idaho.

"I know how disappointed you must be, Shannon, but I fear there is nothing to be done about it. It's already September, and the mountain passes between here and Boise will soon be impassible. Besides, the Boseman Trail has been under constant attack these past few months. We have received word that wood-gathering details from Fort Phil Kearny have been ambushed by bands of twenty or thirty renegades. Forts Fetterman and Reno report the same conditions. Scant security exists outside their walls, and I warned Wilson to choose another route."

"Frank Wilson?"

"Yes, he was elected captain of the wagon train after Clive Bailey left their company."

"I have good friends among the emigrants—are they in danger?" Shannon asked fearfully.

"There is always danger in Indian country," Greer said tactfully. "We tried to sign a treaty with the Sioux for the right to travel the trail but the chiefs walked out of the negotiations. Anyone who travels the Boseman Trail faces peril and possible attack.

"You've heard of the Fetterman massacre, haven't you?" he continued. Shannon shook her head. "William Fetterman was an impetuous young captain at Fort Phil Kearny who was sent out with eighty men to relieve a wood detail under attack. A wily young Sioux named Crazy Horse lured the patrol into an ambush and wiped out the entire force, including the wood-cutting detail."

The Colonel's story so unnerved Shannon that she fell silent, chewing her food thoughtfully. If she had to stay at Fort Laramie, there were many things she had to consider. It looked as if she was marooned for the winter—at least until early summer when the wagon trains started arriving. Fortunately she had some money in one of the trunks the Johnsons left off, but she'd need it to buy passage on the next wagon train. Kindhearted Molly Greer offered her a place with her family for as long as she chose to stay, but Shannon didn't want to impose on the family for several long months.

"Colonel Greer, is there no way to earn my keep?" Shannon asked. "I don't feel comfortable imposing on your kindness."

"Nonsense, dear, you're welcome to stay for as long as you like," Molly smiled warmly. "It wouldn't be the first time we've opened our home to visitors. That's the way of things on the western frontier."

"I appreciate your generosity," Shannon demurred, "but surely there is something I can do."

"Don't worry your pretty head about it, my dear," the Colonel blustered. "We're pleased to have you."

"Papa, didn't you say you were looking for a schoolteacher?" Claire hinted innocently. "Shannon would be perfect for the job."

"I don't think Shannon would . . ."

"Schoolteacher?" Shannon asked, her interest piqued. "Tell me about it."

"If you insist. I've been trying to lure a teacher out here for some time to teach the dozen or so children of officers attached to the post. It appears no one is interested in teaching school in the heart of Sioux country."

"I am," Shannon surprised herself by saying. "I've been given a good education and feel qualified to apply for the job. There is a salary, of course?"

"Of course, and a small house of your own next to

the schoolhouse. "Are you saying you'd consider it?"

"Oh, yes. I'd rather be useful than sit here all winter doing nothing," Shannon assured him.

"Well," Colonel Greer considered, "if you're sure. We certainly could use a teacher. I tried to interest Claire in the job, but it didn't appeal to her."

"When can I start?" Shannon asked eagerly.

"There is a certain amount of work to be done in order to get the schoolhouse and your house in condition. I'll try to lend you a man, but we're woefully short-handed. It shouldn't take more than two weeks to whip everything into shape."

"I'm sure I can manage on my own," Shannon stated.

"We'll help, won't we, Claire?" Molly offered kindly. Forced to it, Claire grudgingly agreed.

When can I move into the house?" Shannon asked.

"Are you so anxious to leave us?" Colonel Greer chided gently. "As soon as it is habitable, you may move."

"It's not that I find your hospitality lacking," Shannon assured him, "it's just that I'd like to get school started as soon as possible."

That evening Lieutenant Goodman came to call. Somehow Shannon wasn't surprised to learn that the lieutenant was a frequent visitor, and that he and Claire were considered practically engaged. For a man supposedly in love, Shannon thought the man's eyes strayed in her direction far too often. Claire must have thought so too, for she glared daggers at Shannon at every opportunity. When Goodman invited Claire for a walk and asked Shannon to join them, Shannon politely declined. She certainly didn't intend to become involved in the couple's love affair.

Blade stood concealed in the dark shadows outside Colonel Greer's quarters. He wondered what Shannon was doing, if the room where the light had just flickered on was hers. So close yet so far, he thought regretfully. They were poles apart, meant to be neither friends nor lovers. Yet he wanted to be both. He lingered outside until the light in the upper window went out, then walked morosely back to his room, recalling with vivid clarity the night he had taken Shannon's virginity and attained paradise.

If Blade were Waken Taken, he might have been able to read Shannon's thoughts, felt her soul and body calling out to him. She missed his comforting presence, his big body next to hers at night. They'd been together so many days and nights that she had grown accustomed to his company, accepted it quite naturally. Shannon's emotions were so tangled where Blade was concerned, she had difficulty sorting them out.

Blade had risked his life to save her, even if his methods were harsh and she'd lost her innocence in the bargain. Yet mere gratitude didn't begin to describe what Shannon felt for Blade. She couldn't really hate him, the attraction between them was too vitally alive for that emotion. It occurred to her that he had made love to her as if he truly meant it, making her first time memorable. Blade was a man like no other. Did it really matter that he was a half-breed?

Clive Bailey was a happy man. He had returned to his trading post to find it prospering under the able management of a man from Iowa named Burt Dunlap. Burt's wife, Iris, sewed ready-made dresses and sold them in the store. But after his return, their services were no longer needed so he let them go before they inadvertently discovered the smuggled guns. Then he had successfully traded the guns to Mad Wolf for a fortune in gold—gold that the renegade had stolen from a stagecoach transporting the precious metal to meet the payroll of railroad workers. Bailey had even demanded and received more than originally agreed upon. He had been angered by Mad Wolf's attack upon him on the prairie and threatened to withhold the gun shipment unless more gold was offered. Not sharing the white man's greed for gold, Mad Wolf readily agreed.

Bailey was so anxious to rid himself of the contraband weapons that he appeared at the rendezvous designated by Mad Wolf shortly after he arrived at Fort Laramie. He learned from the renegade that Blade had left the Sioux village with Shannon Branigan and would probably reach the fort soon.

Bailey had mixed feelings about this news. Little was known about the half-breed except that he had turned up seemingly from nowhere to act as guide. Highly recommended by the army, Blade had been hired sight unseen and arrived in Independence mere days before the wagon train departed. Though Bailey had no complaint with his work, the man appeared too educated for the average half-breed, and much too curious.

Nevertheless, Bailey was relieved to have the guns off his hands and the gold hidden away, enough to last him a long time. One day, before the savages massacred every living person on the western frontier, he would return to civilization and spend his wealth. Still, he couldn't erase Mad Wolf's parting words from his mind.

"Bring Little Firebird to me and the rest of the gold is yours."

It was a tempting offer.

Chapter Ten

*B*lade's footsteps were noiseless as he approached the rear of Clive Bailey's trading post. The wagon in which Bailey had crossed the plains sat forlornly beneath the slim crescent of moon. The night was still, the air crisp with the promise of winter. Blade's midnight foray went unheralded, due in good part to his Indian cunning. With the stealth of a mountain lion he eased into the wagon.

Since the conestoga was nearly empty, Blade had little difficulty exposing the false bottom. A twinge of keen disappointment twisted his gut when he discovered the guns had been removed. They had either already been delivered or were hidden somewhere in Bailey's store. Dropping to the dusty ground, Blade circled the building until he found an unlatched window in the rear. Boosting himself up, he wriggled through the opening, his broad shoulders barely scraping past its narrow frame.

Once inside, Blade found himself in a rear storeroom with no other windows save for the one he had just used to gain entrance. Searching through his pockets he located a match, lit it, and held it aloft. He faced a closed door, which he suspected led into the main part of the store. Blade saw a stub of candle atop one of the bales nearby and carefully lit it from his match. Then he made a thorough search of the storeroom. He found nothing remotely resembling guns or anything else of a suspicious nature. Though Blade doubted Bailey would be stupid enough to hide weapons in the main store, he cautiously opened the door and stepped into the large room crowded with merchandise of all descriptions. Wasting little time, he began a cursory search of the boxes and bags stacked on the shelves and on the floor.

His need for speed caused him to become careless, and he brushed against a tin can perched on the edge of a shelf. It teetered for a breathless moment, then crashed to the floor. Blade's lungs filled with air, then he exhaled slowly as he doused the candle and crouched low behind the counter. He waited breathlessly to see if his blunder had aroused Bailey, whose living quarters were above the store. Suddenly a trap door lowered from above and Bailey, wearing a nightshirt over his breeches and carrying a gun in one hand and a lamp in the other, appeared at the top of the ladder.

"Who's there?" Bailey called out, holding the lamp aloft to illuminate the dark interior.

On hands and knees, Blade crawled to the open door of the storeroom and eased through. He heard Bailey's footsteps descend the ladder, move about the store, then falter outside the storeroom door. Blade realized that if he was found prowling where he shouldn't be he'd risk exposure, be charged with trespassing, and punished. President Johnson had warned him he was on his own in this investigation, and he wasn't certain even Major Vance would help if he got himself in trouble.

Bailey burst into the storeroom just as Blade dove through the window.

Though the hour was late, a single light still burned in a window in an apartment on officer's row. Three short raps on the door brought an immediate response.

"I've been waiting. You're late."

Blade slipped inside and Wade Vance quickly closed the door behind him. This was the second private meeting Blade had had with Vance since his arrival at Fort Laramie. Blade had already revealed his suspicions concerning Clive Bailey and had been given permission to search the trading post for the smuggled weapons.

"They're gone!" Blade announced with a foul oath. "Bailey has already rid himself of the guns. Damn, I wanted to nail that bastard."

"Don't blame yourself, Blade," Vance consoled. "He's a wily son of a bitch. I'd be willing to bet this isn't his first involvement with illegal weapons. I wonder if he has an accomplice?"

"If I hadn't taken time to go after Shannon, I'd have the evidence we need. Now we'll have to wait and see if Bailey goes back east in the spring and brings back more guns," Blade grumbled sourly.

"There is a good chance Bailey will somehow expose himself," Vance offered. "Sit down, Blade, and tell me what happened. Whiskey all right?"

"Whiskey is fine," Blade said distractedly.

Vance poured two glasses of amber liquid and handed one to Blade, who sipped slowly on the whiskey while he told Vance how he'd searched Bailey's wagon and store and found nothing, almost getting caught in the bargain. They chatted a while about their unfortunate luck, then Blade left to snatch a few hours of sleep. Before he departed he assured Vance he'd not give up so easily. Failure wasn't something Blade took well.

* * *

Shannon awoke early, excited by the prospect of inspecting the schoolhouse and moving into her own home. She ate a hasty breakfast, and when Colonel Greer asked if she wished to see where she would be teaching, Shannon nodded her head with an eagerness that amused him.

The schoolhouse sat at the far end of the fort beyond the corral and horse shed. It was a one-room structure already furnished with desks and blackboard in anticipation of the teacher it didn't have. A wide variety of books and supplies were on hand, enough to get them started. A wood-burning stove sat in the middle of the room. It was filthy. So were the windows. So dirty in fact that Shannon couldn't see out of them.

Shannon learned that she'd be responsible for cleaning, carrying water, gathering firewood, and keeping supplies in good order. A teacher's duties seemed endless. She'd be teaching the usual course of study, including reading, writing, arithmetic, spelling, geography, history, and grammar. All this for forty dollars a month and the house she would occupy. It was no great fortune, but Shannon didn't mind. She was sure that not only would the job prove rewarding, but it would occupy her time during the long winter.

The house itself was in no better shape than the school, badly in need of a thorough scrubbing. Shannon realized that if school was to start in two weeks, she had her work cut out for her. Before Colonel Greer left Shannon to return to his duties, he imparted a stern reminder concerning her moral conduct.

"I know there is no need to caution you, my dear, but since you will be teaching our children, your conduct must remain above reproach. I've already done what I could to quell the talk circulating about your unfortunate ordeal with Mad Wolf. The rest is up to you."

"I understand, Colonel, and you'll have no complaint about my conduct."

"Good, very good. I'll leave you to your work now.

There is much to be done before school opens and I'll help you by assigning a man to do the heavy chores."

Shannon strode across the square wearing her oldest dress and carrying a bucket in one hand and a brush in the other, ready to tackle the awesome job of cleaning the schoolhouse and her new lodging. Suddenly she spied Blade leading his gray pony across the parade grounds. He looked big, lean, and dangerous —Nothing like the tender lover she remembered from the Indian village. She wondered where in the world he had found Warrior. They both assumed the animal had perished in the tornado. Shannon stopped, waiting for Blade to approach so she might question him about his horse. She was shocked when he passed her by without so much as flicking an eyelid in recognition.

"Blade, how dare you ignore me!"

Blade halted in mid-stride. He should have known Shannon couldn't let well enough alone. Didn't she realize he was avoiding her for a reason? She caught up with him, glaring at him with a challenge on her lips. "You weren't going to speak to me, were you?"

"Believe me, Shannon, it's for your own good. I'm not the kind of man a proper young woman like yourself should associate with. The new schoolmarm is expected to be more descreet."

"You know about that?"

"News travels fast on a small army post. Is teaching the profession you've decided upon?"

"For the time being," Shannon allowed. "I'm sure I'll enjoy it. Besides, a steady income will allow me to pay my own way to Idaho. And I don't like taking advantage of the Greers' hospitality. Isn't it fortunate rooms are included in the salary? I'm on my way there now," Shannon added brightly.

With devouring thoroughness, Blade's dark eyes feasted on every aspect of Shannon's face and figure. God, she was an enchanting creature! She had no idea what she did to him or how badly he wanted to take her in his arms, to feel her softness melt against his hardness. Unfortunately, here on the frontier he was considered no better than a savage and unsuitable company for a well-bred young lady.

A desire stronger than life propelled him a step closer, aware that people were staring but unable to help himself.

"Shannon—"

"Is there a problem?" Lieutenant Goodman's voice was harsh with disapproval. He had seen Blade and Shannon from across the parade ground and beat a hasty path to where they stood deep in conversation. He was astute enough to sense an undercurrent of emotion pass between them, and he seethed with anger.

"No problem at all," Shannon denied, unable to tear her eyes from the intensity of Blade's gaze. She wondered what Blade might have said if Goodman hadn't interrupted. "Blade and I were having a private conversation."

"Don't you have duties to attend to?" Goodman asked Blade, his voice ripe with censure. "I suggest you refrain from annoying Miss Branigan."

"But Blade wasn't—"

"The Lieutenant is right, Miss Branigan. I'll be on my way."

Shannon knew by Blade's compressed mouth and cold eyes that he was furious, and his valiant effort to contain his temper impressed her. She watched in consternation as Blade walked away, Warrior following close on his heels. The horse reminded Shannon that she hadn't asked Blade where he had found his mount.

"Blade, where did you find Warrior?"

"He wandered into the fort a few days ago," Blade explained tersely. He didn't bother to stop but continued on his way.

"Wait, I—"

"Let him go, Miss Branigan. The breed knows his place."

"Lieutenant Goodman, Blade is a man like any other and better than some I know," she hinted, fixing him with a cold glare. "Why do you insist on belittling him?"

"He is accustomed to it by now," Goodman said with careless disregard. "Please call me Ronald and I'll call you Shannon. I'd like us to be friends."

"I don't think . . ."

"Shannon, this is a small fort and people talk. It isn't proper for you to be seen with Swift Blade. I'm only saying this for your own good."

"Thank you, Lieutenant, but I don't need anyone looking out for my welfare."

"Ronald."

"Very well—Ronald," Shannon allowed grudgingly. Anything to get rid of him. "If you'll excuse me, there is much work to be done before school opens."

Shannon tackled the house first, cleaning several months' accummulation of dust and grime with a vigor that surprised even her. The house was small, consisting of bedroom, kitchen, and parlor, sparsely furnished with the bare necessities. But with the linens Shannon had brought with her and sundry items donated by Molly and various officers' wives, the house would be adequate for her needs—comfortable, even. At least it would be all hers for as long as she remained the schoolmarm.

True to his word, Colonel Greer sent a man to help with the cleaning. Sandy Loomis, a young, fuzzy-faced private, was eager to please, and within two days the house was sparkling clean. Before Private Loomis left at the end of the second day, Shannon received his promise to lend a hand whenever she needed him.

Alone at last, exhausted but satisfied with all she had accomplished, Shannon spared a moment to sink down on the soft surface of the newly made bed. It was beginning to feel like home already. She sighed sleepily. Tired, so tired . . . Her eyelids drooped, her chest rose and fell in steady cadence.

Blade stood outside Shannon's house in the growing dusk with an arrested look on his face. He knew he should turn around and leave just as fast as his legs could carry him. He had no business being here, no business at all—yet his heart told him otherwise. He had been coping admirably until he saw Shannon on the parade ground. Until that moment he had made himself believe she wasn't important to him, had denied in his heart that he needed her. He had intended to return to his room after his duties were completed, but his feet had worked independently of his mind and carried him to Shannon's house.

Though he knew she was forbidden to him, Blade felt driven by a force stronger than life. He had to see Shannon, had to speak with her, needed to tell her he hadn't meant to be so rude when they spoke last. He rapped lightly on the door, and when he received no answer he entered through the unlatched screen, careful that he wasn't seen. He knew Shannon was alone, for he had watched the young private assigned to help her leave a short time ago.

When a cursory inspection showed Shannon in neither the kitchen nor the parlor, Blade approached the bedroom. The door was ajar, and he saw her asleep on the freshly made bed. A large kerchief concealed her rich chestnut locks and a soiled white apron covered her blue gingham dress, but to Blade she was the loveliest sight he'd ever beheld. He stared at her, mesmerized, yet reluctant to awaken her. He should leave, Blade told himself. Being here was definitely not in Shannon's best interests. His decision made, he turned to depart. But as luck would have it, his moccasined feet, usually so noiseless, trod across a loose plank. As the plank gave beneath Blade's weight, it groaned in protest.

Shannon lingered in that place between sleep and wakefulness, aware of movement nearby. The creak-ing plank nudged her fully awake. She opened her eyes and saw him. He had his back turned to her as if he meant to leave without awakening her. She'd recognize that broad back and massive shoulders anywhere.

With a note of constraint in her voice she asked, "Blade? What are you doing here?"

Blade spun around, surprised to see Shannon wide awake and staring at him, her brows raised in a question.

'I—I came by to ask if you needed anything," he improvised, for in truth he had no idea what had brought him here. It was dangerous for them to be alone, dangerous in more ways than one. "Do you need money or—anything? I've some cash set aside that I'd be happy to lend you."

"No, thank you, I'm fine," Shannon replied primly. "My needs are small."

"My needs are enormous," Blade said hoarsely. His words were ripe with implied meaning, sending Shannon's Irish temper soaring. How dare he ignore her one minute then turn around and demand things she wasn't prepared to give!

"Perhaps you should leave," she said coldly, looking away from him.

Being alone with Blade did things to her, made her feel things she had no business thinking about, let alone doing. That one night spent in Blade's arms, experiencing his love, learning what it meant to be a woman, had put forbidden thoughts in her head. She couldn't look at him without recalling all those wonderful things he did to her and the incredible joy his loving brought her. But deep in Shannon's heart, she knew he didn't love her, that he had made love to her only because it was necessary. The only emotion involved was lust.

Blade didn't want to leave, but neither did he want to do anything to hurt Shannon. He turned again toward the door, reluctant yet prepared to oblige if it was what she really wanted. The effort was futile.

Suddenly he whirled to face her, his ebony eyes searching her face.

"I want you, Shannon. I want to make love to you."

Shannon's breath caught painfully in her chest. She hadn't expected him to be so brutally honest and his words caught her off guard. All her senses demanded that she tell him she wanted him with the same intensity as he wanted her. Why was something that made her feel so alive and glorious so sinful?

Shannon longed to give her approval, but the words refused to come. She could only stare at Blade—stare at him so long that she felt swallowed by the passionate authority in the black depths of his eyes.

"Don't you enjoy being made love to by a half-breed?"

"Blade, you don't understand. I can't—"

"Yes you can—and you will!"

In two steps he was beside her, tearing at her clothes, giving her a taste of what it meant to be loved by a real savage.

"Blade, stop—don't do this!"

"Why? Am I too much of a savage for you? Does my loving disgust you?"

For the first time since she met Blade, Shannon felt true fright. She opened her mouth to protest, to scream, anything to dissuade him from the terrible thing he was about to do.

"You bastard! I don't want this!"

"Yes you do. You want it as much as I do."

"No, I—"

Her words died in her throat as his mouth slanted across hers, his hands ridding her of the last remnants of her clothes. His kiss forced her mouth open so he could rake the inside with his tongue, until she ceased struggling and was kissing him back. Then his mouth was on her breast, drawing a nipple deep into his mouth until she cried out, shaking her head from side to side as if to deny her own response.

"Do you know how many times I've ached to have

you since that first time?" Blade groaned hoarsely.

Shannon struggled to resist, but she couldn't. His hands were doing wonderful things to her, his fingers sliding rhythmically inside her until the pleasure became a frantic beat that sang through her veins like liquid heat.

"Oh," she whimpered. "Oh, no."

Rising slightly, Blade's long fingers worked to release his swollen and throbbing manhood. Shannon gasped, realizing that her body had become his to do with as he pleased.

With a low growl and a curse, he sank into her—deep, deeper.

"Say it, damn you! Say you want me!"

"No!"

"Say it! Say it!" Beads of sweat dripped down his forehead as he fought to control the terrible need to thrust and thrust until she cried out, until she wanted him as badly as he wanted her. "Tell me you want me!"

A sob of surrender burst past her lips. "Yes! God help me, I want you!"

Then he was moving inside her, driving, pounding, grinding their loins together in mindless frenzy. He filled her again and again, straining and pounding his way as far as he could go inside her. The intensity became unbearable. A blazing bliss burst upon her, shattering, devastating. Blade tensed, shuddered, cried out. Shannon felt his body throb violently as he filled her with liquid fire.

Shannon whimpered.

The sound seemed to snap something inside Blade, bringing him abruptly to his senses.

"Sweet Jesus, Shannon—forgive me, forgive me. I don't want to hurt you. For a moment I forgot what I am, who I am."

"What are you, Blade?" Shannon asked, choking back a sob.

"I am a man. Red or white, I am a man."

"Yes, you are," Shannon agreed. "I won't ever forget it. Though I'll probably burn in hell forever, I wanted you to love me."

"Does that mean you forgive me? God, Shannon, I don't deserve you," Blade groaned. "Being a half-breed isn't my only sin where you're concerned. I served in the Union Army, I fought against all you loved and cherished."

Shannon winced, not wishing to be reminded of those painful memories and all she'd lost during the war. She may have been slow in learning it, but life did go on. Nothing remained the same forever. She had chosen a new life, just as the other Branigans had done, and there was no looking back. All that counted was tomorrow and what lay beyond the horizon—a new land, a fresh beginning, and freedom to do and be whatever she wanted.

Shannon had much to be grateful for and a good share of the credit was due to Blade. It was true he had stolen her innocence, but only because it was necessary to save her from captivity. Nor could she blame him for what he had just done. He hadn't really forced her, just made her admit how much she wanted him.

"I don't really care what you are, Blade, I only know how I feel when I'm with you," Shannon confessed. How could she fight him when his touch lifted her to such ecstasy? "I wanted desperately to hate you. It seemed the only way I could protect myself from you."

"Look at me," Blade directed, his voice a sensual purr. "What do you see?"

Her gaze went from his mouth—full and sensual now, though she'd seen it taut with rage—to his firm, arrogant jaw. There was a ruthless nobility about his dark features. Her eyes continued to drift down the strong column of his bronze neck to his broad chest—sprinkled with black, softly curling hair at the vee of his shirt—then across his taut abdomen and slim hips, to stare finally at the muscular thighs and bold thrust of his manhood. Blushing, her gaze shot upward to his midnight-black eyes fringed with thick, unbelievably long ebony lashes.

"Don't be embarrassed, Little Firebird." He stared into her eyes, his voice low and grating. "Tell me what you see."

"I see—I see—"

"Go on," he encouraged her.

"A man—a handsome, wonderfully virile man."

"What color am I?"

"Color? I see no color. Your skin is smooth and bronze from the sun. What do you want me to say?"

"That my Indian blood doesn't offend you, that afterwards you will remember that a *man* made love to you, not a half-breed savage."

"I know who made love to me."

Her words seemed to release something in Blade. "Oh God, Shannon, I need you. I'll never get my fill of you! What kind of a spell have you cast over me?"

Shannon's heart pounded rapidly as Blade slowly lifted his hand to her face and lightly ran his finger over her full bottom lip. His hand dropped to cup her breast, caressing it, his thumb teasing the nipple to a taut bud.

"I want to do it right this time."

Shannon felt weak; a hot tingling sensation rushing over her as he gathered her in his strong arms. He bent his head to her throat and lightly ran his tongue over it, tracing the throbbing pulsebeat to her ear, circling it, then gently probing it. Shannon shuddered in response. He nibbled at the corners of her mouth, his tongue teasing. At last his lips claimed hers in a long demanding kiss, his tongue plundering, her own answering, until they were both trembling with intense excitement.

His kiss went on and on as he deftly peeled away the rest of his clothing. When he settled down beside her there was nothing between them but sizzling flesh. Then Blade continued his slow, delicious assault. He nipped at her sensitive breasts, then licked the hurt away, his tongue rolling around one tender peak and then the other. His hand slipped between her thighs, his fingers stroking, tantalizing as his tongue traced her ribs down to her belly, thoroughly exploring her naval. Positioning himself between her legs, his tongue slid down her inner thighs.

Shannon's body was on fire, writhing in ecstasy, her blood spurting hotly though her veins. But when his mouth touched the nest of curls between her legs she froze, shocked and frightened. "Blade, no!"

"I won't hurt you, Little Firebird, let me, let me . . ."

Holding her thighs apart, Blade buried his head in her softness, his tongue a hot brand, flicking, teasing, stroking her erotically. A consuming heat spread over her as her thighs parted naturally, allowing him full access. Slipping his hand beneath her buttocks, Blade lifted her to his hot, devouring mouth, her scent and honeyed sweetness driving him wild. Shannon moaned, unaware that such a sensation was possible. She only knew she wanted it to go on forever.

"Blade, I want you inside me!"

"Not yet, Little Firebird, I owe you this. Don't hold back, love, this is just another way of loving."

Then she was crying out, thrashing her head from side to side as waves of exquisite pleasure carried her away. Her body was still vibrating, her nerve endings on fire when Blade surged full and deep inside her. His powerful thrust affected her like a bolt of lightning.

Blade's response to their fiery union was to groan in her ear, "Oh, God, Shannon, you feel so tight—so warm—so damn good."

His strokes were sensual, skillful thrusts, his hands and mouth everywhere, fondling, arousing, as their bodies clashed and rocked in primitive. violent mating.

He brought her to the trembling brink, then retreated, leaving her gasping, pleading, until a series of deep, penetrating thrusts hurled them both into oblivion, spinning, careening wildly, their cries of ecstasy intermingling. Afterwards, as they floated back to earth, Shannon swore their souls had touched and united.

"My sweet, exciting vixen," Blade crooned in her ear.

"My bold, handsome savage," Shannon sighed in response.

Blade stiffened, then realized she meant it as praise. He shifted his weight to lie beside her, pulling her into the curve of his body.

"I shouldn't have come here, Shannon. I never meant to jeopardize your reputation."

"We are both too hot-headed for our own good," Shannon observed dryly. "We lashed out at one another in self-defense. One thing I learned is that I have no pride where you are concerned."

"It is dangerous for you to be seen with me."

"How do you mean that?" Blade was silent so long that Shannon realized his warning was double-edged. "You're involved in something, aren't you? Something to do with the reason you were prowling inside those wagons."

Blade fell silent, reluctant to involve Shannon in his secret investigation.

"You may as well tell me, because I'm not going to let it rest until I find out. Perhaps I can help you."

"Don't ask, Shannon. I care for you too much to see you harmed."

"I told you I won't let it rest. Perhaps I should ask Colonel Greer."

"Christ, Shannon!" He raked his finger through his hair, snorting in exasperation. "That is the worst thing you could do. When you get something stuck in your craw, you won't let go. I'm an investigator for the government—does that satisfy you?"

Shannon mulled his answer over thoughtfully. "Not really. What are you investigating?"

Silence.

"Well? Perhaps I could do a little snooping and—"

"Gun smuggling."

"Gun smuggling! You suspect someone on our wagon train? Who are the guns intended for?"

"Indians," Blade said. "Renegades like Mad Wolf are desperate for weapons."

"You're working for the government?"

"Yes."

"But you're a—"

"—half-breed," Blade finished. "But I fought for the Yankees, remember?"

"How could I forget?" Shannon muttered. "Did you find what you were looking for?"

Blade paused in thoughtful consideration. If he told Shannon the truth, would that be the end of it? If he lied, would Shannon's prying land them both in trouble? In the end he decided to tell the truth and pledge her to secrecy.

"I found the guns, for all the good it did me."

"You found them in one of the wagons?" Shannon asked. Truth to tell she was more than a little stunned that Blade was actually confiding in her. He had probably decided it was the lesser of two evils. "Whose wagon?" Before Blade could reply, she added, "No, don't tell me, I already know. Clive Bailey. Clive is the gun smuggler. I never did like that man. What are you going to do about it?"

"Nothing," Blade replied sourly. "The bastard got rid of the guns while we were stranded on the prairie."

"Oh," Shannon said in a small voice. "What happens next?"

"I watch and wait for Bailey to make a mistake."

"How can I help?"

"By forgetting I ever mentioned this," Blade said earnestly. "By not telling a soul what I've just confided. I want your promise, Little Firebird."

"Of course I won't tell anyone," Shannon vowed, "but I want to do more than that."

"No, Shannon," Blade warned, regarding her keenly. "I'm serious about this. You can help me by staying out of it."

"Whatever you say," Shannon said meekly. If Blade hadn't been so distracted by the way Shannon's long chestnut hair curled around her breasts he would have been highly suspicious of his easily won victory. Passive compliance was hardly her way.

"Good, at least I—"

"Shannon, dear, where are you? When you failed to show up at dinner time, Claire and I decided to bring you your dinner. You work much too hard, you know."

"My God, Molly and Claire!"

Like a shot, Shannon was out of bed, scrambling into her clothes. Blade was one step behind. "What shall we do? They can't find us here like this."

"I'll slip out the window," Blade hissed, struggling into his pants.

"Shannon! Are you in the bedroom?"

"They'll be here in a minute." Shannon's voice shook with alarm.

Blade gathered up the rest of his clothes, grabbed his boots and dove through the open window.

Shannon turned from the window just as Molly and Claire Greer stepped into the bedroom.

"My goodness, why didn't you answer?" Claire asked suspiciously. Her violet gaze swept the room, missing nothing. Not the mussed bed, the open window, or the red neckerchief Blade left behind as he made his hasty exit.

"I—I must have fallen asleep," Shannon confessed guiltily. She was aware of Claire's keen scrutiny and prayed she suspected nothing.

"You poor dear," Molly crooned sympathetically. "You've worked yourself into a frazzle. Eat your supper and come back to the house later for a bath and a good night's sleep. Tomorrow is soon enough to move in here. The officers' wives are donating food to fill your cupboards."

"How wonderful," Shannon exclaimed, truly grateful.

"You are going to be teaching their children, and they wanted to welcome you properly. Well, I must be off. Are you coming, Claire?"

"I think I'll stay and chat with Shannon while she eats," Claire said, waving her mother off. Abruptly she turned and slanted Shannon a smile that didn't quite reach her eyes.

Shannon knew Claire didn't like her, but she had no idea why. It never occurred to her that the lovely brunette might be jealous, for she had nothing or no one to be jealous over. What Shannon didn't realize was that just her beauty was enough to send Claire into a jealous rage. Claire had been the belle of the post since arriving at Fort Laramie with her father and didn't appreciate the competition one bit. Already Shannon had all the young officers agog, and Claire sensed there was more between Blade and Shannon than met the eye. Blade was more man than Claire had seen in a long time, and she wouldn't have refused a clandestine flirtation.

"Let's go to the kitchen," Shannon said. "The food smells delicious and I'm famished."

Suddenly Claire bent and picked up something from the floor, something that had been partially concealed beneath the bed. Shannon blanched, recognizing Blade's neckerchief immediately.

"What's this?" Claire asked. Her knowing smirk brought a silent groan to Shannon's lips.

"Why, that's the dust cloth I was using," Shannon lied, thinking furiously.

"Hmmm, fancy dust cloth," Claire observed, her eyebrows arched in open defiance.

Though Shannon had no way of knowing, Claire had seen Blade wearing that very same neckerchief just this morning. Claire had no idea what was going on, but she certainly intended to find out. Shannon was competition she neither needed or wanted.

Shannon breathed a sigh of relief when Claire left a

short time later. She had much to ponder and needed
to be alone. She wanted to review in her mind all that
Blade had told her about his investigation and to
explore the ways she might help him.

Chapter Eleven

*B*lade entered *Clive Bailey's trading post, pretending* interest in the merchandise while Bailey was occupied with another customer. Blade made his way through aisles crowded with bags of flour, dried beans, coffee, cornmeal and barrels of salted meat. Past rows of shelves holding tins of food, harnesses, halters, ropes, saddles, and even wagon wheels stood on end against them. Blade skimmed quickly over tables loaded with clothing and yard goods to inspect a display of guns and knives. In addition to all this merchandise, sunbonnets and women's corsets hung from long poles next to pots and pans piled one on top of another. There was even a brass bathtub sitting in the corner.

Blade suspected Bailey did a thriving business, mostly from fur trappers, miners, and wagon trains passing through. Predictably Blade wandered over to inspect the weapons, disappointed when none of them appeared to be those smuggled in the false bottom of Bailey's wagon.

"Are you looking for something in particular, Blade?" Bailey had finished with his customer and walked over to where Blade stood examining the weapons. "That rifle you're holding is a good choice."

"I'm just looking," Blade muttered, turning to face Bailey. "Thought it was time I collected the rest of my pay." He'd already collected half his pay and was to be paid the rest upon reaching Fort Laramie.

"Wondered when you'd come for it. Naturally I deducted a portion for those days you left the wagon train."

"Naturally," Blade said dryly.

The money was important to Blade but not essential. All through those years he had attended school in the East, his father had sent him money regularly, most of which Blade saved. He'd even managed to save a portion of his army pay these past years and though far from wealthy, he certainly wasn't destitute.

"Heard you hired on as scout," Bailey said.

"That's right. With winter coming on I had nothing better to do."

"Hello, Mr. Bailey. Am I interrupting?"

Both men turned, surprised to see Claire Greer standing beside them, smiling brightly.

"What can I do for you, Miss Greer?" Bailey asked respectfully. As the daughter of the post commander, Claire Greer demanded and received deferential treatment from soldiers and civilians alike.

"I heard you brought a selection of new bonnets from back East. Thought I'd look them over."

"Help yourself, miss. I'll be back in a few minutes—I have to get something for the breed." He disappeared up the stairs.

Blade studied the young woman with considerable interest. She was small, pleasingly formed, and undeniably lovely. But not as vibrantly beautiful as Shannon, he decided, picturing Shannon as he had last seen her, her incredible body flushed from his lovemaking and her deep blue eyes hazy with passion.

She stepped closer, her voice a seductive purr

meant to entice. From previous experience Claire knew few men could resist her. "You're the new scout Daddy hired."

The moment Claire spied Blade inside the trading post her mouth had gone dry and a slow heat built inside her. Up close, his blatant masculinity nearly overpowered her. He was big, vital, and so tantalizing he literally took her breath away. She could hardly blame Shannon for succumbing to the half-breed—if in fact she had—for the man was every woman's dream. Being half savage and forbidden to Claire only made him more exciting and dangerously attractive.

"They call me Blade," Blade said, a lazy smile hanging on the corner of his mouth.

He had met many women like Claire Greer in his lifetime. When they saw something they wanted they went after it with single-minded determination. He recognized Claire's avid interest in him and acknowledged her silent message with a cynical smile. Though Claire would never, ever, admit to wanting a half-breed, obviously all he had to do was beckon and she'd fall into his bed. But oddly, he didn't want Claire, beautiful though she might be. He wanted a chestnut-haired vixen whose nose was dusted with freckles and who made love like an angel.

"I'm Claire Greer. My, you are a strong one," Claire gurgled admiringly as her eyes swept the magnificent length and breadth of his muscular form. "I'll wager you're good at just about—anything."

Blade smiled tightly, saying little while Claire continued to ogle him. He recognized an outright invitation when he heard one and prudently withheld a reply.

What neither was aware of was that Shannon had just entered the store to purchase a few necessities not provided by the women of the fort. Her anger sizzled when she saw Claire and Blade engaged in intimate conversation, Claire's hand resting on Blade's bulging bicep, her violet eyes wide with appreciation—and something that could only be interpreted as invitation. When Blade made no attempt to discourage Claire's brazen conduct, Shannon did a slow burn.

How dare Blade flirt with Claire after making love to her as if he really cared! Shannon bristled indignantly. Did it mean nothing to the womanizing savage? She whirled abruptly and left before either Blade or Claire even noticed that she had witnessed their shameful display. A few minutes later Clive Bailey returned.

Immediately Claire stepped away from Blade, pretending great interest in the bonnets hanging from a pole. Blade nearly laughed aloud. Claire's prompt dismissal made it perfectly clear that further contact between them must be in private, away from prying eyes and gossips. Would she be content with quick, furtive kisses and gropings, he wondered curiously, or would she demand all he had to offer? The question was moot, for he never intended to find out.

"There you are, Blade," Bailey said, eying the pair suspiciously, then immediately dismissing his outlandish thoughts. "This pays you in full."

Blade pocketed the money, nodded a curt thanks, tipped his hat politely at Claire, and strode from the store.

"Now, Miss Greer, what can I do for you?"

"I'll come back later, Mr. Bailey," Claire replied. Entranced by the way Blade's trousers clung to his muscular thighs and buttocks, she licked her dry lips and hurried after him. "I suddenly remembered a prior engagement." She swished out the door in a swirl of ruffled petticoats.

The first day of school dawned bright and cool. Notices had been posted for several days and Shannon stood eagerly at the door to greet the students from the fort. She was pleasantly surprised to see two Indian boys amidst the white faces. They had somehow learned of the school and came out of curiosity. The children ranged in age from seven to eighteen, and

Shannon eagerly anticipated the challenge of teaching so diverse a gathering.

After introductions were made all around, she determined that only seventeen-year-old Tommy Pierce and fifteen-year-old Leroy Jones would present any problems. Both were big, burly boys, much taller than herself, and they were already bullying the rest of the children, particularly the two Indian boys, Blue Feather and Running Elk. Thus far the Indian boys appeared well-behaved and attentive despite jeering from the rest of the group.

Shannon had seen little of Blade these past several days, except from a distance. She'd seen him ride out with patrols several times, and despite the fact that she'd been in her own quarters now for days, he'd not come to her again. Not that he'd find a warm welcome, Shannon grumbled sourly. She was still incensed over the outrageous way he had flirted with Claire Greer in the trading post.

The first week of school passed with blessed little trouble. For the most part the children were eager students, a bit boisterous perhaps, but badly in need of formal learning. Some hadn't attended school in two or three years. If not for Lieutenant Goodman, Shannon would have been content with her job. When he wasn't out on patrol or engaged in duties he made a habit of waiting until school let out, then dropping by to "chat" with her, and usually ended up walking her home. Shannon was certain Claire didn't know about it or she'd have the violet-eyed witch breathing down her neck.

That Friday after school was dismissed, Lieutenant Goodman appeared outside the schoolhouse at the usual time. After Shannon waved the children off, he followed her inside without waiting for an invitation.

"You appear to enjoy this job, Shannon," he said. His eyes followed her greedily as she went about her chores.

"I do," Shannon replied, picking up supplies and

depositing them in cupboards. "Sometimes I feel as if I was meant to teach school. Is there something you wanted, Ronald?" Since he had been so insistent about it she had begun calling him by his first name.

"Why, yes, I suppose I do," Goodman grinned ingratiatingly. "Are you planning to attend the dance a week from Saturday?"

"I'm looking forward to it," Shannon admitted. "It's been ages since I've been to a dance and it sounds like great fun."

Several young officers had already approached her offering escort, all of which she politely declined. She thought it wise that she attend her first dance with the Greers. She was so looking forward to it that she even had the dress she would wear picked out. All she needed to do was buy some new ribbon to trim the bodice.

"Good. Save me a dance. I'm taking Claire, but I can dance with whom I please once I'm there. Claire and I aren't engaged yet, even if her father does expect a proposal soon."

He sent Shannon a speaking look, as if to say he'd be more than willing to give Shannon a tumble behind Claire's back if Shannon was willing. She wasn't.

Shannon was searching her mind for a way to rid herself of the obnoxious lieutenant when noise from some kind of a commotion outside captured their attention. "What's happening?" Shannon wondered aloud, walking to the door and peering out. "There appears to be a crowd gathering down the street."

Goodman rudely pushed past her in order to get a better look. "I'll find out."

"Wait for me!" Shannon was right behind him, her curiosity piqued.

"Make way!" Goodman ordered, shoving his way through the knot of people gathered in the middle of the dusty parade ground. They seemed to be staring at something lying at their feet. Shannon followed close behind Goodman as a path opened for him.

When she saw what had caused the disturbance, she

froze, a strangled gasp rushing past her lips. "My God! No!"

A man lay on his stomach on the ground, an arrow protruding from his back. His spent horse stood nearby, its head lowered, blowing and heaving from exhaustion. It appeared the poor animal had been ridden hard and long with little rest or food.

But that wasn't the worst shock about seeing the man lying near death in the square. What struck Shannon forcefully was the fact that she knew the man. It was young Todd Wilson from the wagon train.

"Todd! Todd Wilson!"

Then suddenly Blade appeared from nowhere, kneeling beside Todd, supporting his body as he turned him over with gentle hands. Todd groaned and opened his eyes. They were nearly swollen shut by a vile mixture of dust and blood from a gash over his eyebrow. The expression on Todd's face was so bleak, so utterly despairing that Shannon couldn't stop the cry of dismay that slipped past her bloodless lips.

"Indians," Todd gasped from between lips parched and bleeding from lack of water. "It happened on the Bozeman Trail. They attacked at dawn several days after we left Fort Laramie."

"Todd, what about the Johnsons? And your family? And all the others?" Shannon asked. Anguish and fear twisted her beautiful features into a grimace of pain and disbelief.

"Shannon," Todd said, recognizing her for the first time. "Thank God you weren't with the wagon train. Dead, they're all dead."

"No! Oh God, no," Shannon sobbed, turning away to hide her grief.

"What do you make of it, Blade?" Goodman asked as he crouched beside Blade.

"Sioux," Blade replied tersely. He abhorred the thought that all the people he'd become fond of were dead. Could Mad Wolf be behind this massacre? he wondered bleakly. If so, he'd go out of his way to make damn certain it never happened again.

"Do you know the boy?" Goodman asked.

"Todd Wilson was traveling to Oregon with his family."

"Todd, is everyone dead?" Goodman asked.

"The bastards carried off my sister and Callie Johnson, but the rest are dead—my family, Howie, everyone. They left me for dead, but I fooled them. They stole all the stock, but missed old Cletus here, who was off foraging. Thought I was a goner for sure until he came wandering back a day or two later."

"Hang on, son, the doctor from the fort is on the way," Blade said gently. "Think hard, Todd—to your knowledge is everyone dead, even the Johnson baby?"

The question was never answered, for Todd had passed out. Serious loss of blood complicated by dehydration had sent him spinning into oblivion. It was a small miracle he'd survived this long.

Mercifully the doctor arrived with a pair of stretcher bearers close on his heels. With military authority the doctor quickly dispersed the crowd and knelt to examine his patient. Shannon watched in shocked horror as Todd was lifted onto the stretcher and carried away. Blade was quick to note her distress and offered comfort without a thought to how it might look.

"Don't worry, Shannon, he's in good hands."

Shannon's face was so white, so drawn, that Blade feared she was in shock, but the sound of his voice seemed to bring her out of her state.

"Oh Blade, I can't bear it! All my friends—gone. And poor Nancy and Callie." Suddenly a terrifying thought occured to her. "What about little Johnny Blade?"

It seemed only natural and right for Blade to offer the solace of his arms as he opened them wide. Without considering the right or wrong of her decision, Shannon stepped into his embrace, sobbing into his chest.

Goodman stood with his mouth open, shock and disbelief transforming his handsome features into a mask of hate and disgust. He never would have suspected that a well-bred young lady like Shannon Branigan would seek solace from a savage. But that was exactly what she was doing. Had some kind of bond developed between them during those days they were alone on the prairie? he wondered. No, it must be merely because the half-breed had once saved her life, and it was only natural now that she turn to him in a moment of grief. The girl needed to be set straight on what was proper and what was not.

"Get your gear together, Blade," Goodman rapped out with authority. "I want you along with the burying detail. We'll leave within the hour. Let's hope it's not too late to save the women."

With great reluctance Blade set Shannon aside. When she made sounds of protest low in her throat, he gave her a little shake and said in a voice only she could hear, "Think of how this looks, Little Firebird. Don't give the fort food for gossip."

Shannon was too distraught to care what people thought, but common sense prevailed as she silently watched Blade walk away. Only then did she realize that Lieutenant Goodman was still there, staring at her with stern disapproval.

"I've warned you before about the half-breed, Shannon, and your improper behavior where he is concerned," he lectured. "It's a good thing the townspeople dispersed before witnessing so disgraceful a demonstration. Keep in mind that you are a schoolteacher and your morals should never be in question."

Shannon bristled with indignation. "You don't have to preach morals to me, Lieutenant, I'm fully aware of my responsibility regarding the children."

"Don't be angry, Shannon, I'm only telling you this to prevent you from making a terrible mistake. The breed isn't the kind of man ladies become involved with. You're new to the West and don't know the rules and the harsh realities of frontier life. Think about what I've said while I'm gone." He turned abruptly and left her standing in the middle of the square.

"Are you going after the women?" Shannon called after him.

He halted, turning back to answer her. "It depends on Colonel Greer. We're a mere handful of men gathered here at Fort Laramie, and we have all we can do to make safe the hundreds of miles of Oregon Trail under our jurisdiction, most of it in the heart of the Sioux Nation. If it's within our power, we'll bring the women back, but I can't promise we'll succeed."

Blade scouted ahead of the patrol, his ears attuned to the slightest sound, his eyes alert for signs of danger. Blade strongly suspected that Mad Wolf and his renegades were behind the vile attack on the wagon train, and it occurred to him that if Mad Wolf hadn't gotten the weapons he'd never have attempted so daring a raid. Killing innocent women and children was a cowardly act. It was an attack like this that led to the Sand Creek Massacre in '64, when the army killed one hundred and fifty peaceful Indians in retaliation for Indian atrocities.

That night the patrol bedded down on the prairie and Blade deliberately chose a spot a short distance apart from the main party to spread his bedroll. Lieutenant Goodman approached Blade as he prepared to settle down for the night.

"How soon before we reach the wagon train?"

"A couple more days at least," Blade calculated. "We can travel twice as fast as the wagon train. I'll leave at dawn and scout ahead." Blade turned away, expecting Goodman to leave. When Goodman stood his ground, Blade faced him squarely, one black eyebrow arched. "Is there something else?"

Blade waited for Goodman to speak, his eyes coldly assessing.

"Damn right! You're damaging Miss Branigan's reputation every time you're seen with her. That display today was uncalled for. Don't let it happen again."

"Is that an order, Goodman?"

"If you want to keep your job, stay away from Shannon Branigan. I have the colonel's ear and a word from me is all it will take to send you packing."

"Don't threaten me, Goodman," Blade said evenly, stifling the urge to put the cocky lieutenant in his place. It was imperative that he contain his anger until his investigation was done here.

Deliberately, Blade stretched out in his bedroll and turned his back, putting an abrupt end to the conversation.

Two days later they found the wagon train. Vultures swooping low over the charred wreckage showed them the way. It was just as Todd Wilson described, only worse. Everyone was dead. Men, women, and children, all slaughtered, most scalped. It was a grisly sight, causing even the most seasoned troopers to turn away, sickened.

Under Goodman's direction, the burying detail set to work immediately. The terrible stench of decaying flesh rose above the site like an evil cloud, forcing the men to cover their noses and mouths. Not only were the emigrants murdered, but their goods had been ransacked and their valuables stolen. During the search for victims, Blade was quick to note that the Johnson baby was not among the dead. A survey of the patrol confirmed his theory that Callie had somehow managed to take her child with her. Realistically, Blade knew that there was only a slim chance that they were still alive. It would break Shannon's heart if little Johnny Blade Johnson was dead.

"Do you have any idea who is responsible for this?" Goodman asked Blade once all the dead had been buried.

Blade held up an arrow similar to the one found in Todd Wilson's back. "Renegade Sioux who are unhappy on the reservation and angered by the influx of people moving West. See this notch?" He held the arrow under Goodman's nose, pointing to the feathers at the end of the shaft. "There is only one man I know of who notches his arrows in this manner."

'Who is that?"

"Mad Wolf."

Blade thought he saw something stir in Goodman's eyes, something he was unable to decipher. "That red devil!" Goodman spat. "He will pay for this atrocity. He belongs to Yellow Dog's village, doesn't he?"

"He acts independently," Blade explained. "It isn't fair to blame Yellow Dog, or all Sioux in general, for this attack. If you start killing indiscriminately, you'll be no better than Mad Wolf."

"Stick to what you know, Blade, and leave the soldiering to me. Move out, men!" Immediately the patrol prepared to mount up and ride out.

"Where are we going, Lieutenant?"

"Away from here," Goodman said, wrinkling his nose in obvious distaste. "Surely we can find a better camping place than this. I hope you're as good a tracker as you claim."

"We're going after the renegades?"

"Damn right!"

Blade had been tracking Mad Wolf a full day. It was noon now and Goodman had just sighted a stand of cottonwood trees on the south bank of the Platte River and signaled for a break. Mad Wolf had crossed the river several times but Blade had been able to pick up his trail with little difficulty. His keen perception told him there were about twenty renegades in the raiding party. Hoof prints indicated that the women rode double with two of the Indians, lending Blade hope that they were still alive. But knowing Mad Wolf as he did it was difficult to guess what condition they were in.

Blade downed a hasty meal, then scouted out the area while the others rested. Within minutes he found signs indicating that the renegades had camped nearby, and other signs that led him to believe a struggle had taken place. In short order he discovered scraps of material that looked like pieces of women's clothing.

He pointed them out to Goodman, who swore to avenge the atrocities. After they had eaten, Goodman ordered the patrol back on their horses, but Blade lingered behind, still reading signs. Suddenly he froze, all his senses coming alive. A strange sound coming from a clump of bushes close to the river bank set his hair on end.

His dark eyes swept the surrounding area, but he saw nothing. Yet obviously something had distracted him. On cat's feet he crept toward the bushes, his hand hovering above his gun. Nothing stirred. Could he have been mistaken? No, he told himself, his senses hadn't failed him yet. Then he heard the soft mewling sound again, renewing his faith in his instincts. Someone or something was hidden in the bushes. Perhaps only a wounded animal, he told himself, not daring to hope.

He reached the river bank and knelt, spreading apart the thick branches of undergrowth. What he discovered was no wounded animal—no animal at all. His shout of jubilation caused the patrol to about-face and rush to his side.

"What is it?" Goodman asked, sliding from his horse and hunkering down beside Blade.

"I found the Johnson baby." Blade picked up the small bundle with surprisingly gentle hands.

"Is he alive?"

"He looks all right, probably just hungry. But I'm no doctor."

"What do you think happened?"

"He probably got in the way and Mad Wolf dumped him, expecting him to die."

"And the women?"

"We can only assume they are still alive."

"Then we push on."

"What about the baby?"

Goodman stared at Blade in silent contemplation. "Obviously someone has to take him back to the fort."

A short time later, after Blade had painstakingly

spooned water down little Johnny's parched throat, one of the privates rode back to the fort with the baby strapped securely to his chest, a precaution suggested by Blade. Then the patrol resumed their march, more determined than ever to kill the savages responsible for so many deaths.

Blade found Mad Wolf's camp the next day while he was out scouting alone. The renegade had set up camp in the shadow of a ledge jutting out from a hillside. It was obvious from his lack of vigilance that he thought no one from the wagon train had survived to alert the soldiers from the fort.

Blade crouched in rocks above the campsite, making a visual search of the area. He spotted the two women lying motionless on the ground. From a distance Blade couldn't judge whether they were dead or alive, only that they appeared to have been abused both sexually and physically. Edging closer, Blade heard the men arguing about who would have them first tonight. Having heard more than enough, he melted into the shadows to alert the patrol.

The patrol waited to attack until the Indians were seated around the campfire, smoking and drinking whiskey taken from the wagon train. The attack caught the renegades completely by surprise as they dove for their weapons. Some were killed outright in the ensuing battle, and when the melee ended, Blade was dismayed to discover that Mad Wolf and several of his cohorts had slipped away during the height of battle. Only the dead and dying remained.

"See to the women, Blade," Goodman barked as he turned to check on his own wounded.

With trepidation Blade approached the women, recalling that neither Callie or Nancy had moved during the battle. That alone gave him fair warning of what he would find. Hunkering down, he turned over the woman closest to him. It was Nancy Wilson. She was dead, having suffered more abuse at the hands of Mad Wolf and his renegades than she could tolerate. Realizing that she was beyond human help, Blade moved on to Callie. He was heartened to discover she still lived, though covered with filth and battered nearly beyond recognition.

"Callie, can you hear me?"

At first Blade received no answer, but when he held his canteen to Callie's bloodless lips she drank greedily. "Easy, you're safe now."

Just the sound of a male voice and Blade's hands on her wrenched a scream from Callie's throat. "No! No! Please don't hurt me again!" Then she started shuddering and shaking uncontrollably. Seeing Blade's swarthy face poised above her sent her teetering on the edge of sanity.

Blade held her tightly, crooning words of comfort into her ear. "It's Blade, Callie, Swift Blade. You are safe now, no one will hurt you again."

A long time elapsed before he was able to get through to her. She ceased struggling and crying out but continued to shudder.

"Blade?"

"Yes, Callie, you're safe now."

"My baby, my baby is dead. Howie is dead," she moaned over and over.

"Your baby is alive, Callie. I found him and sent him back to the fort. You will join him soon."

"How are the women?" Lieutenant Goodman stood beside Blade, having seen to his wounded and issued orders for their care.

"Nancy Wilson is dead, but I think Callie will make it with proper care. She should be taken back to the fort as soon as possible."

"You'll be taken care of, Mrs. Johnson," Goodman assured her, placing a hand on her shoulder.

Immediately Callie jerked away, fear and terror twisting her features. "Don't! Don't touch me!"

"It's all right, Callie, Lieutenant Goodman won't hurt you. He'll send you back to the fort with one of his men."

"No, please, can't you take me? I don't want to go with anyone else."

"Perhaps that would be best," Goodman mused thoughtfully. His eyes narrowed and an arrested look came over his features. "Obviously the woman trusts you."

"What about Mad Wolf?"

"We'll find him. And if we don't someone will pay for this."

Goodman's insinuation that someone, even innocent Indians, would be held responsible for Mad Wolf's vile atrocities, frightened Blade. However, there was not much he could do about it, only pray that Goodman would find Mad Wolf. Callie's life depended on how fast Blade could get her back to Fort Laramie and a doctor.

Two days later Blade rode into Fort Laramie. Callie sat slumped against him in the saddle. A curious crowd gathered around them when Blade reined in in front of the infirmary and dismounted. Ignoring the questions flung at him, he quickly carried Callie inside. After a terse explanation and a comforting word to Callie, he left her in the doctor's expert care. The reason Blade didn't linger was because he felt the need to find Shannon without delay. He wanted to be the one to tell her how and in what condition they had found Callie. When he left the infirmary he spied Shannon crossing the parade ground, having already heard that Blade had returned with one of the women. He strode out to meet her.

"Blade, what happened? Who did you bring back?"

"It's Callie, Shannon. I left her with the doctor."

"Thank God. I'm going to her, she'll need someone," Shannon said, pushing past Blade.

"Wait!" Blade grasped her arm, stopping her in mid-stride. "First let me tell you how I found her. Did the private arrive with the baby?"

Suddenly Shannon's face lit up. "Yes. After Johnny was cleaned up and fed he seemed no worse for his ordeal. Mrs. Cramer generously offered to nurse him along with her own three-month-old son. Please, tell me about Callie and Nancy. Is Nancy being brought back by someone else?"

"Nancy is dead. She couldn't take the abuse," Blade said, his voice somber. "Thank God Callie is made of sterner stuff. She's in shock over Howie's death and needs a great deal of care and understanding. Knowing that her child is well and safe will help heal her."

"Poor Nancy," Shannon lamented. "I'll do all I can to help Callie recover. Why did this happen to her? It could have been me. Why didn't Mad Wolf abuse me when he had me?"

"Mad Wolf wanted you for his wife," Blade told her, "that's why he allowed none of his friends to touch you. It would have killed something inside me to see you in the same condition as Callie."

Shannon's heart thumped a wild tattoo inside her breast. Did Blade's words mean he cared for her? More importantly, did she care for him? The answer was a resounding yes. She never would have surrendered to him so easily if she didn't care. She wasn't the kind of woman who offered herself to just any man. She was finally able to admit that when Blade made love to her it mattered little that he carried the same blood in his veins as those men who had killed all her friends and abused Callie.

"Go to Callie now, Shannon. She'll need a friend. I'm anxious to speak with Colonel Greer, and he'll be expecting a report. Mad Wolf escaped and the patrol went after him." He turned to leave.

"Blade, please stop by tonight, I need to—talk to you."

An arrested look came over Blade's features. "Shannon, you know what happens when we're alone for more than a few minutes." If his words were meant to discourage, they failed miserably.

"I'm old enough to make my own decisions."

"Are you sure?"

"Yes," Shannon said with firm resolve.

Blade searched her face for several tense minutes before answering. "Very well, but remember, you're as much to blame for what happens as I am. God knows I tried."

Darkness and shadows played tag with the surrounding plains and hills when Shannon heard Blade's footfall on the porch. She flung open the door before he knocked and he stepped inside. The air outside was crisp and ripe with the promise of winter, and Blade moved close to the stove to warm his hands.

"I'm sorry I had to leave so abruptly the other day," Blade said, "but it wouldn't do for Claire and Molly Greer to find me in your bed. How is school?"

"Forget school for a moment. I want to know what you and Claire found so interesting to talk about in the trading post. She was absolutely enthralled with you. She looked as if she could devour you."

"You saw us?"

"I stayed only long enough to see you engaged in intimate conversation. When she put her hands on you I left. I had no idea she could be so brazen."

"Jealous?" A hint of amusement brought a twinkle to his dark eyes.

"Of course I'm not jealous!" Shannon replied huffily. "You could have bedded Claire right there in the trading post for all I cared. It surprised me that you two even knew one another."

"We had just met," Blade revealed. "And you are right, she is brazen. Not my type at all."

"What is your type? Not that it matters," Shannon was quick to add.

"Look at yourself in the mirror."

"What?"

"Look at yourself in the mirror," Blade repeated, "and you'll see the type of woman who attracts me. Women like Claire Greer are common enough, but there are damn few Shannon Branigans in the world."

Shannon flushed, moving to the uncomfortable-looking sofa close to the stove and sitting down. Blade followed, settling down beside her.

"Do you mean that?"

"I never say anything I don't mean."

"Claire certainly is tempting."

"You're far more tempting."

He looked at her as if he were starving and Shannon the meal.

"What did you want to talk about?" he asked, suddenly recalling the reason he had come here tonight.

Truth to tell, talk was the last thing Blade had on his mind. What he really wanted was to take Shannon in his arms and love her to distraction. But he knew Shannon deserved better; she needed a man who wasn't despised for the mixed blood that ran through his veins. In the East it didn't seem to matter all that much what he was. Besides, few had guessed he was part Sioux. Out here on the Western frontier his Sioux blood forced him to live on the fringes of society, yet he had never once considered remaining in the East forever. Wyoming was home and the plains and hills where he grew up the place where he would eventually settle down and raise his children.

"I wanted to ask you about Clive Bailey. Have you learned anything new?"

"No, and I probably won't until next spring when he goes back East for another load of weapons. *If* he goes back," Blade stressed.

"Maybe he'll confess."

Blade laughed bitterly. "Why would he do that?"

"Perhaps I could get him to talk," Shannon offered innocently.

"No!" Blade blasted, jumping to his feet. "Leave Bailey to me and my contact."

"You have a contact here at Fort Laramie?" Shannon asked, catching his slip immediately.

"Dammit, Little Firebird, when I'm with you I get so confused I don't know what I'm saying. For your own safety, don't involve yourself in this."

"But I want to become involved. When I think that Clive might have been the man who furnished the guns that killed my friends, it makes me angry. Too angry to sit back and do nothing. I can't forget how he almost succeeded in assaulting me out on the trail."

"Leave Bailey to me, Shannon," Blade advised sternly. "One day he will make a mistake, and when he does I'll be there to nail him. I couldn't bear it if you were hurt."

"Do you care so much?"

"More than you know."

He held out his hand, and when she grasped it he pulled her to her feet. Then his arms encircled her, drawing her against his hard, muscular chest, and his parted lips touched hers. Abruptly Clive Bailey was forgotten, for her mind ceased functioning; his kiss was one of such intense longing and hunger that Shannon knew exactly where it would lead.

"I'm going to make love to you, Little Firebird."

"I know."

His tongue slid across her lips, urging them apart, and when they did, he plunged it into her mouth. His hands glided restlessly, possessively, up and down her back and breasts, sliding across her bottom, pressing her tightly to his hardened thighs, and Shannon felt herself falling slowly into a spinning whirlpool of sensuality and passion. Surrendering to the power of his virility, she wound her arms around his neck and clung to him.

In a dreamlike daze, she felt her gown falling away, and then the brush of his hardened palms against her swollen breasts. Arms like steel bands surrounded her, lifted her, carried her to her bedroom and gently stood her on her feet while he removed the rest of her clothes.

"You're perfect," Blade proclaimed, his voice tinged with awe. "Your body is so beautiful it hurts my eyes."

Then he was kissing her again, exploring her mouth with his tongue, his hands like burning brands on her bare flesh. Suddenly she felt herself floating, then felt the cool sheets against her skin. Abruptly the warmth, the security of his arms and body withdrew. Her lids flew open, alarmed, until she saw him standing beside the bed, and a tremor of admiration quaked through her. His skin was like oiled bronze, the heavy muscles of his shoulders and arms and thighs rippling gloriously as he removed his pants and boots. He was wonderfully made and splendidly male, she thought, shocked when she felt no compulsion to turn away in embarrassment.

Then Blade was lowering his body beside her, pulling her hips into vibrant contact with his straining loins, molding her body to the rigid contours of his. He cradled her head as he drove his tongue into her mouth again and again. When he stopped, Shannon groaned in keen disappointment, taking his head between her hands and gently caressing his eyes, his cheekbones, with trembling fingertips. Then she leaned up and kissed him, and a knot of tenderness swelled in Blade's chest.

"You're beautiful, too," Shannon offered shyly.

"Only women are beautiful," Blade grinned foolishly.

"Then you're wonderfully handsome."

"For an Indian," Blade added with a hint of bitterness.

"For a man," Shannon corrected.

"Oh God, Shannon, if only . . ."

"If only what?"

"I have no right to say it."

"Blade, please."

"If only you were mine."

"You've already made me yours."

"I'm a half-breed . . ."

"Dammit, Blade, forget that and love me."

"Shannon," he groaned, his hands rushing over her back, her thighs, caressing her buttocks. "Shannon," he repeated, unable to stop saying her name as he rolled her onto her back and covered her body with his. "Shannon," he moaned hoarsely as her arms went around him and she lifted her hips, molding herself to his engorged manhood. Her name was like a melody in his head, singing through his veins, as she welcomed the first hot thrust of his body into hers.

"Blade!" Shannon cried out as his hips flexed again and again, stroking, caressing, bringing her to a shattering completion.

Desperately straining for his own reward, Blade dragged his lips from hers, leaning up on his elbows in order to watch her face as her tremors subsided. Then, he thrust into her again, and yet again, his body jerking convulsively as he spilled his seed into her.

Chapter Twelve

*"**M**ust you go?" Shannon asked, stretching luxuriously.* Her body was pleasantly exhausted, yet she'd never felt so vibrantly alive.

"I'd like nothing better than to lie here beside you all night, but we both know that's impossible," Blade sighed, planting a kiss on Shannon's lips before levering himself from bed. "I'm leaving in the morning to find Lieutenant Goodman. I don't trust that man. He's so consumed with hate, I fear he'll seek vengeance on any Indians unlucky enough to cross his path. We don't need another Sand Creek Massacre. There is already enough unrest in the area. Think of me while I'm gone, Little Firebird."

Blade walked through the dark night to Major Vance's quarters. Earlier he had made arrangements to speak with Vance before his departure the next morning. Blade's discrete knock brought an immediate reply.

"You're late," Vance said shortly. Blade walked inside and closed the door behind him.

"I was—detained."

Vance sent him a searching look. "I saw that little display the other day with the Branigan girl. What's going on, Blade? A flirtation at this time could jeopardize our investigation."

Blade flushed. What he felt for Shannon was more than mere flirtation. "You know I wouldn't do anything to hinder the investigation. Shannon is—special to me. But that's as far as I can allow it to go. Her family would never accept me. Have you found out anything new?" he asked, changing the subject.

"I wired the president today. I told him our investigation has hit a snag and nothing more is likely to be accomplished until next spring. What are your plans for the present?"

"My immediate plans are to ride by the village and make certain my mother and grandfather are well and that nothing is amiss. Then I'm going to rejoin Lieutenant Goodman's patrol. I may as well stick close to the fort this winter."

"Good luck. I'll see you when you return."

"I'd like to ask a favor of you, Wade."

"Of course, Blade, anything."

"Keep an eye on Shannon while I'm gone. Trouble seems to follow her."

"That Southern belle means a lot to you, doesn't she," Vance asked shrewdly.

"You've been a good friend to me, Wade, so I don't mind telling you, I love Shannon." His blunt confession startled Vance. "But I can't let her know. She deserves much better than I can offer her."

From her porch Shannon watched Blade ride out of the fort the next morning. She was just leaving for the schoolhouse. She always arrived early on these cold mornings in order to build a fire in the stove before the students arrived. But seeing Blade leave took a little of the bounce out of her step. She had no idea when he would return and instinctively knew she'd miss him dreadfully.

Later that morning when Shannon took roll call, she noted that the two Indian boys were missing. She thought nothing of it, for they came and went at will. She had learned early on that they came from Yellow Dog's village and often went with the men on hunting expeditions.

A few days later, Shannon had just dismissed school for the weekend when Lieutenant Goodman's patrol rode into the fort. She saw at a glance that Blade wasn't with them and wondered if he had somehow missed them, though she thought it highly unlikely, given his tracking skill. Wondering at his absence, she walked across the compound to visit Callie.

Being reunited with her child had done wonders for Callie's spirits. Little Johnny prospered with Mrs. Cramer, who had offered to keep and feed the infant until Callie was fully recovered. It hurt Shannon to see Callie in such dreadful shape, but at least she was alive. Since Callie was reluctant to speak of Howie or her harsh treatment by Mad Wolf, Shannon carefully avoided mentioning those painful subjects, and because Callie tired easily, Shannon left after a short visit. She ran into Claire Greer outside the infirmary.

"Have you heard the news?" Claire gushed excitedly.

"You mean about Lieutenant Goodman's patrol returning? I saw them ride in earlier. Did they find Mad Wolf?"

"I'm not certain," Claire admitted, "but it's all over the fort that they wiped out the village that gave Mad Wolf sanctuary."

Shannon blanched. "Are you referring to Yellow Dog's village?"

"I don't know," Claire shrugged carelessly. "Ronald is with Father now."

"Dear God, no!" Shannon cried, turning and running toward headquarters. She had to know whose village had been attacked. If her fears proved correct, Blade's mother and grandfather could be badly wounded—or dead!

Shannon rushed headlong into headquarters, demanding to see Colonel Greer.

"I'm sorry, ma'am, the colonel is in conference," the sergeant occupying the front desk said politely.

"I'll wait," Shannon insisted stubbornly.

Shannon began to pace, glancing beyond the sergeant to the closed door, assessing her chances of getting past him without being stopped. When the man returned to his work, Shannon made her move. Suddenly she darted past the desk, flung open the door, and pushed her way inside. There were three men in the room—Colonel Greer, Lieutenant Goodman, and Major Vance.

"What's the meaning of this, Shannon?" Colonel Greer thundered when he recognized the intruder.

"I'm sorry, sir," the sergeant apologized. He was close on Shannon's heels, but not fast enough to prevent her from disrupting the conference. "I'll remove her immediately."

"No!" Shannon resisted. "Not until I find out about Yellow Dog and his people. Is it true? Did Lieutenant Goodman's patrol attack the village? Didn't he realize they were peaceful Indians?"

"Come along, young lady," the sergeant said with stern reproval.

"It's all right, Sergeant Miller, let her stay," Greer said.

"Yes, sir. If you need me I'll be right outside the door."

"You know Lieutenant Goodman, of course, and this is Major Vance. Now, Shannon, what is this all about?"

"Rumor has it that Lieutenant Goodman's patrol attacked a Sioux village. Was it Yellow Dog's village? They are peaceful people, Colonel, nothing like Mad Wolf and his cohorts. They had no weapons other than bows and arrows. The village consists mostly of women, children, and elderly braves."

"You're wrong, Shannon," Goodman claimed. "We tracked Mad Wolf to the village. We know he was hiding out there, yet they insisted they hadn't seen him in weeks. I allowed them sufficient time to turn him over to me and when they failed to comply I ordered the attack."

"On defenseless women and children!" Shannon charged, recalling gentle Singing Rain and wise old Yellow Dog with fondness. And Blade. God, he'd be devastated if his entire family was wiped out. "I was there, remember? I know what the village is like. They didn't harm me. Did you find Mad Wolf in the village?"

No answer.

"Well, did you?" Shannon demanded to know.

"Er—no," Goodman admitted sheepishly. "Mad Wolf could have slipped away during the battle."

"Or he wasn't there in the first place," Shannon snorted derisively.

"Why are you defending those savages?" Goodman challenged. "Could it be because you're smitten with the half-breed?"

"My personal life is no concern of yours, Lieutenant," Shannon retorted. "It's the lives of innocent people we're discussing."

"Shannon, this has gone far enough," Colonel Greer warned sternly. "I trust Lieutenant Goodman. His judgment has always been above reproach. I'm convinced he did what was right given the circumstances."

"Were Yellow Dog's people armed with guns?" Major Vance asked. Perhaps Colonel Greer trusted Goodman's judgment, but he didn't, nor did Blade.

"I'm sure they were," Goodman replied somewhat uncertainly.

"Were any of your men wounded?"

"Four, sir."

"Gunshot wounds?"

"Er—no, arrow wounds, I believe."

"I see," Vance said with an unmistakable hint of censure.

"So do I," Shannon concurred. "I can see I'm

wasting my time here. Good day, gentlemen." Whirling on her heel she stormed from the room, past a startled Sargeant Miller and out the door.

Shannon knew exactly what she had to do now. No matter where he was, she had to find Blade. With firm resolve, Shannon hurried in the direction of the livery, intending to rent a horse and leave immediately. Fortunately it was Friday and she had two whole days to find Blade. He'd need someone with him when he learned of Lieutenant Goodman's attack upon his grandfather's village.

"Miss Branigan—Shannon—where are you going?"

Shannon spun around to find Major Vance a few steps behind her. "Not that it's any of your business, Major, but I'm going to find Blade. He'll be utterly devastated when he learns of Lieutenant Goodman's foul deed."

"I agree," Vance said with real concern.

"You do?" His words left Shannon momentarily speechless.

"I do. Few here know, and we prefer it that way, that Blade and I are close friends, have been for a good many years."

"You're Blade's contact!" Shannon blurted out before she could catch herself.

"My God, what did Blade tell you!"

"Everything—or nearly everything. He really had no choice, you see. I encountered him searching through the wagons after the wagon train left Independence. I kept badgering him until he was forced to admit he worked for the government. I even offered my help, but he adamantly refused."

"I should hope so," Vance said slowly. "You are quite a woman, Shannon Branigan. No wonder Blade is—er, so fond of you. But he is right, of course, this isn't child's play. The last man sent by the government is dead. But to get back to the subject, how do you propose to find Blade? Do you know where to look?"

"N-no," Shannon admitted, "but I'll find him."

"He told me he was going to see his mother and grandfather before rejoining Lieutenant Goodman's patrol."

Shannon's eyes grew wide with alarm. "Oh no, he could be there now. I'd better hurry."

"Shannon, you can't go alone."

"Do you have a better idea, Major?"

"Yes, wait till morning and I'll go with you. It's too late to start out now anyway."

"You'd do that?"

"I told you I was Blade's friend, and yours too, I hope. Well, is it a deal?"

"Very well," Shannon agreed reluctantly. "Until morning."

Blade's face was watchful as he rode toward the Sioux village. He was anxious to see his mother and grandfather again, yet a profound sense of foreboding disturbed him, and he didn't know why. For one thing it was quiet, too quiet. By now he should have encountered a hunting party, or heard dogs barking in the distance, or the echo of children's laughter. It was as if he was the only living thing in the vast empty prairie.

A cold north wind whistled down from the distant mountains and Blade shivered. He sensed it in every fiber of his being—something was wrong, terribly wrong. Even his bones ached with the knowledge. The village was nestled in a narrow valley between two hills, but no smoke arose to greet him, no happy voices carried to him on the wind.

Digging his heels into Warrior's sides, Blade urged him into a gallop as unspeakable fear gripped his insides. He knew, somehow he knew what he'd find, yet denied it with every heartbeat. Then, abruptly, the village lay before him and the most horrible nightmare imaginable became shocking reality. There was nothing left of the village but smoldering embers.

Bodies lay scattered everywhere—men, women, children, even babies still strapped in their cradle boards. The breath slammed out of Blade's chest and the air around him vibrated from the terrible, blood-curdling cry of outrage and denial that erupted from his lips. For several long minutes Blade was unable to move. Then, fighting his emotions, he forced himself to the gruesome task of examining each body for signs of life.

Tears rolled down Blade's cheeks when he found Singing Rain's body. He howled in outrage and flung his arms heavenward, his fists clenched, screaming out his rage.

"Why?" he challenged Wanken Tanken, the Grandfather Spirit. "Why did you allow this to happen? Why my sweet gentle mother? Why these people who wanted only peace?"

Then he began the death chant, gathering ashes from the ground and smearing them on his face and chest. He felt no pain when he slashed his arms in several places, ignoring the blood as if it didn't exist. That was how Shannon and Major Vance found him the next day, still kneeling beside his mother, his face a bleak mask of despair, keening the Sioux death chant.

Sensing their presence, Blade's chanting stopped abruptly. He turned to face them. Shannon paled. Blade's face was devoid of all emotion, his eyes desolate and empty; he seemed not to recognize them. Never had Shannon beheld such profound anguish, such overwhelming grief—except, perhaps, when her family had discovered her father dead by his own hand.

"Blade, I'm so sorry," Shannon said, touching his shoulder gently. Her soft voice seemed to release him from his hypnotic state.

"Shannon," he groaned as if in pain. "They killed her. She never hurt a soul. Singing Rain was kind and gentle." Though Indians were taught from birth never to show emotions, Shannon could see the glimmer of tears in his dark eyes.

"I know, Blade, I loved her too. I—I don't see your grandfather," she ventured.

"He's not among the dead. Neither is Jumping Buffalo. I can only hope they escaped this carnage."

"I'll help you bury the dead, Blade," Major Vance offered.

"It is our custom to place the dead on burial platforms," Blade said bleakly.

"There are too many, it wouldn't be possible," Vance reasoned. "Burial is the best we can do."

"Yes," Blade concurred. "Except for my mother. I will build a platform and prepare her body. She will be mourned properly, in the Sioux manner."

Even Shannon lent a hand with the burying, at times gagging from the stench. But for Blade's sake she swallowed her revulsion and bravely pitched in where needed.

Singing Rain's burial platform was built alongside the Platte in a stand of sturdy cottonwood trees. With a tenderness born of love, Blade wrapped her body in a blanket and placed it on the platform. He stood below a long time, bidding her a silent farewell while Shannon and Vance looked on, sharing his grief.

"You'd better leave now," Blade told them. "There is nothing more you can do here."

Shannon hardly recognized this harsh stranger speaking to her as if he'd never seen her before. This man had eyes as cold and empty as death. Nothing remained to remind her of the tender lover who had taken her gently and made her first time memorable.

"I don't want to leave you, Blade. Come back with us," Shannon pleaded.

"Shannon is right, Blade, come back to the fort," Vance cajoled.

"If I went back with you now, I'd probably kill Goodman. I will stay and search for Grandfather. If he still lives, he will need me. Give me time to mourn my mother properly. After my time of mourning is over, I'm going to find Mad Wolf and end his miserable life."

"Is there nothing I can say to change your mind?" Shannon asked. She couldn't let it end like this.

"I'll wait for you by the horses, Shannon," Vance said, determined to give the couple privacy.

Blade watched him walk away before turning back to Shannon with his answer. "There is nothing you can do."

"Would it make a difference if I told you I loved you?" Shannon asked, her voice low and tender.

If not for the sudden flair of warmth in Blade's eyes, Shannon could have sworn he hadn't heard her. "My heart is empty," he told her.

"Let me help you."

"Perhaps—later. There is much for me to do now. There must be survivors and I will find them. Winter is around the corner and they'll need food and shelter. My people need me more than you do right now."

"I—I thought you cared for me."

He looked at her then, really looked at her, his face pale beneath the ashes. "Love has no place in my heart now. Perhaps one day I will be free to love, after I have mourned my mother and helped my people. Find someone else, Shannon. Someone who can give you everything you deserve."

"I won't accept that," Shannon said stubbornly. "Promise you'll let me know if you find your grandfather. I won't leave here unless you give me that much. Please, Blade, I care what happens to you."

"I'll try, but I give no promises."

Shannon turned away, her face contorted with anguish. With a terrible dread, she realized that nothing she said was getting through to Blade. Forcing one foot in front of the other, she slowly walked away.

The shock of seeing Shannon walk away did something to Blade. He realized he might never see her again, never taste her sweetness or know her love, and he couldn't let her go without a word of how he felt.

Conquering his grief, he stopped her with a touch. Then she was in his arms.

"Let me sample your sweetness one last time, Little Firebird," he groaned, for a brief moment becoming the Blade she knew and loved. "I can't let you go without kissing your sweet lips."

He lowered his head, capturing her lips with a slow, hungry kiss. Their breaths merged and became one as his tongue parted her lips, tasting, taking, drinking passionately. She savored him fully with the sweep of her tongue, tasting his desperation, his rage. It was not the sweetness of his love she tasted in his demanding kiss, but the pain of their parting. Then it was over. His eyes opened and reality intruded. When she looked up at him his eyes had turned as cold and bleak as his heart.

"Good-bye, Little Firebird."

Sobbing, Shannon whirled and ran blindly to where Major Vance stood with the horses. She didn't look back, she couldn't—it seemed too final. Yet she knew in her heart they would meet again, that their lives were irrevocably intertwined. They might be worlds apart, but they were soulmates in all the ways that counted.

"Keep in touch, Blade," Vance called over his shoulder as he helped Shannon mount. "If you need help you know where to find me."

Blade said nothing, nor did he turn to watch them leave. He had already resumed his mourning.

During the following weeks, Callie recovered from her injuries and moved in with Shannon. Though the house was small, it was adequate for two women and a baby. Todd Wilson had also recovered from his wounds and found work. Eventually he hoped to earn enough money to join a wagon train passing through next summer. He hadn't given up his dream of settling in Oregon.

While Shannon taught school, Callie insisted on doing the cleaning and cooking. Shannon hadn't pressed her on her plans for the future, but one night after little Johnny had been fed and put to bed, Callie confided in Shannon.

"I've been doing a lot of thinking, Shannon, about my future," she said slowly. "I want to go back to Ohio. Without Howie there is no future for me in Oregon. I know my parents will be willing to take me and the baby in. I'm all they have."

"Are you certain, Callie? You're welcome to stay with me as long as you like. I won't be going anywhere till next summer."

"I want to leave now, Shannon. I hate this country. It's a constant reminder of—of the attack, and Howie's death and—everything. But I have no money, not even the clothes on my back are mine. The ladies here have been kind to me, but they look at me as if I'm some kind of freak. Sometimes I think I would be better off dead."

"Don't talk like that, Callie," Shannon scolded. "Your child needs you. Besides, it will be spring before travel is possible."

"Haven't you heard? The railroad has reached Cheyenne. It's now possible to travel by train to the East in winter as well as summer. Everyone is talking about it."

"I—I suppose I've been preoccupied lately," Shannon said lamely.

"It's Blade, isn't it? I knew a long time ago you had feelings for him. Do you think he'll ever return?"

"I don't know. But you're right, Callie, I do love Blade. I know he's a half-breed, but it doesn't matter. He's an incredible man no matter what he is. But enough of me. If you had the money, how would you get to Cheyenne?"

"It's a moot question, but if I *did* have money I'd take the stage to Cheyenne. It comes through once a week, weather permitting."

"You are serious, aren't you? If money is all that is holding you here, then your worries are over. I'll give you the money."

Generous to a fault, Shannon never considered that she'd be stranded at Fort Laramie if she gave Callie her meager savings.

"Shannon, I couldn't!"

"Of course you can. I have my pay to live on."

"That's not enough to get you to Idaho. What about your family?"

"My family will understand and even send me money if I need it. I have a job and a roof over my head. Besides, I'm not certain I *could* leave knowing I'd never see Blade again. If I remain at Fort Laramie there is a good chance he'll come back."

"I'll repay you, Shannon, as soon as I reach Ohio. My parents are well-to-do, I'll mail you the money."

A week later Callie and Johnny Blade boarded the stage for Cheyenne. Shannon missed them dreadfully almost at once. She almost wished Blade had given her a child those times they made love. At least she'd have a small part of him to love and cherish. It was the emptiness that was unbearable. And the fierce, desolate loneliness.

Chapter Thirteen

*O*ne blustery day in late November, Shannon entered Clive Bailey's trading post. She hadn't spoken to him at length since he tried to rape her that night Mad Wolf abducted her. The man made her skin crawl. It so happened that Bailey's assistant was helping another customer and Shannon was forced to deal with Bailey whether she wanted to or not. Since Shannon had given most of her money to Callie, she had little to spend on herself and planned to refurbish one of her more festive dresses with new ribbon. Molly Greer had persuaded her to attend some of the holiday parties being planned.

Clive Bailey hadn't actively pursued Shannon since she arrived at the fort. It wasn't because he didn't want her still, but because he feared Blade. Bailey wasn't blind; he had seen them boldly embracing in the square that day and had in fact suspected something was going on between them long before Shannon was abducted by Mad Wolf. But with the breed gone, Bailey saw no reason to avoid her.

Bailey thought it strange how the breed just up and disappeared one day. Rumor had it that it was his village Lieutenant Goodman had destroyed and that Blade had remained with the survivors to help them prepare for the winter.

"Why, Shannon, how nice to see you," Bailey greeted her amiably. "How are you enjoying your new job?"

"I like teaching, Mr. Bailey," Shannon said coolly. She walked directly to where the ribbons were displayed, wasting little time on amenities.

"I know I haven't always acted like a gentleman where you're concerned, Shannon, but I'd like us to be friends. I—I wasn't myself out there on the prairie."

Shannon fixed him with an icy glare. "I'd like four yards of blue ribbon." He could apologize all he wanted, but she wasn't going to forgive him.

"If we could be friends again, I promise to treat you with utmost respect and courtesy," Bailey vowed as he measured out the ribbon.

Shannon wanted to laugh in Bailey's lying face, until it occurred to her that this could be the opportunity she had been waiting for—an opportunity to help Blade and Major Vance prove Bailey was guilty of selling guns to the Indians. All she had to do was disguise her distaste for the man and pretend forgiveness. Once he trusted her, she could cultivate his friendship and use her cunning. It should take little persuasion on her part to cajole him into bragging about his exploits.

Pasting a false smile on her face, Shannon said coyly, "If you're truly sorry, then I suppose we can be friends." Don't act too eager or he'll get suspicious, she warned herself.

A sly grin curved Bailey's thin lips. It was good to know he hadn't lost his charm. Perhaps if Shannon knew how rich he was, she'd be more kindly disposed. But he'd not make the same mistake he made out on the prairie. This time he'd take it slow and easy and still have her in his bed. It suddenly occurred to Bailey that Shannon was stranded at Fort Laramie with only her meager pay to sustain her and might look favorably on a wealthy suitor.

"Thank you, Shannon, I appreciate that concession. "Perhaps you'll save me a dance at the ball Saturday night."

"Perhaps I will," Shannon allowed, digging in her reticule for the money to pay for the ribbon.

"No, it's my gift to you, to make amends for offending you. I can well afford it," he boasted, puffing out his chest importantly.

"You must do a good business here," Shannon hinted with feigned innocence.

"I do well enough, but this isn't the source of my wealth. I have—other interests."

Now we're getting somewhere, Shannon thought gleefully. But before she could probe further, a customer approached, demanding Bailey's attention.

"Excuse me, my dear—duty, you know."

Shannon left then, but not for home. She walked briskly to Major Vance's office, relieved to find him in.

"Shannon, what can I do for you? Sit down, it's good to see you again."

"Have you heard from Blade, Major Vance?" Shannon asked hopefully.

"I'm sorry, Shannon, he hasn't been in touch. We must give him time to get over his grief."

"I know, I just thought . . ."

"You care for him a great deal, don't you?"

It took Shannon several tries to swallow the lump in her throat. "I love Blade."

"I don't want to offer encouragement where none is due, but I'm certain Blade feels the same about you."

Instead of cheering her, a bleak sadness settled over Shannon's features. "He thinks he's not good enough for me. I'm afraid I'll never see him again and I don't know if I can bear it. But that's not why I'm here. It's about Clive Bailey."

"Clive Bailey? What about him?"

"I'm going to help you prove he's the man selling guns to the Indians."

"What!" Vance exclaimed, jumping to his feet. "You'll do no such thing, young lady!"

"It's too late. I've already renewed our friendship, if you could call it that. Fortunately he's a confirmed womanizer." She thought it best not to reveal that he had tried to molest her on more than one occasion. "He thinks I'm impressed with him. The man is a vain brute, and I know I can get him to boast about his exploits."

"I won't hear of it," Vance pronounced with quiet authority.

"You can't stop me. I want to do this—I have to do it, for Blade. I'll keep you informed of my progress. And—and if you hear from Blade, please let me know." She turned to leave, everything settled in her mind.

"You're correct, Shannon, I can't stop you," Vance allowed, "but I can ask you to be careful. Come to me if you need help, or for any reason."

Snow covered the ground in thick white clouds. It was a proper setting for the first ball of the Christmas season. The dance was well under way when Shannon walked into the clubhouse with the Greers. The main room was gaily decorated in keeping with the season and the dance floor already bursting with dancers. It was the first dance Shannon had attended since she had declined to attend the last one. She didn't feel comfortable dancing while still mourning her friends killed in the Indian raid. Because Fort Laramie had never been attacked by Indians, it was known far and wide as a gay and spirited post, hosting many frivolous balls and parties.

Immediately Shannon was swamped by young men eager to fill her dance card. Actually, Shannon felt little like dancing. She worried about Blade and missed him dreadfully. But she agreed to accompany the Greers for a good reason. She hoped the festive atmosphere and her company would entice Clive Bailey into revealing more of his illegal activities.

To her surprise, Shannon found she was enjoying herself. She danced with Major Vance, Colonel Greer, Lieutenant Goodman, and most of the officers from the fort. When it was Clive Bailey's turn to lead her onto the dance floor, he did so with a smug arrogance that set Shannon's teeth on edge.

"Do you like to dance, Shannon?" he asked politely. His words said one thing while his eyes hinted at another.

"Oh yes. Before the war we had the grandest balls and fetes at Twin Willows," Shannon said wistfully.

"Is Twin Willows your plantation?"

"Was our plantation. We lost it. Lost everything," Shannon said bitterly. "A Yankee is living there now."

"Would you like it back?"

"Like it back? I—I don't understand?"

"I could buy it back for you. One more trip East and I'll be rich enough to buy you anything you want. You don't belong in this wilderness, teaching school to support yourself. I can dress you in pretty clothes, buy your home back if you like, give you jewels . . ."

"Clive, what are you suggesting?"

"We've become good friends these past weeks," Clive hinted with an eagerness that stunned Shannon. "I think we could deal well with one another. I'm asking you to be my wife."

Bailey had considered the possibility of marrying Shannon for some time now. It wasn't such a bad idea when one thought about it. Once he left the Western frontier, he'd need respectability and Shannon was just the woman to give it to him. If she didn't want to go back to Georgia, they could go to California. One more trip East and he'd be set for life.

Shannon was dismayed. Never in her wildest dreams had she expected a marriage proposal from Clive Bailey. He had come calling and she had forced herself to accept his friendship, pretending to enjoy his company, but that was as far as it had gone. He had chatted politely over tea while Shannon chafed impatiently for him to leave. Nothing else had transpired to even suggest he might want her for his wife.

"You want to marry me?"

"Is that so strange? You're a beautiful woman. Any man would be proud to have you for his wife. I can give you everything your heart desires."

Shannon's mind worked furiously, casting about for an answer that would satisfy him and still not compromise herself. There must be some way to get out of this predicament and still expose Clive Bailey, she reasoned. "How do I know you'll do all you say?" she challenged. "How do I know you're not lying about your wealth? After the war we were poor as church mice. I won't be poor again. The man I marry must be able to provide me with all I lost."

They had stopped dancing several minutes ago and now paused before an open window. Shannon had become so flushed after Clive's unexpected proposal that he had edged her toward the window when their dance was over.

"If I can prove to you I'm not lying about my wealth, will you consider my proposal?"

Before Shannon could form an answer, her next partner arrived to claim her. Later, Clive offered to walk her home and Shannon accepted. She was anxious to find out exactly how Clive Bailey intended to prove his worth.

"It's a beautiful night," Shannon said, wrapping herself more snugly in her coat. "See how brightly the moon reflects off the snow?"

"I'd rather look at you," Clive said, devouring her with his greedy eyes.

Though the only thing new about the blue velvet dress Shannon wore was the ribbons, she did indeed look lovely tonight. The fitted bodice was cut low enough to entice, yet high enough to be considered modest. The deep blue velvet matched her eyes and complimented her pale skin and rich chestnut tresses, which she wore piled atop her head in a most becoming style. A new ribbon circled her miniscule waist, and she had sewn tiny bows over the full skirt. She looked fetching and seemed totally unaware of it.

"Clive, what did you mean you could prove you had wealth? Do you have money in the bank?"

Shannon's blunt questions seemed to amuse Clive rather than annoy him. He thought her quite practical to want to know exactly what he could offer her.

"Better than that, my dear, I have gold—lots of it, all nice and safe where no one can find it."

"How do I know you're not lying?" Shannon challenged.

"I told you I'd prove it, and I will. Just as soon as you agree to our marriage, I'll show it to you."

"I—I have to think about it," Shannon hedged. They had reached her door now and she fumbled in her reticule for her key. Once the door was open, she said, "Goodnight, Clive. Thank you for walking me home."

"You'll think about what I said?"

"I—yes, of course."

"May I kiss you goodnight?" he asked, moving to take her in his arms.

A shudder of revulsion passed through her body. If his mere touch repulsed her, what would his kiss do? Shannon wondered distractedly. Yet she had no alternative but to let him kiss her. It would seem odd if she refused to kiss a man whose proposal she was supposedly considering. Shyly she offered her mouth.

The kiss wasn't as bad as Shannon thought it would be—it was worse. She wanted to gag, but didn't dare. When Clive tried to pry her lips apart with his tongue, they remained staunchly closed. She broke it off as soon as she could, murmured a hasty good-night, and slipped through the door, closing it firmly behind her.

God, what was she getting herself into? she wondered shakily, leaning against the door to catch her breath. Tomorrow she'd see Major Vance and ask his advice. Perhaps she was getting in too deep. Why wasn't Blade here when she needed him? Until she met Blade, her life had been empty, as well as amazingly uncomplicated. Just looking at him brought her a special kind of happiness, something she never knew existed. Sighing bleakly, she realized that no amount of wishing would bring Blade back to her. She walked slowly through the darkened parlor to the bedroom; she had purposely left a fire burning in the stove so she wouldn't come home to a cold house.

After being gone for hours, Shannon thought the room exceptionally warm, but she didn't possess the energy to analyze that confusing fact. She was tired; it had been a long, exhausting night and she had much to think about. Shrugging out of her coat, she slowly began to undress. An oath escaped her lips as her fingers fumbled with the hooks at the back of her dress.

"Do you need help, Little Firebird?"

He stepped from the shadows—a tall, powerful man with bold, chiseled features. He was everything she remembered, and more. Thick, rippling muscles corded his arms and thighs, and his big hands were as gentle as she remembered as they brushed hers aside to unfasten the hooks she found difficult to manipulate.

"Blade, where did you come from?" Whirling, she ended up in his arms.

"From the looks of things, I didn't arrive any too soon. What in the hell were you doing with Clive Bailey?"

Blade, forget Bailey. Just kiss me. I can't believe you're real."

He bent his head to taste lightly, meaning only to prove he was flesh and blood. But his intent was burned away by the volatile flame that ignited within him the moment their lips met. The feel of his lips against her mouth was the most exquisite sensation

Shannon had ever experienced. Fire shot through her, searing her senses. She sighed in abject surrender, her eyes closing. His tongue was slow and hot and gentle, sliding between her lips, touching her teeth, the roof of her mouth, the inside of her cheeks.

Blade had never wanted Shannon more; he needed to thrust his love deep inside this beautiful, head-strong, unpredictable woman. He needed her strength and strong spirit to make his life whole again. The Grandfather Spirit had ordained their fates even before their births. Suddenly the tenderness and care yielded to a hard, fierce passion and Blade drew a ragged breath, pulling away so he could continue unhooking her dress. There was an urgency about him that communicated itself to Shannon and she responded by tearing at his clothes.

A slow smile curved Blade's sensuous lips. "Easy, love, we've got all night."

"I can't wait, Blade. I've dreamed of being with you like this, but I never thought it would happen again."

Her clothes fell away like magic and she stepped out of them, watching Blade as he tossed aside his trousers. Then he pulled her into his arms, holding her against him, savoring the feel of her smooth flesh against his own hair-roughened skin. His kiss was like a shaft of hot steel that pierced deeply into her, throbbing and pulsing low in her belly. She gripped his shoulders tightly, afraid he'd disappear if she let him go. His mouth parted from hers, his eyes dark, burning ebony as he gazed deep into hers. He swept a tendril of hair from her face, his voice both tender and hoarse.

"You aren't the only one who has dreamed of this moment, Little Firebird. I had to come back, if only for this brief time. I need you—you're my life, my breath, my very existence. I'm going to make love to you and when I'm done we're going to make love again—and again."

His words drifted off as he acted upon them, his

palm cupping the fullness of her breast. Instinctively her flesh responded to his touch, and the coral nipple hardened against the caress of his hand.

"You're incredible," he mouthed against her lips as his hand moved down in a trail of fire that left her gasping for breath.

Suddenly Shannon was swept off her feet as Blade carried her to the bed, stretching his lean length beside her.

His hand wandered boldly over her body, followed closely by his lips, tasting her skin with his tongue, drawing a damp trail from her mouth to a hardened nipple, sucking it into his mouth. His warm breath sent a delicious shiver through her as gentle hands explored her soft woman's triangle, stroking and probing with bold insistence and tenderness.

Desiring to bring him the same joy he gave her, her hand moved down to close around him. A jolt passed through him at her touch and a low growl came from throat. His hand continued its exploration of the golden down at the top of her legs, his fingers slipping into the dark, moist cavern, and Shannon cried out at the intense pleasure his stroking fingers evoked. When he took his fingers away she knew an empty ache that only Blade could fill.

He whispered her name in a raw, shaky voice and slid his mouth downward along the delicious surface of her skin to that place between her legs where his hands worked so diligently. She cried out, jerking in spasms as his hands slid beneath her buttocks and he teased her with the first touch of his tongue. She writhed and twisted and arched against him as his tongue probed and parted, delving deeply, tasting. Her body surged against him and she moaned, tossing in wild abandon.

He allowed her no mercy, for he was determined to have all of her. He sought the tiny bud of greatest pleasure, his tongue a flame setting her afire. Then she burst and exploded, waves of absolute rapture erupting through her with shattering intensity. Suddenly he gripped her ankles, parted them wide, and settled his weight in the cradle formed by her thighs. Then she felt the huge hot shaft of him probing hard against her, and she was soaring. Moments later Blade joined her and they flew to towering mountain tops to touch the stars. It was several minutes before either could talk.

A tiny sigh slipped past Shannon's lips. "I felt you in every part of me."

His fingers tenderly brushed the chestnut curls away from her forehead. "Little Firebird, you *are* a part of me. What am I going to do without you?"

Alarmed, Shannon cried out, "What do you mean? You're not leaving again, are you?"

"I must. Yellow Dog needs me. Those survivors from the village have no food, no shelter. They'll starve to death this winter if I don't return to help them."

"You found your grandfather! Is he well?"

"As well as can be expected given his great age. Jumping Buffalo helped him escape the carnage, but it has been difficult for him. My mother's death was a bitter blow."

"What did you learn about the attack?"

"Little outside of what I already knew. Mad Wolf wasn't in the village. They hadn't seen him in weeks. Lieutenant Goodman refused to believe Yellow Dog and ordered the destruction you saw. The survivors have nothing—no food, no clothing, no shelter."

"If what you say is true, then why did you return to Fort Laramie?"

"For one thing, I promised I'd let you know about Yellow Dog. And I came to buy blankets and food."

"And that's all?" Shannon asked with keen disappointment.

"No, Little Firebird, I came to see you. I had to see you again before . . ."

Though Blade longed to tell Shannon he loved her, he deliberately refrained from saying the words. Too many obstacles stood in their way, too many years of hatred between their people made marriage impossible. Marriage between them would make her an outcast among her own kind.

"Blade, do you love me?" Shannon asked bluntly. Though Blade had never given voice to the words, Shannon's heart told her he did love her and she longed to hear him say it.

"What if I did?" Blade challenged, deliberately hardening his heart against the pain of knowing he could never have her. "What good would it do us? Would it make our good-bye any less painful?"

"You're leaving for good?" Shannon asked in a small voice.

"Grandfather needs me. I'm going to live with the Sioux for as long as I'm able to help. I have nothing to offer you. Go to Idaho, Shannon. Your family is expecting you. Find a husband who can offer you more than his heart."

"I don't have to go to Idaho," Shannon said stubbornly. "My family would understand. I have a job and can support myself for as long as need be. If you loved me, if you wanted me, I'd wait forever."

"I'm not that selfish, Little Firebird. I wouldn't ask for that kind of sacrifice. Marriage between us is forbidden. I couldn't bear to see you condemned by your people. My Indian blood makes me an object of scorn and hatred. I am a savage."

"I don't care what people say. You're my savage. I'll live my life as I see fit. I'd leave with you now if you'd let me."

"My sweet, sweet love. I can't ask such a sacrifice of you. Winters are harsh in Wyoming Territory and I'd be a fool to take you with me no matter how desperately I wanted you," Blade confided in a hushed tone.

"Then I'll wait," Shannon vowed staunchly.

"Many things could happen to change your mind," Blade predicted. "I'll not ask you to wait for me, but if you're still here when I return . . . " His words trailed off, ripe with hope yet asking nothing.

"Love me again, Blade. Love me for all the empty tomorrows."

"I will, Little Firebird, but you're not going to distract me so easily this time. First tell me what you were doing with Clive Bailey."

A long sigh escaped Shannon's lips. She had thought Blade sufficiently diverted and had forgotten all about Clive Bailey. But he was too astute for that.

"How much did you hear?"

"Enough to know you have some devious plan in mind. I know you detest the man, yet you deliberately led him to believe you'd marry him."

"How do you know that?"

"I was listening at the window where you and Bailey conveniently stopped to talk," Blade revealed. "I heard him bragging about his wealth, and I heard your probing questions. What in the hell are you trying to prove?"

"I only wanted to help," Shannon said, growing animated. "I know I can get him to confess to selling guns to the Indians. He's already offered to show me the gold he received from their sale. Major Vance isn't too happy about what I'm doing, but . . ."

"Wade knows about your prying?" Blade roared, appalled. "I'll have his hide when I see him tomorrow."

"Don't blame Major Vance, Blade. He told me to stay away from Clive, but I wouldn't listen. If not for those guns your mother would be alive today. I want to expose him for the slimy toad he is. I want to help in any way I can."

"The only way you can help is by steering clear of Bailey. Please, Little Firebird, I couldn't bear it if anything happened to you."

"Then you do love me!" Shannon cried, jubilant.

"You little fool, of course I love you. Are you happy now that I've admitted it?"

"Ecstatic."

"Will it make the pain of parting any less?"

"It will comfort me while you're gone," Shannon said softly.

"Then I love you, Shannon Branigan. I will go to my grave loving you. If I never see you again, my love will sustain me. And if you love me as much as you say, you'll promise to stay away from Clive Bailey. Leave him to me and Wade."

"But—"

"No buts, I mean it."

"Very well," Shannon acquiesced, "if it means so much to you."

"I care what happens to you, and Clive Bailey can go to hell. Wade and I will handle him when the time comes. Since that's all settled," he said, smiling lazily, "we can concentrate on more important things, like making love again. We've hours yet till dawn."

His hand cupped her bare buttocks, bringing their bodies together in searing rapture. Their breaths merged and became one as his parted lips sought and found hers. The naked hunger that flared between them was both sweet and violent. Her world tilted crazily beneath the urgency of his kisses, carried along in a turbulent storm of passion.

She reached with her hand to hold him, felt him throbbing hot and hard in her grasp, felt his warm seed against her palm, drew in his male scent.

"Now, Blade, now," she groaned as she raised her body above him and sheathed the pulsing, thickened length of him into the searing heat of her flesh. She fit him like a glove, hot and liquid, moving against him in wild frenzy.

She rode him into ecstasy, making him moan and arch against her while he sucked her firm nipples, drove into her quivering satin with relentless fury. Suddenly he reversed their positions, deliberately slowing the pace, using all his strength to hold back his own release. He wanted it to go on and on, he wanted always to be buried deep inside her. They clung together in desperate yearning as he delved deeper and deeper, consumed by the demand for fulfillment.

Shannon's body stiffened with pleasure so intense she had to bite her lips to hold back a scream. Blade felt the tiny tremors deep inside her. "Ah sweet, so sweet," he breathed as if in agony. "I can feel your spasms; so tight, so damn good! Ah, Shannon, I can't hold back!"

"I—love—you," Shannon gasped, unable to control the words that flew from her lips.

His restraint burst into shattering release, her words beating against his brain as his body shook with wave after wave of shuddering rapture. When they returned from their incredible journey, they stared at one another for long moments, holding each other, awed into silence by the explosive bliss they had shared.

Unable to speak, Blade's thoughts ran rampant. Even if they never saw each other again, he had enough sweet memories to last forever. He had but to close his eyes and Shannon would be there. No one could deprive him of the certain knowledge that he was the man who had led her into womanhood and taught her the meaning of passion. In his arms she had become a woman—his woman. And she had given him a taste of the kind of love few people experienced in their lifetime.

"Blade, what are you thinking?"

"That I'd like to wake up with you in my arms like this every day of my life."

Shannon was determined not to cry the next morning when Blade bid her good-bye. If only he hadn't made it sound so final, as if he never expected to see her again. He didn't know her very well if he thought she'd change her mind about waiting for him. For her, love came only once, and she'd wait forever if she had to, until Blade was ready to commit himself to her for all time. She understood about his grandfather and his need to help his people, and she prayed he wouldn't decide to stay with the Sioux permanently. He had lived in the white world for ten years, and Shannon counted on the pull of civilization and the love they shared to bring him back to her.

Chapter Fourteen

Shannon's cool reception during the following weeks left Clive Bailey reeling in confusion. Christmas came and went. Shannon returned Clive's expensive gift with a polite note and declined his company at the New Year's Eve dance, chosing instead to go with a timid young lieutenant who'd make no demands on her. Unfortunately, Clive did manage to corner Shannon at the dance, much to her chagrin.

"Why are you avoiding me, Shannon?" he asked when he found her alone in a rare moment between dance partners.

"I—I'm not," she faltered lamely, recalling her promise to Blade.

"Have you forgotten your plantation? I have the means to restore it to you. I meant it when I said I'm wealthy. I can prove it to you if you'd let me."

Shannon's answer was forestalled when her escort came to claim her for the next dance.

Later, when Shannon went to freshen up in the ladies' room, she was intercepted by Claire. The lovely brunette continued to remain openly hostile to Shannon despite her warm friendship with the elder Greers.

"Once again you have all the men panting after you," Claire accused her. "I hope you're satisfied."

"You have no reason to be jealous of me, Claire," Shannon insisted.

"Jealous! Is that what you think? Don't be ridiculous. I saw you talking with Clive Bailey tonight. He seems quite smitten with you. You could do worse, you know. You're without kin here at Fort Laramie, and you'd do well to marry the man if he'll have you. Or are you still pining over the half-breed?"

"I have no idea why you hate me, Claire, and truthfully, I don't care," Shannon retorted. "What I do, or with whom, is none of your concern."

"But it is. I don't like the way Ronald looks at you, or the way you flirt and carry on with every officer at the fort."

"You're imagining things. I wouldn't have Lieutenant Goodman on a silver platter. He was responsible for an unprovoked attack on innocent people."

"They were Indians, for God's sake! What makes you think they were innocent?"

"Blade found his grandfather alive and learned the truth from him. Mad Wolf wasn't in the village."

"You've seen Blade!" Claire smirked knowingly. "You've been consorting with the half-breed behind our backs. The parents of your students won't be pleased. How will you support yourself without a job?"

Shannon wanted to shout out her love for Blade, to tell the world how proud she was to love such an extraordinary man. But she needed the job, and it definitely wasn't the right time to reveal her sentiments.

"You'll look mighty foolish making an accusation you can't prove. I'm a good teacher, and you will have a difficult time convincing folks to fire me."

Claire sniffed disdainfully, realizing the truth of

Shannon's words. Truth to tell, she *was* jealous of the little witch. She'd give anything if Blade looked at her the way she'd seen him look at Shannon. He fairly reeked of power and sexuality and Claire envied any woman who experienced love in the arms of a vital and aggressive male like Blade.

Claire wasn't the innocent everyone thought her to be. She had tasted passion at an early age, having succumbed to a lusty private at her father's last duty station. Since then she'd kept her liaisons secret, threatening to cry rape if word leaked out. She deliberately chose young enlisted men intimidated by her father's rank and frightened of the consequences should they be found out. Not even Lieutenant Goodman knew of her dalliances, for she had fooled him into believing he had taken her virginity the first time they made love. Claire would have liked to add Blade to her list of conquests, but he'd never exhibited the least interest in her as a woman.

"If you will excuse me, Claire, my escort is waiting." Shannon rose and left the room. If looks could kill, she thought, she'd be plucking daggers out of her back.

February 1868 brought an unexpected thaw in an otherwise bleak winter, much to Shannon's delight. But that was not all that pleased her, though she was somewhat shocked by the idea. Talk of allowing women to vote was sweeping Wyoming like wildfire. It was a well-known fact that Wyoming was trying to attract emigrants, especially women. Precious few women were willing to brave the ferocious plains Indians and severe weather.

It was astounding to think that women's suffrage would come to such a wild and far-flung place as Wyoming before women were permitted to vote in more civilized states in the East. It was a highly controversial issue, widely debated by both men and women alike. Generally women favored getting the vote, but the male population debunked the idea, saying it would cause women to leave home and hearth and invade male-dominated domains.

Molly Greer was thrilled at the prospect of being able to vote and solicited Shannon's help in organizing women's groups urging for the passage of a suffrage bill. Though little more than an idea at this time, territorial secretary Edward M. Lee and legislator William H. Bright were said to be penning such a bill in hopes of attracting more settlers. There were under one thousand females in all of Wyoming over the age of ten, as compared to nearly sixty-one hundred males.

In the East, women such as Anna Dickinson and the beautiful Redelia Bates lectured long and fervently in behalf of women's rights and Molly held out the hope that one day they would come to Wyoming to speak.

Meanwhile Shannon concentrated on teaching the children under her charge, enjoying the challenge of a profession she had never before considered. She knew Mama, Tuck, and her siblings would be proud of her accomplishments and wished they were there to see her.

Shannon spent considerable time worrying about her maverick brother, Devlin, though. He was so hot-headed, so darn unpredictable, and she hoped he hadn't gotten himself into trouble. If only her father had lived to keep his family together instead of—but it was too late to wish for what might have been.

Not a day went by that Shannon did not think of Blade. Was he surviving the severe winter? Did he have sufficient food and adequate shelter? Was he warm? Did he miss her as much as she missed him?

One day in March, Shannon set out for Clive Bailey's trading post shortly before closing time. She was baking bread and found she lacked enough salt for her mixture. Donning her coat and boots she trudged through the muddy square to the store. She knew the hour was late but hoped the trading post would still be open, for she wanted to set her bread to rising before she retired for the night.

To Shannon's dismay, she found the store deserted when she entered. A lamp on the counter was left burning, but Clive was nowhere in sight. She nearly decided to take the salt she needed and pay Clive the next day when the murmur of voices coming from the storeroom behind the counter piqued her interest. Naturally curious, she sidled as close as she dared and listened. The only voice she recognized belonged to Clive Bailey. The other man spoke barely above a whisper, too low and furtive to identify.

"I want my money, Bailey—now!"

"Mad Wolf lied, he only paid me half of what he promised," Bailey responded slyly.

"You greedy bastard! I know how much you got for the guns and I want my cut."

"I took all the risks," Clive contended.

"And I made certain our operation wasn't discovered. I got rid of the government agent when his snooping brought him too close to the truth."

"I'm not the only one his discovery would have incriminated. Besides," Clive revealed, "I have plans for the money. I'm going to get married. After one more trip East for another load of weapons, I plan to settle down on a Southern plantation and live the life of a rich planter."

"Marry? You? Do you have a woman back East waiting for you?"

"No, not back East," Clive gloated. "I'm going to marry Shannon Branigan."

Harsh derisive laughter followed Clive's startling disclosure. "You're either a fool or mad. She wouldn't have you with twice the amount of gold in your poke. Quit stalling, where is the money? I don't have time to argue with you over my share of the gold."

Shannon was so shocked by what she heard that she stood rooted to the spot. She had no idea another man was involved in Clive Bailey's illegal venture. She'd be willing to bet neither Blade nor Major Vance was aware of it either. Who could it be? One of the townspeople? A trooper from the fort? Major Vance needed to know about this latest development immediately, she told herself. She turned to leave and in her haste brushed against a hoe leaning against a shelf. It tottered sideways then crashed to the floor. Shannon froze.

"What's that!"

"I don't know," Clive hissed. "Wait here while I take a look."

Shannon just made it to the other side of the counter when Clive burst through the door.

"Shannon! How did you get in? I thought I locked the door. Business was slow tonight, so I closed early in order to sort through some merchandise in the storeroom."

"You must have forgotten to lock the door, Clive," Shannon said, gulping nervously. No matter how hard she tried, she couldn't stop herself from casting furtive glances toward the storeroom. "The door was open and I walked right in."

"Did you need something?"

"Why, yes—salt. When I saw no one about I decided to help myself and pay later. I brushed against the hoe and it fell to the floor. I'm sorry, did I do wrong?"

"No, no, you merely surprised me. As I mentioned before, I was in the storeroom when I heard something. I thought it was a thief. Or one of those pesky Indians who always hang around the fort. They're a thieving lot."

He reached behind him and plucked a packet of salt from the shelf. "Here is your salt, my dear."

Shannon fished in her pocket for a coin and placed it in his hand. "Thank you. Well, I'd best be off—I've got bread to bake."

"Shannon," Clive said, lowering his voice to a mere whisper. "Have you thought any more about my proposal? Why have you avoided me these past weeks?"

Shannon prepared a curt answer, then thought better of it. It suddenly occurred to her that she was in a position to help Blade and Major Vance whether they liked it or not. She was the only one who knew about the second man involved in smuggling guns, and she could learn so much more if she pretended interest in Clive's marriage plans.

"As a matter of fact, I've given your proposal serious thought," she said slowly. "I don't want to spend the rest of my life in poverty. What you offer is tempting indeed. It's not that I've been deliberately avoiding you, but I needed time to think without interference."

"Then you'll marry me?" Clive crowed, his eyes shining excitedly. He had dreamed of possessing the chestnut-haired beauty from the moment he'd set eyes on her.

"I'll give you my answer at the spring dance next week" Shannon hedged. Surely by then she and Major Vance would have all the evidence needed to convict and hang Clive Bailey and his secret partner. "But I will tell you this much," she hinted coyly, "your proposal has much to commend it. Being alone in this wilderness is definitely not to my liking. I must go now, Clive."

Clive walked her to the door. Shannon was dismayed when he pulled her into his arms and kissed her hungrily. Her first reaction was to claw at his eyes until he released her, but she restrained herself. A woman considering a man's marriage proposal wasn't supposed to feel disgust in his arms. So she pretended to enjoy it, enduring it until he was finished. Then she pulled away and darted out the door.

Bailey locked the door behind Shannon and hurried back to the storeroom, a silly smile pasted on his face.

"What did she want? Did she hear anything?"

"I'd forgotten to lock the door. Shannon merely wanted to purchase some salt."

"You were talking too low for me to hear what was said. Did she act as if she heard our conversation?"

"Shannon couldn't have heard anything," Clive

insisted. "She was standing on the other side of the counter."

"What makes you so sure? Perhaps I should follow her. If she goes any place but home, we can assume she heard and is going to report our conversation."

"What are you going to do?" Clive called out as the man left through the back door.

"Nothing," he hissed over his shoulder, "unless I think the little bitch knows what we are up to—" His words were lost to the wind as he slipped into the shadows.

Shannon strode across the parade ground at a brisk pace, unaware that she was being followed. It was growing darker and colder by the minute, and she hoped Major Vance was at home this late in the evening. Unfortunately, he was out. Shannon was told by his orderly that he was at a staff meeting, which was running late. Shannon thought her information important enough to interrupt, so she headed directly to headquarters. Sargeant Wilson sat behind the desk in the outer office.

"Can I help you, Miss Branigan?" he asked warily, recalling the last time Shannon had burst into a meeting without waiting for permission.

"Is Major Vance in his office? I must see him, it's important."

"I'm sorry, ma'am, but the major is in a staff meeting."

"Would you please tell him I'm out here?" Shannon requested. "I need to see him immediately."

Sargeant Wilson balked, unwilling to disturb his superior officers.

"Inform the major that Miss Branigan is here, Sargeant." Lieutenant Goodman walked into headquarters in time to hear Shannon's plea.

"Yes sir," Wilson saluted. Though somewhat reluctant to interrupt the meeting, he did as he was ordered, knocking, then entering the staff room. He returned within a few minutes followed by Major

Vance, a worried frown creasing his brow.

"What is it, Shannon? Sargeant Wilson said you wanted to see me, that it was urgent."

Aware that both Sargeant Wilson and Lieutenant Goodman were listening, Shannon was unwilling to divulge crucial information before witnesses.

"Could we speak in private?" She licked her lips nervously. "It's about—er, something we're both concerned about," she hinted.

Wade Vance knew immediately what Shannon was referring to. Though she had been warned time and again not to interfere, she obviously hadn't listened and in the process had learned something vital to the investigation of Clive Bailey. Unfortunately, he was in the midst of a staff meeting and couldn't leave.

"Go home, Shannon. I'll be through here shortly, then we can discuss whatever it is you have to tell me. I'll drop by in about an hour."

Shannon nodded, much relieved. It was a burden being privy to information of such major importance. Vance watched her leave headquarters, a speculative look on his face, before returning to his meeting. Lieutenant Goodman remained behind a few minutes longer talking with Sargeant Wilson, then he too took his leave.

Blackness swallowed Shannon as she strode across the parade ground, shivering in the cold wind that whistled out of the north. Few were about this time of night; most everyone was inside enjoying supper in comfort. Shannon's head was pounding with everything she'd heard tonight. If only she had been able to recognize the second voice! Suddenly a gust of wind caught at her coat, and she pulled it closer about her. She couldn't help but think that in Georgia it would already be warm and the evening breeze redolent with spring flowers.

A shrouded figure stepped out of the shadows, but because Shannon had her head bent against the wind she failed to see it. She suspected nothing, had no time to be frightened, as the figure crept up behind her. A single tap from the butt of his gun rendered her unconscious. With a sigh she crumbled into the arms of her assailant.

Major Vance approached Shannon's house a full hour later than he intended. Unfortunately Colonel Greer had kept him in the meeting longer than expected. To his dismay, Shannon's house was dark. Had she grown tired of waiting and retired for the night? Strange . . . he could have sworn Shannon's information was urgent enough to warrant her waiting for him. He supposed it could wait until tomorrow, he reasoned, turning away. He'd catch her before she left for school in the morning.

No one answered when Vance knocked on Shannon's door early the next morning. Thinking she'd already left for the schoolhouse, he walked the short distance to the schoolyard, surprised to find children milling about outside on such a cold, damp morning.

"Is Miss Branigan inside?" he asked one of the older boys.

"Naw, teacher ain't here yet," he returned. "It ain't like her to be late."

"Is that why you're all standing about outside?"

"Yeh. Why do ya suppose teacher is late?"

"I don't know, son, but I aim to find out. Why don't you and the other students go on home for now. I'll find Miss Branigan. Tell your parents you've been granted a holiday."

A cheer followed his words and the children quickly scattered. Vance lingered for a time, checking the door—it was locked—and looking through the windows. Shannon was nowhere in sight, nor had she been inside the schoolhouse to start a fire in the stove. A frisson of fear crept up Vance's spine, and his intuition told him something dreadful had happened to Shannon. Obviously she had information that placed her life in danger and was paying dearly for her prying. He had assumed Shannon had given up the notion of helping solve this case long ago.

Vance prayed he was wrong. He hoped he and Shannon had merely missed one another. He hurried off, hopeful, yet knowing in his heart she wouldn't be there.

He was right. Shannon wasn't at headquarters, nor had she been seen since the previous evening. He immediately dispatched a detail of men to search the fort. Two hours later, they returned to report that Shannon Branigan was nowhere to be found. Vance felt justified in returning to Shannon's house and forcing the door open.

A careful inspection proved that Shannon had never returned to her house last night. The bed hadn't been slept in, and ingredients for making bread were spread out on the table. The ashes in the stove were cold, indicating that Shannon hadn't cooked breakfast that morning. Not only was Vance concerned over Shannon's disappearance, he feared for her life. He had no proof as to the identity of the person or persons who had taken Shannon, but he strongly suspected that Clive Bailey was somehow involved. Vance hurried to Colonel Greer's office to ask permission to form a patrol to look for Shannon. He wished Blade was here, for if they ever needed his tracking skills it was now.

Shannon opened her eyes to absolute darkness. She tried to move, and couldn't. Her arms and legs were tightly bound. Panic—sheer, stark panic—seized her when she opened her mouth to scream and tasted the gag. A cloth covered her eyes as well, so she couldn't see where she was. Still groggy from the blow to her head, Shannon tried desperately to recall what had happened. The last thing she remembered was walking home from headquarters, then everything went blank. She moved her head and a terrible pain pierced her brain. Her groan of agony died in her throat, suppressed by the gag.

In a burst of insight, Shannon recollected what had happened. Someone had struck her on the head and

NAME: _____

ADDRESS: _____

_____

_____

TELEPHONE: _____

E-MAIL: _____

_____ I want to pay by credit card.

__ Visa   __ MasterCard   __ Discover

Account Number: _____

Expiration date: _____

SIGNATURE: _____

*Send this form, along with $2.00 shipping
and handling for your FREE books, to:*

Love Spell Romance Book Club
20 Academy Street
Norwalk, CT 06850-4032

*Or fax (must include credit card
information!) to:* **610.995.9274.**
*You can also sign up on the Web
at* www.dorchesterpub.com.

Offer open to residents of the U.S. and
Canada only. Canadian residents, please
call 1.800.481.9191 for pricing information.

brought her—where? Where was she? And why? Once her head cleared somewhat, it became obvious why she had been attacked. Someone didn't want her to tell Major Vance what she knew. And that someone was Clive Bailey and his cohort. The shuffle of feet brought all her senses to attention. A squeaking hinge warned her that someone was very near. She learned just how near when a man spoke to her.

"You couldn't let well enough alone, could you, Shannon?"

Clive Bailey!

"I wanted to marry you, but it was all an act on your part, wasn't it? You were just fishing for information. Are you the government agent sent by Washington?"

Shannon shook her head in vigorous denial.

"What are we going to do with her?"

"She has to die."

This from a second person in the room whose hoarse growl Shannon identified immediately as belonging to Clive's partner.

"It's such a waste," Clive sighed regretfully. "Wait, I have a better idea! Mad Wolf offered gold for Shannon once,—I'll bet he's willing to do so again. He wanted her damn bad. I did too. Maybe I'll poke her a time or two before she leaves here."

"I wouldn't mind it myself," the nameless man concurred. Lust colored his words and Shannon shuddered. "But not here, not now—it's too dangerous. Come morning everyone will know Shannon is missing. I want her delivered to Mad Wolf as soon as possible. Do you know where to find him?"

"I'm fairly certain I'll find him and his renegades at their secret camp. I know the way,—it's where I delivered the guns."

"It has to be done tonight, before a search is instigated," the man said thoughtfully. "Stuff the girl in a gunny sack and throw her across your horse. At this late hour, no one will be about to see you. I'm depending on you to find Mad Wolf and make the deal."

"You can count on me."

"Just remember, half the money is mine."

Mad Wolf! Dear God, not again, Shannon thought bleakly. Why hadn't she listened to Blade and avoided Clive Bailey? Then Shannon sensed that she was alone again and began straining against her bonds, but it was futile. She was trussed up tighter than a Christmas goose. Sheer exhaustion soon put an end to her struggles. Unless she thought of something quickly, she'd end up Mad Wolf's captive again.

Two hours later, Clive Bailey and his partner returned. Despite Shannon's valiant struggle, she was stuffed into a gunny sack and carried from the room that she since realized must be the storeroom of Bailey's trading post. The air left her lungs when she was tossed across the back of a horse. The animal was walked for a length of time before a man she assumed was Clive Bailey mounted behind her and galloped off into the night.

Since Major Vance was the only man besides Blade who knew of Clive Bailey's involvement in gun smuggling, he went alone to the trading post to see what he could find out. The store was still closed when he arrived, and the ruckus he raised at the door failed to bring the owner. Vance felt no guilt over forcing the door open. A thorough search of Bailey's living quarters, the store, and the storeroom yielded nothing. But the very fact that Bailey was absent was proof enough for Vance. He firmly believed Bailey was responsible for Shannon's disappearance. An hour later, Vance received Colonel Greer's blessing to lead a column of men out of the fort to look for Shannon.

"Major Vance, I'd like to join you."

"We're leaving immediately, Lieutenant Goodman."

"I'm ready, sir. I'd like to help catch the scum who abducted Miss Branigan. She's an exceptional young lady."

"Permission granted, Lieutenant. Saddle up. We ride out in five minutes."

The closer Blade got to the fort, the more anxious he became. Would Shannon still be waiting for him? He hadn't seen her for over three months—three hellish months of bitter cold, hunger, and deprivation. In the end it had proved too much for Yellow Dog. He died a month ago of pneumonia and complications from wounds received in the massacre. Personally, Blade thought his grandfather had died of a broken heart. Singing Rain's death had caused him untold anguish; he had mourned her with the deep, abiding sorrow of a father whose children had all preceded him in death.

After Yellow Dog's death, Blade joined the diminished tribe on a buffalo hunt. The meat was needed for food, the hides for tipis and clothing. Everything was used, nothing wasted. Even the stomach and intestines were cleaned and used, the stomach as a pouch to carry water and the intestines to store mixtures of food. The horns were fashioned into vessels of every description. But the choicest parts were the tongue and liver, which were consumed raw.

They had been fortunate to find such a large herd, for each year buffalo were becoming more and more scarce. Once the buffalo had been processed, his tribe began a long trek to Powder River country where they were to meet with other Sioux for a council meeting held each spring. They had expected Blade to join them, assuming his grandfather's place as chief. But since neither his mother nor his grandfather were living, Blade found no reason to remain with the tribe. He had great love and respect for his mother's people, but he'd lived in the white world too long to cling to his Indian ways and become a part of the tribe.

He had remained with the Sioux long enough to see the exodus of the tribe to the Powder River, where he fully expected their small numbers to be integrated into another tribe. He had explained his decision to the council and to his friend Jumping Buffalo, and promised to do all in his power to help the plight of the Indians.

Blade hadn't forgotten his obligation at Fort Laramie. Both the President and Wade Vance were counting on him. And Shannon was waiting for him. He couldn't bear the thought of never seeing her again.

Blade knew he loved Shannon. Three months without her was a lifetime of pure hell. They were meant to be together, and he fully intended to tell her so—only he'd have to make her understand that they couldn't be together until Clive Bailey was behind bars. Selling guns to renegades harmed innocent people, whites and Indians alike. When this was all over, he'd ask Shannon to marry him and hope she loved him enough to bear the stigma attached to marrying a half-breed.

Chapter Fifteen

Blade had just crested a hill when he saw the column of troops below. Assuming it was a patrol from Fort Laramie on routine surveillance, Blade's first inclination was to let it pass without calling attention to himself. But when he recognized Major Vance at the head of the column, he realized that something serious must have transpired to bring Vance out of the fort. He also noted that Lieutenant Goodman rode with the men and that pack horses carried supplies enough for several days.

Some sixth sense warned him that he'd live to regret it if he didn't intercept the patrol. Digging his heels into Warrior's sides, he plunged down the incline, meeting the riders as they came around the bend. Surprise, followed closely by relief, crossed Vance's features when he recognized Blade. He halted the column, waiting for Blade to approach.

"Blade, you couldn't have shown up at a better time!" Vance exclaimed jubilantly.

Vance's words did little to dispel Blade's premonition of disaster. "What is it, Major? I haven't heard of any attacks in the area. The Sioux are engaged in spring hunt and have little time for raiding."

"It's not Indians, Blade, at least I don't think it is. It's—" His words fell off when Lieutenant Goodman rode up to join them. It was all Blade could do to keep from seizing the man and squeezing the life out of him.

"Have the men fall out for a ten-minute rest," Vance ordered crisply. Reluctantly, Goodman turned to carry out orders, leaving Blade and Vance alone.

"I feel the same way about the man," Vance said, admiring Blade's restraint. "Besides, we can trust no one except Colonel Greer. And even he isn't aware of your position with the government. I'd like to keep it that way until we catch the culprit who is smuggling guns across the prairie." Vance dismounted. "Walk with me out of earshot and I'll explain."

They walked to a rocky ledge where Vance stood shuffling his feet and staring off into space. He knew Blade would be devastated to learn Shannon had been abducted, and he wanted to break it to him gently. But Blade would have none of it.

"All right, Wade, spit it out. What aren't you telling me?" Suddenly Blade froze, his bronze features drained of all color. He knew! He *knew*! "It's Shannon, isn't it? Something has happened to Shannon."

Amazed at Blade's perception, Vance nodded, his face grim. "Shannon is missing, Blade. A search was organized as soon as I learned of it. She is nowhere in the fort."

"Did you question Clive Bailey?" Blade asked, his heart pounding furiously. He blamed himself for telling her about his investigation and Clive Bailey's involvement, even though she had more or less forced the truth from him.

"Bailey is missing also," Vance revealed. "That's not all. The night before she was discovered missing, Shannon came to see me. Said she had something urgent to discuss. I could only assume it concerned Bailey. Unfortunately I was in a staff meeting and couldn't leave.

"I sent her home, telling her I'd see her later that evening. But when I arrived, her house was dark. I assumed she had grown tired of waiting and retired for the night. I left, but returned early the next morning. Her house was empty and her bed hadn't been slept in."

"Do you think Bailey has her?" Blade asked fearfully. For a man who didn't frighten easily, he was scared out of his wits. "Wouldn't he suspect he'd be under suspicion?"

"Bailey has no reason to believe he is suspected of anything," Vance responded. "When he returns, I've no doubt he'll have a good explanation for his absence. He often visits nearby Indian villages to trade. Do you have any idea where he'd take Shannon?"

"If Shannon learned something to connect him to gun smuggling, he might just decide to kill her," Blade said, choking on his words. "Is there any possibility that Mad Wolf might have taken Shannon? When he wants something bad enough he rarely gives up."

"I've thought of that, but no one has seen him this past winter, though he might have returned to the summer hunting grounds by now. Do you know where his camp is located?"

"No, but it will be in a place well hidden and not easily accessible. I think we should operate under the assumption that Bailey has Shannon and try to pick up his tracks. Who is doing the tracking?"

"Lieutenant Goodman, and he's doing a damn poor job of it," Vance complained disgustedly.

"I'll take over," Blade said. He did not ask permission but accepted responsibility on his own. "The sooner we get started the better. But I promise you one thing, Wade, if Bailey has Shannon and he's harmed even one hair on her head, I'll derive great pleasure from killing him."

* * *

Released from the gunny sack once they were well away from the fort, Shannon now rode behind Clive, her hands bound securely around his waist and her gag still firmly in place. Thank God Clive had seen fit to remove her blindfold, Shannon reflected gratefully. They rode almost continuously through the night, stopping for two hours near dawn to rest the horse and allow Clive a brief nap. Shannon was left tied to a tree, unable to move or speak.

"I suggest you get some sleep," Clive hinted nastily, "for tomorrow you'll belong to Mad Wolf and there will be little enough rest for you after that. Hell, I'm hoping he'll let me have a poke for bringing you to him. I'd take you here and now except I need some sleep and we're not far enough from the fort for me to relax."

Though Shannon couldn't speak, her blue eyes flashed her hatred for her captor, her revulsion, her utter contempt. But her furious glances slid off him like water off a duck's back. Tossing a blanket over her, Clive rested his head on his saddle and promptly fell asleep. They were on their way again shortly after sun-up.

Clive knew exactly where he was going, having been to Mad Wolf's encampment before. He only hoped the renegade would be there and not off somewhere raiding. Clive was reluctant to kill Shannon himself, but if it came to that he would suffer no guilt over performing the deed. He needn't have worried. Mad Wolf was at his encampment along with a dozen or so of his followers.

Mad Wolf's eyes widened in astonishment when he saw Clive Bailey ride in with Little Firebird bound and gagged behind him. He waited outside his tipi until Clive halted before him, untied Shannon's arms from around his waist and dismounted, dragging Shannon behind down him. He waited for Mad Wolf to speak first, not wishing to anger the hot-headed renegade. Mad Wolf's piercing black eyes never left

Shannon's face as he addressed Clive in halting English.

"Why have you brought Little Firebird to my camp?" He knew but wanted to hear it from Clive's lips. Mad Wolf felt nothing but contempt for the trader, aware that a greedy man like Clive Bailey would betray his own mother if the price was right.

"I thought you wanted her," Clive answered, licking his lips nervously. Indians made him edgy, especially renegades like Mad Wolf. "I went to great trouble to bring Shannon Branigan to you. I expect to be rewarded accordingly."

"Have you harmed her?"

"I haven't touched her, you can see for yourself she is in perfect condition. You promised me gold if I brought her to you."

"We will smoke first, then you will have your gold," Mad Wolf said haughtily. "Bring the woman." He turned and entered his tipi, leaving Clive no choice but to follow. Grasping Shannon's arm, he pulled her after him.

Blade, I need you! Shannon silently implored. Just thinking Blade's name gave her a shot of courage. He rescued her once from Mad Wolf, perhaps . . . But no, Blade was miles from here, helping his grandfather hold their tribe together. He had no way of knowing she needed him. Shannon knew what Mad Wolf planned for her couldn't be pleasant, but somehow she would survive. Somehow she and Blade would be reunited. But would he still want her after Mad Wolf had defiled her?

Once inside the tipi, Shannon was shoved rudely to the ground. She felt hands fiddling with her gag and looked up to see Mad Wolf pulling the offending material from her mouth. "Water," she croaked, desperate to wet her parched throat. The gag hadn't been removed since she left the fort.

Mad Wolf grunted, handing her a skin pouch holding water. She raised it to her lips and drank greedily.

When she had drank her fill she set the pouch down and faced Mad Wolf squarely. "I won't stay here. This—this slimy toad can't sell me. He doesn't own me, no one owns me."

"Quiet, woman, or I will bind your mouth again." Then he promptly ignored Shannon as he regarded Clive Bailey through shrewd black eyes.

"What is your price for the woman, Trader?"

Never had Shannon felt so degraded as when they discussed her attributes in terms that made her cheeks flame. After several minutes they struck a bargain, settling on a sum that brought a gasp to Shannon's lips. Where would Mad Wolf get so much gold? She was stunned beyond words when Bailey boldly asserted, "I want the woman one time before I sell her to you. It's part of the deal. Either I have her or no deal."

Mad Wolf's eyes narrowed dangerously. "I could kill you here and now and keep both Little Firebird and the gold."

"But you won't," Clive stated smugly. "Who will supply you with guns if I'm dead? By now you should be low on ammunition. I have plenty at my store."

Mad Wolf's hardened features showed none of the utter contempt and hatred he felt for Bailey. He'd kill him in a flash if he didn't need what the trader could give him. As for Little Firebird, he no longer wished to make her his wife. She had scorned him, a great warrior, and bedded a half-breed instead. He still wanted her; just looking at her swelled his loins with lust. He'd have Little Firebird, oh yes—as his whore. And this time he'd share her with his friends. The trader wanted her too. And unless Mad Wolf wished to halt the supply of arms and ammunition at a time when they were essential to their survival, he must grant the trader's request, though it galled him to do so.

"You may have Little Firebird, trader, for one night," Mad Wolf conceded grudgingly. "Then she is ours."

"No!" Shannon howled, rage rendering her incautious as she surged to her feet and charged a thoroughly startled Mad Wolf.

The Indian's reaction was swift and vicious as he raised his arm and backhanded Shannon, putting his considerable strength behind the blow. Shannon went flying. Dazed and hurt, she lay in a limp heap against the tipi wall.

Abruptly Mad Wolf stood. "Come," he said to Bailey, who stared at Shannon as if he wanted to fall on her immediately and ravish her. "First we will drink white man's whiskey, then you can have your fill of the woman."

"But I want her now," Bailey whined, rubbing his swollen crotch in an obscene manner. "I don't know if I can wait."

"White men! Pah!" Mad Wolf snorted derisively. "You are all weak, sniveling creatures with no restraint, no willpower. We will drink first, then we will all have the woman. Come, the whiskey is good. It was taken during our last raid."

Bailey knew better than to argue. Eventually he'd have Shannon; it cost him little to humor Mad Wolf. Slanting Shannon a glance ripe with salacious promise, he followed the renegade from the tipi.

Reeling dizzily, Shannon knew her time was growing short. After Bailey used her, Mad Wolf and his friends would defile her body, perhaps even kill her if she resisted. *Blade! Blade!* she cried out in silent supplication. *Nothing they do to me will change the way I feel about you.*

While Shannon cringed in terror inside the tipi, Mad Wolf and his warriors sat in a circle passing bottles of whiskey back and forth and getting drunk. Even Bailey felt tipsy, but not too inebriated to forget about the woman waiting for him inside the tipi. Suddenly he reeled to his feet. "Enough!" His face was set in determination, his voice harsh with impatience. "I want the woman and I want her now." He staggered toward the tipi, noting with satisfaction that Mad Wolf made no move to stop him.

Mad Wolf merely grunted in response, too sated with whiskey to care. Soon Little Firebird would be at the complete disposal of him and his warriors. What did it matter when the trader took her?

With a careless wave of his hand, Bailey dismissed the guard Mad Wolf had placed in front of the tipi and entered, closing the flap behind him.

"Don't touch me, you vile bastard!" Shannon spat as Bailey stalked her. "Blade will kill you for this."

"Swift Blade! Bah! I should have known that savage couldn't keep his filthy hands off you. You let him poke you and here I thought you were so damn innocent. Now you'll find out how it feels to have a real man between your legs."

"I'm not going to make it easy for you," Shannon warned, preparing for the fight of her life.

"That's just the way I like it," Bailey responded, grinning viciously as he removed the rope from his belt and walked slowly toward her.

"Do you see either Bailey or Shannon?" Major Vance hissed in a low voice.

Due entirely to Blade's expert tracking, the patrol found Mad Wolf's encampment. It was cleverly located in a tall stand of cottonwood trees beside a bubbling creek below a ridge of rolling hills. It came as no surprise when Bailey's tracks led them directly to Mad Wolf's camp. Blade, Vance, and the patrol were huddled behind one of the ridges above the encampment, looking down on the renegades and circle of tipis.

"No, but one of the horses tethered with the Indian ponies is shod," Blade whispered in response. "We can only assume that Bailey is here somewhere, perhaps in one of the tipis."

They exchanged uneasy glances, both aware of what that statement meant in regard to Shannon but neither willing to give voice to their fears.

"They're drunk," Vance observed, nodding toward the Indians below.

"You're right, Wade," Blade concurred. "They're probably drinking whiskey stolen from wagon trains they raided. Signal your men. We won't find a better time to attack. I owe that bastard, and if he's harmed Shannon, I'll—"

Suddenly a piercing scream rent the air. Blade spat out an oath, his face grim, his eyes wild with fear.

The Indians merely laughed among themselves, exchanging knowing leers as they glanced toward the tipi that Bailey had just entered. Blade surged to his feet. Nothing or no one could stop him now.

"I'm going in."

Vance was close on Blade's heels, signaling his men to follow. Lieutenant Goodman was only a few steps behind. Mad Wolf and his renegades never had a chance. Seated around the campfire, they had consumed large quantities of whiskey and lolled about in a drunken stupor when the soldiers came howling down from the surrounding hills.

Those Indians who were sober enough to defend themselves made a valiant effort to counter the attack, but the outcome was inevitable. Blade didn't linger to see the Indians cut down by the patrol or Mad Wolf fall victim to Wade Vance's bullet. He fought his way from tipi to tipi, looking for Shannon, thrusting himself inside one tipi after another, then out again when he didn't find her, praying he'd get to her in time.

Shannon heard the commotion outside but was too occupied with fending off Bailey's drunken attack to think about what it meant. Bailey had finally subdued her, throwing her to the ground and falling heavily atop her. Unfortunately, she hit her head when she fell and was knocked senseless. She had no idea that Bailey tied her hands together in front of her, raised her skirt to her waist and shoved his trousers down below his hips. Nor did she see or hear the man who slipped silently through the tent's opening and tore

Bailey off of her seconds before he thrust himself inside her.

"What! You!" Bailey gasped, eyeing the rifle pointed at him with misgiving. "What are you doing here?"

"The government is on to you, Bailey," the man hissed. "I can't let you be taken alive and spill your guts about me. I don't trust you."

"No, I swear—"

The man pulled the trigger. Bailey spun around, dead before he hit the ground. The killer then turned his sights on Shannon, who was just beginning to regain her senses. He was astute enough to realize that he couldn't allow her to live and tell the authorities about him. Even though she didn't know his identity, it would only be a matter of time before she figured it out. But before he could squeeze the trigger, Blade threw open the flap of the tipi. Bailey's killer dove for the back of the tent, scooting beneath the buffalo hide and into the open just as Blade burst inside.

Adjusting his eyes to the dimness, Blade spied Clive Bailey sprawled on the ground. His trousers were shoved down past his hips and it took little imagination to realize what he had been doing. A large hole punctured Bailey's chest, and he was apparently dead. Then Blade's eyes fell on Shannon. Quickly he knelt beside her, his face a mask of agony as he flipped her skirt down over her legs. Shannon moaned, thick layers of cotton slowly peeling away from her fuzzy brain.

"Shannon! Little Firebird, please be all right." He gathered her in his arms, rocking her back and forth as he crooned in her ear. "If Bailey wasn't already dead, I'd kill him all over again."

Shannon's dream was so delicious, she resisted opening her eyes. Strong, tender arms held her— Blade's arms. She smelled his special scent, inhaled his clean, woodsy aroma. She heard his voice—low, vibrant, tender, coaxing. Never had a dream seemed so real. When he brushed her lips with his, Shannon knew she wasn't dreaming.

Her eyes fluttered open. "Blade? I—I thought I was dreaming. Is it really you?"

"It is me, Little Firebird."

"How is it you always arrive in time? How did you know where to find me?"

"I met the search party on my way to the fort," Blade explained. "Major Vance told me everything. We both suspected Bailey immediately. Fortunately I picked up his tracks and followed them here to Mad Wolf's camp."

"Clive Bailey intended to sell me to Mad Wolf," Shannon revealed.

"Why? What did you do to arouse his suspicion? I could have sworn he had no idea we were on to him."

"Is everything all right in here?" Major Vance entered the tipi, paused a moment before Bailey's body, then said, "Did you kill Bailey, Blade?"

"No," Blade replied. "I wish to God I had been the one."

"Perhaps Shannon—"

"Bailey is dead?" Shannon said, shocked. She lifted her hands in a helpless gesture and only then did Blade realize she was bound.

"The bastard," he ground out, making short work of the ropes. "Shannon couldn't have shot Bailey, she was unconscious and bound when I arrived. But I'm almost positive there was someone else inside the tipi. He crawled out the back beneath the buffalo hide just as I burst inside."

"Who was it?" Vance asked sharply.

"Damned if I know," Blade shrugged, helping Shannon to her feet. He was more concerned about Shannon than he was with Clive Bailey. "Are you hurt, Shannon? Did they . . ."

"I'm fine, Blade," Shannon assured him somewhat shakily. "Except for the lump on my head. Whoever killed Bailey arrived in time to—to stop him from hurting me. Do you have any idea who it could have been?"

"I haven't a clue."

"If one of my men is responsible for Bailey's death, I'll find out soon enough," Vance said. "The fighting is over and things are well in hand. A few of the renegades survived, and I'm taking them back to the fort. I've already set men to digging graves."

"Mad Wolf?" Blade asked, his voice tense.

"Dead," Vance replied. "Killed him myself. Bring Shannon out when she is ready." He turned to leave.

Suddenly Shannon thought of something. "Major, wait! There is something you and Blade should know."

"You don't have to talk about it now, Shannon," Vance said gently. No one could ever doubt Shannon's courage.

"I have to tell you now," Shannon insisted, quietly determined. Both men regarded her with keen attention. "Clive Bailey had a partner."

"We know," Vance smiled indulgently. "That big Swede who was killed by Mad Wolf."

"No, someone else."

Now she really had both men's undivided attention. "My God, Shannon, who?" This from Blade who appeared stunned by her disclosure.

"I never saw his face," Shannon told him, "nor did I recognize his voice. He disguised it. But believe me, there is another man. I wouldn't be in this predicament if I hadn't learned of it by accident."

"Tell me about it," Vance said earnestly.

Taking a deep breath, Shannon told them everything, exactly as she remembered it.

"Damnation, that man could be with us now, a part of the patrol. It certainly would explain Bailey's mysterious death," Vance surmised. "The man probably thought Bailey would talk in order to save his own skin and made short work of him."

"Jesus, he could have killed Shannon!" Blade exploded. Raw fear contorted his features.

"Sir, the men have buried the dead and await your orders."

Lieutenant Goodman stuck his head through the tent flap, spied Shannon, and came the rest of the way inside. "Is Miss Branigan all right?"

Blade's dark eyes blazed with hatred when he saw Lieutenant Goodman. If not for that bloodthirsty Indian-hater, his sweet mother would still be alive and his grandfather in good health. But wisely he realized this was not the best time to confront the slimy bastard. As sure as he breathed, Blade knew that one day Goodman would pay for his evil deeds.

"Miss Branigan is fine, Lieutenant. We're almost ready to leave. There is another body to bury." He motioned to Clive Bailey. "See to it."

Goodman looked with distaste at Bailey's stiffening body. "He got exactly what he deserved." Then grasping him by the heels he dragged him from the tipi. Major Vance followed him out.

"Can you ride, Little Firebird?" Blade asked, concern coloring his words. Shannon looked shaken and pale and on the verge of collapse.

"Do we have to leave tonight, Blade? I'm exhausted."

"I'm fairly certain Wade will make camp tonight before returning to the fort tomorrow. The men have been riding hard all day. Wait here while I find out his plans."

A short time later Blade returned. "Wade ordered the patrol to camp a mile or two down the trail. I told him you were too exhausted to travel and that we'd stay in Mad Wolf's lodge tonight. We'll catch up with the patrol in the morning."

"What will the men think, you and me alone here?"

"We won't be alone," Blade smiled. "Wade put Goodman in charge of the patrol and told the men he will remain behind to protect you. No one need ever know we will be sharing the tipi."

"But won't Major Vance think—"

"Wade knows how I feel about you, but if you'd feel more comfortable alone . . ."

"No, I want you with me tonight!" Shannon cried. She never wanted to be without Blade again. "I love you, I don't care what anyone thinks. I need you, Blade, don't leave me alone."

"Never again, love. I'll always be with you."

Chapter Sixteen

After a hastily prepared meal, Shannon sat beside the campfire with Blade and Major Vance discussing Clive Bailey and speculating on the identity of his partner. Vance revealed that none of the men in the patrol had admitted to entering the tipi and killing Bailey, a clear indication that Bailey's unknown partner was running scared and had killed Bailey in order to silence him.

Once they had exhausted the subject, Vance tactfully excused himself and disappeared into another tipi a short distance away. Blade took Shannon's hand and led her inside Mad Wolf's lodge. Earlier he had built a fire to keep them warm and laid down a thick mat of buffalo robes for their bed.

Inside the tipi, firelight eased the dark shadows, dispelling the gloom and distasteful memories. With Blade beside her, the tipi seemed almost cozy now, its welcoming warmth and Blade's presence suffusing her with a rosy glow. Shannon knew Blade was going to make love to her tonight, and God knew she wanted it, yet an unexpected shyness brought a rosy flush to her cheeks.

"Little Firebird, you look exhausted. You've been through a terrible ordeal. I should leave you to your rest."

Her porcelain paleness, the violet circles around her eyes, and her fragile beauty caused Blade to have second thoughts about his plans for the night. He cursed himself for being a selfish bastard and thinking only of personal gratification at a time when Shannon needed his loving the least. Whenever he was near Shannon he could think of nothing but how much he loved her, how desperately he wanted and needed her. It had been so long—too damn long.

Suddenly Shannon found her tongue. "No, don't leave, I can't bear to be alone tonight! I want you, Blade, I want you to make love to me."

"Oh my sweet, sweet love. I want to make love to you, more than anything in the world. If you're sure . . ."

"I've never been more certain of anything in my life."

With shaking hands she reached out and pushed the jacket from his shoulders. It was all the invitation Blade needed as he pulled her into his arms. His kiss was slow and gentle, his mouth softly yielding yet demanding as his tongue slipped between her parted lips and his hands slid along her spine to cup her buttocks. He kissed her and kissed her again, covered her face with kisses, her throat, the hollow between her breasts. Through the fabric of their clothing his hard, probing strength pressed against her as his mouth continued to search hers with desperate urgency.

"Help me," Blade groaned as his strong hands fumbled with the buttons on Shannon's bodice. "I want you naked beneath me, responding to my touch. Your passion drives me wild."

In response to his plea, Shannon began tearing at

her clothes, as eager for their mating as Blade. When her last garment fell away, they attacked Blade's clothes with furious haste until he was as gloriously naked as Shannon. Dark, powerful chest; corded ribs; strong, muscular arms; long, sturdy legs—she had nearly forgotten what a magnificent specimen of virile masculinity Blade was. Her appreciative gaze was riveted to that splendid symbol of sexuality springing from the black thatch between his legs. Unconsciously Shannon licked her lips, overwhelmed by the living, breathing statue of flesh and blood perfection standing before her and the glorious ecstasy he was capable of giving her.

Blade flushed with pleasure, happy to know he pleased Shannon so well. He certainly was well satisfied with her. She was a vision of beauty and perfection, wonderfully proportioned and masterfully painted in hues of ivory and rose.

Shannon's expressive blue eyes devouring his body caused Blade to swell with pride. He felt invincible, embued with an enormous need to give Shannon more rapture than she'd ever known before. Almost reverently, he touched her right breast with one hand, toying with her tautening nipple while his other hand slid down her flat belly to cup the rich chestnut vee between her legs.

"Blade," Shannon gasped. She was stunned by the heat exploding through her body at his intimate touch. Clinging to him, she began to tremble.

"I know, Little Firebird, I feel the same things you're feeling."

When his long, skilled finger invaded her wet warmth, Shannon's legs buckled and Blade swept her into his arms, sitting down on the mat and placing her on his lap. He kissed her breasts until they were pink and tingling; sucked and licked her nipples till they grew pebble hard and achingly distended. Immersed in erotic pleasure, his skilled hands worked magic on her heated flesh, arousing her, thrilling her.

"Ride me, love," Blade whispered, stretching out

on his back, putting his hands to her waist and lifting her astride him.

He urged her up to a kneeling position, then slowly, carefully, brought her back down on his straining erection. Shannon's body quivered with pleasure as she gripped his ribs, pushed down hard and settled herself on his engorged flesh, taking all of him inside her.

"Damn, you feel good," Blade moaned in sublime rapture. "So warm—so tight!"

Tossing her head back in pure joy, Shannon rocked her body in a slow, undulating motion, nearly destroying Blade's determination to restrain himself. He wanted to grasp her waist and plunge into her, hard, demanding, driving himself in deep, wild thrusts to possess her totally. Exerting extraordinary control, he allowed Shannon to set the pace. Her passion exploded, her legs squeezing his slim hips as she ground her pelvis against his, her hands clawing at his back, her mouth nipping at his neck and shoulders. Suddenly Blade reached the limit of his endurance as he grasped her buttocks in his big hands, sliding her up, then down along the rigid length of his pole with savage, naked fury.

"Blade—oh, God—I'm—"

"Let go, Little Firebird, it's time. I want to watch your lovely face soften and glow in passion when you come to me."

Then he drove her over the edge.

"Blade, I love you!"

Blade groaned and shook as her contractions tightened around him, speeding toward his own fierce release.

Shuddering uncontrollably, they floated back to earth, still entwined, Shannon resting on Blade's chest, his hands running the length of her spine and back.

"My God," he rasped reverently, trying to sort through the maelstrom of emotions he had just experienced. What in the hell made him think he could get along without Shannon? he wondered. Without her to brighten his life he'd shrivel up and die. He had never experienced such a tempestuous, white-hot climax. Each time with Shannon got better. She aroused emotions in him that he never felt with any other woman.

"Blade, I've never felt anything like that," Shannon whispered, echoing Blade's thoughts. She sounded as awestruck as he was. "Don't ever leave me."

"Never," Blade vowed, hugging her close. "You're my life, my reason for living. You're mine, Shannon Branigan."

"And you're mine, Swift Blade. Do you have a last name?" she asked curiously. "What was your father's name?"

"Stryker. In the East I was known as Blade Stryker."

"How soon can I be Mrs. Stryker?"

"If I had my way, it would be tomorrow, but I'm afraid we'll have to wait," Blade said regretfully.

"Wait! For what?" Shannon raised herself on her elbows, staring at Blade as if he'd lost his mind.

"You're going to be in enough danger without my contributing to it. Bailey's partner will surmise that you've told Wade Vance about him, and he'll live in fear that you'll recognize his voice. He might decide to eliminate that problem. Now do you understand why your life could be in danger?"

Wide-eyed, Shannon nodded.

"Fortunately, no one knows I'm a government agent or that I'm working with Wade, which means I'll be able to continue the investigation unhindered. I suspect Wade will be closely watched, though, since our man seems to know that you went to the major with your suspicions."

"Then he's in danger too."

"Possibly," Blade allowed.

"I still don't see what all this has to do with us and

the way we feel about one another."

"I'll be better able to keep an eye on you if no one suspects there is anything between us," Blade explained. "There are times when I might have to leave the fort, and if we were married you'd be subject to ridicule from the townspeople. Be patient, my love, my job here will be finished soon. Bailey and Mad Wolf are dead, but other renegades will take Mad Wolf's place as long as guns are placed in their hands by men like Bailey and his partner."

"Blade, you never said why you left your grandfather. What happened to those of his people who survived the attack?"

"Yellow Dog is dead," Blade said, his eyes sad and remote. "The winter was hard on us. Food was scarce, and we had no proper shelter and much sickness. Grandfather died of pneumonia in February."

"I'm sorry, Blade," Shannon said sincerely. "What of the others?"

"Jumping Buffalo is taking the people to Powder River country where I imagine they'll join with other Sioux. They are too small a group now to survive on their own. White Elk is a friend of Yellow Dog and will welcome them into his tribe."

"How long before we can be together?" Shannon asked abruptly.

"Not long, I hope," Blade promised. "This partner of Bailey's is bound to make a mistake and give himself away. Until he does I'm going to watch you like a hawk. Nothing, *nothing,"* he repeated fiercely, "is going to happen to you. I love you too much to see you harmed."

"I didn't think I'd ever hear you say those words," Shannon sighed happily.

"I never thought I'd say them," Blade grinned sheepishly. "You deserve better, Little Firebird. I'm a half-breed and a Yankee officer, everything you despise. That you love me at all is a miracle."

"No, Blade, you're the miracle. You made me forget

the war and all the sadness I endured because of it. I realize now that both sides suffered. You joined the Yankee army out of deep conviction and I respect you for your belief. I'm no longer that shallow, hot-headed girl who listened to no one. I'm a woman now, capable of understanding and forgiveness. Mama would be proud of me."

"I'm proud of you, Shannon."

"Do you think . . ." She blushed furiously, suddenly aware of what she was about to ask."

"What, Little Firebird? What were you going to say?"

"I was going to ask you to love me again. If you're not too tired," she added with a twinkle.

A lazy smile curved Blade's full lips. "Tired?" he scoffed. "I'm a man in his prime, sweet little love, not yet thirty years old. I could make love to you all night and still have the energy to go out and slay all my enemies tomorrow."

"You talk too much, Blade Stryker."

Shannon stared wistfully out the schoolhouse window, as distracted as her students. She'd been back at the fort for days, and an early spring snowfall covered the land. At first all the pristine white snow had enthralled her, but as the dreary season progressed Shannon yearned for the soft Georgia spring she'd grown up with. The heavenly scent of flowers and gentle ocean breezes were as remote as Blade had been since their return.

Then she thought of this sprawling, wild country just bursting with opportunity and remembered exactly why her family had chosen to travel to the Western frontier. And now that Blade loved her, she never intended to leave, unless it was to follow him elsewhere.

Thinking about Blade turned her musings in another direction. Since returning to the fort, she'd rarely seen him. She knew he and Major Vance were secretly involved in unmasking Clive Bailey's partner. The man was a sly one, wonderfully clever at covering his tracks. By now he must be aware that Major Vance was on to him. Shannon had spoken to Blade but briefly during these past few days, and he'd told her they still hadn't a clue to the man's identity. Shannon sincerely hoped something would break soon, for she missed Blade desperately.

Thus far there had been no evidence to suggest Shannon was in danger, yet Major Vance had insisted on assigning a man to protect her. Sargeant O'Brien, a battle-scarred veteran of many campaigns, had been given the task of seeing that Shannon came to no harm. Shannon felt uncomfortable being accorded special treatment but made the best of it. She felt unqualified to argue with Major Vance's logic.

After school was dismissed that afternoon, Shannon remained a few minutes longer than usual, tidying up for the weekend. When she turned from her task, Blade was leaning lazily in the doorway.

"Blade!"

Uncaring who might be watching, Shannon ran into his outstretched arms. "You feel wonderful, Little Firebird. I've missed you."

"You have no idea how much I've missed you," Shannon returned, truly content for the first time in days. It felt so right to be in Blade's arms.

Suddenly Shannon peered over Blade's shoulder. "Where is Sargeant O'Brien? What will he think, seeing us like this?"

"Wade dismissed O'Brien tonight. I'm to take his place," Blade said, his voice hinting of a night filled with rapture. "I need you, Little Firebird."

Closing the door behind them, Blade pulled her closer, his warm mouth covering hers in a kiss ripe with tender yearning and sweet promise. His tongue slid temptingly along her parted lips, slipping inside to explore the moist insides of her cheeks. He deepened the kiss, sucking her tongue into his mouth, savoring her sweet nectar. When the kiss ended Shannon felt totally drained, leaning limp and breathless against Blade's massive chest. Blade grinned knowingly as he set her back on her feet.

"You're far too tempting, Little Firebird. When I'm near you I forget everything but the need to have you in my arms, to bury myself in your sweet flesh. Do you understand now why I've been avoiding you? I need to keep my wits about me until Bailey's partner is apprehended."

Shannon flushed becomingly. Blade rarely waxed so eloquent about his feelings. "Have you and Major Vance learned anything new?"

"We still don't know the identity of Bailey's partner. The man is damn clever. But I suspect he'll be going after the gold that Bailey owed him one day soon. Naturally he'll assume it's hidden someplace in the store and when he shows up to claim it either Wade or I will be there waiting."

"What will happen to the trading post now that Bailey is dead?"

"A new man will take over soon. The Post Trader's Store is owned by the army but leased to civilians."

"Will the new owner be told about the gold?"

"No, and I see no need to tell him, since the gold is no longer there."

Shannon's mouth flew open. "You found the gold?"

"Wade and I searched the store thoroughly before the new owner took over. We found the gold in a space under the floor beneath a loose floorboard. Wade has it well hidden in his quarters."

"You think Bailey's partner will break into the trading post to look for the gold?"

"I'm sure of it. Wade and I take turns keeping watch on the trading post night and day. Sooner or later the man is going to try to remove that gold."

"Be careful, Blade," Shannon whispered shakily. "I couldn't bear it if anything happened to you."

"Don't worry, sweet, I'm always careful. After

Wade relieves me tonight I'll come to you. It's Wade's turn to stand guard outside the trading post, so we'll have a few hours together."

"I'll leave the rear door unlatched."

"No, it's too dangerous. I'll knock. It will probably be late."

"I don't care how late, I'll wait," Shannon promised, eyes shining brightly. "But I think you're exaggerating about my danger."

"Perhaps, but I'm not taking chances where you're concerned."

He kissed her again, a short, passionate assault upon her senses. She felt the hard proof of his desire rise against her and she quivered with excitement.

"Tonight, Little Firebird. Go home now. Trust no one but me, Wade, and Sargeant O'Brien."

Shannon left the schoolhouse in a daze of happiness, thinking of tonight and having Blade to herself for a few stolen hours of bliss. She'd soak in a hot tub first, then . . ."

"Shannon!" Startled, Shannon whirled as Molly Greer hailed her from across the road. Smiling, she waited until the older woman hurried across the street to join her.

"My dear, where have you been hiding yourself? Surely school isn't keeping you from visiting friends. You've not attended a suffrage meeting in ages."

Most townspeople knew Shannon had been carried off by Clive Bailey, but few knew why or any of the details. It was due primarily to the Greers' staunch friendship that gossip about Shannon was squelched before it really got started.

Colonel Greer had been informed that Clive Bailey was dealing in illegal weapons and that he intended to sell Shannon to Mad Wolf, but little else. Vance stopped short of telling Greer that he and Blade were special agents working out of Washington. Vance was permitted to tell no one until given permission to do so by the president.

"I'm sorry, Molly, I've been rather busy with tests and—and things," Shannon said lamely. "I'll try to attend the next meeting."

"My dear, there is no need for shame or pretense between friends. I don't know the entire story where Clive Bailey is concerned, but I'm certain you were not at fault for what happened. No one would dare accuse you in my presence. I insist you attend our meeting tonight."

"Tonight?" Shannon hedged. "I . . ."

"Oh please—you were so helpful in organizing our group, I know you're interested."

Shannon didn't have the heart to refuse. Especially after Molly's vote of confidence. Besides, suffrage was a subject close to Shannon's heart. She felt strongly that women should have a say in their futures. Women were the backbone of civilization and shouldn't be treated as mere property or an extension of some man. It was time they received recognition for the special place they occupied in society. Since Blade said he wouldn't show up until late, Shannon decided she'd have plenty of time to attend the meeting.

"Of course I'll attend the meeting, Molly. And—and thank you."

"No need for thanks," Molly said briskly, aware of what she was being thanked for. "Seven-thirty, dear. I'll send an escort."

"There is no need."

Molly merely smiled and waved, the matter already settled.

Shannon was annoyed to see Lieutenant Goodman at her door that evening, sent by well-meaning Molly Greer to act as escort. She despised the brash lieutenant for his cowardly attack on Yellow Dog's village and was quick to convey her contempt.

"Good evening, Shannon," he greeted her pleasantly when Shannon opened the door. "Are you ready? Mrs. Greer asked me to see you safely to the meeting."

"I'm ready," Shannon said with cool disdain. She lifted her coat from the hook by the door and Goodman took it from her hands, placing it over her shoulders with a flourish.

Shannon set a quick pace once they left the house.

"I'm happy to see you survived your—er, recent ordeal with little effect. Have you any idea why Clive Bailey abducted you?"

"I really don't wish to talk about it," Shannon said tightly. "Look, Lieutenant, why don't we stop pretending."

Goodman went still, his eyes narrowing to mere slits. "What do you mean?"

"I don't like you and you know it."

An audible sigh escaped Goodman's lips. "I know you are upset about the raid, but those red devils had it coming. I never took you for an Indian lover. You're lucky to be alive."

A strange chill settled over Shannon and she shuddered. Either her ears were deceiving her or Lieutenant Goodman's words held a hint of menace. Fortunately, she was saved from further conversation, for they had reached the Greer house. Shannon quickly disappeared inside.

"I'll be waiting to walk you home," Goodman called to her departing back.

The meeting went well. Shannon learned that Anna Dickinson, famous suffrage leader, promised to travel to Cheyenne in the near future to speak on behalf of women's rights.

"The women's rights issue is a controversial subject at the present time," Molly told the group assembled, "though truth to tell, there is little opposition to the movement in the state legislature. There are so few women in Wyoming that most men foolishly discount our impact upon politics."

"Our influence out here on the Western Frontier is very different from Eastern sisters'," Carrie Lincoln, a young major's wife, contended. "You all remember how it is back East. Women are modest, submissive, educated in genteel and domestic arts. A wife is rarely heard outside the family circle. She is a private person, never public."

Everyone nodded in agreement as she continued. "On the western frontier women are the mainstay of the family. We work the fields beside our men and have opinions of our own."

"I'm certain most men now realize that women's lives have changed and broadened and that change is necessary if the frontier is to be conquered and civilized," Molly said sagely.

"Yes," agreed Sarah Hanks, another suffragette. "Women establish schools and churches to help tame the frontier. States do not provide financing for schools," she said bitterly. "It is the Ladies Aid Societies that raise money and make it all possible. Indeed, I've heard tell that even dance-hall girls show up at some meetings for women. Our ranks are open to all."

"But there are men in Wyoming against allowing women to vote," Shannon spoke up. "They cite the harm we could do at the polls. They argue that homes and families will be ruined, women unsexed, and divine law disobeyed."

"Yes," Molly agreed, "but fortunately the Wyoming legislature agrees that the benefits to our sparsely populated state far surpasses the drawbacks. Mark my words, ladies, the women's rights ammendment will pass the legislature and very soon we will be allowed to vote and hold office."

When it came time to leave, Claire Greer raised such a ruckus over Lieutenant Goodman acting as escort to Shannon that Shannon declined his company on the short trip home. When Molly offered to provide another escort, Shannon politely refused, since she had walked home many times in the past without mishap.

"I'm sorry about Claire, dear," Molly apologized as

Shannon stepped outside. "I'd forgotten how possessive she is of Lieutenant Goodman. It was remiss of me to send him in the first place."

"Claire has nothing to worry about, Molly," Shannon assured her. "I despise the man."

"Aren't you being a little hard on him, dear? He only did what he felt was right. I don't like to see innocent people killed either, but we do what we must."

Shannon chose not to respond as she bid Molly a hasty good-bye and hurried off across the parade ground. It was already ten o'clock and she worried that Blade might have arrived and become upset when he found her gone.

Blade sat hunched behind a clump of bushes several yards from the rear entrance to the trading post. Major Vance wasn't to relieve him until eleven, freeing him to go to Shannon. Blade wasn't certain how much longer he could keep up this pretense. He wanted to claim Shannon for all time, wanted to let the whole world know she was his. But Wade Vance had convinced him to wait until they had their man behind bars, that Shannon was already in enough danger without announcing to everyone that she loved a half-breed. Vance argued that people would likely shun and ridicule Shannon if they were to marry now. School teachers held a special place in the community and were expected to project an untarnished image to their pupils.

Suddenly Blade tensed, every instinct alert. His sharp ears picked up a rustling in the bushes behind him. Then he relaxed, thinking that Wade, knowing how much he wanted to be with Shannon, had arrived early to relieve him. It was the first serious mistake Blade had made in a long time, and it nearly cost him his life.

"You're early, Wade, but I can't say I'm not glad you're here."

Blade glanced over his shoulder, expecting to see Vance hunkering down beside him. By the time he recognized the glint of moonlight on the knife blade it was too late to do more than twist his body so that the point missed that vulnerable spot on the back of his neck and buried itself instead deep in his shoulder. Blade spun around to confront his assailant, his own knife unsheathed and ready. To his chagrin he faced nothing but air, for his attacker had already melted into the shadows. Blade tried to rise, grunted in pain, then tried again. This time he made it to his feet and staggered forward. He reached the street in front of the trading post and fell to his knees.

Shannon hurried across the square, for some reason apprehensive. She wished now that she had allowed Molly to provide another escort. A prickling sensation slid down her spine. Was someone following her? Casting a furtive glance over her shoulder, she saw no one. The street was deserted. Her imagination was working overtime, she told herself with a nervous laugh. Suddenly she saw someone stagger out from behind the trading post, and froze. It looked like—it *was.*

Blade! Something was wrong with Blade! Blood rushed to Shannon's frozen limbs as she lurched forward, but in so doing tripped over her long skirt, stumbled, and fell. Just as she hit the ground, an explosion rent the night air and a bullet went whizzing harmlessly past her head. If she hadn't fallen, she would surely have been killed!

Blade heard the shot and knew immediately what it was and what it meant. He had seen Shannon approaching and realized that whoever had tried to kill him also wanted Shannon dead. Mustering what little strength he had left, he staggered to where Shannon lay on the ground a short distance away. He assumed she'd been shot and howled in outrage. Great waves of relief washed over him when she rose unsteadily to her feet, looking confused but unhurt.

"Blade, what happened?" Shannon asked, bewildered.

"Someone tried to kill us," Blade said with difficulty. He was growing dizzy now from pain and loss of blood, though fortunately his wound wasn't life-threatening.

With the last of his waning strength Blade pulled Shannon into his arms. "You're hurt!" she cried. Her hand came away from his back wet with blood. "I'll take you home, it's only a few steps to my house." She placed an arm around his waist to support his sagging weight.

They had taken but a few steps when Major Vance suddenly appeared at their side. "What in the hell happened here? I was just on my way to relieve you, Blade. I heard a shot. Is anyone hurt?"

"Someone shot at me," Shannon offered tersely, "but I don't know who it was."

"What is the matter with Blade?" By now Blade was leaning heavily against Shannon.

"Stab wound," Blade gasped, rousing himself sufficiently to explain. "My fault, let my guard down. I thought it was you coming to relieve me. Sorry."

"Here, let me help," Vance said, taking the burden from Shannon. "Where were you taking him?"

"To my house. It's just a few steps away."

Shannon unlocked her door and stepped aside while Vance eased Blade inside.

"Take him to the bedroom," Shannon said crisply.

After carefully inspecting Blade's injury, Vance pronounced him in no danger of dying. Already the blood had congealed around the edges of the jagged wound.

"You're lucky," he told Blade. "I'll send the doctor around, because the wound needs disinfecting and stitching. Did you see who did it?"

"No," Blade said weakly. "He was gone before I got a look at him."

Vance frowned worriedly. "It appears that our man

now knows you are a government agent, Blade. He probably thought it was me lying in wait in the bushes. Too bad it's such a bright night tonight—he couldn't help but recognize you. I suspect he received quite a shock when he learned it wasn't me he was attacking."

"I fear you're right, Wade," Blade concurred. "Our man is cunning as well as dangerous. Now he knows we're both on to him."

"Don't try to talk anymore, Blade. I'm on my way to get the doctor."

"Don't bring him here!" Blade insisted, trying to rise from the bed. "I can't be seen at Shannon's house in this condition."

"It makes no difference now, Blade," Shannon observed. "I'm tired of sneaking around. I told you before I'm not ashamed of our love."

Blade looked appropriately grateful but unmoved. "Wade can help me back to my quarters. At the outside I'll be laid up a day or two. I'm determined to catch this man, Shannon. Until then we must be patient. One day we'll be together as we want to be."

"Major Vance, I'd like to speak to Blade in private," Shannon requested. "Would you wait in the other room, please?"

While Vance cooled his heels in the small parlor, Shannon lit into Blade. "I don't care what people say. You're as much white as you are Indian. I love you."

"God knows I love you, Little Firebird, never more than at this moment. But I have a job to do before we can be together. I made a commitment to the president that I aim to fulfill. If Mad Wolf didn't have those guns, he might never have raided that wagon train. And Goodman wouldn't have retaliated by attacking Yellow Dog's village. Honor demands that I avenge all those senseless deaths and bring those responsible to justice."

"Is revenge more important to you than I am?" Shannon asked quietly.

"Shannon, you misunderstand. Nothing is more

important to me than you, but this matter goes far beyond what we feel for one another. It isn't just a thirst for vengeance I crave, but justice. And I fear for you, Little Firebird. I'm not going to place your life in jeopardy by involving you in this any more than you already are. Now that my identity is known, the danger will be even greater."

"We can face anything if we are together," Shannon stated with quiet dignity.

"I can't take that chance."

"Blade, unless you stop this charade where we're concerned, we're through. I can't go on like this. I hate sneaking around. I hate pretending."

"Damnation, Shannon, you don't mean that!"

"Every word."

"I'm sorry, Little Firebird," Blade said, his voice ripe with regret. "I'm convinced my way is best. If only you'd—" A groan of pain prevented him from finishing the sentence, reminding Shannon that he was wounded and needed immediate attention.

Very calmly, almost too calmly considering her breaking heart, Shannon walked to the door. "Major Vance, you can take Blade back to his quarters now."

"Shannon, I—"

"Please don't say any more, Blade."

Then Vance came in and Shannon stood aside while Blade was helped to his feet and led out into the crisp night air. Before darkness swallowed him up, he glanced over his shoulder at Shannon, his eyes so filled with anguish and mute appeal that Shannon nearly capitulated. But her upbringing demanded she stand firm in her conviction. How could a love like theirs be wrong? Why should it be hidden, as if she were ashamed of Blade and his mixed blood?

When two people loved, nothing mattered but being together, and everything else be damned. Though she didn't doubt Blade's love, his thinking was seriously flawed. Until he came to his senses Shannon wasn't budging. Unless Blade was ready to openly acknowledge their love, she was prepared to deal with a life without him. She wouldn't like it; life without Blade would be like no life at all. But it was better than pretending their love didn't exist.

Chapter Seventeen

*B*lade's wound healed rapidly, just as he'd predicted. Shannon saw him ride out with a patrol a few days later and was amazed at his stamina. With spring finally upon the land, Indian activity had increased and patrols went out regularly to make the trail safe for emigrants. The first wagon train would be arriving in a matter of weeks. But even before that, travelers could be expected at the fort; some would stay, others travel on to different destinations.

One of those who arrived early, traveling with a party of buffalo hunters who stayed a few days and moved on, was an Englishman named Nigel Bruce. Bruce had been sent abroad by his parents with a monthly remittance to sustain him during his long absence. There were many "remittance men" in America, most biding their time until they were allowed to return home. A few were guilty of grievous crimes in their homeland, while others had merely disgraced their families and were shipped abroad until the furor died down. Such was the case with Nigel Bruce.

Blond and handsome, Nigel's fondness for gambling, women, and drink—not necessarily in that order—proved his undoing. He had seduced the daughter of a prominent family on a whim, then balked when she became pregnant and demanded marriage. Consequently she threw herself into the Thames, and in so doing lost the child but fortunately not her life. She was shipped off to a convent and Nigel Bruce was quietly sent to America until the London gossips wagged their tongues in another direction and the hapless young man learned his lesson. Making the most of his exile, Nigel vowed to see as much of America as time permitted. He arrived at Fort Laramie in late April, saw Shannon walking across the parade ground, and decided to stick around a while.

Another new arrival at Fort Laramie was Poker Alice, so named for her expertise in the game. A small brunette with huge dark eyes and voluptuous curves, Alice came up from Cheyenne with a wagon load of dance hall girls and enough money to build a saloon. She looked over Fort Laramie with a critical eye, saw Blade striding across the square and promptly proclaimed business opportunities excellent in the male-dominated fort.

Shannon saw little of Blade during the following days. Much of the time he was out on patrol or occupied with duties. No further attempts were made on her life, and Major Vance assumed their man was keeping a low profile to avoid capture. Since he was needed elsewhere, Vance dismissed Sargeant O'Brien from guard duty. Vance and Blade also discontinued their surveillance of the trading post. They concluded that Bailey's partner had somehow learned the gold was out of his reach and had given up on it.

Two weeks after their tempestuous parting, Blade appeared at Shannon's door one night. It was all

Shannon could do to keep from throwing herself into his arms. With great effort she made her voice deliberately cool and remote.

"It's rather late, Blade. Is there something you wanted?" Damnation, didn't he know how much this was hurting her?

Blade's answer was to push past her and barge inside, slamming the door behind him. "We need to talk."

"Not if you've come to persuade me to continue this stupid pretense. I'm not ashamed of our love, why are you?"

"Ashamed? Never!" Blade vowed. "I told you before it's not the right time to—"

"Will there ever be a right time? You're no closer now to learning the identity of the gun smuggler than you ever were. Please leave, Blade."

"Dammit, Shannon, I miss you. I need you. What do I have to do to convince you?"

"Marry me, tomorrow, in the post chapel."

"I—it's not in your best interest right now."

"Good-night, Blade," Shannon said tightly. "If you've come merely to slake your lust, forget it. I'm not making myself available to you. I suggest you try one of those new girls who just arrived. I understand they're entertaining in their wagon until the new saloon is built."

"You know better than that," Blade said with quiet insistence. "What we have is special."

· As if to prove his words he seized her waist and drew her close, lowering his mouth to hers. The fury of his kiss forced her head back, the power of it parted her lips as he staked a harsh claim to her mouth. He wrapped his arms around her, surrounding her with his scent of excited, sexual male. He stole her breath and replaced it with his own. Resisting with all of her might, Shannon decided being in love was frustrating, maddening, painful.

"I want you, Little Firebird," Blade whispered, nibbling deliciously on her ear.

Shannon felt hot quick tears prick her eyes, and she blinked them away. If she gave in now and allowed him to make love to her, her pride would suffer serious damage. It took all the willpower she possessed to jerk herself from his arms. She had to stop him from doing what her heart pleaded for him to do.

"Please stop, Blade. You're making this difficult for both of us."

"You don't mean that."

Deliberately she turned her back on him.

"I won't make love with you. There is nothing more to discuss."

Flinging her around to face him, Blade's face grew granite-hard, his eyes remote. He always meant for them to be together, but not until Shannon was damn certain she knew what she was doing by marrying a half-breed. Shannon was impulsive and too damn stubborn for her own good. Someone had to keep a level head when they were together. Her cold denial made him want to lash out at her, to hurt her as she had hurt him by rejecting their love.

"Perhaps you're right, Shannon. Those new girls did look mighty tempting. Can't hurt to give one or two of them a try."

Whirling on his heel, he slammed out the door and into the night, leaving Shannon numb with disbelief.

Shannon met Nigel Bruce quite by accident, or so she thought. Actually, Nigel had been waiting for just such an opportunity for days. He bumped into her during a sudden rainstorm, introduced himself, and offered to share his umbrella, which he never was without, no matter what the weather. At first Shannon was reluctant, but the young man's intriguing smile and open friendliness quite charmed her.

"Please allow me to see you home, Miss Branigan," Nigel said once he learned her name. "I'd be no gentleman if I allowed you to get soaked and become ill." He offered his arm and held the umbrella high over both their heads. Shannon saw no reason to refuse and soon they were chatting quite amicably.

Two days later she found herself seated next to Nigel at a dinner party given by Molly Greer. It was that same night, while walking home with Nigel, that she saw Blade lounging outside Poker Alice's wagon. The diminutive brunette wore a sheer clinging gown that indecently displayed her charms as she leaned against the hard wall of Blade's chest.

Damn him! Shannon thought scathingly. If he was trying to make her jealous, he was succeeding. The bright moonlight provided enough light for Shannon to see Blade smiling down into Alice's eyes. Abruptly she turned her head, too pained to watch whether or not he accompanied Alice inside the wagon.

Actually Blade had no intention of making love to Alice, though that might have been his objective originally. His heart just wasn't in it. He wanted only one woman—a chestnut-haired vixen too stubborn to heed what her mind and body told her. Then, from the corner of his eye he saw Shannon walk past on the arm of that remittance man from England. Though Blade had nothing personally against Nigel Bruce, whom he had met a day or two earlier, it made him green with envy to see him with Shannon. If she was trying to make him jealous, she was succeeding.

"Well, Injun, are you comin' inside with me or not?" Alice asked, wiggling against Blade provocatively. It titillated her senses to think of Blade as an Indian and she fantasized about him making love to her with savage brutality.

Gazing down into Alice's eyes, Blade pretended great interest—until Shannon and her escort were well out of sight. "Sorry, not tonight, Alice, maybe another time." He started to walk away.

"I'm the best," Alice claimed saucily.

Blade turned around and winked outrageously. "Why don't you let me be the judge of that? I'll be back."

"Soon, Injun, make it *real* soon," Alice called after his departing back.

Other renegades had taken Mad Dog's place harassing the army and the emigrants, notably the Sioux chief, Red Cloud, who constantly sapped the strength of Fort Phil Kearny. In late 1867 Red Cloud felt he had sufficiently weakened the garrison at Fort Kearny to attack. With more than one thousand warriors, he rode toward the fort, only to encounter Captain James Powell and a work detail on the way. The soldiers sought shelter behind an oval of wagon boxes and held off Red Cloud's forces for four and a half hours until reinforcements arrived. Consequently Red Cloud called off his attack on the fort during the battle that was thereafter known as the Wagon Box Fight.

The following summer word was received at Fort Laramie that all the forts along the Bozeman Trail were ordered abandoned by Washington, due mostly to Red Cloud's demand that they be closed. Red Cloud adamantly refused to talk peace unless Forts Reno, Phil Kearny and C.F. Smith, deep in Sioux hunting territory, were abandoned. There was talk of Red Cloud and his minions coming to Fort Laramie in the fall to sign a peace treaty after Washington's unprecedented step in yielding to Indian demands. Actually it was no great loss to Washington, for the forts were soon to be made obsolete by a railroad.

Blade burned each time he saw Shannon with Nigel Bruce, which was quite often. Shannon found she enjoyed the Englishman's company and he posed no danger to her where her heart was concerned. That part of her belonged to Blade no matter how she tried to deny it.

As the days passed Blade grew exceedingly frustrated. His investigation had stalled and he was losing Shannon because of it. Adding to his discontent was the fact that his favorite hunting knife had mysteriously disappeared. It had been a gift from his grandfather and he always carried it attached to his belt. But one day it turned up missing. He spent considerable time looking for it and decided it must have dropped from its scabbard while he was out on patrol. After a day or two he bought a new one.

Since nothing new had materialized in their investigation, Blade decided it was time to have a private conversation with Wade Vance to plan their next move. Blade crossed the parade ground to Vance's quarters, wondering if Shannon was entertaining that damn English remittance man tonight. Just the thought of her in another man's arms sent him into a jealous rage. If he was smart, he'd let Poker Alice soothe his terrible anguish. But he didn't. Strangely, Blade didn't want Alice. There was only one woman he wanted in his arms and in his bed.

Wade Vance answered Blade's knock, ushering him into his spartan quarters and offering him a drink. Blade accepted the partially filled glass and sprawled into a chair next to an open window. A hint of summer wafted in on a gentle breeze, reminding Blade of those years he had spent on the prairie with his mother's people. Vance poured himself a whiskey and sat opposite Blade.

"Have you learned anything new?" Vance asked hopefully.

"Nothing," Blade said sourly. "And frankly, I'm fed up with the entire matter. I'm losing Shannon because of it and it scares the hell out of me. I never thought I'd be lucky enough to find a woman like Shannon. It's difficult to believe she could love a half-breed like me."

"Shannon is smart," Vance volunteered. "She knows a good man when she sees one. Don't let this investigation come between the two of you, Blade. I'm perfectly willing to carry on alone. I was thinking that it's time I confided in Colonel Greer. It's possible one of his men is our culprit. Tomorrow I'll have a talk with Greer and inform him that you're a special agent working directly for the president."

"Is that wise?" Blade questioned thoughtfully.

"At this point we have no alternative. This man is dangerous. He's biding his time now, but he's killed once and will do so again. He's already tried to kill both you and Shannon. I think Colonel Greer deserves to know what is going on. If one of his men is involved, he might be able to provide a suspect."

"What about the gold?" Blade wondered.

"It's safe in my footlocker for the time being. Tomorrow I'll put it in Colonel Greer's hands for safekeeping. It will remain there until I take it to Washington. I wonder where Mad Wolf got all that gold?"

"Robbed a payroll wagon probably," Blade grunted. "Thank God no one knows it's here."

"That's one of the reasons I wanted to confide in Colonel Greer," Vance said. "The gold will be much safer in his office safe. If you want out of this, Blade, there will be no recriminations. I'll explain everything to the president when I report to him in the fall."

"I always finish what I set out to do," Blade said with quiet determination.

"What about Shannon?"

"I'll make things right with her somehow," Blade vowed. "I have to. I love her, but she stubbornly refuses to consider the consequences of marrying a half-breed."

"Shannon doesn't seem the type to rush recklessly into something without giving it careful thought. Go to her, Blade. Do what you must, but don't lose her."

In the difficult weeks ahead, Blade would have good reason to remember Wade Vance's parting words. But now only one thought existed in his mind as he left Wade's quarters.

Shannon.

He had to see her again, speak to her, hold her—make love to her. With grim purpose he crossed the parade ground, slipped past the sentry when his back was turned and, keeping to the shadows, approached Shannon's house. He smiled when he noted a light shining through the window. He stepped from the concealing shadows, then hastily withdrew again when the door opened and a man stepped through the opening.

"It's been a most pleasant evening, Shannon, thank you," Nigel Bruce said graciously.

Jealousy jolted through Blade when he saw that the Englishman held Shannon's hand in a most possessive manner.

"You're entertaining company, Nigel," Shannon returned. "You're just what I need right now."

Clenching his fists, Blade fought the urge to take Nigel Bruce by the scruff of his neck and toss him off the porch.

"There is a spring ball next week. Would you allow me the pleasure of your company?"

Shannon nearly refused, then thought better of it. Why shouldn't she have a good time while Blade was cavorting with whores? It wasn't as if Nigel could take Blade's place, but he was amusing enough to distract her from her dismal thoughts.

"I'd be happy to go with you, Nigel." Though she agreed readily enough, her heart wasn't really in it.

Expecting a refusal, Nigel was thrilled by Shannon's unexpected acceptance. "Splendid!" He was so pleased with himself that he grabbed Shannon and kissed her soundly on the lips before she realized what was happening. Then he turned abruptly and bounded down the steps. He passed within inches of Blade, whose rigid self-control was within seconds of shattering.

Shannon stood in the doorway staring thoughtfully after Nigel. She was shocked when Blade suddenly materialized from the deep shadows, his bronze features and midnight eyes grim with cold fury. He frightened her and she turned to flee into the house.

When she turned to slam the door in his face, he was close on her heels. Grasping her waist, he pushed her through the opening and followed her inside. He shoved the door shut with his foot and stood glaring down at her.

"It didn't take you long to replace me, did it?" he spat disgustedly. "Have you bedded the remittance man yet?" He hated himself for taunting her so cruelly, but he couldn't stop the words from tumbling past his lips.

"How dare you!" Shannon's Irish temper exploded, hitting Blade squarely. "I'm no longer any of your concern. I begged you to marry me, but you refused. It's my business now who I see or don't see." Not one to mince words, Shannon was ever forthright in expressing her mind.

"It wasn't my idea to break our—our—"

"—affair," Shannon said bluntly, for lack of a better word.

"Dammit, Shannon, what we had was no shoddy affair," Blade said defensively, fighting the self-accusing thoughts plaguing him.

"Prove it!" she challenged. "Marry me."

"I will, but not now."

"Good-bye, Blade. Mama always said I inherited the Branigan pride, and I've choked down enough pride for your sake. I can swallow no more. Keeping our love secret and sneaking around shames me, and I'll have no more of it."

"God, you're beautiful when you're angry, Little Firebird." Blade grinned with easy arrogance as their gazes locked in silent struggle, each aware of something binding and powerful building between them. Shannon's breathing grew shallow and labored. Blade hadn't so much as touched her and yet she felt the heat of his caress, tasted the flame blazing inside him.

Before Shannon could stop him, he pulled her up against him and his lips were on hers. He caught her with her mouth open and took full advantage of it.

While she struggled and shoved impotently on his hard, unyielding chest, Blade kissed her with a power and passion that was so blatantly sensual, Shannon felt hot spurts of blood surge through her veins despite all her efforts to remain unresponsive.

One muscular arm hooked firmly around her; her soft curves molded against his ungiving length. He kissed her hungrily, aggressively, his tongue plunging deeply into her warm, moist mouth. Finally, just as he intended, she quit struggling and her moans of outrage changed to soft little sighs of rapture.

"Can you honestly say another man stirs you the way I do?" Blade asked when he finally released her.

Shaken, Shannon remained stubbornly mute, unable to move or deny his words. "I thought not," Blade smirked smugly.

Finally Shannon found her voice, a strangled sound deep in her throat. "Why are you doing this to me?"

"Because I want you. Because I can't stand this coldness between us—and because I love you."

"But apparently not enough," Shannon observed with bitter emphasis.

"More than you know," Blade acknowledged cryptically. "I want to make things right between us."

"How do you intend to do that?" Shannon challenged skeptically. "Are you prepared to give up on this investigation?"

The time came for Blade to make a decision and he did, in his usual forthright manner. Life without Shannon was no life at all.

"No, but I'm ready to tell the world how much I love you, that you're mine until the end of time."

"Oh Blade, I love you so much," Shannon cried, her eyes bright with unshed tears.

"Show me how much, Little Firebird," Blade groaned, his need for Shannon an aching torture.

With an agile combination of hard muscles and strong shoulders, Blade swung Shannon up in his arms and carried her to the dimly lit bedroom.

Carefully, he lowered her atop the soft surface of the bed. Leaning over her, he cupped her flushed face, gently brushed her eyes, nibbled her bottom lip and whispered into her mouth, "I'm going to light a lamp so I can see all of you."

He was back in a few minutes and sat on the bed facing her, one long leg folded beneath him, the other foot balanced on the floor. For a long breathless moment, he did no more than gaze at her, lightly caressing her upturned cheek, thinking how incredibly lovely she was. He leaned over her, kissed the moist corner of her mouth and said, "I'm going to love you, Shannon Branigan, and tomorrow we'll see the chaplin and arrange for our marriage."

"Yes, oh yes," Shannon agreed eagerly as his arms came around her and his hands moved lovingly over her body.

She made no effort to assist as Blade began removing her clothes—first her shoes, then her stockings, gliding them languidly down her legs and off. Next her petticoat came away with effortless ease. Then Blade was kissing her again, his hands moving deftly beneath the folds of her skirt. His breath was hot against her cheek, igniting a fever deep within her. Shannon arched to him, threw her head back and sighed as his questing fingers skimmed her trembling thighs. Instinctively her knees fell apart and she shivered in delicious expectation.

Shannon felt as though she might burst into flame, and with breathless whimpers urged him to touch her where she burned the hottest. With an impatient gesture Blade removed her dress and tossed it aside.

With practiced skill, Blade kissed and caressed the trembling woman in his arms until she was squirming and thrashing, begging him to end his loving torment. When his heated lips climbed the soft mound of her breast and closed around its arching peak, sucking on the hard nipple, the air exploded from her lungs. She was aware only of the sweet aching pleasure his lips gave her as they moved over her chest to her other nipple, his teeth raking tantalizingly over the sensitive crest. Boldly his tongue toyed with her before taking her fully into his warm wet mouth to suck vigorously.

Shannon murmured in protest as Blade's warmth left her, but he returned in moments, pressing her to his naked flesh, once again kissing and sucking her breasts. Shannon was almost beside herself with ecstasy. At last his lips released his sweet treasure and slid down over her delicate ribs. Her eyes flew open when his hands rested on her hips, lifting her to the hot, teasing warmth of his mouth.

"I want to taste you all over," Blade murmured against the trembling flesh of her belly.

"Blade . . ."

Opening his mouth he touched his tongue to her.

Shannon called his name again and spasmed from intense pleasure. Abruptly his hands slid around to grip her bare bottom, wanting to take her all the way with his mouth. Holding her close he sank his face deeply into her, feasting, stroking her with his tongue until she was panting and tossing in wild delirium. The sweet tension was unbearable, spiraling hot and molten upward from where he was kissing her. It felt so marvelous she never wanted Blade to stop, would surely die if he did.

"Blade, please, please . . ."

Blade's hands tightened, cupping her rounded bottom, teasing, lashing, until he took her over the top. Her climax came in jerking spasms, her fingers digging into his bronze back. He stayed with her while total ecstasy claimed her, until the last tiny tremor passed and her body went limp. With gentle, trembling hands, Blade placed Shannon atop him, soothing, patting, pressing kisses to her damp temple until her pulse slowed and her breathing returned to normal.

"Come with me, Little Firebird," he whispered as he lifted her hips and sank full and deep into her.

"I don't think I can," Shannon sighed, limp and sated.

"It's all right, love, just relax," Blade said, smiling with wicked delight. Did he know something she didn't?

Then he began a slow, steady surging of his hips and miraculously, a wild sweet pleasure built inside Shannon. She gasped, amazed that desire could flare again so swiftly.

And so it went throughout the night. Sometimes their mating was as hot and wild as an inferno, other times slow, lazy, sweet. They made love, rested, then made love again—and again—until sheer exhaustion plunged them into a deep dreamless slumber, still clinging to one another, arms and legs entwined.

Blade was annoyed to discover he had overslept the next morning. He intended to be gone long before daylight. But sleeping with Shannon in his arms had been so incredibly wonderful that he had slept peacefully for hours. He dressed hurriedly and quietly so as not to disturb Shannon. Guilt assailed him when he thought how thoroughly he had exhausted his Little Firebird. She had been extraordinarily sensual last night, so wonderfully wanton, so delightfully sexual. God, he loved her! She looked like an angel lying in bed, her skin flushed from his loving, her mouth swollen from his kisses. He didn't have the heart to waken her.

Before Blade let himself quietly out the door, he scribbled a brief note and placed it on the pillow beside Shannon. He meant what he said when he told her they would talk to the chaplain today about their wedding. But first he wanted to change his clothes and tell Wade Vance about his decision.

Blade had just reached his quarters when he was grabbed from behind. His hands were tightly bound and he was forcibly restrained before he realized what was happening. Snapping his head around, Blade was stunned to see Lieutenant Goodman grinning evilly at him while three burly enlisted men held him prisoner.

"You're under arrest for murder, Injun."

Chapter Eighteen

Shannon stretched luxuriously, her body tired beyond belief yet feeling more content and at peace than she could ever remember. Knowing that Blade loved her and that they would soon be man and wife made up for all the heartache she'd suffered in the past. The terrible war, losing her beloved father and brother, being forced from the home she loved, were all sad memories she intended to bury. With open arms Shannon embraced the future. A wild new land, a steadfast love, and the promise of tomorrow all beckoned to her.

She spied Blade's note immediately. His special scent still clung to the pillow as she snatched up the single sheet of paper. A dreamy smile curved her kiss-bruised lips as she read his words. He'd be back after he talked with Wade Vance and informed him of their plans to wed immediately.

Since it was Saturday, Shannon took her time bathing and dressing, reliving every delicious detail of their night together. She had thought it physically impossible for a man to love a woman so many times in so many ways, but Blade had proven just how little she knew. His stamina was amazing, she thought, giggling.

Shannon ate a leisurely breakfast, devouring every morsel; her appetite was enormous. But as morning edged toward noon, she began to fret. A nagging fear tugged at the corner of her brain, an unexplained dread that could only be rationalized in her woman's intuition. As she paced her small parlor, anxiety rode Shannon, and some sixth sense told her Blade needed her. She had no idea where to begin looking for him, but Major Vance's quarters seemed like as good a place as any.

As Shannon strode across the parade ground, she noted the increased activity, more than was warranted for a Saturday morning. Alarm bells went off in her head, though she was unable to give her fear a reason.

"Shannon, have you heard the news?"

Shannon whirled to see Claire Greer hurrying toward her, bursting to tell someone her scandalous news. Shannon's heart beat like a triphammer; she didn't want to ask but knew she must.

"What news, Claire? What happened?"

"Major Vance was murdered in his quarters last night."

"Oh, no!" came Shannon's shocked reply. She was truly fond of the man and devastated to learn of his death. She could well imagine what it would do to Blade, for they had been close friends for years. No wonder he hadn't shown up yet. She turned to leave. Blade would need her now.

"Wait. There is more," Claire said, placing a restraining hand on Shannon's arm.

Impatient to leave, Shannon slanted an inquiring look at Claire. "Well, what is it? Have they arrested the killer?"

"Yes, and you'll never be able to guess who it is."

"Claire, I don't have time for guessing games."

"The half-breed was arrested early this morning and charged with Major Vance's murder."

A look of absolute horror crossed Shannon's features. Claire smirked in smug satisfaction.

"Blade? Impossible!" Shannon denied vehemently. "Blade wouldn't kill anyone, especially Major Vance. They were close friends."

"Friends?" Claire repeated, openly skeptical. "They hardly knew one another. Blade kept mostly to himself. No one knows him well enough to say whether or not he is capable of murder. He's part savage, for heaven's sake!" Claire emphasized, as if that explained everything.

"I don't have time to stand here arguing with you, I've got to go to Blade," Shannon called over her shoulder as she sped off. She went directly to the guardhouse, demanding to see Blade.

"I'm sorry, Miss Branigan, the prisoner isn't allowed visitors," the sargeant in charge informed her.

"But I must see Blade. He's innocent!" Shannon persisted doggedly.

"You'll have to get permission from Colonel Greer."

Turning on her heel, Shannon hurried away to find Colonel Greer. Fortunately she located him in his office.

"Colonel Greer!" she cried, bursting into the room. "It's not true! Blade didn't kill Major Vance. He's innocent!"

"This is none of your concern, Shannon," Greer said sternly. "I know you harbor a certain fondness for the breed—after all he did rescue you from Mad Wolf—but none of us really knew him before he joined your wagon train as scout. He appeared out of nowhere. Doesn't that seem strange to you?"

Shannon was on the verge of blurting out all she knew about Blade—his investigation, his connection to Major Vance, and that he couldn't have killed the man because he was with her—but at the last moment she thought better of it. If Blade wanted Colonel Greer to know, he would have told him by now. Why hadn't he? she wondered. Didn't he realize the seriousness of the situation?

"Can I see Blade, Colonel?" Shannon asked hopefully.

"It would serve no purpose," Greer replied absently as he began sorting through papers on his desk. His gesture was meant to signal the end of the interview. "If you will excuse me, I have reports to see to."

"Please, Colonel Greer," Shannon begged, refusing to budge, "at least tell me why you think Blade killed Major Vance?"

"You certainly are persistent," Greer sighed wearily. He'd had a hectic morning, ever since Major Vance's body was found in a pool of congealing blood and his quarters literally torn apart.

"If I'm insistent, it's because I know Blade is innocent."

Greer regarded Shannon keenly, started to say something, then changed his mind, saying instead, "The evidence is irrefutable. Blade's knife was found imbedded in Wade Vance's back. You know the one I'm talking about, it has a carved bone handle and is quite impressive. He wore it in a scabbard hooked to his belt and seemed quite fond of it. And if that isn't enough, Major Vance's money belt was found in Blade's room."

Shannon was stunned. She knew exactly which knife the Colonel referred to, Blade was rarely seen without it. But strangely, she couldn't recall him wearing it last night. In fact, she was certain he wasn't. "I'm sure there is an explanation," she offered lamely.

Blade was with her the entire night. He couldn't have killed anyone. She would have shouted it to the world, but she needed to speak with Blade first. She didn't want to do anything to hurt him.

"If there is, Blade didn't offer one," Greer muttered, growing impatient. "I'm sorry, Shannon, you'll simply have to leave now. I'm much to busy to continue this conversation."

"I won't leave until you give me permission to see Blade," Shannon insisted stubbornly. "What harm can it do?"

Colonel Greer frowned, annoyed. Apparently, the only way he was going to get rid of Shannon was by granting her request. Didn't she know it wasn't going to change a thing? Blade was guilty of murder and would pay with his life. Taking out a sheet of paper, he scribbled a few words and handed it to Shannon. "Show this to the guard. It's a visitor's pass. You'll be allowed to see Blade for a few moments."

"Thank you, Colonel. This means a lot to me." She turned to leave.

"Shannon, wait. Just how involved are you with the half-breed?"

Shannon knew this was no time for confessions or admissions. "Blade is—my friend. I want to help him." She whirled and hurried off, the visitor's pass clutched tightly in her fist.

Once the guard, Sargeant Tyler, was shown the pass, Shannon had no difficulty gaining entrance to the guardhouse. She smiled at the smitten sargeant so engagingly that he even agreed to allow her a few moments of privacy, though he couldn't imagine why Shannon was so concerned about a half-breed. True, most of the soldiers liked and respected the man, but obviously he had kept his true nature hidden.

"Be careful, Miss Branigan," Sargeant Tyler warned. "The man is a killer."

Disdaining to give an answer, Shannon walked through the door into the dim corridor that led to the cells. There were three tiny cubicles, only one of them occupied. Blade lay on a bare mattress atop a narrow bunk, his long legs hanging over the end. There was nothing else in the small cell except a bucket placed discreetly in a corner, a table on which sat a pitcher and tin cup, and a three-legged stool. Shannon couldn't bear to think of Blade in such dismal surroundings. She approached the bars, her steps nearly soundless, but Blade heard her and sprang to his feet instantly.

"Damnation, Shannon, what are you doing here?"

"It isn't true, Blade! Why don't you tell them you were with me last night? Isn't it time Colonel Greer was informed about your investigation and friendship with Major Vance?"

"Do you think I would ever say anything to hurt you? No one must ever know I was with you last night."

"That doesn't make sense, Blade. All that matters is that you are cleared of murder charges. Can't you tell them Major Vance was your friend? That you were working together by order of the president?"

"With Wade dead there is no one to testify in my defense. It doesn't seem possible that—that he's gone. I knew our man was clever, but when he killed Wade he went too far."

"Tell Colonel Greer about the investigation," Shannon urged. "There must be someone willing to speak up for you."

"Only three people knew," Blade said tightly. "Me, Wade, and President Johnson."

"Then wire the President if that's what it takes!"

"You don't understand. I'm on my own in this. President Johnson warned that he'd be unable to help if I got myself into a bind. He's in enough trouble with congress for concentrating too much effort on the Western frontier and not enough on the reconstruction of the South. They are upset that he granted an unconditional pardon to all persons involved in the Southern rebellion that resulted in the war. The latest news is that congress is charging him with violating the Tenure of Office Act and have begun impeachment proceedings. My problems are insignificant compared to his."

"Not to me," Shannon whispered shakily. "Tell Colonel Greer, let him decide."

"They have strong evidence against me." Blade

seemed in shock over Major Vance's death and Shannon thought his reasoning seriously flawed. It wasn't like him to give up so easily. "My knife was found embedded in Wade's back."

"I know, Colonel Greer told me. How could such a thing happen?"

"I noticed my knife missing a few days ago but assumed it was lost."

"Someone planned this very carefully," Shannon mused thoughtfully. "Do you have any idea who did it?"

"No, except—never mind, there is no proof to confirm my suspicions. You'd better go, love, it's senseless to become involved with me now. There will be a speedy trial and—well, no sense speculating."

Blade didn't need to elaborate. Shannon knew exactly what he meant, and she didn't intend to let it happen. "If you don't tell the Colonel you were with me last night, I will. There is no way you could have killed Major Vance while you were making love to me."

"I'll deny it," Blade said grimly. "I'll say you're merely lying to save my life. Do you think I'd knowingly allow you to ruin your reputation?"

"Blade, please . . ."

"I won't hear of it."

"Time is up, Miss Branigan."

Sargeant Tyler stood at the end of the hallway as he called his warning, then discreetly withdrew, allowing Shannon a few moments to say good-bye.

"Kiss me good-bye, Little Firebird. I'm sorry about —everything. I never intended for it to end like this."

"It won't," Shannon vowed stubbornly. "I love you. Nothing is going to happen to you."

Straining against the bars, she lifted her lips as Blade's mouth descended to meet hers. His kiss was slow and sweet and gentle, filled with longing and remorse. He acted like a man already condemned. Evidently he hadn't counted on Shannon's strength and daring, for she had no intention of letting him die.

During the next two days, Shannon tried to see Colonel Greer and was turned away every time. She was deliberately being barred from the colonel's office and resented the fact that he was avoiding her. With Blade's trial set to take place soon, she needed to act swiftly. Shannon tried calling on the colonel at his house, but even that didn't work. Molly Greer stood staunchly by her husband's side on this issue, advising Shannon to leave this nasty business to the army.

In all the confusion, Shannon forgot about the spring dance until Nigel Bruce reminded her. How could she dance when Blade was languishing behind bars, in danger of losing his life? She thought to refuse Nigel but quickly changed her mind. It occurred to her that the dance offered a perfect opportunity to find a few minutes alone with Colonel Greer. Nigel was thrilled when Shannon told him she hadn't forgotten and was in fact looking forward to attending the dance with him.

Shannon waited anxiously for the day of the dance to arrive. She couldn't wait to tell Colonel Greer the truth and watch his face when he learned just how wrong he was about Blade. She didn't care what Blade said, she couldn't stand by and say nothing in his defense.

Dressed in her best gown of shimmering green satin, Shannon had never looked lovelier. She had managed to save it throughout the war and bring it with her. The puff sleeves stopped just above the elbow and her waist appeared miniscule compared to the bouffant skirt that swirled around her green dancing slippers and trim silk-clad ankles. Her rich chestnut hair crowned her head like a halo, a perfect frame for her splendid features. Nigel was stunned by her beauty and said so.

It was such a pleasant May evening that Shannon needed only a light wrap as they walked the short distance to the clubhouse. Shannon did not lack for dance partners during the evening, though it rankled to know that of all the men present, only Colonel Greer seemed to avoid her.

It was nearly eleven o'clock when the opportunity to confront Colonel Greer presented itself. Shannon observed him slipping out a side door to enjoy a cigar. She promptly sent Nigel after punch, and the moment he disappeared into the crush of people she hurried off after the colonel. She found him standing alone, blowing smoke into the scented May night.

"Colonel Greer, may I have a word with you?" Her voice was soft and pleading.

"Shannon!" An annoyed frown furrowed the colonel's brow. He had spent considerable time this evening avoiding Shannon and he'd nearly succeeded, until the urge for a smoke drove him outside. He was none too pleased to find himself at Shannon's mercy after all. "This is neither the time nor place to discuss anything of a serious nature." If his words were meant to discourage, they failed miserably.

"There is no proper time or place when a man's life is at stake," Shannon returned quietly.

"My dear," Colonel Greer said placatingly, "why have you appointed yourself Blade's defender?"

"Because Blade is innocent. Bringing him to trial is a travesty of justice. And I intend to tell you why."

"Must you? The dance—see me Monday."

"Please, Colonel, hear me out."

A frustrated sigh hissed through Greer's teeth. "Very well, Shannon, just make it brief. Molly will have my hide if I desert her too long."

"Has Blade said anything in his defense?"

"He'll have the opportunity at his trial next week."

"Then it's up to me," Shannon mumbled, half to herself. "Blade is a special investigator for the president. He and Major Vance were working together on a case."

At first Greer looked incredulous, then he threw back his head and laughed. "My dear, how do you come up with such outlandish stories? Don't you think I'd know if that were true? In the first place, it's highly unlikely that you would be privy to such confidential information and I would not."

"I learned by accident and was sworn to secrecy," Shannon explained. "They were investigating a man suspected of smuggling guns to the Indians. Only recently, they learned that two men were involved instead of just one. Clive Bailey is dead and couldn't name his partner, but if you find him you'll find Major Vance's killer."

"Clive Bailey was a scoundrel," Greer concurred thoughtfully. "Taking you against your will was a despicable act, but there is absolutely no proof that he was involved in gun smuggling. I'm afraid this whole thing is but a figment of your imagination and too far-fetched for belief. Now I'm going to ask you a question. Are you in love with Blade?"

Shannon flushed. "Yes, I love Blade," she admitted, her chin tilted at a stubborn angle. "I'm not ashamed to admit it."

"Ahhh, that explains this compulsive need to defend him," Greer said astutely. "I fear you've picked the wrong man to love, my dear."

"Blade was with me that night—all night—and couldn't have killed Major Vance!" Shannon blurted out.

Greer blanched, properly scandalized by Shannon's baldfaced statement. "I'll forget you said that, Shannon. I realize you are distraught and apt to say things you don't mean."

"Everything I just said is the truth."

"You actually believe what you told me about Blade and Vance being special investigators, don't you?"

"I'd swear to it on the graves of my father and brother."

"Hmmm, very well, if you feel that strongly about it I'll wire Washington, but meanwhile Blade's trial will proceed as scheduled. If Washington confirms what you've just told me he will be freed. But—truthfully, I don't put much faith in it."

"All I ask is that you make an effort to learn the truth," Shannon responded. "Will you notify me when you receive a reply?"

"You'll be the first to know *if* I receive a reply," Greer stressed doubtfully.

"Here you are, Shannon, I've been looking for you."

Nigel appeared at Shannon's side holding two cups of punch. "I had the devil's own time getting these in the crush of people around the refreshment table."

"I—it was stifling inside. I needed air," Shannon offered lamely. "Evidently Colonel Greer was of a same mind."

Nigel greeted Greer in a friendly manner, then said to Shannon, "Shall we go inside?"

"Would you mind if we left, Nigel? I've suddenly developed a headache."

"Of course not, Shannon. I'll get your wrap," Nigel said, concern coloring his words. He slanted an accusing look at Colonel Greer, then took Shannon's arm and led her inside.

"I'm sorry I spoiled your evening," Shannon apologized as they strolled across the parade ground.

"You didn't spoil anything, Shannon," Nigel assured her. "Did Colonel Greer say something to upset you?"

"I—no, certainly not. It's just this nasty headache."

"Ah, yes, the headache," Nigel echoed, not at all convinced.

By now they had reached Shannon's door. "I wish you a speedy recovery. May I kiss you goodnight? I've never met a woman like you before, Shannon, and I want us to be more than friends. I'll be going back to England one day soon. Perhaps I can convince you to come with me as my wife."

Shannon blanched. She never meant for things to progress this far with Nigel. The kindest thing she could do now was to put a quick end to his hopes.

"I'm sorry, Nigel, if I led you on, but you can never be more than a friend to me. It would be best for all concerned if we don't see one another again. My heart is engaged elsewhere."

"There is no hope?" Nigel asked, strangely bereft. He knew he could change his life around with Shannon as his wife.

"None," Shannon said. "I love him more than my own life."

"Do I know the man?"

"I—no." What good would it do to tell Nigel about Blade? Shannon reasoned.

"Then I reckon I'll be moving on in a day or two," Nigel said slowly. "I suddenly have the overwhelming urge to visit California before I return to England."

Shannon had no idea what sin Nigel had committed back in England to disgrace his family, but she recognized the spark of decency in him. He wasn't a bad sort and was almost always a perfect gentleman where she was concerned. She hoped that when he had lived down his disgrace and learned his lesson, he'd go home and make a brilliant match.

Shannon vowed not to bother Colonel Greer again until he received an answer to the telegram sent to Washington in Blade's behalf. But when the morning before the day of the trial arrived and she still hadn't heard a word, Shannon dismissed school at noon and presented herself at Greer's office. Evidently, he was expecting her for she was ushered into his office immediately.

"Blade's trial is tomorrow, Colonel. Did you send the telegram?" Shannon asked. Preliminaries had no place in a conversation when a man's life was at stake.

"I sent it," Greer acknowledged curtly.

He had in fact sent a telegram after he spoke to Shannon. A fair man, the notion of convicting an innocent man didn't sit well with Greer. If there was a modicum of truth in Shannon's allegations he wanted to know. Greer assumed an answer would be forthcoming immediately if Blade was in truth a special investigator for the President. But nearly a week elapsed with no response to his inquiry. Naturally he treated the President's failure to reply as a clear indication of Blade's guilt. He assumed that if Blade was a special agent the President wouldn't hesitate to come to his defense.

Colonel Greer's telegram reached the hands of President Johnson's personal secretary at the worst possible time. Distraught over impeachment proceedings and his testimony before a congressional committee, the secretary, loathe to bother the President at so crucial a time, made a decision to lay the telegram aside until after the trial. It didn't sound at all urgent, asking only if a half-breed named Swift Blade was a special investigator for the President. He took it upon himself to withhold the telegram from President Johnson until after the vote, which was scheduled for May 26. An earlier vote on May 16 fell one vote short for passage.

Of course neither Shannon nor Greer could have known that, as Shannon asked, "Have you received a reply?"

Greer regarded Shannon with pity. "No, Shannon, I've heard nothing. Blade's trial will proceed as planned. Since military law prevails at Fort Laramie he'll be tried by a panel of officers consisting of myself, Captain Delaney and Lieutenant Goodman. You can be certain we will weigh the evidence carefully before passing sentence. Justice will be served."

"Justice! I know the kind of justice Blade will receive," Shannon spat, turning on her heel and slamming out the door. "Before God I swear you will not hang Blade!"

Blade's face was carefully blank as the charges were read against him.

"How do you plead?" Colonel Greer asked.

"Not guilty," Blade replied, his voice firm and unshakable.

In swift order the court's evidence was presented. The argument for conviction was strong, the evidence found at the scene incriminating. Intuitively Blade realized it would take no less than the President of the United States to save his life, otherwise he would surely die. That thought sent his heart plummeting to his feet. The President was hundreds of miles away.

When Blade was finally allowed to testify in his own defense, he revealed his status as special agent working with Major Vance to stop gun smugglers from selling illegal weapons to the Indians.

"Do you have proof of that?" asked Lieutenant Goodman.

"I have no written proof," Blade returned, "if that is what you're asking. But if you will wire the President I'm certain he will verify my words."

"I did just that, over a week ago," Greer revealed.

Immediately Blade brightened. Surely President Johnson wouldn't let him die, would he? "Then this trial is unnecessary. I would never kill Wade Vance, he was my friend. I had no motive. Once I am free I swear I will find the real killer."

"The President never answered my telegram," Greer said with harsh denial. "You weren't important enough to warrant an answer."

The trial progressed swiftly after that. Lieutenant Goodman laughed outright when Blade claimed he had been an officer in the Union army during the war and afterwards. Captain Delaney had always liked Blade, but the evidence against him was too strong for the conscientious officer to ignore. After the testimony he had no choice but to agree with the persuasive Lieutenant Goodman and a reluctant but convinced Colonel Greer. Blade was unaminously convicted of premeditated murder with robbery as the motive. It had been pointed out during the trial that Vance's quarters were thoroughly ransacked and his money belt found in Blade's room.

Colonel Greer's voice was properly subdued when he pronounced sentence. In two days Blade was to be hung by the neck until dead. The news spread like wildfire throughout the fort. Shannon was nearly prostrate with grief when she heard. She found it impossible to believe someone as honorable as Blade could be condemned to death. He was too young, too vital; she loved him too much to even consider his death. So she didn't.

Instead, Shannon calmly planned Blade's escape. The Branigan courage had been ingrained in her since birth. That and her love and absolute confidence in Blade's innocence lent her the strength and daring necessary to undertake so bold a task. Two days wasn't much time, but God willing it would be enough.

She had no idea fate was already at work in her behalf. It came in the form of a slim young man who rode into Fort Laramie in the company of several trappers.

Chapter Nineteen

Shannon was pleasantly surprised when Colonel Greer agreed to see her the morning after Blade's trial. When once again she pleaded for Blade's life and argued his innocence, Colonel Greer expressed true remorse for having to end a man's life. But since he found no evidence to suggest Blade wasn't guilty of the crime, he felt dutybound to follow the dictates of the law.

"Justice will be served, my dear," he said grimly. "I appreciate your feelings, but the trial was a fair one. Is there anything else I can do for you?"

"I'd like to see Blade before—before—"

"I don't think that is wise, Shannon."

"Please, I must see him."

Unbidden tears came to her eyes, producing just the picture Shannon wished to convey. A compassionate man, Colonel Greer expressed true sympathy for Shannon and her ill-fated love, and felt compelled to oblige.

"Ten minutes, Shannon. You can have ten minutes with Blade. I'll write you a pass."

Having been granted that much, Shannon squared her shoulders and asked for more. "I'd like to speak with Blade alone."

"It's against my better judgment, but you have my permission," Greer allowed. "I'll note in the pass that you are to be given ten minutes privacy."

Two more days, Blade thought with bleak resignation. The day after tomorrow his life would end as if he had never existed, and there wasn't a damn thing he could do about it. His one regret was leaving Shannon. Their times together had been too few, their moments of ecstasy too brief. Yet he was grateful for what they did have; few couples were lucky enough to find so much. Then another terrible thought assailed him. What if Shannon was carrying his child? It would be difficult for her to raise a child alone, but mercifully she had a family she could go to for support. Unfortunately, that thought offered little comfort, for he'd not live to see the son or daughter he sired.

Damnation! Blade cursed, striking the bars in frustration. Why hadn't the President answered Colonel Greer's telegram? Surely the man wouldn't let him hang for a crime he didn't commit, would he? Blade refused to believe he'd been abandoned, preferring to think that a last-minute reprieve would arrive fully explaining his position and exonerating him.

Suddenly the guardroom door swung open and Shannon stood poised on the threshold. His heart beating furiously, Blade watched her walk down the long corridor leading to his cell. Evidently she had convinced Greer to allow them a few moments alone, for Sargeant Tyler did not accompany her.

"Shannon, you shouldn't have come," Blade said, devouring her with his eyes. This last sight of the woman he loved would have to last him into eternity.

"Don't say anything," Shannon whispered, deliberately turning her back to the guardroom door. "Listen carefully. I'm going to get you out of here."

"Dammit, Shannon," Blade hissed from between clenched teeth, "stay out of this! I forbid you to do anything rash."

"Forbid all you like, Blade, I won't let you die. I love you. If there is a way to set you free, I'll find it. Not tonight, maybe, but tomorrow night, I swear it."

"There is nothing you can do, Little Firebird," Blade said, smiling wistfully. "If the president refused to acknowledge me or my work, what do you expect to accomplish?"

"Miracles," Shannon said cryptically. "The president doesn't love you as I do. I'll think of something. Just be prepared to act swiftly."

"I'd never forgive myself if something happened to you."

"I'd never forgive myself if I didn't try to stop this travesty of justice."

"Time is up, Miss Branigan." Sargeant Tyler stood at the end of the dim corridor, holding the door open for Shannon.

"Kiss me, Blade, and wish me luck," Shannon whispered almost frantically. She had to free Blade! If he perished, something inside of her would wither and die along with him.

Their parting kiss was sweet and slow and so filled with love. Shannon couldn't stop the tears that gathered in her eyes.

"Good-bye, Little Firebird," Blade choked out. He was so certain he would never see her again that his eyes filled with tears.

"Not good-bye, Blade, never good-bye. We'll meet again, maybe not soon, but we *will* see each other again. Tomorrow night, be ready." Without another word, she turned and walked away.

Though Blade knew in his heart there was little Shannon could do to free him, he loved her all the more for her indomitable spirit and incorrigible optimism. He adored her for her unflagging courage and giving nature. If will alone could free him, Shannon would surely find a way.

Shannon spent the remaining hours of that day, including those she should have spent sleeping, formulating then discarding dozens of plans to free Blade from jail. Each one was worked out meticulously in her mind, then promptly rejected. When morning arrived Shannon had finally settled on a strategy that *could* work—provided she found an accomplice. Alone, she hadn't a prayer of freeing Blade, but with an accomplice her chances improved dramatically. The problem was locating someone willing to break the law. A wide smile lit Shannon's features when she finally came up with the name of a man who just might be persuaded to join her in her madcap scheme.

"I came as soon as I received your message, Shannon. What is so urgent? Why must I tell no one?"

Shannon had asked one of her Indian students to take the message to Nigel Bruce, knowing it would be more difficult to trace that way.

"Come inside and close the door, Nigel. I don't want anyone to hear us."

"This *is* serious, isn't it?"

"A man's life is at stake."

"A man's life! Are you referring to the half-breed they call Blade? There are rumors circulating about the two of you but I put no faith in them." Shannon flinched at the hint of reproach in Nigel's voice.

"I don't know what you've heard, Nigel," Shannon said slowly, "but I want you to know the truth. I love Blade and he loves me. He is no more guilty of murder than I am. He is a special investigator for the president, but Colonel Greer refuses to believe him."

"I understand the evidence against him was quite convincing," Nigel said, more than a little shocked by

Shannon's astounding confession.

Nigel did not feel the same hatred for Indians the American harbored, but murder was a vile crime. Still, he trusted Shannon, had faith in her judgement, and if she said Blade was innocent, he tended to believe her.

"Someone deliberately made it look as if Blade committed the murder by planting false evidence," Shannon explained. "Blade may be capable of many things, but cold-blooded murder isn't one of them. Major Vance and Blade were friends, as well as being involved in an investigation that I cannot divulge at this time. You'll just have to trust me."

"I must confess I'm shocked by—what you have just told me," Nigel said. Thinking of Shannon with another man wasn't pleasant. Truth to tell, he had hoped . . . ah well, it just wasn't meant to be. "I do trust you, but I'm puzzled by your reason for confiding in me."

"I need your help, Nigel," Shannon said. "I can't do it alone."

"Do what? Surely you don't—no—not even you would dare," he sputtered, becoming excited at what Shannon was suggesting.

"I simply can't let Blade die without trying. I still believe the president will vindicate Blade, but it may be too late. We have to act tonight. I've already alerted Blade."

"Bloody good show!" Nigel crowed, properly impressed. "By God, I wish your heart weren't engaged elsewhere. I'll never find another woman like you."

"Then you'll help me?"

"Why not? I'm ripe for a bit of adventure. Should prove quite interesting. I don't know Blade well, but if you love him, he can't be a bad sort. Since there is no longer any hope for me where you are concerned, I'll be moving on soon. I may as well make a grand exit. Tell me your plan."

"How are you at stealing horses?"

"I understand one of my ancestors was a horse

thief, so I imagine I shall take to it naturally. Where is the horse I'm to steal?"

"It's Warrior, Blade's gray pony. He's stabled in the corral with the cavalry horses. I suggest you identify him in daylight, then go in for him after dark. Leave by the postern gate and take him across the river. Tether him in the grove of cottonwoods growing there. I'll give you a list of supplies to pack in the saddle bags. You must accomplish all this by ten o'clock tonight and be concealed behind the guardhouse when I pass by."

"What will happen then?" Nigel asked eagerly. His admiration for Shannon's fertile mind grew by leaps and bounds. Everything had been well thought out.

"Here's what we must do," Shannon said, leaning close. Then she proceeded to tell Nigel exactly what to expect.

"Grand, just grand!" Nigel exclaimed. "It should work if luck is with us."

"It *will* work. Luck has nothing to do with it," Shannon retorted. "You don't know how much your help means to me, Nigel." Her eyes grew misty with gratitude. "I'll always be grateful to you for your willingness to help and your trust."

"It will be a noble adventure, one I can tell my grandchildren about one day."

Shannon's head was awhirl as she carefully went over her plans for Blade's escape later that evening on the way to Molly Greer's house for the weekly women's suffrage meeting. When she arrived, she was more than a little shocked to see Poker Alice and several of the other saloon girls in attendance. It was to Molly's credit that she didn't turn them away, for they were all committed to women's rights, no matter what their calling.

As usual, the meeting adjourned shortly before ten o'clock and Shannon kept a strict eye on the time. As was her habit, she lingered a few minutes after the meeting, not wishing to rouse suspicion. While Molly was bidding the others good-night, Claire sidled up to Shannon, a nasty smile pasted on her face.

"Too bad about the half-breed," she smirked. "I always knew he was dangerous, him with his bold black eyes." She shuddered delicately. "I'll wager those big bronze hands have more power in them than five men put together. I'm certainly glad I never— knew him well. Not like you did," she hinted maliciously.

"Obviously you don't know what you are talking about," Shannon charged, curbing her famous temper. "I know Blade better than you do, and I know he's not capable of murder."

"I'll bet you do know him better," Claire hinted lewdly.

Shannon bristled angrily and would have lit into Claire despite her resolve if Molly hadn't joined them just then. "A rewarding meeting, wouldn't you say?" Molly was never happier than when espousing a cause.

"I was mortified when those loose women showed up," Claire said, feigning outrage.

"We all want the same thing, dear," Molly replied with mild reproof. Then she turned to Shannon, her eyes soft with sympathy. "Are you all right, Shannon? I know you were fond of Blade, and I admit I was shocked myself by what he did."

"Blade saved my life and I'll never believe him guilty of murder," Shannon said stubbornly. "Thank you for caring, Molly."

"Why, you're like my own daughter, Shannon. I'll always care about you."

Claire turned away in disgust, making an unladylike sound deep in her throat.

Mindful of the time and what lay ahead, Shannon said, "It's getting late, and I should be going. Goodnight, Molly, Claire."

"Goodnight, dear. Come to dinner next week."

"I will. Ask me any night," Shannon responded.

Her trek home across the dark parade ground led Shannon past the guardhouse, just as planned. All was quiet; the grounds were deserted except for the usual guards patrolling the outer perimeter of the fort. Shannon hoped Nigel had gotten Blade's horse out of the corral without mishap and was already in place waiting to implement the second phase of their plan.

As Shannon drew abreast of the guardhouse door, she suddenly threw herself to the hard-packed earth with sufficient force to knock the wind from her. Lifting her dirt-smudged face she cried out in a voice just loud enough to alert the guard inside the guardhouse. "Help, oh please, help me!"

The night was balmy, the guardhouse door open to catch the breeze, and the sergeant on duty responded instantly to a female in distress. Rushing out the door, he nearly stumbled over Shannon where she lay stretched out on the ground.

"Miss, what happened? Are you hurt?"

The young, newly promoted sargeant never had a prayer against Shannon's feminine wiles.

"I—I think so," Shannon said, her voice quavering. "I tripped over my hem and twisted my knee. I—I don't believe I can walk."

Recognition dawned as the sargeant helped Shannon rise. His arm steadied her as she swayed against him. "Why, Miss Branigan, what are you doing out by yourself this time of night?"

"I attended a meeting at the Greers'," Shannon explained, "and was on my way home. I don't think I can manage on my own . . . will you help me?" Her voice held a note of helplessness few men could resist.

A confused look spread over the sargeant's face. Southern-born and raised, his chivalrous nature demanded that he aid a lady in distress, while his sense of duty mandated that he not leave his post.

Sensing his dilemma, Shannon gazed up at him, fluttering her long lashes in a captivating manner. "Please assist me back to the Greers' house—it's closer," she suggested helpfully. She looked so appealing, so adorably dependent on him, that Sergeant Becker failed to consider the consequences. Besides, he'd only be away from his post a few minutes and the prisoner was locked securely behind bars.

"Of course I'll help you, Miss Branigan," offered the smitten young man. "Lean on me and I'll assist you back to the Greers'."

The moment Shannon limped away, leaning heavily against Sergeant Becker, a figure detached itself from the shadows at the side of the guardhouse and slipped inside the open door. Working against time, Nigel Bruce quickly pulled open the center drawer of the desk and found the keys to the cells exactly where Shannon had said they would be. On her previous visits she had observed where the duty officer kept them. Stealthily Nigel entered the cell area. Only one cell was in use, the occupant lying on the bare mattress.

"Blade, wake up, old boy!"

Years of training brought Blade instantly alert. He rolled to his side. "Who is it?"

"Nigel Bruce, old boy."

"What in the hell are you doing here this time of night?" Blade asked, his eyes narrowed suspiciously.

"Letting you out of here."

"What! How—"

"It's Shannon's idea, old boy. I'm just along for the adventure. Hurry, we haven't much time." The cell door swung open with a groan of protest. "Your horse is tethered across the river in a grove of cottonwood trees. You'll have to make your way there on foot."

"Where is the guard?" Blade asked, peering anxiously toward the guardroom.

"Shannon lured him away. She's quite a woman. But you must hurry," Nigel urged, "or all her planning will have been in vain."

Blade acted swiftly once the cell door was open, proving he had lost none of his skill or cunning.

Before leaving the cell he rolled the pillow and blanket to look as if a man were lying on the narrow bunk. Then Nigel carefully locked the cell door and followed Blade into the deserted guardroom. While Nigel replaced the keys exactly where he'd found them, Blade located his guns in a cupboard. Beside them he found his stolen knife, the one that had killed Major Vance. He strapped on his weapons and was ready to leave.

"I don't know how to thank you, Bruce," Blade said as they slipped out the door and around to the rear of the guardhouse where darkness protected them.

"You have Shannon to thank." Nigel grinned, relishing the grand escapade. "I merely lent my help."

"Will you give Shannon a message for me?"

"Of course, old boy, though I reckon it's the same one she asked me to relay to you."

"Tell Shannon I—I love her—and thank her for giving me back my life."

"I'll relay your message. Now I have one to deliver to you. Shannon said to tell you she'll wait for you to return for her—forever if necessary."

"I'll return, somehow I'll come back for Shannon. Farewell, Nigel Bruce." He extended his hand.

"Good-bye, Blade, good luck. Use the postern gate. It's unguarded."

Then Blade was gone, melting into the shadows. When Nigel turned around for a last look he had already disappeared, his moccasined feet moving silently and stealthily through the black night.

Meanwhile, Shannon arrived at Colonel Greer's house. The colonel was home and expressed great concern as he helped Shannon into the house. He summoned Molly to see to Shannon's injury, then turned his cool gaze to Sargeant Becker.

"Weren't you assigned duty at the guardhouse tonight?"

"Yes sir, but Miss Branigan needed help," the flustered young man explained. "I did what I felt was proper under the circumstances."

"We'll discuss this tomorrow, Sargeant. Return to your post."

Minutes later, Sargeant Becker reached the guardhouse. Nothing looked amiss, but just to be certain he looked in on the prisoner. Blade appeared to be sleeping soundly, much to Becker's relief, and he returned to the guardroom. At midnight his replacement, Sargeant Lark, arrived and Becker sought his bed in the barracks. When Sargeant Lark checked the prisoner, he found all in order.

"Prison break!" The word spread rapidly through the fort. The prisoner was discovered missing when breakfast was brought to him. It was to have been his last meal. No one could explain his mysterious disappearance. A thorough investigation was under way, but Colonel Greer was convinced it had happened when Sargeant Becker left his post during those few minutes he had gone to Shannon's aid. If Greer didn't know for a fact that Shannon was at his house, he would have sworn she was responsible. But Shannon couldn't have done it alone, and Greer could think of no one willing to break the law to free a convicted killer.

A patrol was sent out immediately after it was discovered that Blade's horse was missing from the corral. But the half-breed was too clever for the soldiers; he had covered his tracks well. Still suspicious of Shannon, Greer ordered her brought in for questioning.

"I won't deny I'm glad Blade escaped," Shannon admitted when she faced the irate commander. "But I don't know who did it or how. I was at your house all night, remember? Molly insisted I spend the night after I fell."

"Quite convenient, you falling when you did, and in front of the guardhouse," Greer observed, his tone strongly accusatory.

"Are you suggesting—"

"Shannon, I don't want to think you could be guilty of such a thing, and I can prove nothing. It might interest you to learn that Sargeant Becker will face a court martial because of you. He left his post without authorization, resulting in the escape of a prisoner."

"I—I'm sorry," Shannon said, truly regretful for using the young sargeant so shamelessly. But if she hadn't, Blade would be dead by now. Desperate times called for desperate measures. "I didn't think he would get into trouble by helping me."

"By the way," Greer asked slyly, "how is your injury?"

For a moment Shannon looked blank, then quickly covered her confusion. "Much better, thank you. Molly is an excellent nurse, and those cold compresses worked wonders."

"Hmmm, yes," Greer said, staring at her so intently she nearly lost her composure.

Recovering with admirable aplomb, Shannon asked, "Is that all, Colonel?"

"For the time being. You may go now."

Remembering to favor her right knee, Shannon limped from the room.

Nigel left Fort Laramie later that morning. Before he departed, he managed to slip unseen into Shannon's house and relay Blade's message. Then he walked out of Shannon's life. With both Nigel and Blade gone, she felt truly alone. Blade was everything to her—friend, family, lover. Her world revolved around him. Now she had no one.

While all this was happening at Fort Laramie, a historic occurrence was taking place hundreds of miles to the east in Washington. On May 26, 1868, Congress once again failed to impeach President Johnson. And since that worry no longer plagued the president, his secretary saw fit to show him the telegram from Colonel Greer that had been laid aside these past weeks. Almost simultaneously the President learned through military channels that Major Vance had been murdered and a half-breed named Swift Blade sentenced to hang for the crime. A telegram was dispatched posthaste to Fort Laramie explaining Blade's position as special investigator and clearing him of all charges.

Shannon was the first to learn of this when Colonel Greer appeared at the schoolhouse shortly after classes were dismissed for the day. She was more than a little shocked to see him standing in the doorway looking properly abashed.

"Shannon, I've come to apologize," Greer said before Shannon could find her voice. "I've just received a telegram from the president."

"Is it about Blade?" Shannon asked, growing excited.

"Yes, as you might guess, it does concern Blade. President Johnson has explained Blade's position and insists he is incapable of murder, especially the murder of Major Vance. The president has demanded we drop all charges and clear Blade's name immediately."

"My God, Blade would be dead if he hadn't escaped, and now you tell me the president has finally remembered he had a special investigator named Blade! What took him so long?"

"I don't blame you for being upset, my dear. I shudder to think how close I came to executing an innocent man. President Johnson said a letter of explanation will follow. Everything you said about Blade is true, Shannon, and I apologize. His full name is Blade Stryker and he was an officer in the United States Army before he accepted this assignment. I've taken measures to clear his name immediately, just as the President ordered."

"Little good it will do now, Colonel. Blade is gone."

"That's something else I wanted to speak to you about. I feel I can talk to you as I would to my own daughter. Perhaps it's for the best that Blade is gone from your life. Rumor has it that the reason you defended him so staunchly is because you are lovers. I will ask you to neither confirm nor deny that charge.

"For all his good qualities, Blade Stryker is still a half-breed. You are astute enough to know that a half-breed is not a good thing to be here on the Western frontier, especially with Indians on the move again. I strongly urge you to join your family in Idaho and make a new life for yourself where no one knows you."

Shannon grew angrier with every word she heard. No better man existed than Blade—how dare people judge him on the color of his skin! When she opened her mouth to protest, Colonel Greer added quickly, "I know you fancy yourself in love with Blade, but in time you will find someone more suitable to marry."

"Blade is the only man I'll ever love," Shannon said with firm conviction. "I don't want another man. And I'm certainly not leaving now. One day Blade will return and learn he is no longer a wanted man. I'll wait."

"Then you leave me no choice but to give you the bad news," Greer said regretfully.

"What—what do you mean?"

"The townspeople are concerned over your involvement with a half-breed. They've asked me to hire another schoolteacher. Since there is only one week remaining in the current school year, you may finish out the term, and I've persuaded them to allow you to live in this house until the new teacher arrives. Now that the railroad has reached the Western frontier it will be less difficult to find good teachers."

Shock rendered Shannon speechless. She couldn't believe people were so narrow-minded—until she recalled how just months ago her hatred for Yankees was so fierce she would rather kill one than talk to one. Knowing Blade and his family had taught her that all Indians weren't alike, just as all Yankees weren't like Harlan Simmons. She was just as proud of

Blade's Indian blood as he was. Every one of his ancestors had a hand in making him the extraordinary man he was.

"I'm sorry the townspeople feel the way they do," Shannon replied sadly, "but you can tell them for me I'm not leaving town until I'm good and ready. As for the house, I'll accept your offer to remain until the new teacher arrives."

"I regret things turned out this way, my dear. It makes me thankful Claire found a proper young man like Ronald Goodman. I'd best be going, Shannon. I merely dropped by to apologize for my bad judgment regarding Blade."

"What about Major Vance's killer? He's still roaming free somewhere."

"We haven't a clue to the man's identity," Greer said regretfully. "I'm in the process of conducting a thorough investigation. If the man is still at Fort Laramie, he will be caught." It rankled to think that gun smuggling was going on under his nose and he knew nothing about it.

"Perhaps the killer will try to spend the gold," Shannon offered.

"Gold. What gold?" Greer asked sharply. "This is the first I've heard of any gold. Perhaps you'd better explain."

Realizing that she knew more than Colonel Greer did about Blade's investigation, Shannon revealed everything she knew about Clive Bailey, his gun-smuggling activities, and the gold he received from Mad Wolf in payment.

"I understand more clearly now," Greer said when Shannon finished. "There was no gold in Major Vance's quarters, so we can safely assume the killer has it. I'm glad you told me, my dear—at least I have something concrete to go on. And I'm certain the president's letter will enlighten me even more."

"Colonel, before you go, will you tell me if Molly feels the same about me as the other townspeople do?" Somehow it would hurt more if Molly sided with everyone else in their low regard for her.

"Definitely not. Molly thinks of you as another daughter. You're always welcome in our home. I feel as Molly does. Now I really must go."

When school let out for the summer, Shannon truly missed her students. She'd miss this snug little house when the time came for her to leave, she thought with a twinge of sadness. She had no idea where she would go or what she would do when that time came. She had the money she had saved from her salary and also the money Callie had sent in payment for the loan, but it wouldn't last forever. Opportunities for work at Fort Laramie were virtually nonexistent for women. There was always marriage, but there was only one man she would consider marrying.

Blade had promised he'd come back and Shannon vowed to wait for him. Unfortunately, he had no inkling that he'd been completely cleared of murder charges and was free to come and go as he pleased. Shannon considered looking for Blade but had absolutely no idea where to look. If her money gave out before Blade showed up, Shannon reflected, she'd be forced to make a decision. Fervently she prayed it wouldn't come to that.

While Shannon waited out the summer for Blade to return, a group of Sioux chiefs rode into Fort Laramie to sign a treaty. Man-Afraid-Of-His-Horses and Spotted Tail were two of the great chiefs who attended. Under the terms of the treaty, they would settle permanently on the huge Great Sioux Reservation in the Black Hills country of the Dakota Territory, retaining the right to hunt in the Powder River region. Both the Black Hills and the Powder River would be forbidden to white exploration. Chief Red Cloud was the only great chief left to sign the treaty, and he was expected to arrive at Fort Laramie later in the year to do so.

Meanwhile, Shannon continued to attend meetings of the women's rights group and to take an active part in their activities. Only Molly and one or two of the other officer's wives welcomed her without reservation, while the others treated her with cool disdain, including Claire Greer. Surprisingly, the saloon girls, including Poker Alice, continued to attend the meetings. The group wired both Anna Dickinson and Redelia Bates, inviting them to Fort Laramie to present suffrage lectures.

In August, 1868, Shannon wrote a letter to her brother Tucker explaining why she hadn't joined them in Boise. But no sooner had she posted her letter to Tucker than she received one from him urging her to come to Idaho before winter. Their letters must have crossed somewhere in the mountains.

Also in August the new schoolteacher arrived, a man named Curtis Black. Much to Claire's chagrin, Molly Greer, an unfailingly kind and compassionate woman, offered Shannon a place to stay.

During all this time Shannon heard nothing from Blade.

Shannon's move to the Greers' house went smoothly. She met Curtis Black, who was a pleasant young man four or five years her senior, and spent considerable time with him explaining how far her students had progressed during the past year and going over lesson plans. When school commenced, Shannon suffered a pang of regret and loneliness, feeling at loose ends with nothing to occupy her time. Her spirits plummeted even further when she realized she'd have to make a decision soon regarding her future. She couldn't rely on the Greers' hospitality and good nature forever, and her finances were too meager to allow her permanent independence.

In early September the entire fort was atwitter with the news that the fierce Sioux Chief Red Cloud and most of the Sioux nation were on their way to Fort Laramie, where Red Cloud would sign a peace treaty. Within the week the Sioux began gathering, dotting the hillsides surrounding the fort with hundreds of tipis. Ferocious-looking warriors wearing loincloths and wrapped in colorful blankets wandered in and out of the fort at will; the trading post became a favorite gathering place where they traded hides for tobacco and other necessities.

Security measures were doubled and vigilance observed to avoid unpleasant incidents between the townspeople and Indians. But the huge influx of Indians made the touchy situation ever more difficult. Most of the women remained safely inside, venturing out only when absolutely essential that they do so.

Colonel Greer was much harried and harassed, attempting to keep peace and still maintain strict control over a potentially explosive situation. He had a responsibility to see that nothing interfered with the signing of the treaty. Red Cloud was the last in the line of chiefs to sign, and once he did the Great Sioux nation would be forced to the reservation designated by the treaty. Still, Colonel Greer found time for a few private words with Shannon one day at dinner after Molly and Claire had excused themselves. Shannon waited politely for the colonel to speak.

"I'm aware of your—er, fondness for Blade Stryker, my dear, so I thought I would consult with you first before disposing of his belongings. Though his quarters are small, they are desperately needed right now with the fort straining at the seams. It was remiss of me not to have his personal items removed sooner. I thought perhaps there is something of Blade's you might like as a keepsake."

"You talk as if he's not coming back," Shannon accused him.

"Would you return if it meant you might be caught and hung?"

"Blade has been cleared of murder charges."

"But he doesn't know that." Colonel Greer shrugged. He was too busy to argue. "What would you like done with his belongings? Shall I have one of my men collect them and deliver them to you?"

"No," Shannon said thoughtfully. "I'd like to do it myself." She couldn't bear the idea of someone else pawing through Blade's personal property.

"Very well. Please do so tomorrow, if possible. I've hired a new scout and he'll be needing the room."

It was nearly dusk when Shannon made the fateful decision to visit Blade's room immediately to collect his belongings instead of waiting until the next day. She expected to be there and back in less than an hour, long before the Greers missed her.

Chapter Twenty

Shannon made her way to Blade's room at the rear of the smith's shop. It could be worse, Shannon reflected, and was actually better than some quarters assigned to scouts. Most army scouts were full-blooded Indians or half-breeds like Blade and received little in the way of amenities. Shannon arrived without mishap, passing unnoticed across the parade ground. She was amazed at the hundreds of campfires ringing the fort, and it occurred to her that the Indians could easily wipe out the entire population of the fort and town if they wanted to. It gave Shannon an uneasy feeling in the pit of her stomach.

This was the first time Shannon had been to Blade's room, and it looked as if nothing had been disturbed since he left. It was rather small, with a window and door facing the river and another door leading into the main part of the smith's shop. Her imagination worked overtime as she closed her eyes and sniffed, savoring his special scent that still lingered in the air.

The cot, table, chair, dresser, and stove appeared

untouched since Blade had last occupied the room. Shannon spied a deerskin pouch hanging on a hook and took it down, intending to pack it with Blade's belongings. Piling everything on the cot, she discovered that his possessions consisted only of a change of clothes, another pair of moccasins, a blanket, and an ornate necklace made of hammered silver disks and turquoise. The necklace reminded her so much of Blade that it was like a physical blow to her middle. With the necklace clasped tightly in her hand, she sat on the cot and fondly recalled everything she loved about Blade—every incredibly handsome feature, each deliciously sensuous inch of hard smooth flesh. She remembered the rapture they shared, the love that bonded them for all time, and how very much she needed him.

Time stood still in that small room as darkness descended and Shannon's fancy led her into a world where she had but to reach out to touch Blade, or call to him and he'd appear at her side. "Blade . . ." But wishing would not bring him back. If it could, he would have reappeared weeks ago.

Absently Shannon glanced out the window and was startled to see how dark it had grown. She hadn't bothered to light the lamp, and she could barely see her hand in front of her. She chided herself for lingering overlong with her reminiscences. She should have returned to her room at the Greers' long ago. Heaving a wistful sigh, she rose from the cot, picked up the deerskin pouch, and had her hand on the doorknob when the sound of voices drifted to her from the livery. The voices were so clear, the speakers could have been standing mere inches away. Shannon paused, knowing she shouldn't eavesdrop but too curious to care. Returning the pouch to the cot and placing her ear to the door, Shannon heard enough to freeze the blood flowing through her veins. She would have recognized that low, hoarse whisper anywhere!

"I can give you guns. As many as you want."

"We cannot pay in gold as Mad Wolf did."

From his tone and accent Shannon knew immediately that the second man was an Indian.

"I will trade guns for prime pelts," the first speaker whispered hoarsely. "You have them, don't you?"

"We have them. Where are the guns?"

"You will get them soon. They are being brought across the prairie by a trader, hidden in his wagon beneath his other wares. He will take the pelts back East in his wagon and sell them for me. Clive Bailey was but one of many such men working with me."

Shannon couldn't believe her ears. At the same time that Red Cloud was at the fort to sign a peace treaty, renegades were bargaining for illegal weapons. Peace efforts were a mockery as long as men continued buying and selling weapons to wage war against one another. Just the thought that she was so close to learning the identity of Major Vance's killer sent a tremor of emotion racing down Shannon's spine. Without a care for her personal safety, Shannon eased open the door, staring intently into the blackness of the livery. But to her chagrin, the man's face was concealed in shadows. The Indian she did not recognize, so wasted little time on his features. Then something caught her eye. The glint of shiny metal. She lowered her gaze to the man's chest and caught her breath in sudden shock. The man wore an army uniform! The distinctive buttons gave him away.

Straining her eyes, Shannon tried desperately to see through the shadows to the man's face, unaware that a dark figure had slipped through the window behind her as soundlessly as a jungle cat. He saw Shannon and froze, momentarily stunned, then crept up behind her. He peered through the door, seeing what Shannon saw, instinctively sensing the danger to them both should Shannon see him and cry out. He heard the man speak of guns and payment, but his face registered no surprise, only a deep sense of satisfaction.

Suddenly Shannon felt another presence in the room. Abruptly she whirled, and found herself imprisoned within a pair of arms stronger than steel bands.

Raising her eyes she looked into the fathomless black eyes of the fiercest-looking Indian she had ever seen!

Fright, sheer black fright overwhelmed her. Shannon was more frightened of the ferocious warrior imprisoning her in his arms than she had been of Mad Wolf. She opened her mouth to scream, and found it clamped tightly shut by a big, bronzed hand. Terror-stricken, she struggled against the Indian, but he held her in place against the hard wall of his chest with effortless ease. She fought this new peril so fiercely that she paid scant heed to the words spoken into her ear and did not understand the message her captor was attempting to convey. She sensed grave danger. Not just from the Indian, but from the men on the other side of the door.

Shannon renewed her struggles, disregarding the Indian's whispered warning in her ear; nothing he said made sense. She wanted to scream and scream and scream. Her small sharp teeth bit ruthlessly into the hand gagging her, gaining scant satisfaction when her captor grunted in pain. But his grip did not weaken. He muttered something that sounded like an apology, then Shannon knew no more.

Holding Shannon against his chest, the Indian quietly waited and watched until the two conspirators left the area. Then, hoisting her over his shoulder, he carried her out the door and into the night.

Shannon moaned, afraid to open her eyes, yet knowing she must. Her jaw ached, and she recalled with painful clarity that big hand coming at her before losing consciousness. He hit her! Her eyes flew open. The first thing she saw were flames dancing against a wall made of hides. Shannon knew then that the Indian had brought her to his tipi. She turned her eyes slowly to study her surroundings. To her right, so close she could reach out and touch him, stood the Indian. His bare legs, as sturdy as twin oaks, were spread wide apart, his moccasined feet planted firmly on the hard ground beneath him.

Slowly Shannon's gaze traveled upward, over the massive calves and hard, muscular thighs. She paused briefly at his slim hips, her gaze wandering unbiddingly to his loins where the small patch of buckskin barely contained the bold thrust of his sex. Convulsively, Shannon gulped, finding the sight oddly disconcerting as well as terrifying. What did this Indian intend to do to her?

Jerking her gaze away from the strangely arousing sight, Shannon's eyes continued their erotic journey. His arms, corded with ropy muscles, were crossed over an impressive bronze chest twice the size most normal men possessed. The flesh beneath the smooth tawny skin of his neck and shoulders rippled with suppressed strength. Long ago Shannon had learned the Sioux were a handsome people, more so than other Indians of different tribes, but she knew of only one man who could compare with this handsome savage standing proud and tall before her.

"Blade . . ."

The name slipped past her lips before her eyes slid upward to behold his dark, bold features, so fierce looking now with his long braids and painted face.

"Do you see anything you like, Little Firebird?"

There was laughter in his voice and tender amusement in his eyes as he squatted down beside her.

"Blade, you frightened the daylights out of me!" Her voice was taut with anger. "Why didn't you tell me it was you?"

"I did, several times, but you were struggling so hard you didn't hear me."

"You hit me!" she accused him sourly, suddenly reminded that her jaw still ached from the blow.

"Forgive me, love. I feared the men in the livery would hear if you cried out."

"You knew about them? One of the men is Major Vance's killer, but I couldn't see his face," Shannon lamented. "I still don't know who he is."

"I do," Blade said with quiet menace. "I followed Broken Lance to the livery. By then I had already guessed the identity of the gun smuggler and Wade's killer. I've had weeks to think about it."

"Tell me, who—"

"Later, Little Firebird, after you have greeted me properly. I've dreamed of this moment for months."

Stretching out beside her, Blade gathered Shannon in his arms. She rose up to meet him, winding her arms around his neck, lifting her mouth as his swooped down to capture hers in a long, drugging kiss. It was a ravaging kiss, fraught with need too long denied, searing, urgent, hungry.

"Sweet, so sweet," Blade whispered against her lips in taut agony. "I love you, Little Firebird, I love you."

"Show me, my love, show me how much you love me."

Her hands found their way along his body. With something akin to wonder, her fingertips moved along his lean ribs to his muscled waist and down his side to hair-roughened thighs. They explored the ropy muscles of his back and shoulders before combing through the soft hair on his bronze chest and pausing at the base of his throat. Their breaths merged as his parted lips sought and found hers again and again. For a long time they just held each other and kissed. Then, very slowly, Blade began to undress her, worshipping with hands and mouth each part of her body he had bared. His hands caressed her breasts, his fingers toying with her nipples. She felt the sensation deep in her loins and moaned.

With a flip of her wrist, Shannon released Blade's breechclout, her glimmering blue eyes admiring every magnificent inch of his hard flesh, turgid with desire for her. He sucked his breath in sharply as Shannon took him into her hand. He was big and hard and throbbing with a pulsing heat that made her ache with the need to feel him deep inside her.

He suckled upon the hard nubs of her nipples, making her whimper. Gently he sank his teeth into the delicate flesh, then laved them tenderly with the rough moistness of his tongue. She made a sound in her throat that was half moan and half plea. The sound seemed to unleash something wild in Blade as he flung himself atop her, pressing forcefully into her as she parted her legs for him. With a cry of joy she welcomed his hard pulsing length, rising up to meet him. He used her fiercely, piercing deeply as she eagerly responded with wild, tempestuous thrusts of her hungry body.

"Ahhh, Little Firebird, you're so hot and tight, so damn good. I don't know if I can wait."

The anguished groan that followed his words told Shannon he was losing control; they had been apart too long. Then she felt the hot spurt of his seed bathe her throbbing womb, and she turned savage beneath him. She soared. Up. Up. Up. Until she could go no higher. Then she was whirling downward into a warm darkness that rose up suddenly and claimed her.

Crying out in ecstasy, Blade felt his seed leave his body in hot, violent spurts. In his entire life he had never known such fulfillment with a woman. Shannon was perfect in every way, and she was his.

Rolling his weight off her, he wrapped his arms around her, holding her close. "I love you, Shannon." Those simple words expressed every emotion he felt in his heart.

Sighing softly, Shannon replied, "If I ever doubted it, I don't now."

Blade managed to pull a fur coverlet over them as they lay together, arms and legs entwined, basking in the afterglow of love's bliss. Shannon must have dozed then, for she awoke with a start to find Blade kneeling between her legs, gently cleansing her inner thighs and the soft folds of her woman's flesh with a wet cloth. At first she felt embarrassed to find him performing so intimate a task, but when she looked into his dark eyes she knew there could be no shame between two people who loved each other as they did. When Blade finished, he cleaned himself, then settled down beside her again.

"You shouldn't have crept up on me tonight like you

did," Shannon complained, "I would have come with you willingly had you asked."

"I didn't know you were inside the room when I climbed through the window," Blade explained. "I hadn't expected anyone to be there, since there was no light shining through the window."

"Why were you there?" Shannon asked curiously.

"I followed Broken Lance to the livery and entered my old room in order to hear more clearly what was being said without exposing myself. I was shocked to find you there eavesdropping."

"You looked so fierce I didn't recognize you. What made you follow Broken Lance? Did you know he wanted to buy guns? Are you here with Red Cloud's people?"

Blade smiled with fond indulgence. "One question at a time, Little Firebird. First let me thank you for giving me back my life. I was shocked to learn it was Nigel Bruce who had come to set me free. Is he still at Fort Laramie?"

"No, he left the next day, and I've neither seen nor heard from him since," Shannon explained. "Now tell me about you."

"I've been with Red Cloud since I left Fort Laramie last spring. The survivors of Grandfather's village joined him shortly after I returned to the fort. My friend Jumping Buffalo and his wife Sweet Grass made me welcome in their tipi."

"I'm happy you found your friends," Shannon said, brushing away a tear. "But I'm happier still that you came back. How did you know to follow Broken Lance? I assume he's the Indian who met with the gun smuggler in the livery."

"Broken Lance was one of Mad Wolf's followers," Blade revealed. "When I found him with Red Cloud I decided to gain his confidence, hoping that one day he would lead me to Bailey's partner and Wade's killer. It wasn't difficult once word got around that I was a fugitive and wanted for murder at Fort Laramie.

Jumping Buffalo was most helpful in circulating gossip.

"Soon Broken Lance was bragging about obtaining illegal guns and killing emigrants despite the peace treaty Red Cloud was about to sign. I wanted to clear my name and the only way I could do that was by catching the real killer.

"When Red Cloud began his journey to Fort Laramie, Broken Lance joined him, and so did I. But evidently Broken Lance didn't trust me enough to tell me about the meeting tonight. Jumping Buffalo knew of my investigation and alerted me when he saw Broken Lance sneak away from camp. I followed him here."

"Weren't you going to let me know you were at the fort?" Shannon asked with growing dismay. She had a nagging suspicion that Blade would have come and gone without her even knowing if he hadn't stumbled on her in his room.

"It would have served no purpose. I couldn't take you back to the reservation with me to starve and spend the rest of your life living in poverty," Blade said with quiet dignity. "The government might have good intentions, but graft and corruption flourish among the ranks of those in charge of Indian affairs. It has happened before and will happen again. Food and clothing meant for the Sioux will find their way into unscrupulous hands, leaving the Indians destitute."

"Can't you warn Red Cloud? Perhaps he shouldn't sign the treaty."

"Not signing the treaty could result in slaughter on both sides. Innocent women and children will die. The proud Sioux nation and all other Indian tribes will cease to exist. It is better to survive in any condition than to have your numbers decimated and your people scattered to the four winds. I can't ask you to become a fugitive like me and live as I am forced to live."

"My God, what am I thinking? You're no longer a

wanted man!" Shannon cried, wondering how she could have forgotten to mention something so vitally important as Blade's freedom. But when he made love to her, she could scarcely remember her own name, let alone anything else. "President Johnson wired Colonel Greer shortly after your escape from the guardhouse. He explained everything and demanded that your name be cleared. You're free to come and go as you please. Furthermore," Shannon continued excitedly, "Colonel Greer has launched an investigation of his own and let it be known that you are a special agent. He wants to catch Major Vance's killer as badly as you do."

At first Blade was merely stunned, then angry—damn angry. The telegram might have come too late if Shannon hadn't found a way to free him. But after his temper cooled and he had time to think about it, he was too damn happy to hold grudges. He whooped in pure joy. He was alive and free and held the woman he loved in his arms.

"You know what that means, Little Firebird?" he asked, raining exuberant kisses over Shannon's face and neck.

"It means we are free to love and spend our lives together," Shannon said, smiling blissfully.

"It won't be easy," Blade predicted. "If you marry me, you'll suffer undeserved prejudice. Our children will be openly ridiculed by their peers."

"No one will ridicule our children!" Shannon declared fiercely. Her hands cradled her stomach as if Blade's seed already grew there.

"You're a ferocious warrior, Little Firebird," Blade laughed. "Are you certain you want to marry me? It might be easier for us in the East, but I have no desire to leave the land of my birth."

"I left the East once. It holds nothing but sad memories for me. I'd be proud to be your wife, Blade. Anywhere you want to live is fine with me."

"Then we will be married as soon as Major Vance's killer is in custody."

"Damnation, I nearly forgot! You know who the killer is. Who, Blade, who is he?"

"I've known for some time but had no proof. I suspected him even before I left the fort, which is why I knew exactly who I would find here tonight with Broken Lance."

"Don't keep me in suspense!"

Blade paused thoughtfully. "You're better off not knowing until the man is in custody."

"Blade Stryker, you'd *better* tell me!" Shannon demanded hotly. "I'm in this as deeply as you are."

"Very well, Little Firebird, I can't deny your involvement or your right to know. The man who arranged for guns to be delivered to the renegades is Lieutenant Goodman. The same man who killed Clive Bailey and Wade Vance."

"Lieutenant Goodman! But—but that's preposterous," Shannon stammered, stunned. "He hates Indians. He'd never sell guns to them."

"Greed knows no loyalty. No doubt he tried to salve his conscience, if he has one, by killing as many Indians as possible. Goodman is the man I saw talking to Broken Lance. I saw him clearly, Shannon, while you were struggling in my embrace."

"My God, the Greers will be devastated. Claire was going to marry him. Colonel Greer positively dotes on the man."

"Something tells me Claire will not only survive, but will quickly find a replacement for Goodman," Blade predicted sagely.

"What's going to happen now?"

"I'm going to make love to you again," Blade said, a rakish smile hanging on one corner of his wide mouth.

"Blade, be serious! What I meant is, what are you going to do about Lieutenant Goodman?"

"Who?" Blade asked distractedly. He had already forgotten the man as his hands made a bold foray along the sensitive skin of her breasts.

"Blade, you're incorrigible."

"So I've been told."

Then his drugging kisses put an end to her questions. After rendering her breathless, his lips left hers to wander where his hands had been, blazing a trail of fire along her ribs, pausing to lavish loving attention on the smooth tautness of her belly. Then he continued his downward journey, amply rewarded by a surrendering sigh from Shannon when he pushed her thighs apart and buried his dark head in the tangle of blond curls at their apex.

"Blade, oh God, that's so good."

Her body jerked convulsively when his tongue probed delicately into the tender folds of flesh.

"I want to love you with my mouth, and every way possible tonight," Blade said, lifting his head to stare into her passion-glazed eyes. "You're mine, Shannon Branigan, and I want you to remember it always."

"How can I forget when you remind me in so many wonderful ways?" Shannon panted, nearly beyond speech.

Then words were no longer possible as Blade's bold, thrusting tongue sent her tumbling over the edge of ecstasy.

"Wake up, sleepyhead," Blade said, swatting Shannon's rear playfully. "I reckon by now Colonel Greer will have a detail out looking for you, if he can spare the men. Today Red Cloud is to sign the peace treaty and Greer will need every available man to keep order at the fort."

Shannon was up instantly, shrugging free of the coverlet and reaching for her clothes. There wasn't a part of her body that didn't ache, nor an inch of her sensitive skin that didn't tingle with pleasurable memories.

Blade watched with renewed interest as Shannon rose like a nude goddess from the mat. How could he possibly want her again after exhausting himself so thoroughly, loving her so completely—too many times to count—quenching his hunger until he had no more to give? His need for Shannon truly amazed him, and instinctively Blade knew he would always need her.

"Don't look at me like that," Shannon warned with a teasing smile.

"I can't help it. You're beautiful."

"You're not so bad yourself."

Her appreciative gaze slid over Blade like warm honey. She thought him handsome in buckskin trousers and shirt. Instead of moccasins he now wore leather boots. His pitch-black hair was unbraided and hung down to his incredibly wide shoulders. Lean, hawkish features stared at her from a dark bronze face.

"Let's get out of here," Blade suggested wryly, "before I lay you down and make love to you again. And I sincerely doubt I'm up to it."

Hand-in-hand they left the tipi and walked through the Indian encampment. Shannon could feel the dark, curious eyes follow their progress but placidly ignored them. When she was with Blade nothing or no one could harm her. They strode into the fort and were immediately confronted by a detail of six men riding across the parade ground. Sergeant O'Brien was in charge. When he saw Shannon he brought the detail to a skidding halt.

"Miss Branigan! Colonel Greer is beside himself with worry. He ordered a detail of men sent out to search the Indian camp."

He slid a inquiring glance at Blade, recognizing him immediately. "Are you responsible for Miss Branigan's disappearance, Blade?"

"I reckon I am," Blade admitted, slanting an amused look at Shannon.

"We haven't time for conversation now, Sergeant O'Brien," Shannon said, tossing her head impatiently. "It's imperative that we see Colonel Greer at once."

Without offering an explanation, Shannon took Blade's arm, pulling him along with her. Sergeant O'Brien turned his mount and followed, dismissing the rest of the detail with a wave of his hand.

Blade and Shannon were allowed immediate entrance to Colonel Greer's office. "Shannon, you're more trouble than all the men under my command!" the irate officer declared. He looked worried, and Shannon felt guilty for not thinking to send word of her whereabouts. Then Greer saw Blade and his expression lightened.

"Hello, Colonel," Blade said quietly. "Shannon told me I'm no longer a fugitive."

"Blade! Blade Stryker! I suppose you're responsible for Shannon's sudden disappearance. Have you two no sense at all? Haven't I enough to worry about without sending out men to comb the area for one wayward girl?"

"I'm sorry," Shannon said in a small voice. "I didn't mean to worry you. It was thoughtless of me. But what we have to tell you will more than make up for the distress I caused."

"Well, get on with it. This is a hectic time." He looked at Blade. "Are you with Red Cloud's people?" Blade nodded. "Look, Blade, I'm sorry as hell about —everything. But I know the truth now and will cooperate fully with your investigation." Having had his say, he waited for Blade to speak.

"My investigation is finished, Colonel," Blade revealed, drawing a skeptical look from Greer.

"You know who killed Major Vance?"

"Yes. The man is clever. He recruits traders traveling back and forth across the Oregon Trail to carry illegal weapons for him. When they arrive they are sold to renegades at a great profit."

"That's despicable! Who is it?"

"You're not going to like this, Colonel," Blade warned cryptically. "You may not even believe it."

"Spit it out!"

"Our man is Lieutenant Goodman."

"What! Preposterous! The man hates Indians. He'd never deal with them. Ronald Goodman is going to be my son-in-law."

"If you search Goodman's quarters, you'll find the

gold stolen from Wade Vance's room. Furthermore, Shannon and I overheard him negotiating an arms deal last night in the Smith's Shop with a renegade named Broken Lance."

Colonel Greer was stunned. Goodman was on his way to becoming a fine officer; he had big plans for his daughter's fiance that included a promotion and a bright future in the army. How could this be? How could they all have been taken in by the man? "Are you certain? Absolutely certain?" Greer looked as if he had aged ten years in ten minutes.

"Send someone to search Goodman's room, and you'll have your proof," Blade suggested, knowing how difficult this was for Greer.

Blade and Shannon waited in the Colonel's office while a search was conducted in Goodman's quarters. Not satisfied to assign the job to just anyone, Colonel Greer went himself, taking Sargeant O'Brien and a young private with him. They returned less than thirty minutes later, each man carrying a sack of gold. The crushed look on Greer's face told the story.

"Sargeant O'Brien, when Lieutenant Goodman returns from patrol, place him under arrest and bring him directly to my office. Neither of you speak of this if you value your rank."

Both men saluted crisply, but the private seemed unable to tear his eyes away from the gold. Sargeant O'Brien had to literally drag him from the room by the arm.

Once they were gone, Colonel Greer seemed to collapse inwardly. "I'd like both of you to remain when I confront Goodman. Meanwhile, Blade can explain much that was missing in the president's letter and tell me how he happened to be in the livery last night to hear Goodman and the renegade."

Eager to oblige, Blade related all the details of the investigation he and Wade Vance were conducting before his tragic death. He also revealed his movements during the past months and how he knew Broken Lance was meeting with Goodman last night.

He carefully omitted any mention of Shannon or where they had spent the night. But Greer was no fool. He knew Shannon loved Blade and was reasonably certain Blade returned her feelings. Since Shannon had no father, Greer intended to make damn certain Blade did the right thing by her.

Blade had just finished his rather lengthy explanation when Goodman burst through the door. "What is this all about, Colonel? Why am I under arrest?"

Chapter Twenty-One

Lieutenant Goodman's eyes narrowed suspiciously when he saw both Shannon and Blade sitting in Colonel Greer's office. He guessed immediately that he had been found out and wondered how it had happened. He decided to brazen it out by pretending innocence no matter what the charges against him. He sincerely doubted there was enough evidence to convict him of anything.

His eyes widened in fear and disbelief when he saw the sacks of gold sitting on the Colonel's desk. They should have been resting in their hiding place in the closet of his quarters.

A frisson of dread shivered down his spine as he repeated, "What is this all about? Why am I under arrest?"

"You're under arrest for the murders of Major Vance and Clive Bailey," Colonel Greer said with quiet authority. "Then there is the additional charge of selling illegal weapons to Indians."

"What! That's preposterous!" Goodman sputtered, stunned and flustered by the evidence against him. "You know me, Colonel, I'm not capable of murder."

"It's too late for denials, Lieutenant. The gold taken from Major Vance's quarters was found hidden in your rooms. If further proof is needed, there were two witnesses to your meeting with Broken Lance last night."

Goodman slid a venomous glance at Blade and Shannon. They hadn't said a word since he entered the room. "That can't be! The Smith's Shop was empty when—" He stuttered to a halt, suddenly realizing what he had just admitted. His shoulders slumped in utter dejection as he lost all his bluster.

Until that moment Colonel Greer had held a slim hope that this was somehow all a hoax, that Goodman would offer a plausible explanation to clear his name. But that hope was dashed by Goodman's fatal slip of the tongue.

"Both Shannon and Blade heard you and Broken Lance discussing weapons," Greer said with grim resignation. "Somehow you learned that Major Vance and Stryker were working together to halt the illegal sale of guns to renegades and risked murder rather than be unmasked and charged with the crime. You killed Vance and neatly arranged for Blade to take the blame. It almost worked, but fortunately Blade escaped from the guardhouse and became friendly with Broken Lance. It wasn't long before everything was finally brought out into the open."

"They lie! The gold was deliberately planted in my quarters," Goodman said lamely.

"Your feeble excuses don't hold water," Greer replied disgustedly. "How could you do this? You had a brilliant future ahead of you in the army. I approved of your marriage to my daughter. Why, Lieutenant, why?"

"I did it for Claire," Goodman tried to convince the Colonel. "She deserves the best things in life and army pay allows for few luxuries."

"Don't blame your greed on my daughter," Greer rebuked harshly. "Take him away," he ordered, deliberately turning his back. Sargeant O'Brien moved quickly to obey, completely baffled by all that had transpired.

Goodman swiveled to confront Blade and Shannon before he was hustled out the door, his face mottled with rage. "You'll pay for this. One way or another you will pay!" Then he was taken away, still cursing and spewing threats.

"I didn't want to believe it," Greer said, shaking his head slowly.

"It's never easy when someone you trust betrays his friends and the uniform he wears," Blade sympathized.

"Yes," Greer said, clearing his throat as he put the matter firmly behind him. In his position he couldn't afford maudlin sentiments. "What are your intentions now that this investigation is over?"

"I have plans for the future," Blade replied, squeezing Shannon's hand.

"Might I ask if they include Shannon?"

"I have no future without Shannon," Blade stated simply.

"Do you intend to marry?"

"If Shannon will have a half-breed for husband."

"Of course I'll have you," Shannon replied proudly. "You're the man I love. Nothing else matters."

"Since Shannon has no father or male relative nearby, I'm going to speak frankly," Greer said. "For Shannon's sake, I suggest you settle anywhere but near Fort Laramie. This is a small post and feelings run high against Indians and half-breeds. Once you marry people will lose all respect for Shannon. She'll suffer because of it and I don't want that to happen."

"It's not my intention to remain at Fort Laramie, Colonel," Blade revealed. "For some time now I've had my eye on a valley near Cheyenne. If it isn't taken,

I plan on homesteading there, building a house for Shannon, and buying cattle with the money I've saved. The land is perfect for raising Texas longhorns."

Greer nodded approvingly. Shannon had a more difficult time coming to grips with the notion that Blade wanted to become a rancher. It was the first she had heard of it.

"Before you leave," Greer continued, "I'd like to arrange with the chaplain to perform the marriage. If that is what you'd like," he added hastily.

"Yes, I'd like that," Shannon said eagerly.

"Then run along to the house and inform the women while Blade and I settle the details."

Shannon left headquarters in a daze. She had dreamed so long about being Blade's wife, but she hadn't thought it would ever happen. Finally they would be together always, never to be separated again.

"It won't be easy, Blade," Greer warned once Shannon was gone. "No matter where you go, there will be prejudice—unless you go back East and live as a white man as you did during the war years."

"There is nothing back East for me and Shannon," Blade argued. "Wyoming is my home, and I'll stay regardless of the way people feel about me. Shannon is a fighter. She'll survive."

"Then let's go find the chaplain. You can be married tomorrow."

By the time Shannon left headquarters, the fort was abuzz with rumors of Lieutenant Goodman's arrest. Snippets of gossip and cutting remarks flew around her as she crossed the parade ground. People seemed to be more concerned that Shannon had spent the night with a half-breed than they were about finding a killer. Injun lover, white squaw and whore were among some of the choice words directed at her.

How could these same people she considered her friends turn on her so viciously? she wondered bleakly. With head held high, Shannon was determined no one should know how deeply their remarks hurt her. No matter what people said or thought, it was worth it to be with Blade. She sincerely hoped things would improve in Cheyenne, but even if they didn't she would survive. Hadn't Mama always preached that love had the power to conquer all adversity?

Molly Greer was staunchly supportive as she helped Shannon pack her meager belongings. If it made any difference to her that Shannon loved a half-breed, she wisely kept it to herself, though Shannon thought her enthusiasm overly restrained. When Shannon happily announced she was to be married soon, Molly had offered to help refurbish one of her gowns to make it more festive. Though the older woman offered no advice, Shannon knew by the expression on her face that she desperately wanted to say something.

"Go ahead and speak your mind, Molly," Shannon encouraged her. "We're friends. What is it you want to tell me? It won't hurt my feelings."

Sighing distractedly, Molly said, "Yes, there is something. I heard about Lieutenant Goodman. It's all over the fort. It's so difficult to believe he is capable of murder. The man ate at my table, courted my daughter. Are you certain, Shannon, absolutely certain the man is guilty? Could it be a case of mistaken identity?

"I know you and Blade are responsible for his arrest, but Lieutenant Goodman seemed like such a nice young man. He and Claire were to be married soon. The poor girl is devastated."

"There is no mistake, Molly," Shannon said as gently as possible. "Lieutenant Goodman has admitted before witnesses that he is guilty of cold-blooded murder. He also sold illegal weapons to renegades. Even if he hadn't confessed, the evidence against him is overwhelming."

"Oh dear, oh dear," Molly murmured, rubbing her temples distractedly. "I think I'll lie down a bit. I seem to have developed a terrible headache."

After Molly left, Shannon continued sewing bows on her wedding dress, a soft pink silk that had seen better days but was the prettiest she owned except for the green ballgown, which was inappropriate for a wedding. Her thoughts turned inward as she dreamed about what it would be like married to Blade, living in their own house and raising their children. Suddenly the door nearly flew off the hinges as Claire burst inside.

"You bitch!" she spat accusingly. "You and your Indian lover spoiled everything. If not for you, I could have married Ronald and gotten out of this godforsaken wilderness. I hate it here! Ronald promised me clothes, jewels, everything I desired. Who cares if he sold guns to those nasty Injuns!"

"You knew," Shannon whispered, utterly stunned. "You knew about the guns. Did you also know about the murders?"

"I knew nothing," Claire hissed, "and you can't prove I did. You ruined my life, and one day I'll ruin yours—just you wait and see." Whirling on her heel, she flounced out of the room.

The needle poised in her hand, Shannon sat back, her mind working furiously. Claire was devastated all right, but not because she was shocked by Goodman's cold-blooded acts of murder. Claire thought only in terms of material possessions and what she had lost. Shannon seriously considered telling Colonel and Molly Greer what she suspected but finally decided to let the matter drop. She hated to hurt and disillusion the Greers, who had taken her in and treated her with kindness. With Goodman behind bars, Claire could do no further damage.

The following morning, Shannon and Blade were married by the army chaplain in the small post chapel. Among the few people who attended were Colonel and Molly Greer. Claire Greer was conspicuously absent, but Shannon hardly noticed. It was the happiest day of her life.

Blade thought Shannon looked exquisite in her pink gown. It made her skin shine like pure alabaster and emphasized the dark blue of her eyes. Never would he have believed that he would be marrying so beautiful an angel. Half-breeds rarely aspired so high. That Shannon loved him at all was a miracle. As they exchanged vows, Blade promised himself that she would have nothing but the best; he would make her life perfect in every way.

Shannon thought Blade the handsomest man she'd ever seen. His bold, brooding looks might not be conventional, but his dark striking features and powerful frame were difficult to ignore and impossible to forget. He looked wonderful, she reflected dreamily, dressed in new clothes and his braids shorn to a respectable length.

In a surprisingly short time, the ceremony was over and Blade was kissing her, his dark eyes suspiciously moist and misty. Then Colonel Greer was wishing them well, with Molly adding her own subdued words of congratulations.

Once again Claire absented herself, refusing to appear at the sumptuous wedding dinner generously provided by the Greers. But Blade and Shannon were too entranced with one another to notice or care. Afterwards Blade loaded their belongings and supplies in the wagon he had purchased, tied Warrior to the back, and drove away from Fort Laramie.

"I didn't want us to spend our wedding night with the Greers, or in my tipi," Blade said as they left the perimeter of the fort. "I want it to be special, something we'll always remember. That's why I suggested we leave immediately. I'd rather celebrate the first day of our married life under the stars, where the Grandfather Spirit will shine his blessing down on us."

"I wouldn't have it any other way," Shannon agreed blissfully.

They plodded south at a leisurely pace for a destination only Blade seemed aware of. At dusk they approached a winding creek, and Blade pulled the wagon into a glade of cottonwood trees.

"Perfect," Shannon sighed, raising her eyes heavenward where the stars played hide and seek among the cottonwood branches.

Blade grinned, lifting his arms to help Shannon down. Effortlessly, she slid into his embrace, their bodies touching and igniting a blaze that seared their senses. With a sigh of regret Blade set her aside. "Soon, Little Firebird, soon," he promised in a low voice. "You build a fire while I find our dinner."

Her heart beating with wild anticipation, Shannon soon had a fire started. Blade returned a short time later with two plump rabbits already gutted and skinned. Shannon expressed admiration as he spitted and set them over the fire. Soon delicious smells wafted through the glade, joining that of the biscuits browning in a large skillet.

Though she was starving, Shannon had great difficulty swallowing. Lord knew she had no reason to be nervous on her wedding night—she already knew Blade was the best of lovers, gentle, tender, yet fierce in his passion.

"Aren't you hungry, Little Firebird?" Blade asked, putting his own food aside.

"Not very," Shannon answered with a hesitancy not lost on Blade.

"I'm famished, but not for food. We can always eat later. Come," he said, his urgency communicating itself to Shannon. "The stream isn't deep, and the water is warm." Snatching up soap and towels, he grasped her hand and led her toward the water.

"You want to go swimming?" Shannon asked, dismayed.

"It will relax us, you'll see," he promised. His roguish grin needed little interpreting.

He dropped the soap and towels at the gentle rise

that sloped down to the water, turned Shannon around and unfastened the back of her dress. His fingers trembled as he slipped it down over her shoulders then turned her about to face him. His gaze swept over her bared flesh, his eyes avid with appreciation and wonder. Reverently he touched the pure alabaster of her breast with the tips of his fingers.

"Your skin is so soft and white," he murmured huskily. His own large hand was like a dark splotch against her flesh.

Shannon offered her mouth and he took it, his kiss a sensual exploration of taste and texture. Then his mouth bent to the high curve of her breast, his breath scorching her skin. He found a ripe nipple, suckling her like a babe, and she rewarded him with a low moan deep in her throat. His hands grew urgent now as he slid her dress down over her hips, then removed her underclothes. He lifted her out of the circle of fabric and kicked it aside.

A gentle breeze lifted her hair, caressed her long legs and lithe body, perfectly slender yet temptingly full, her waist so tiny he could encircle it, her breasts so round and thrusting their weight filled his hands. He wanted her now, this very instant, but he forced himself to wait.

"Your clothes," Shannon whispered, tugging on his shirt.

In a very short time he stood before her in all his naked splendor. The shifting light of the campfire behind them cast a red glow over the muscles of his shoulders and arms. Every well-sculptured inch of his magnificent body reminded her of a Greek statue she'd once seen gracing a neighbor's garden.

Then Blade scooped her into his arms and waded into the water. It *was* warm, Shannon thought as Blade walked out a short distance and set her on her feet. The water came only to her waist.

"I forgot the soap," he said, dashing back to the shore. He returned before Shannon even realized he was gone. "I'll wash you first."

He washed her arms, then her back, his rough palms creating a tantalizing friction on her sensitive skin. He devoted tender attention to her breasts, using the soap in a circular motion, then rinsing with agonizing slowness. Shannon gasped when his soap-lubricated hand disappeared beneath the water and slid up along the inside of her thigh. Her legs parted underneath the water as he caressed the soft center of her. His fingers slipped inside her and he kissed her passionately, smothering her tremulous sounds of delight. The tumult of their passion churned the water around them. Suddenly his fingers were gone, causing Shannon to groan in protest.

"Not yet, love," Blade teased, "I haven't had my bath." He handed her the soap.

Shannon savored the delicious texture of his skin and the muscles beneath her fingertips, loving the way they quivered at her touch. When she reached below the water and boldly massaged his swollen sex, Blade's steely control snapped. He took the soap from her hands and tossed it to the shore. Then he grasped her hips, lifted her and slid his hard pulsing length deep inside her. Once firmly seated, he began to thrust furiously, raining flurries of wild kisses along her forehead and temples, down her jawbone to her throat, finding an aroused nipple and sucking it into his mouth.

"Blade, oh Blade," Shannon moaned as if in pain.

Her legs grasped his waist tightly and her body moved in perfect tempo with his. He was driving her frantic. She could feel tiny tremors begin deep inside her as he drove them both to an explosive climax.

"Now, Little Firebird, now," Blade urged, his strokes a fierce assault on her senses. "Come with me now."

His words were the final assault on her tenuous control as her soul left her body and soared to a place beyond the horizon reserved only for lovers. The moment Blade felt her contractions, he galloped to his own tumultuous reward.

"I love you, Shannon."

Traveling at a leisurely pace, it took three days to reach Cheyenne. Each night they celebrated their love beneath the stars and Shannon had never felt more content or happier. If only life could forever remain as uncomplicated as it was right now, she reflected wistfully. She wanted to raise her children in a place without prejudice, live with Blade where people didn't judge him on the merits of his Indian blood but by the kind of man he was. Immersed in her rosy dreams of the future, Shannon didn't realize Blade had stopped the wagon on a ridge overlooking a tranquil valley.

"There it is, Little Firebird," Blade said, his voice filled with pride. "Down there is where I'll build our house. Our cattle will graze these hills surrounding us, our children romp among the wildflowers. Look!" he pointed out, "see that stream winding through the valley? It's our guarantee that water will always be close at hand."

"It's beautiful," Shannon sighed. "So—so peaceful."

"That's what we'll call it," Blade said in sudden inspiration. "Peaceful Valley."

"How far are we from Cheyenne?"

"Not far, ten or twelve miles."

"Where will we live until the house is built?"

"We'll find something in town. I intend to put cattle on the land first, then build the house during the remaining days of summer, though I reckon it will be next year before it is finished. I want to do it right. You don't belong in a crude hut."

"Do we have enough money?" Shannon asked hopefully.

"I'm not penniless, love. Not rich either. But I've saved most of my army pay and nearly all the money left to me by my father. He was quite successful at trapping. We'll manage until the ranch starts paying for itself. Then we might even take a trip to Idaho to visit your family. Would you like that?"

"Yes, Blade, oh yes. They'll love you, I know they will."

They rented a room at the Cheyenne Hotel until they could find proper lodging. By the summer of 1868, Cheyenne had grown to a busy, thriving city. The town sprang up, like most frontier cities, along the railroad as it progressed westward. It was located on Crow Creek just east of the point where the Great Plains met the Laramie Mountains.

They soon learned that the city teemed with unruly elements, mainly as a result of the nearly one thousand men who came to build the railroad tracks, and that vigilante action was necessary to maintain order. Cheyenne was nicknamed "Hell On Wheels" because of the hard-drinking, gun-toting men who passed through the frontier town. Justice, or what passed for justice, was dispensed with a short rope and a long drop.

Blade bought his first small herd of cattle not long after he filed claim on Peaceful Valley and its surrounding hills. He hired two willing hands in town and began work on the cabin he and Shannon would occupy. The following weeks were lonely for Shannon. With Blade gone so much, she had more time on her hands than she knew what to do with. She hated being idle. She always had something to do at Twin Willows, and at Fort Laramie her time had been devoted to teaching school. She applied for a teaching position, but was informed that all vacancies were filled for the coming school year. When she casually mentioned to Blade that she wanted to find work in one of the shops in town, he promptly put an end to her aspirations. With typical male arrogance he insisted he was capable of supporting her without her working. Fortunately Shannon found a worthwhile outlet on which to expend her energy.

Since Cheyenne was a town of some five thousand people, views were varied and strong concerning women's right to vote. It was no secret that the state legislature was close to passing the amendment, and Shannon offered her considerable talents and experience to the local suffrage group. She began by attending suffrage gatherings, where she quickly met influential women who welcomed her into their ranks with open arms. Before long she was performing small services for the group and in quick order became indispensible to the cause. To her astonishment, she found that people of both sexes listened with interest to what she had to say about the movement.

In October, 1868, Shannon wrote a letter to her mother.

Dear Mama,

I'm married! Blade and I were married by the post chaplain at Fort Laramie and are living in Cheyenne. I'm ecstatic—we're both ecstatic! Blade is homesteading a piece of land outside Cheyenne he has named Peaceful Valley, and he is busy building our first home. Until it is finished, probably next spring, we are living at the Cheyenne Hotel.

I haven't heard from you recently. I hope things are going well for all of you in Boise. If you've written to me at Fort Laramie, it will probably take a while for your letter to find me in Cheyenne. I wish I could tell you I've heard from Devlin, but I have no idea where he is.

I'm so eager for you all to meet Blade. I love him so much. You'll see that he is everything I said and more. I worried about our reception in Cheyenne, but so far all has gone well.

I've gotten involved in the women's rights movement and am quite caught up with my work. I realize women's suffrage is a new concept to you, Mama, but knowing you, I am certain it is something you would

> *embrace wholeheartedly. Blade is proud of all I have*
> *accomplished in behalf of the movement. We all think*
> *Wyoming is close to passing the amendment granting*
> *women the right to vote.*
>
> > *Give the family our love and write soon.*
>
> > *Your devoted daughter,*
> > *Shannon*

The next few weeks were busy ones for Shannon, and when she was asked to speak before a group, she was amazed at how easily she was able to do so. When one believed so strongly in a cause, one found words to express those deep feelings. Not even the hecklers who tried to shout her down annoyed her; nothing could shake her confidence or her staunch conviction in the cause.

Blade proudly endorsed Shannon's work for women's rights and even encouraged her to participate fully. Since he was gone much of the time and involved with their ranch, he was happy that Shannon had found an outlet for her overabundant vitality. If he worried about Shannon's acceptance once the townspeople learned she was married to a half-breed Sioux, he never mentioned it, for thus far the subject hadn't arisen. Few people had even seen the mysterious Blade Stryker. Blade prayed the day would never come when Shannon would be hurt by cruel people too blind to see past the accident of a man's blood. But to be on the safe side, he increased his efforts on the cabin. Unfortunately winter came early in 1868, and by late October Peaceful Valley lay deep in snow.

Blade decided they should remain at the hotel for the winter. It was a time of peace and contentment for Shannon. When snow covered the ground and the wind howled around the corners, she and Blade spent long blissful hours making love, or just holding each other when the more physical side of their love exhausted them. They attended performances at the newly built opera house and found they needed no other companionship when they had each other.

At Christmas Shannon would have been thrilled to announce she was expecting Blade's child, but was bitterly disappointed when pregnancy was not in the offing. Blade was properly sympathetic but confessed he'd like to have her to himself a while longer.

"Children will come, Little Firebird," he teased. "They are bound to when we spend so much time trying to make one. Not that I'm complaining. I find it most pleasant work."

"Work! You call making love to me work?" Shannon accused him with mock anger.

"Work that gives me more pleasure than anything I've ever done in my life."

Then he was kissing her and the room grew quiet but for the small cries and moans made during those moments of shared ecstasy.

The year 1869 arrived, and with it more snow and cold. It wasn't until April that severe weather finally gave way to a glorious spring. The Great Plains burst into a carpet of tall grass and flowers. Blade returned to Peaceful Valley to round up his cattle and count his losses from the severe winter. According to his calculations, he still had considerable work to do on their house. It wasn't to be a cramped one-room cabin, but four spacious rooms built to withstand nature's worst onslaught.

The suffrage movement in Wyoming was bolstered by the appearance of Eastern suffrage speaker Anna Dickinson. Her lecture was well received and given fair and full coverage in both the Wyoming Tribune and the Cheyenne Leader. Shannon was so impressed that she remained after the lecture to meet the famous speaker. They spent several lively hours before Miss Dickinson boarded her train discussing the issues and the importance of women's right to their future well-being.

Inspired by Dickinson's fervor, Shannon soon became a leading proponent of women's suffrage and her work was widely recognized and acclaimed in

Cheyenne and its environs. Her confidence in the cause and her unshakable belief in female independence soon made Shannon a popular speaker at local gatherings.

One day in early summer Shannon was asked to lecture in the town hall. She was excited at the prospect, for many people from out of town were expected to attend, including legislator William Bright. Bright would introduce the suffrage bill written by Territorial Secretary Edward M. Lee to the legislature for passage later that year. Blade surprised Shannon by expressing a desire to attend the gathering and hear her speak. Usually duties at the ranch prevented him from attending any of her lectures.

"I've never heard you speak, Shannon, and I'm damn proud of you. I want to be there for you this time."

"Can you spare the time?" Shannon asked, pleased by Blade's obvious pride in her.

"I'll make the time for you," he promised. "I haven't said anything before because I wanted to surprise you, but the cabin is nearly completed. Next week you can choose the necessary furnishings and we can move in soon. Will that make you happy?"

"Ecstatic!" Shannon vowed, throwing herself into his arms. "And just in time, I might add. I want our baby to be born on our own land." She had refrained from telling Blade until she was absolutely certain that she was expecting his child.

"Baby!" Blade exploded, the air rushing from his chest. "Are you sure?"

"As sure as I can be. By my calculations, our child will be born in about seven months. You—you're not disappointed, are you?" she asked tremulously. "Truthfully, I never thought it would take so long, considering how frequently we make love."

"Disappointed! Nothing you do would disappoint me. I'll love all the children you give me."

"Even if they are all daughters?"

"Even then," Blade laughed. "But somehow I doubt a fiery creature like you will give me all daughters. Though I wouldn't mind one or two if they looked like you."

Then he drew her into his arms and kissed her with so much feeling, such gentle tenderness, that Shannon had to blink away the tears threatening to spill down her cheeks.

"I love you, Blade Stryker. If we had time, I'd show you how much."

"Later, Little Firebird," Blade replied, his voice husky with promise.

Shannon's lecture that evening thoroughly entranced Blade—not merely because she was his wife and he loved her, but because she was magnificent. Mesmerizing, enthralling, totally inspiring, were some of the words that came to mind. If the bill for women's rights were to be ratified tomorrow, Blade suspected every man present tonight would wholeheartedly endorse its passage. After the lecture, legislator William Bright and his wife, a staunch supporter of women's suffrage, lingered behind to offer Shannon congratulations on her inspiring speech. When Blade joined her, she was surrounded by a large group of admirers.

"I'd like you to meet my husband, Mr. Bright," Shannon said, her voice tinged with pride.

Blade looked so handsome tonight that Shannon felt the envy of every woman present. She was aware that Blade was being ogled by staid matrons and beautiful young women alike. They were pressing forward with shocking eagerness in order to inveigle an introduction and take a closer look at the wildly handsome Blade Stryker.

Blade was conversing with Mr. Bright and Shannon was speaking with his wife when something so unexpected happened that it left Shannon shaken and speechless.

A woman pushed boldly forward until she was standing nearly toe to toe with Shannon. Recognition hit Shannon like a bolt of lightning.

"You've made quite a name for yourself, haven't you, Shannon?"

"Claire, how—how nice to see you again," Shannon said with as much dignity as she could muster. "Is Molly with you. What are you doing in Cheyenne?"

"Mama and I are here to take the train East for a visit. We heard you were speaking and decided to attend, only Mama didn't feel well tonight and I came alone. I couldn't let this opportunity pass," Claire hinted with quiet menace. Then she directed her malevolent gaze at Blade. "Hello, Blade."

"Hello, Claire," Blade returned warily. Intuition warned him that Claire intended to make trouble. He was right.

"You've come up in the world," Claire said breezily. "From army scout to a man of property. And a wife who has built a reputation as a lecturer and staunch supporter of women's rights. You've even acquired a last name. I wonder," she hinted slyly, "if these good people are aware that you are a half-breed—that you're related to those murdering, lying Sioux who are raiding and killing again despite the treaty they signed last year."

A collective gasp rose from the people crowded around Blade and Shannon, and their faces contorted with shock and dismay. More than a few backed off, their admiring glances swiftly turning to fear and revulsion. Noting the effect her words had on those within earshot, Claire smiled in smug satisfaction. She had waited a long time to get even with Shannon and Blade for ruining her life, and a way had presented itself when she least expected it.

Claire's words about the Sioux breaking their treaty was all too true. Once again a solemn treaty had proved as worthless as the paper it was written on. By the end of 1868 the Union Pacific Railroad had crossed southern Wyoming and new towns had sprung up along its right-of-way, stretching into the Sioux reservation. Now talk of gold in the Black Hills had provoked a rush into Sioux territory, provoking anger and retaliation. The mighty Sioux had called a council and were beginning to gather together a formidable army.

Blade could have strangled Claire for spoiling Shannon's triumph. The men and women who just moments ago had looked at her with pride and respect now considered her an object of scorn and ridicule. One by one they turned their backs on her.

"Why are you doing this, Claire?" Blade asked, his eyes so cold and ruthless, it wasn't difficult to imagine him in Indian garb stalking an enemy.

"I want everyone to know the kind of man Shannon married," Claire replied heartlessly. She flinched beneath Blade's stony glare but continued, undaunted. "I'll wager your friends don't know you were imprisoned for murdering an army officer and sentenced to die for the crime. I suspect they'd also be interested to know that you escaped the night before you were to hang."

"Blade was cleared of those charges, and you know it!" Shannon cried, the depth of Claire's hatred astounding her. But Shannon might as well have shouted her words into the wind, for the damage was already done.

Around them people were breaking into groups, whispering and pointing, their eyes round with shock. The room was abuzz with words like half-breed, savage, murderer, white squaw, and worse. For herself, Shannon didn't give a fig what people said, or the vile names they called her. It was Blade she was concerned about. He didn't deserve the hate and enmity directed at him. It sickened her to note that those very same women who only moments ago had regarded Blade with admiration now eyed him with awe and speculation—as if wondering if he was also a savage in bed.

Mercifully there were staunch friends among the group. Elizabeth Davis, the banker's wife, seemed unconcerned that Shannon was wife to a half-breed.

So was Cora Allen, one of the women who had taken Shannon under her wing when she first arrived in Cheyenne. Both women knew Shannon incapable of marrying a killer. Blade Stryker might appear dangerous, but he didn't look like a man capable of murder. To William Bright's credit, he did not jump to conclusions but waited patiently for an explanation.

Meanwhile, satisfied that she had done all the damage she could for one day, Claire slipped quietly away.

Chapter Twenty-Two

*B*lade was well aware of the hostility directed at him, and the knowledge that it included Shannon nearly tore him apart. There were elements in Cheyenne that would go to any lengths to do them harm, and he felt overwhelming relief that their new home was nearly habitable. Soon they would be safe and snug in their own little valley where Shannon and the babe she carried would be free from abuse and ridicule. Suddenly Blade became aware that Mr. Bright was still standing beside him, looking at him with unfeigned curiosity. Blade was somewhat shocked that the man had remained after Claire's venomous attack and felt duty-bound to offer an explanation.

"There is an explanation for all this, Mr. Bright."

"I'd be interested to hear it," Bright replied.

Blade then launched into a brief but concise telling of the events that led to his arrest for murder. Not only did Mr. Bright hang on Blade's every word, but his wife and both Elizabeth Davis and Cora Allen appeared enthralled. Everyone else had left, eager to spread gossip about the half-breed married to a white woman and mixing socially with the townspeople.

"You fought with the Union Army," repeated Bright with a hint of admiration. "A captain, no less. Few of us have had the privilege of meeting the president. I, for one, am proud of your work. You are a credit to our great country, Mr. Stryker, and I find scant sympathy in my heart for people who despise you for your Indian blood.

"And you, Mrs. Stryker, are a courageous woman. Few women are brave enough to flout tradition to marry the man they love. It's no wonder you make so brilliant a spokeswoman for women's rights," Bright concluded. "I wish you both the best. You deserve it."

"Thank you, Mr. Bright," Blade said with heartfelt gratitude.

"Don't fret, dear," Mrs. Bright added, "the townspeople will come around in time. Those that matter, anyway. Your work for woman's rights is more important than petty prejudices."

Her words were endorsed by both Elizabeth and Cora. Soon afterwards they all left for their respective dwellings.

It was only a short distance to their hotel, but Blade and Shannon couldn't help overhearing the snide remarks directed at them as people passed them by on the street, or fail to notice the scornful glances following in their wake. Blade's fierce black looks soon discouraged the most persistent of their revilers, but Shannon was nevertheless grateful when they reached the hotel.

To their dismay, they learned just how fast gossip traveled in Cheyenne when they were detained by the desk clerk on the way to their room. Though his words were politely rendered, his tone held a definite sneer.

"The management requests that you vacate your room by the end of the week. We are a high-class hotel and do not cater to half-breeds and their squaws."

Blade went still, his mouth a thin white slash in his

bronze face. The chords in his neck bulged and his huge hands clenched into fists at his side. Shannon felt his anger building and feared the explosion that was bound to follow. Her restraining hand on the taut muscles of his shoulder brought Blade's temper slowly back to merely simmering. The clerk blanched. For a moment he had thought he was about to meet his maker. Then he began to breathe again when he saw the violence drain out of Blade. Color returned to his face, but instinctively the clerk knew he still trod on dangerous ground.

"I suggest you apologize to my wife," Blade said tightly, his tone barely civil. "I don't care what you think of me, but my wife is a lady and deserves to be treated as one."

The clerk swallowed convulsively, smart enough to know when descretion was called for. He turned to Shannon, his voice properly obsequious. "I meant no disrespect, Mrs. Stryker. I'm merely following orders."

"And enjoying it, I'll wager," Shannon snapped with bitter emphasis.

"We'll be gone by the end of the week," Blade said curtly, much too incensed for prolonged conversation.

If not for Shannon's delicate condition, he would be demanding satisfaction for the insult to his wife. Taking her arm, he propelled her toward their room with all the calm of an active volcano.

Blade felt little concern for his own feelings, it was Shannon he worried about—Shannon and his unborn child. He had known when he married her that he was courting trouble by placing her in a potentially explosive situation. What he had failed to consider was his volatile temper. When Shannon was insulted and degraded because of him he wanted to lash out, to punish. He should have never married Shannon, never have placed her in a situation where she was open to ridicule by her peers.

Once inside their room, Shannon sagged against

Blade's broad chest, shuddering with emotion. It hurt, hurt dreadfully, to see Blade treated in so disparaging a manner. She could kill Claire for bursting the bubble she had existed in these past months. Though Blade hadn't deliberately tried to hide his Indian heritage, the subject just hadn't come up. Blade was a proud man, and it saddened her to hear him belittled and insulted by people not fit to wipe his boots.

"Don't worry, Little Firebird," Blade consoled, hugging her tightly. "I won't let anything happen to you or our child. I'd kill first."

"What are we going to do?" Shannon asked. "If we have to be out of here by the end of the week, that doesn't leave us much time."

"It's no longer safe to leave you in Cheyenne while I tend to our ranch," Blade decided.

"I still have friends," Shannon reminded him.

"And enemies. No, love, we're moving out to the ranch. The house is nearly completed and we can make do. During the next few days, we'll buy furniture and supplies and be ready to move by the end of the week."

"I'd hate for people to think they are running us out of town," Shannon said, her head tilted at a stubborn angle.

"It doesn't matter what people think," Blade vowed with tender concern. "Nothing matters but you and our child. I shouldn't have placed you in this intolerable situation. I knew from the beginning that our marriage was a mistake, but I loved you too much to consider the consequences."

"There is no way I'd let you get away from me, Blade Stryker! Now kiss me and forget all about that little unpleasantness." Twining her arms around his neck, she pulled his head down to hers.

Blade needed no encouragement to kiss his beautiful wife. His eyes smoldering like brilliant black ebony, he took her mouth, lavishing tender attention on the moist corners before sliding his tongue between her teeth to taste her sweetness. Then he began to undress her, his hands trembling in his great need to lose himself in her sweet flesh.

"Each time I make love to you is like a wonderful new experience," Blade groaned against her lips. "I'm shaking like a boy with his first woman. I love you, Shannon Branigan."

"You talk too much, Blade Stryker. Please take me to bed."

"Are you sure my loving won't hurt the baby?"

"Positive. My mother had six children and continued to—to share my father's bed until the final weeks of her confinement."

"Six children," Blade repeated, his eyes crinkling with amusement. "Shall we try to beat that number or merely match it?"

"Let's concentrate on this one before we make any decisions," Shannon returned tartly.

She squealed as Blade lifted her high in the air and placed her square in the center of their big bed. Before he followed, he quickly stripped himself bare as Shannon watched in rapt appreciation, her eyes frankly admiring as she studied the enormous width of his bronze chest, then lower, to his loins. She saw that he was ready for her, more than ready, his manhood throbbing against her hip as he positioned himself beside her.

"Don't look at me like that, Little Firebird, or our evening will end before it begins."

Shannon giggled. "Do I always affect you like that?"

"Always."

"I'm glad, because you do the same to me. Now love me, my magnificent warrior."

"That's something you'll never have to beg me to do," Blade assured her and grinned with wicked delight.

Then he joined their bodies, filling her so full of himself that Shannon thought she would explode from the joy of it. Then she did, shattering into a million pieces as she soared to the stars.

* * *

During the following days, Shannon prepared for their move to the ranch. Blade insisted on accompanying her on her errands and shopping trips, refusing to allow her out of his sight. On the street, people went deliberately out of their way to avoid them, and it was impossible to ignore the crude remarks directed none too subtly at them. Shannon thought Blade's restraint remarkable. The thin line of his mouth and smoldering black of his eyes gave mute testimony to his rage.

"Blade, I'd like to stop at the general store to purchase a length of flannel for baby clothes," Shannon said as she stopped before the large wooden building housing the general store.

Blade glanced inside, saw only two women browsing, and nodded his consent. "While you're shopping, I'll go next door to the hardware store." He watched until she was safely inside, then hurried to complete his own errand.

Shannon attracted scant attention when she entered the store. Mr. Samms, the shopkeeper, waited on one customer while another sorted through a stack of dishes. Shannon went directly to where the bolts of cloth were displayed, lingering a long time while she selected thread and trim to match the flannel she had chosen. Her selections complete, Shannon thought it odd that no one came to wait on her. Glancing around, she saw that the store was now empty except for Samms. The other customers had already been waited on and departed.

"Could you please cut me a length of this blue flannel?" Shannon asked when she saw Samms idly leaning over the counter poring over a newspaper. Was the man deliberately ignoring her?

Samms did not stir, nor did he bother to acknowledge Shannon's request.

Shannon tried again. "Mr. Samms, please cut me three yards of blue flannel."

Just then two women walked through the door, and Samms sallied forth to serve them. Fuming in impotent rage, Shannon picked up the bolt of cloth and marched purposefully to where Samms stood hovering over the women. She shoved the bolt beneath his nose.

"Three yards, please."

"You'll have to wait your turn," Samms grunted rudely.

"I was here long before these other customers entered the store," Shannon claimed.

"Squaws wait their turn," Samms said. With surly disdain, he turned away.

Shannon gasped, struck dumb by the crude insult. The two ladies Samms had been helping sniggered behind their hands, waiting with bated breath for the outcome of the confrontation. They didn't know Shannon personally, but thought it scandalous that a white woman would debase herself by marrying a half-breed. What delicious gossip they would have to repeat when they left the store!

"Now, ladies, what can I help you with?" Samms asked with a polite smile that failed to include Shannon.

"I strongly urge that you wait on my wife."

The voice was low, deep, and dangerous. The note of suppressed violence in Blade's tone sent a convulsive shiver down Samms's spine.

"It's all right, Blade, I—I decided I no longer want the flannel," Shannon said, attempting to defuse a potentially volatile situation. "Let's go home."

"I'm not ready yet to leave, Shannon. I've suddenly acquired a great fondness for that particular shade of blue flannel. Make it five yards, Samms." He glared defiantly at the shopkeeper, daring him to refuse.

Ezra Samms was many things, but he wasn't a fool. He knew when to back down. Insulting a defenseless woman was one thing, but challenging an irate half-breed was quite another. There was more than one way to rid the town of unsavory elements, and there were plenty of people who felt as he did.

Taking the bolt of cloth from Shannon's hands, Samms measured out the required length, all the while glaring at Blade with thinly concealed contempt. Samms wasn't the only one eying Blade. Though both women customers pretended disgust and shock at being in such close proximity to a half-breed, they ogled him shamelessly. Certainly neither would admit it, but the pure masculine appeal of Blade Stryker had them all atwitter.

With deliberate rudeness, Blade tossed a coin at Samms, picked up Shannon's purchases, and guided her from the store.

"I'm sorry that happened, love," he said regretfully. "Had I known, I'd never have left you alone."

"Why can't people treat you like a man instead of something vile?" Shannon complained bitterly. "You're twice as handsome, twice as brave, honest, trustworthy—"

"Shannon," Blade protested, smiling in amusement. "Lord knows I have my faults. You must remember that you see me in a different light. Most people choose to ignore my white blood and despise that part of me that is Sioux. Let's get out of here, love. I'll load the wagon and we can leave for Peaceful Valley tomorrow. Would you like that?"

"I'll be happy wherever you are," Shannon assured him.

Blade stopped the wagon on the crest of a hill overlooking the land he had aptly named Peaceful Valley.

"It looks so tranquil," Shannon sighed, awed by the quiet beauty of the valley.

The cattle Blade had bought grazed contentedly on the surrounding hills, and it excited Shannon to think that this majestic valley belonged to them. Though Blade had brought Shannon out here several times, she had no idea what the house looked like. He wanted to surprise her.

"Look to the right and you can see the chimney rising amidst the cottonwoods."

"Oh, Blade, let's hurry," Shannon urged, bristling

with impatient enthusiasm. "I can hardly wait to see our new home."

Shannon was properly impressed. The house was quite grand compared to most cabins erected by homesteaders, which were usually no more than crude huts. What impressed her most was the knowledge that Blade had built the cabin himself, with only occasional help from day workers hired in town. Built of chinked logs, the four-room structure featured real glass windows and a stove in each of the three bedrooms and parlor. The kitchen was reached through an enclosed walkway at the rear. Shannon was especially pleased with the cookstove Blade had purchased for her and brought out earlier.

"It—it's wonderful," Shannon exclaimed, literally dancing from room to room. "Some rugs on the floor, furniture, curtains—it will be cozy in no time. A perfect place to raise our children. Thank you, Blade, I love it. I love you."

"I want you to be happy, Shannon. I know you'll miss your work with the women's suffrage group, but it is safer for you out here."

"Of course I'll miss it," Shannon admitted. "But as important as women's rights are to me, a cause can't compare to what I feel for you. Besides, the women's rights amendment will soon be brought to a vote and my work finished. I only hope what I did helped."

"You were quite impressive, love, and I'm not the only one to think so. Mr. and Mrs. Bright were favorably impressed by your lectures. I'm sorry it had to end the way it did. If it wasn't for that vindictive bitch—"

"Forget Claire. She can do nothing more to hurt us. As long as we have one another nothing can harm us."

During the following weeks, Shannon's happiness knew no bounds as she set about making the house into a home. Once their few pieces of furniture were in place and rugs and curtains adorned the floors and windows, the rooms lost their cold emptiness and reflected the love that dwelled within the four walls.

As long as the weather remained mild, Blade continued to work on building the ranch. He had found two hands in town willing to work for a half-breed and when they weren't out riding the range they helped Blade construct a woodshed and corral. Stables would come next, but probably not until next spring.

At first Blade was reluctant to leave Shannon alone for longer than very short periods of time. But when two weeks passed without incident, he felt more comfortable leaving her at home when he was needed elsewhere on their land. As a concession to his fear, he made damn certain Shannon had a rifle within reach at all times. He offered to teach her to shoot and was pleased to learn she was already quite adept, having been taught by her brother Tucker before he went off to war.

One day while Blade was out riding the range, Shannon saw someone approach the house and reached for the rifle. When she saw it was a lone Indian, she relaxed somewhat, but kept the rifle trained on the man as he rode his pony boldly into the yard. It looked as if the Indian had traveled a great distance, for his pony pulled a travois loaded with his possessions.

The Indian halted a short distance from the house. "What do you want?" Shannon asked.

"Swift Blade," the Indian said tersely.

He was close enough for Shannon to notice that his face was gray with fatigue and etched with lines. He looked near exhaustion; his shoulders were stooped as if the weight of the world rested on them. He was tall and handsomely built; if not for his near state of collapse he would have been almost as imposing as Blade. Intuitively Shannon knew the Indian belonged to the mighty Sioux nation, for none other were as majestic and impressive as the Sioux.

"You know my husband?"

"I know your husband, and I know you, Little Firebird."

Lowering the rifle, Shannon took a closer look at the Sioux brave. "You're Jumping Buffalo!"

Shannon didn't know him well. She had been in Yellow Dog's village but a short time. However, Blade spoke often of his friend and had pointed him out to her before they left the Indian village. She wondered what had brought him to Peaceful Valley. He appeared exhausted and half-starved. She leaned the rifle against the house to show him she wasn't frightened.

"Come inside, Jumping Buffalo. You must be tired and hungry."

Jumping Buffalo hesitated, turning to glance behind him at the travois. "Sweet Grass is ill."

It was the first inkling Shannon had that Jumping Buffalo wasn't alone. "Your wife is with you?" She looked worriedly at the travois. "Please bring her inside. Perhaps there is something I can do for her," Shannon urged. "What is wrong with her?"

"Sweet Grass miscarried our child on the trail three days ago," Jumping Buffalo replied. "She has lost much blood."

"Oh!" Shannon gasped, rushing forward, "the poor thing." She didn't know Sweet Grass but felt great compassion for any woman who lost a child.

Jumping Buffalo was standing on the porch to greet Blade when he returned a short time later. Sweet Grass had been settled comfortably on a cot in one of the spare bedrooms and fed a nourishing beef broth. While she slept, Shannon prepared supper. Jumping Buffalo had taken himself outside, feeling confined by wooden walls. Clasping arms, the friends embraced. They were talking quietly when Shannon called them in to eat.

"How is Sweet Grass?" Blade asked as he hugged Shannon and planted a kiss on her cheek.

"Resting. She's very weak, but I think she'll be all right."

Jumping Buffalo seemed reluctant to sit at the table but was finally persuaded by Blade to join them. The meal Shannon had prepared was simple but nourishing and tasty. Jumping Buffalo ate as if it was the first solid meal he had consumed in days, causing Shannon to slant an inquiring glance at Blade. She waited with her usual impatience for him to explain what had brought the half-starved family to their door. Not until the meal was over did Blade satisfy her curiosity.

"Jumping Buffalo says things are bad on the reservation," he explained, his voice taut with emotion. "Large numbers of buffalo no longer roam the plains as they once did. Food is scarce and supplies promised by the government have not arrived. Most of the problem lies with corrupt Indian agents who sell meat designated for Indian consumption and pocket the money.

"The Sioux are leaving reservations in increasing numbers, following the buffalo or stealing cows to feed their families. The final indignation came when the white man invaded Indian territory in search of gold. Jumping Buffalo could not bear to see Sweet Grass starve to death, so he came to me for help."

"How did you know where to find us?" Shannon asked Jumping Buffalo.

"Swift Blade told me about this valley many moons ago," Jumping Buffalo said slowly. "I knew he would be here."

"What will the rest of the Sioux nation do when winter comes and there isn't enough to eat?" Shannon asked, wishing there was something she could do to help.

"Many will perish," Jumping Buffalo said with stoic resignation. "I did not wish my wife to die."

"According to Jumping Buffalo, Red Cloud is raiding again in retaliation for the broken treaty. He's attacking wagon trains and stage coaches, and disrupting the westward progress of the railroad. Jumping Buffalo is tired of war. He desires peace for his family."

"Then he and Sweet Grass must stay here," Shannon insisted staunchly. "You said yourself you needed more help. They can live with us until a cabin is built for them."

Blade smiled, knowing full well what his tender-hearted wife would say once she learned of Jumping Buffalo's sad plight. "I hoped you'd feel that way. I've already offered him a home and work and he accepted."

Chapter Twenty-Three

During the next several days, Sweet Grass grew strong enough to leave her bed for short periods of time. She was a shy, pretty woman who spoke little English but whose sweet, gentle nature quickly earned a place in Shannon's heart. The two women soon found ways to communicate, and before long Sweet Grass was helping Shannon with the chores.

Blade took charge of Jumping Buffalo, acquainting him with ranch work. One day he took Jumping Buffalo to Cheyenne to attend a cattle auction. The moment they returned, Shannon knew it had been a mistake. Blade's face was like a thundercloud. Bruises covered both men's faces and Shannon wasn't surprised to learn they had been in some kind of altercation. Blade told her about it later that night as they lay cuddled in bed.

"I should have known better than to take Jumping Buffalo with me to Cheyenne," he said bitterly. "Indians aren't welcome there these days."

"I hoped all the prejudice against us would have died down by now."

"Not with men like Ezra Samms stirring up tempers. He refused to serve Jumping Buffalo when he went to trade for supplies."

"What happened?"

"I held Samms at bay while Jumping Buffalo gathered what he needed and left his trade goods," Blade confided. "I thought nothing more of it until Samms and some of his friends confronted us as we left the auction."

"How terrible," Shannon gasped. "Did they hurt you badly?"

"A few bruises." Blade grinned cheekily. "I've had worse. Jumping Buffalo and I managed to crack a few skulls in the melee. I'd say we gave as good as we got."

"When will people realize men are men no matter what their race?"

"That sounds strange coming from a Southerner who kept slaves," Blade teased. "What happened to that Yankee-hater who was shocked to find a half-breed in charge of a wagon train?"

"She grew up," Shannon replied thoughtfully. "She was rather shallow, wasn't she? Until she learned to love a man who taught her to respect men for what they are, not who they are."

"And I rewarded you by planting my seed inside your belly," Blade returned, placing his hand on the gentle rise of her abdomen.

Shannon was five months into her pregnancy, and every day new changes were taking place in her body. Her breasts were exquisitely sensitive to Blade's touch, and he was all too aware of it as his hand moved upwards to tease the swollen mounds and ripe, pouting nipples.

"Tell me if I'm hurting you, love," Blade whispered against her lips.

Just then the babe made its presence known, kicking strongly against the wall of Shannon's stomach.

Blade felt it and inhaled sharply. "Our son is protesting, Little Firebird. Should I stop?"

"He's protesting because you're going too slowly," Shannon answered saucily. "Oh Blade, you drive me wild with wanting."

"Don't ever change, my love. I always want you hot for me, just the way I am for you."

Then he slid his mouth down her throat, lingering lovingly at each breast, over the quivering mound of her stomach. He nudged her legs and they parted eagerly as Blade found her with his mouth, loving her in the most intimate of ways.

When Sweet Grass was well enough, she moved out of the house into the tipi Jumping Buffalo had erected on the bank of the stream a short distance from the house. Blade had offered to build them a cabin, but Jumping Buffalo declined, voicing his preference for the buffalo-hide tipi he was familiar with. A fiercely proud man, he had arrived at the ranch with all his worldly possessions strapped to the travois. His one concession to civilization was agreeing to share meals with Blade and Shannon. Since the two ranch hands, Milo Flenor and Slim Masters, often ate the evening meal with Blade and Shannon, Blade convinced Jumping Buffalo it was perfectly acceptable for him and Sweet Grass to do the same. It wasn't too great a burden for Shannon to cook for six people, especially since Sweet Grass lent a hand. With Shannon's blessing, Sweet Grass soon took over the cooking chores completely.

One night not long after Blade's confrontation in town with Ezra Samms, unwelcome visitors arrived at Peaceful Valley. It was a Saturday night and both Milo and Slim had gone into town to drink and carouse, leaving the two couples behind to share the evening meal. The first hint of trouble came when the sound of pounding hooves interrupted their supper. Reacting instinctively, Blade grabbed his rifle and cautiously opened the front door. Jumping Buffalo stood at his side to lend his support while the two women peered over their shoulders.

"Who is it, Blade?" Shannon asked. A shiver of apprehension jolted down her spine. Why couldn't people leave them in peace?

"Don't know, it's too dark."

When the men reined in before the house, Shannon saw that they wore bandanas over the lower portion of their faces and wide-brimmed hats pulled low over their eyes. She counted five riders. Wildly fearful, she clutched Sweet Grass's hand.

"What do you want?" Blade asked. His words were harsh with chill warning, his dark eyes boldly challenging.

"We come to give ya fair warnin', Injun," one of the men drawled. "Leave the area, ya ain't welcome here." His muffled voice sounded abrasive through the bandana covering his mouth. "We don't need yer kind settlin' around these parts. Afore long you'll have yer whole dang tribe livin' out here with ya. Next thing ya know yer Sioux relatives will be attackin' Cheyenne."

"This is my land," Blade responded, yielding nothing. "I desire only to live here in peace with my family. I strongly urge that you leave before I'm forced to do something neither of us will like."

"I wouldn't do nothin' rash, Injun," the man advised ominously. "Wouldn't want yer little woman to get in the way of stray bullets, her breedin' and all, would ya?"

Blade's jaw clenched with barely suppressed rage. It was one thing to threaten him, but when that threat included Shannon he saw red. "Shannon, take Sweet Grass inside," he ordered tersely. His black eyes never wavered from the riders as he spoke.

Shannon's heart quickened in terror. "Blade—"

"Do as I say!"

"Be careful."

"Turn around and ride out of here," Blade said with deadly purpose once Shannon and Sweet Grass had retreated inside the house.

"Heed my warnin', Injun. Take yer squaw and yer heathen brother and get outta here if ya know what's good fer ya."

They turned as if to ride off and Blade heaved an inward sigh, thinking they had survived the worst of it. He was mistaken. The worst was yet to come. Whooping and hollering, two riders carrying torches burst forth from the trees behind the house. To Blade's utter horror they tossed the torches at the house as they charged past. Then they joined the others in a wild exodus into the night. Whether or not they intended to burn the house down, Blade had no way of knowing. But it turned into a nightmare he wasn't likely to forget soon.

One of the torches hit the wall and fell harmlessly to the ground, where it eventually burned itself out. The other, through either malicious intent or accident, found its way through the bedroom window, which had been opened to admit the mild night breeze. Within seconds the billowing curtains were afire. Minutes later, the whole room was ablaze. Blade and Jumping Buffalo did what they could to douse the inferno, but it soon became apparent that their meager efforts were doomed to failure. Carrying a trunk containing their clothes and what few valuables they possessed, they were forced to retreat, abandoning the house to the flames.

Shannon watched in stunned disbelief as the house on which Blade had expended so much time and money was reduced to ashes. Nothing had been saved but a single trunk and a chair or two. The cookstove she was so proud of was now a melted mass of iron. Gone, all gone—everything they had worked so hard to achieve was destroyed in a single act of violence.

Shannon wept against Blade's chest, the strength of his strong arms little consolation. If not for his pregnant wife, Blade would have ridden after the cowardly bastards who hid their faces behind bandanas. With Jumping Buffalo's help, the night riders might not have gotten away so cleanly. Seven to one weren't bad odds when pitted against warriors trained by the Sioux.

"Everything's gone, Blade, everything," Shannon said in sudden fury. "Damn them to hell! But they haven't beaten us. They just think they have!"

Shannon didn't realize it, but those were almost exactly the same words she had spoken when her family was forced to leave Twin Willows.

"We'll build again, Little Firebird," Blade promised, inspired by Shannon's fire and spirit despite all she'd just lost.

"They'll come back," Shannon predicted, "but next time we'll be ready for them."

That night they slept in the bunkhouse, which miraculously was spared. Nor was Jumping Buffalo's tipi destroyed. Blade felt certain the tipi wouldn't have survived destruction if Jumping Buffalo hadn't placed it in a spot neatly screened by thick foliage growing near the stream.

When Milo and Slim returned from town, they were shocked to learn what had taken place in their short absence. They knew when they hired on that Blade was a half-breed, and at first were hesitant about accepting employment. But since they both needed work, they decided to give it a try. It wasn't long before they learned to respect and admire Blade as a man.

Since there was little they could do to restore the ranch house at the present time, Blade sent the two men out to move the cattle from the distant south pasture to a place where they could be more easily watched. Blade had spent nearly every cent he owned on livestock and the cabin, and he couldn't afford to lose his cattle should the night riders decide to return.

Shannon and Blade were engaged in searching through the smoldering rubble of their home later that day when Milo and Slim rode in hell for leather.

"They're gone, boss, every last one of 'em!" Slim cried as he reined his horse to a skidding halt. "Me and Milo searched the entire south pasture with nary a trace of them cows anywhere. They were rustled, boss. Those men who came last night musta swung 'round and driven off the herd."

Blade, who rarely cursed, mouthed a string of oaths that turned the air blue. He left Jumping Buffalo to protect the women and rode out with the hands to find the cattle. He returned at dark, and Shannon could tell by the slump of his shoulders and the grim set to his mouth that their cows were truly gone. But it wasn't until later, in the privacy of the bunkhouse, that Shannon learned of the disastrous decision concerning their future that Blade had been forced to make.

"You're not going to like what I have to say, Little Firebird," Blade began, wrapping an arm around her waist and pulling her into his lap.

"Then don't say it," Shannon returned, placing a finger against his lips.

Blade kissed her fingers one by one, but the determined look on his face told her he wouldn't be deterred.

"You shouldn't have married me, Shannon Branigan. I'm a selfish bastard for deliberately placing your life in danger. You're going to Idaho."

"Idaho? You'd move to Idaho?" Shannon asked, stunned. Wyoming was Blade's home, and she was surprised that he would even suggest leaving. Blade was neither a quitter nor a man easily intimidated.

"No, my love, *you're* going to Idaho. To join your family. I'm staying here."

"What! You're mad, I'll do no such thing," Shannon declared. Her chin was tilted just enough to emphasize the stubborn line of her fine jaw.

"I knew all along I was doing you a grave disservice by making you my wife. I assumed we could live in peace here in our valley, away from town and people who would hurt you. But I see now I was mistaken.

You won't be safe anyplace as long as you're with me."

"You're sending me away?" An unladylike sound erupted from her lips as she swore in sudden panic. "What about our child? Do you care nothing for him?"

"It's because I care too much that I'm sending you away. I can't bear to see you hurt. Your family can protect you in Idaho. No one need know you are married to a half-breed."

"You've lost your mind, Blade Stryker, along with the sense you were born with!" Shannon scolded hotly. "I never thought you were the kind to give up."

"Give up? You think I'm giving up? No, love, I'm staying. I'll fight with everything I have to hang on to my land."

"And I'll be right beside you," Shannon declared with unshakable confidence.

"You're too damn brave for your own good, that's one of the reasons I want you in Idaho. Your life is too precious to me, and I won't see you suffer on my account. When things are settled here, I'll come for you."

"I'm not going, Blade," Shannon said with quiet determination. "I won't run away simply because some ignorant people don't want us here. I've never told this to anyone, but I've often thought my father a coward for killing himself at a time when his family needed him most. He could have faced his problems like a man, but he chose the easy way out. I'm not like him. I refuse to run away. We'll face this together."

"Your father wasn't right in his head when he took his life," Blade reminded her. Though Blade couldn't understand it—taking one's life was never the answer—he nevertheless felt compassion for the man who had been Shannon's father. "If he were in his right mind, he would never have considered leaving his wonderful family. Don't judge him harshly, Little Firebird. War does strange things to people. I thank God you had the strength of will to overcome the tragedy in your young life."

"Then you agree with me? I can stay?" Shannon asked, an unmistakable ring of triumph in her voice.

"Sometimes I think you're much wiser than I am," Blade conceded.

Suddenly a horrible notion occurred to Shannon. "You're not just saying all this because you're tired of me, are you? Is that why you want to send me away?"

"My God, how could you think such a vile thing? Without you I have no life. I want only what's best for you and our child."

"Then this discussion is over," Shannon said with a dazzling smile. "What's best for us is that we remain together. Now stop spouting nonsense and tell me what our plans are for the future."

"I love you, Shannon Branigan. Though I may live to regret it, I'll not send you away."

"You couldn't send me away, for I'd not go."

He kissed her then, lingeringly, lovingly, his hand resting on her stomach where his babe kicked strongly against his palm.

"We can't stay here," Blade mused when Shannon was once more nestled against his side. "Winter is coming, and it's too late to rebuild."

"Do we have enough money to rebuild?"

"There is still money in the bank, but not nearly enough to both rebuild and replenish our herd. I was counting heavily on selling our cattle to the army. There should be sufficient funds to pay our room and board over the next few months but little left for luxuries. With a baby to feed, I'll simply have to find work."

Shannon kept a wise silence, wondering who in Cheyenne would hire Blade when he wasn't even welcome in town. Most of the ranches in the area weren't taking on help with winter approaching. And Blade was hardly the type to tend store or do menial work. Nor was he likely to join the Sioux. His life was no longer with the Indians who raised him. He was astute enough to realize that the days when Indians roamed free on the plains were swiftly coming to an end. In order to survive and prosper, Blade had to make a place for himself in the white world.

"I could always go back to Fort Laramie and get back my old job as scout," Blade suggested thoughtfully. "But it won't be any easier for you there than it will be in Cheyenne."

"I can manage as long as we're together," Shannon declared. "What people say can't hurt me."

"It's the violence they're capable of that frightens me," Blade answered guardedly.

Shannon ground her teeth in mute rage. "We're going to stay in Cheyenne. If we don't make a stand now, it will be the same no matter where we go. We can't run away from your heritage. Our child will have Sioux blood running through his veins. I want to instill pride in him, not shame."

"Fortunately not everyone feels about Indians and half-breeds like Ezra Samms and people of his ilk."

The next day Blade hitched up the wagon and drove Shannon to Cheyenne. Jumping Buffalo and Sweet Grass elected to remain at Peaceful Valley for the winter and look after things. Their tipi was snug and warm and Blade promised to provide adequate supplies to last through the bitter months.

It wasn't easy to find a place to live in Cheyenne. Those who were sympathetic to Blade's plight feared reprisal from the rowdy element of town. It wasn't until Shannon appealed to Elizabeth Davis, who had remained a staunch friend, that adequate housing was found. Elizabeth was appalled by what had happened at Pleasant Valley and generously offered them her son's home for as long as her son and his wife remained abroad on their extended honeymoon. The house was newly built and completely furnished. They moved in immediately. But in order to preserve his self-respect, Blade persuaded Elizabeth to accept a modest monthly rent.

One of the first things Blade did in Cheyenne was visit the sheriff to report his stolen cattle and malicious destruction of his house. Sheriff Hall made a note of the skimpy information Blade provided but promised nothing in the way of results. Since Blade could identify none of the men, it was virtually impossible to bring them to justice.

"What are your plans for the future, Stryker?" the sheriff asked. "Are you staying in town?"

"My wife is expecting a child, I can hardly allow her to spend the winter in a tipi or bunkhouse. I've rented a house in town and hope to find work. I won't be satisfied until cattle graze on the hillsides of Peaceful Valley again."

Hoping to spare her mother worry, Shannon had written to Tucker instead, pouring out her anguish at the destruction of her home. Tucker's reply arrived one day while Blade was out looking for work, and Shannon was feeling particularly low.

Monday, November 8, 1869, Boise City, Idaho

My dearest Shannon,

I was greatly troubled by your recent news from Cheyenne. Although I think you are wrong about letting Mother know what is happening there, I will abide by your wishes and not show her the letter.

I'm afraid I have to agree with your husband. I think you should come to Boise, at least until after the baby is born. If things are even half as bad as your letter led me to believe, you would be better to leave that town behind. But I can almost hear that stubborn tone in your voice and know that I'm no more likely to convince you to leave Cheyenne than Blade was. So I am resigned to the fact that you won't be coming to Boise any time soon. However, I have already told Maggie that we're coming to see you next summer. I mean to make certain my sister is all right, and I think it's time one of the Branigans met your husband. . . .

Shannon's reading was interrupted by the sound of rapid footsteps. She looked up to see Blade standing in the doorway, his face like a thundercloud.

"What happened?" Shannon asked worriedly.

"Nothing for you to fret over."

"You may as well tell me."

"It was a mistake coming to Cheyenne. You could have been on your way to your family now if—"

"I thought we settled all that," Shannon said emphatically. "I love Peaceful Valley, and I want to raise our children there."

"I'm not even certain I can support our children," Blade complained bitterly. This terrible frustration was a feeling completely alien to Blade. "I've had no luck finding work. I nearly had a job at the Bar K Ranch today until Ezra Samms showed up and talked the trail boss out of hiring me."

"I'd like to wring that man's miserable neck," Shannon muttered darkly. "There's not a better man around than you. Surely there is someone in this town who recognizes your worth."

"Shannon, I—" His sentence was interrupted by a knock at the door. They exchanged startled looks, then Blade reached for the rifle leaning against the wall. These days he trusted no one. "Step aside, love, I'll get it."

The moment the door opened and Blade set the rifle down, Shannon knew it was perfectly safe to show herself.

"What brings you here, Sheriff Hall?"

A frisson of fear traveled up Shannon's spine. What had Blade done to bring the sheriff to their door?

"Business, Stryker. May I come in?"

"Certainly. Have you met my wife?"

Sheriff Hall stepped inside, closing the door behind him. "I've not had the pleasure."

After introductions were made, Shannon offered refreshments, which the sheriff politely declined. "I can't stay—duty, you know."

"May I ask the reason for your visit?" Blade aske
guardedly.

"I've done a lot of thinking since I saw you last, an
I did some digging into your background. I sent a wir
to Colonel Greer."

One black brow rose in an inquisitive arch. "
assume there is a reason for your sudden interest i
me."

"I'm getting to it. Greer wrote that you were
captain in the army and special agent to the presiden
Not everyone in Cheyenne is aware of that. Didn'
know it myself. You were involved in an investigatio
that halted illegal gun sales to renegade Indians."

"I'm also a half-breed," Blade reminded him. "
was raised by my Sioux mother. My grandfather wa
Chief Yellow Dog."

"I know that," Hall returned.

"What is the point of all this?"

"The point is that I want to hire you for m
deputy," Hall surprised Blade by saying. "I could us
a man like you. Hell, man, the whole town could use
man like you. Since the railroad pushed through i
1867, we get more than our share of undesirables i
town. A few weeks ago, Calamity Jane and the gan
she rides with showed up on a Saturday night and sho
the town up pretty good. Cattle Kate Watson and he
band of outlaws were seen in town recently.

"There is still an unruly element in Cheyenne, bu
at least we no longer have to rely on vigilante action t
keep order. With Cheyenne now the designated capi
tol of Wyoming Territory I'll need good men on th
side of the law. What do you say, Stryker? I thin
you'll find the pay decent enough."

Blade looked properly stunned and was momentari
ly tongue-tied. Not so Shannon.

"It's about time someone in Cheyenne recognize
Blade's worth," she declared with a hint of censure
"My husband will make a wonderful lawman."

Shannon's blessing was all Blade needed to loose
his frozen tongue. "You've got yourself a new depu

y," he said, offering Hall his hand. "When do I start?"

Hall grinned, vastly pleased with himself. "Is tomorrow too soon? The new territorial government organized in April this year and is meeting soon in Cheyenne. I'd like to see the rowdies gone, or at least under control by then. I suspect there will be demonstrations against women's suffrage when the legislature debates giving women the vote."

"Expect me bright and early tomorrow, Sheriff."

"Good-bye Mrs. Stryker. It was a pleasure meeting you. I heard you lecture once and was quite impressed."

"Good-bye Sheriff, and thank you—for everything."

"I knew something would turn up," Shannon crowed triumphantly once Sheriff Hall was gone.

"The pay will support us through the winter," Blade acknowledged, "but it will hardly provide enough to rebuild our ranch. Some way, somehow, I intend to see Peaceful Valley restored and prospering."

"You will, Blade, nothing is impossible."

"It would be simple if everything could be accomplished on your faith alone," Blade contended wryly. "Who would have thought someone like me would be lucky enough to have a wife like you? Each day I thank the Grandfather Spirit for putting you on that wagon train. And to think I argued against having you along."

"You were quite rude," Shannon giggled, recalling it as if it were yesterday. "I thought you didn't like me."

"If I remember correctly, you were properly shocked to learn I was a half-breed. But you were wrong about my not liking you. I was attracted to you from the beginning. Each time I saw you I wanted to throw you down and make love to you. Just like now."

"Doesn't my stomach disgust you?"

"How could it when it's my child resting beneath your heart? You're still beautiful to me. Even more so

than before, if that's possible. Tell me, Little Firebird
is it still permitted to take my wife to bed?"

"Not only is it permitted, but it is desirable,"
Shannon assured him. "We have a few weeks yet to
enjoy loving each other."

It was all the encouragement Blade needed. Lifting
Shannon carefully in his arms he carried her to their
bedroom. Their loving was slow and sweet, and oh so
gentle. He enclosed her in a world that extended no
farther than his embrace and powerful strength of his
hard body.

Chapter Twenty-Four

The next morning Blade was sworn in as deputy and his duties were explained to him. The one drawback to the job was having to leave Shannon alone on those nights he was on duty. Especially with her time drawing near.

Some of Cheyenne's citizens were first stunned, then appalled to learn Blade Stryker had been appointed Sheriff's deputy. Since Cheyenne had been named territorial capital, more people had come to settle. Many of them were personally familiar with Indians and the terrible atrocities attributed to them.

On the other hand, there were people happy to see Blade affiliated with the law. Dark and dangerous, he gave the impression of being fully capable of handling the most hazardous of duties. And paradoxically, most breathed a sigh of relief to find Blade aligned with law and order.

When Elizabeth Hobart Morris, the leader of the suffrage movement in Wyoming, arrived in town a few weeks later, Shannon persuaded Blade to take her t[o] hear the lecture despite her advanced state of preg nancy. The legislature was to convene in a very shor[t] time, drawing attention to suffrage and at the sam[e] time providing free publicity for Wyoming. It was a[n] undisputed fact that more women were necessary fo[r] the survival of Wyoming, and state officials used th[e] women's rights issue as a focal point in their plan t[o] lure female emigrants.

Truth to tell, the male population of Wyomin[g] treated suffrage as a great joke. Lacking foresight, n[o] one male citizen thought the day would ever com[e] when there would be enough women in Wyoming fo[r] their vote to matter. Then there were those men in th[e] all-Democratic legislature who hoped to use the su[f] frage issue to embarrass Republican governor John A[.] Campbell, who they believed would veto the bill. Ha[d] the opponents of women's suffrage realized that th[e] bill would be introduced, debated, and passed s[o] quickly and with so little resistance, they would hav[e] organized a vigorous, effective opposition. But at th[e] time of the legislative debate the usual arguments— that homes and families would be ruined, wome[n] unsexed, and divine law disobeyed—were not raised[.]

The night that Shannon and Blade attende[d] Elizabeth Morris's lecture, the press was well repre sented—the result, Shannon suspected, of the pres ence of legislator Bright and Secretary of State Lee[,] who wrote the suffrage bill. Shannon was pleasantl[y] surprised to hear William Bright hail her after th[e] lecture. She was shocked he even remembered her.

"Mrs. Stryker, it's good to see you again. And yo[u] too, Mr. Stryker," Bright greeted them in a friendl[y] manner. "I hope things have been going well for you.["] His gaze dropped to Shannon's protruding stomac[h] clearly outlined beneath her coat, and his eyes lit up[.] "I see congratulations are in order."

Shannon blushed, while beside her Blade puffed u[p] with typical male pride. "Mrs. Morris was wonderfu[l] wasn't she?" Shannon exclaimed.

"Yes, but so were you, my dear. Your last lecture was quite inspiring. Wyoming is lucky to count you among one of its citizens. People would do well to remember that it is the women who will ultimately tame the West." He turned to Blade. "Have you met Secretary Lee?"

Introductions were made and Blade was stunned to learn Secretary Lee knew all about him.

"Word gets around," the secretary said. "If President Johnson trusted you, Wyoming can do no less."

It was a grand moment for Blade, one he savored for a long time to come.

In early October word was received in Cheyenne that Red Cloud and his Sioux were gathering on the plains in protest of the Washita Massacre which had taken place the previous year. The tragic massacre occurred when soldiers of the 7th Cavalry, under the flamboyant Lieutenant Colonel George Armstrong Custer, had the luck to pick up a fresh trail of raiding Indians in the snow. They followed the trail to a Cheyenne encampment on the Washita River, which happened to be the village of Black Kettle, and surrounded the camp late at night. At dawn the cavalry burst into the sleeping camp like avenging furies. Unfortunately, Black Kettle was among the more than one hundred Indians dead.

This time, however, the army paid a price for its victory. Warriors from nearby camps, roused by the firing, joined the battle and forced Custer to retreat with his Indian captives. Unlike Sand Creek in 1864, the Washita Massacre produced no investigation by white officialdom. In fact, the headstrong Custer was heartily commended by his superiors for his bold action. The Indians waited for some word from Washington that the terrible deed would be investigated and Custer punished, and when none came they decided to retaliate with their own justice.

Telegraph lines were cut, passenger trains attacked, and anything moving on the prairie considered fair game. Travel and communications were disrupted to the point that it became dangerous for anyone to leave the city limits. The citizens of Cheyenne lived in terror, expecting hordes of Indians to ride into town and slay them in their sleep. A cry went up demanding that government officials do something about the potentially explosive situation.

The new Indian threat couldn't have come at a worse time where Blade was concerned. Slowly but surely he was being accepted as a valuable citizen of Cheyenne—only to find himself once again the target of hate directed at Indians in general and him in particular. Entirely because of this undeserved hostility, Blade offered to relinquish his badge.

"You need someone people trust to dispense the law," Blade argued when he presented his resignation to Sheriff Hall.

"I trust you," Hall said, looking Blade straight in the eye. "The town is damn fortunate to have you, Blade. I'm damn fortunate. Let's hear no more about resigning. Those of us who know you aren't concerned about your mixed blood."

"I appreciate that, Thad. You'll never have reason to doubt me."

"I know, Blade, you're—"

"Excuse me, I'd like to speak to Deputy Stryker."

While Blade and Sheriff Hall were talking, a man had entered the office. Blade stepped forward. "I'm Blade Stryker."

"I've come from the secretary of state. Secretary Lee would like to see you in his office as soon as possible."

"He wants to see me?" Blade repeated curiously.

"Right away, if you have the time."

"Go on, Blade," Hall urged. "It must be important for the secretary of state to send for you."

When Blade was ushered into Secretary Lee's office a short time later, he was reminded of that day he was summoned by President Johnson and set off on an adventure that gained him a wife he loved beyond all reason. Much had transpired since that fateful day over two years ago, and he wondered where this visit would lead him. If it meant parting from Shannon, he would have no difficulty refusing.

The first thing Blade noted was that Secretary Lee was not alone. Legislator Bright was with him. Bright greeted Blade warmly. "You remember Secretary Lee? You met at the recent suffrage lecture."

"Mr. Bright, Mr. Lee," Blade acknowledged. "What is this all about?"

"I'll come right to the point, Stryker," Lee began. "I'm authorized to speak in behalf of the governor. Please sit down and listen carefully."

Blade poised gingerly on the edge of the chair, waiting impatiently for Lee to continue. Instinctively he knew Lee's words would bring his peaceful existence to an end and he didn't like it one damn bit.

"Mr. Bright filled us in on your background. In view of your work for the president, the governor feels strongly that you are the one person who might help in this touchy situation with the Sioux. The townspeople are edgy and upset over the latest development on the prairie and are demanding the governor do something to lessen the tension."

"What is it you want from me?" Blade asked guardedly.

"I understand you are acquainted with Chief Red Cloud." Blade nodded, his eyes wary. "How well do you know him?"

"Well enough."

"You're aware, of course, that the Sioux are rallying under Red Cloud. Even as we speak, they gather to decide whether to attack en masse and where to strike next. They could launch an attack upon Fort Laramie or, God forbid, Cheyenne. We want them back on their reservation. We can't lure people to Wyoming until the Indians are under control."

"I am but one man—what can I do?" Blade inquired. Surely they didn't expect him to change the mind of a great chief like Red Cloud.

That was exactly what they wanted him to do. "We want you to convince Red Cloud that returning to the reservation is the best thing to do. Cavalry from three forts are preparing to ride against them. Hundreds of lives will be lost."

"What makes you think he'll listen to me?"

"Perhaps we're grasping at straws, but we're desperate. Winter is just around the corner," Lee contended, "and the Sioux have shown no inclination to return to their reservation before snow flies. You've lived in both worlds, and we feel you're qualified to advise Red Cloud. Let's hope he's wise enough to listen. The way things stand now, citizens of Cheyenne are afraid to leave their homes and are appealing to the governor for help."

"It's serious, Blade," Bright added. "Wyoming needs families and not even giving women the vote will persuade them to venture to our territory if Indians continue to threaten their existence."

"When I volunteered my services to the president, I had no wife or family to hinder me," Blade said with slow deliberation. "Things have changed. My wife is expecting our first child in a matter of weeks, and I don't feel comfortable leaving her alone and unprotected. The town isn't exactly friendly to me these days," he added wryly.

"I understand your concern and the bitterness you harbor, Stryker," Lee acknowledged. "And I'm asking that you put it all behind you. Once the citizens of Cheyenne learn what you are willing to do in their behalf, their feelings will change."

"I can't leave Shannon. I *won't* leave her," Blade resisted stubbornly.

"Don't worry about Shannon, Blade," Bright injected. "I spoke with Elizabeth Davis and Cora Allen first and both volunteered to see to her welfare in your absence. Both are great admirers of you and your lovely wife. Each generously offered to take Shannon into her home during your absence. And I personally will see that she wants for nothing."

The two men waited eagerly for Blade's answer. "Even if I agree, there is no guarantee Red Cloud will listen to me."

"You are Chief Yellow Dog's grandson. Red Cloud will accord you the courtesy of listening," Lee said. "That is all we ask. We expect no miracles. We will be grateful for whatever you accomplish."

"What do you offer Red Cloud in return for his compliance?" Blade asked. "You can't expect him to take his people back to the reservation without offering some incentive."

Bright and Lee exchanged thoughtful glances. "Food," Lee said. "Enough to last them through the winter."

"And warm clothing," Bright added. "If they return to the reservation, they will be provided with everything they need to survive the winter."

"They have heard those promises before," Blade challenged.

"This time you have my personal guarantee," Lee solemnly vowed. "In fact, you may tell Red Cloud that once I receive confirmation that they are on their way to the reservation, cattle and supplies will be sent immediately."

Blade searched Lee's face for a long time. Something in his expression must have satisfied Blade for he said, "I believe you, but I can't give you an answer until I speak with Shannon."

"Fair enough," Lee agreed somewhat reluctantly. "But I feel obliged to stress the need for haste. Red Cloud is poised to strike and many lives will be lost."

"I understand." Blade rose to leave.

"Thank you for coming, Stryker."

Blade strode out the door, closing it quietly behind him.

"What do you think?" Lee asked once Blade left the room.

"Blade Stryker is a proud and honorable man who wants what is best for both white and Indian. He is astute enough to realize that the day has come when Indians are no longer free to roam the plains and prairies," Bright reflected thoughtfully. "He is hesitant to leave his wife at this time, and I can understand his reluctance. We will have to content ourselves to wait until tomorrow for our answer."

Blade let himself into the house, his face carefully composed to conceal his anxiety from Shannon. Attuned to his every mood, however, Shannon knew immediately that something troubled him.

"Something happened," she said, kissing him warmly. "I can tell by the look on your face."

Blade managed a smile. "You know me so well, Little Firebird. Come," he urged, "sit on my lap."

"Do you think you can hold me?" she giggled delightedly.

"I'll manage."

Snuggling contentedly against Blade's broad chest, his large hand resting on her protruding stomach, Shannon waited for Blade to speak. She wasn't fooled one bit by his bravado. Something bothered him, something that concerned her.

"How much longer? The little one kicks strongly against my hand. He's anxious to enter the world, I think."

"The doctor says your son should make his appearance in a month."

"You're so certain it's a boy? It matters little to me as long as the babe is healthy. There is always time for sons."

"It's a boy," Shannon said with firm conviction. "I know we haven't discussed it much, but I'd like to name him after my brother Grady."

"And so you shall," Blade promised somewhat distractedly. He knew he had to broach the subject of his leaving somehow, but didn't know how to begin.

"Blade, you may as well tell me what is troubling

you. Perhaps I can help. Has Ezra Samms been causing problems again?"

"No, love, men like Samms I can handle. I've just come from Secretary of State Lee's office. Both he and Mr. Bright expressed their desire to speak with me."

"Whatever for?" Shannon asked curiously.

A shiver of dread laced through Shannon. She had assumed Blade was finished with dangerous missions like the one undertaken in the president's behalf. Yet what else could the secretary of state want with Blade if not to send him off on some hazardous duty? Blade's answer confirmed her worst fears.

"The territorial governor has requested that I speak to Red Cloud on his behalf. He wants me to convince Red Cloud to take his people back to their reservation. He fears blood will be shed on both sides if something isn't done."

Shannon searched Blade's face and recognized his indecision; the need to help was a powerful force inside him. However, his reluctance to leave her gave mute testimony to the dilemma he faced. Shannon knew she had only to utter one word of discouragement and he'd refuse the governor's request. She also knew that deep down inside him, Blade felt the driving compulsion to help his mother's people survive the taming of the West.

"Did you agree?" Shannon asked slowly.

"I'm to give him my answer tomorrow. I wanted to talk it over with you first. I won't do anything without your approval."

Shannon wanted desperately to tell Blade not to go, to stay with her, to never leave her, not even for a moment. But the words lodged like stones in her throat. It had to be Blade's decision. Pride demanded that he do what he thought necessary to maintain a peaceful coexistence between white and Indian.

"I can't tell you what to do, Blade."

"I'd only be gone for a week or two. I intend to be right beside you when our baby is born."

There was little doubt in Shannon's mind that

Blade had already made his decision; he awaited only her blessing—or her plea for him to remain at her side.

"This is important to you, isn't it?" was all Shannon said. It was difficult to utter the words he wanted desperately to hear.

"Lives are at stake, Shannon, both Indian and white lives. The red man's days are numbered. If I can convince Red Cloud to return to the reservation, it will prevent much bloodshed. If they don't return," Blade added ominously, "cavalry from three forts are poised to ride against them."

"You must do what your heart tells you," Shannon advised, still reluctant to give her blessing.

"Dammit, Shannon, I don't have to go if you're dead set against it. I can refuse the governor's request if you ask me to. You must know you'll always come first with me."

Shannon could see how tortured Blade was over this and with sinking heart knew exactly what she must do to ease his pain. Obviously he was being torn apart by his need to help the Sioux and his unwillingness to leave her alone at a time when their child could make its appearance momentarily.

The silence lengthened, until Blade could stand it no more. "I have to go, Little Firebird." His voice was so filled with anguish that it nearly broke Shannon's heart. "I don't want to leave you, but it won't be for very long. I wouldn't be able to live with myself if I didn't at least try to talk to Red Cloud."

"Of course you must go," Shannon finally said. Blade would never know how much it cost her to say those words. "Will Red Cloud listen to you? I couldn't bear it if—"

"Nothing will happen to me, love. I'm well known to Red Cloud. Whether or not he will follow my advice is another matter entirely. I can only try."

"When will you leave?"

"As soon as you're settled in with Elizabeth Davis. Obviously you can't stay here alone, and when Mr.

Bright told Elizabeth of my mission, she wouldn't hear of you remaining by yourself in your condition. Cora Allen feels the same way, but I thought you might prefer Elizabeth because her house is larger."

"I'm not afraid, Blade. I want to stay right here. You said yourself you'd be back in plenty of time for the birth."

"And so I shall, but I won't allow you to remain here alone."

"And I won't leave," Shannon returned, tilting her chin at a defiant angle.

She looked so adorable that Blade couldn't help but plant a kiss square on her mouth.

"What was that for?"

"Because I love you, and you're magnificent when you vent your Irish temper."

"Then you'll let me stay here in your absence?"

"No, I'll settle you in with the Davises before I leave."

The corners of Shannon's slanted downward. She didn't delude herself into thinking Blade would give in to her wishes, so she pretended acquiescence. "Very well, Blade, I'll go—but not until you leave. I want to spend every minute alone with you."

Blade hesitated, fully aware of Shannon's penchant for doing exactly what she wanted. Although Mr. Bright promised to watch over her, leaving Shannon alone did not rest comfortably with Blade.

"Will you promise to go to Elizabeth's the moment I'm gone?"

"I—yes," she lied without a hint of remorse. In Shannon's opinion, staying by herself for two weeks or less was hurting no one.

The wind whistling across the prairie was cold, biting, and relentless. Blade dug his heels into Warrior's side, urging him into a gallop as he crested a hill. He reined in abruptly, pausing to scan the horizon. He had been riding for nearly a week searching for Red Cloud's encampment, and finally his search was over.

Stretched out in the valley before him were hundreds of tipis. It was as if the entire Sioux nation had followed their chief from the reservation.

Picking his way carefully down the hill, Blade rode boldly into the village. Those people milling about turned to follow his passing, their eyes dulled by cold and hunger, and something else—hopelessness. The gaunt emptiness of their gazes tore at Blade's heart. The white man had reduced the once proud Sioux to a mere shadow of his greatness. In his grandfather's day the mighty Sioux warrior, hunter and superb horseman, ruled the plains. Today, their number greatly diminished, the people faced starvation and extinction. Never was Blade more aware of it than he was today.

As custom demanded, Blade reined in before the distinctively decorated tipi belonging to Red Cloud and waited for the mighty chief to come out and acknowledge him.

Red Cloud looked less than impressive when he finally stepped outside the tipi. A threadbare blanket was wrapped about his gaunt frame, his cheeks were hollow, his eyes bleak. Blade dismounted. A light sprinkling of snow crunched beneath his boots as he planted his feet on the ground.

"Swift Blade, grandson of Yellow Dog, what brings you to my village? Do you come to join the Sioux in their fight to drive the white man from their land?"

"I have come to talk with the chief of the great Sioux nation."

For several tense minutes, Red Cloud stared at Blade, his face a monument carved in stone. Then he abruptly turned, held back the flap to his tipi and motioned Blade inside. Seating himself cross-legged before the fire burning at the center of the enclosure, Red Cloud waited for Blade to settle himself before taking up a pipe and filling it with tobacco.

"We will smoke and talk, Swift Blade, grandson of Yellow Dog."

After the pipe was lit, Red Cloud took several long

puffs, then passed it to Blade, who did the same before handing it back. Then Blade waited patiently for Red Cloud to begin the conversation.

"Do you speak as a white man or an Indian, Swift Blade? You chose the white world many years ago. You fought in their war while the Sioux waged their own war."

"I speak as one who respects whites and Indians alike. The blood of my mother flows proud and strong through my veins. Yet I cannot deny the blood of my white father who sent me into his world so that I might learn his culture."

"And you made your choice," Red Cloud contended stonily.

"Yes, I chose to live as a white, but I haven't turned my back on my Sioux heritage. I care for my mother's people. That is why I have come."

"Speak what is in your heart, Swift Blade, but if you come to plead for the White Eyes you speak in vain."

"What I say comes from the heart, Red Cloud. I know the white man. They are as numerous as the blades of grass on the prairie; step on one and two more spring up to take its place. Nothing will stop them in their westward migration. The railroad stretches from coast to coast bringing more and more people into Indian territory. You cannot stop them, Red Cloud. Unless you take your people back to the reservation, none will survive the terrible onslaught that is sure to follow. Three forts are prepared to ride against you."

"All the things you speak of are already known to me, Swift Blade. I know the day when the Sioux and other Indian nations ride free on the prairie is long past. Do you think I want to see my people wiped from the face of the earth?

"But we are a proud people," Red Cloud continued. "Old ways die hard among a people steeped in tradition. We fight when we know we cannot win. We make peace only to have treaties broken. My people starve because the white man kills the buffalo that once were more numerous than stars in the heavens. How can we stop that which we don't understand? We fight, even though it means our death."

"You don't have to fight, or die, Red Cloud. Go back to the reservation and live in peace. The governor has promised meat and grain and warm blankets to see you through the winter."

Red Cloud snorted in derision. "They have been promised before."

In the interest of peace, Blade went out on a limb, hoping the branch wouldn't break behind him. "I personally guarantee that once you lead your people back to the reservation, you will receive the supplies I spoke of. If they fail to arrive as promised you may hold me personally responsible."

Red Cloud studied Blade's face with great interest, waging a battle inside himself. Swift Blade's words indicated that he was trusted and respected by the white chief of the territory. But did he speak as a friend to the Sioux or as a white man with a forked tongue? Swift Blade's grandfather had been a respected chief, but the grandson had lived as a white man long enough to adopt white ways. He looked like a white man and obviously thought like one. Yet Red Cloud genuinely liked Swift Blade and wanted to believe him, wanted him to be right about the food and supplies.

"Your promise is of little use to me once I return to the reservation and the supplies fail to arrive," Red Cloud said sourly.

"I do not lie. I am as much Indian as I am white."

"That is what I fear," Red Cloud muttered, his eyes narrowing thoughtfully as he stared at Blade. "Nevertheless I have come to a decision."

"You'll take your people back to the reservation?" Blade asked hopefully. His easy victory surprised him.

"We will return to the reservation," Red Cloud conceded.

Elation seized Blade, until he heard Red Cloud's

next words. "And you will accompany us. When the supplies arrive, you will be free to leave. If they do not arrive . . ." His sentence trailed off ominously, his omission more potent than his words.

"No," Blade refused quietly. "I cannot go with you. My wife will have our first child in a few weeks. She needs me."

"Your wife is white," Red Cloud said with a hint of censure. "Her own kind will see to her safety in your absence. You say you care for the Sioux and are concerned about what happens to them. I say you are more white than Indian, that you care only for your white friends."

"I have few white friends," Blade said with bitter denial.

"Nevertheless, you will make the journey with us to the reservation," Red Cloud declared, his words brooking no argument. "We will see if your white chief is a man of honor."

Chapter Twenty-Five

Shannon didn't regret her decision to remain by herself in the small house she shared with Blade during his absence. She felt closer to him in the place where they had been so happy, and Lord knew she needed that small comfort at a time like this. With her baby due in a matter of weeks, it was an effort just dragging her heavy body from place to place, and she rarely left the house. Fortunately, she did not lack for company. William Bright and his wife called on her often during the weeks of Blade's absence. Elizabeth Davis and Cora Allen were also frequent visitors.

Though each of her friends tried to talk her out of remaining alone, Shannon was adamant in her refusal to move. She hoped Blade wouldn't be too angry at her, for she had given a half-hearted promise to go to Elizabeth's house. Shannon's thoughts were consumed by Blade. She wondered if he had found Red Cloud and if he was already on his way home. Was he successful or had he failed to convince Red Cloud to return to the reservation?

Heaving a wistful sigh, Shannon gazed out the window at the wind-driven snow that splashed against the window pane. She hated to think of Blade out in this kind of weather, but she was comforted by the knowledge that he was trained to survive the elements. With aimless purpose, she turned from the window and walked to the stove, bending with difficulty to feed sticks of wood into its belly. She straightened slowly, placing her hands at the small of her back to ease the nagging pain that had plagued her these past several days. A knock at the door brought a frown to Shannon's face. She was surprised that anyone would come calling in this dreadful weather.

A strange lethargy held Shannon captive as she slowly made her way to the door. Something inside her flashed a warning to her brain as she opened the door, but it failed to prepare her for the unwelcome sight of Claire Greer. Claire stood on the doorstep, shivering with cold.

"Claire, what in God's name are you doing here? I thought you were visiting in the East."

"I was," Claire said, rudely pushing her way past Shannon. Shannon had no option but to shut the door behind her as a blast of frigid air rippled her skirt and chilled her ankles. "I returned just yesterday and decided to call on you before going on to Fort Laramie."

"What is it you want?" Shannon asked with cool disdain. The woman had caused her and Blade trouble enough to last a lifetime.

Claire's lip curled in derision as she ran her eyes insultingly over Shannon's rounded form. "So, you're going to bring another half-breed into the world," she observed crudely. "From the looks of you, it won't be long."

"Just say what you've come to say and leave," Shannon said tersely. It took all of her willpower just to be civil to the witch.

"I hear you lost your ranch to fire." Claire's smirk set Shannon's teeth on edge.

"I hope you're pleased with yourself."

Ignoring Shannon's remark, Claire continued relentlessly. "Rumor has it your husband is off trying to talk the Sioux into returning to the reservation. I'm surprised the governor saw fit to trust a half-breed with so important a mission. A savage like Blade is as likely to join the Indians as he is to persuade them into something they obviously don't want to do."

Claire shivered delicately, pretending fear and revulsion, but she didn't fool Shannon one bit. The avid expression on Claire's face and the feral light in her violet eyes gave mute testimony to her attraction to Blade.

"I could have had Blade once," Claire bragged, "but I wanted nothing to do with him. He begged me to—be friends with him, but wisely I refused."

Shannon knew the woman lied. "I don't believe you, Claire. If this is what you came to say, you can leave now."

"The reason I came was to tell you what your interference has done to my life. Ronald Goodman was tried in Washington, found guilty, and sent to prison. I attended the trial."

"It's no more than he deserved."

"We could have had a wonderful life. But for you and your husband, I could have had wealth and power, everything I've always wanted in life."

"I'm sorry for you, Claire, but not for the reasons you think. I'm sorry because you feel no remorse for what Goodman did, because you encouraged him, and because you're a cruel, vindictive woman. Your parents are good people. I wonder what happened to produce a daughter like you?"

Uncontrollable rage seized Claire and she struck out viciously. Unfortunately Shannon was standing close enough to receive the brunt of Claire's blow as she reeled backwards. Unable to maintain her balance she tottered dangerously for a moment, then crashed heavily to the floor. Something inside her seemed to snap as pain rippled a path from back to front, tearing her apart. No one had to tell Shannon her baby was about to make its somewhat premature entrance into the world.

Another contraction caused Shannon's face to contort with pain. Claire stood over her, gloating, making no effort to help.

"Claire, help me up," Shannon pleaded, extending a hand. "The baby—the pain—"

"Your pain is nothing compared to the agony you caused me," Claire sniffed unfeelingly. "I refuse to lift a finger in your behalf. It's no more than you deserve."

"Then get Doctor Clarke, or stop by Elizabeth Davis's house and tell her I need her." Another strong contraction prevented further speech.

"Do it yourself," Claire returned with careless disdain.

"For God's sake, Claire, the life of an innocent child is at stake. Forget what you feel for me."

"The world doesn't need another half-breed. Goodbye, Shannon. I'm glad we had this little chat."

Claire opened the door and the force of the wind took it from her hand and banged it against the wall. She didn't bother closing it, vanishing swiftly into the swirling snow that blew unhindered inside the house, chilling Shannon to the bone.

Dragging herself painfully across the floor, Shannon found the strength to pull herself up, using the wall for support. With great difficulty she forced the door shut, the wind nearly defeating her. The weather had grown bitter, and Shannon realized that it would be a grave mistake to venture out in search of help now. She also knew the birth of her child was mere hours away, and no one was likely to come calling to check on her in such foul weather. Nor could she depend on Claire to send help.

Marshaling her meager strength and pacing herself between contractions, Shannon gathered towels, sharp knife and twine and took them into her bedroom. Then she filled a basin with water, dropped the knife into it and set it to boil on the stove in her bedroom. With several younger brothers and sisters, Shannon wasn't ignorant of the birthing process— was quite knowledgeable, in fact, having watched Callie Johnson give birth. She prayed for an easy birth, for beyond simple procedures she knew nothing. Then she prepared for a long wait. At times the pain caused her to grit her teeth and cry out, but fortunately it was still bearable.

Surprisingly, she found time to change into a gown and robe and build up the fire in the stove. Truth to tell, Shannon was amazed at her presence of mind despite such crushing pain. She hadn't expected the pain to be so overwhelming and tried desperately to be brave. But she was inexperienced, alone, and afraid. Morning turned into afternoon, and a lowering sky and murky snow brought on a strange twilight. By late afternoon, Shannon's pain was nearly constant and the need to push urgent within her. Intuition told her it was time and she couldn't do a blessed thing to stop it.

Carefully she carried the basin of hot water to the bedside table, then removed her robe and lay down. She had expended the last of her endurance, accomplished more than she thought humanly possible given the circumstances. Only the knowledge that Blade expected her to deliver their child safely kept her sane. Then she offered up a short prayer, placing herself and her child in God's hands. She hadn't lost the deep faith instilled in her since birth and now she relied on that faith to see her through this ordeal.

The pain was terrible now. She was bearing down and grinding her teeth in agony. Though the room was warm, cold sweat dotted her brow and soaked her gown. She strained, and was rewarded with more pain. From deep in her throat a scream formed, bursting past her white lips in a shrill explosion of sound. She had no idea that the sound carried above the whine of the wind, echoing through the house to two people who stood just outside the front door, braving snow and ice to bring Shannon a message.

"My God, what is that?"

William Bright looked at Elizabeth Davis with something akin to horror.

"Shannon!" Elizabeth cried with growing alarm. "Something is wrong with Shannon!"

Bright pounded on the door, calling Shannon's name.

Receiving no reply, Elizabeth turned the knob, surprised to find it give beneath her fingers. She rushed inside, Bright close on her heels. Shannon was nowhere in sight. Then a strangled cry coming from the bedroom sent Elizabeth rushing in that direction. Bright hung back, unwilling to enter Shannon's bedroom unless he was needed. Elizabeth took one look at Shannon, saw that she was in the last stages of labor, and called over her shoulder, "Get the doctor, quick!"

Exhausted but happy, Shannon held her son close to her heart. So much love went into making this precious scrap of humanity, Shannon thought wistfully, wishing Blade had been there to witness the miracle of birth.

By the time Doctor Clarke arrived, Elizabeth had everything well in hand. Grady Farrell slid into the doctor's capable hands minutes after his hasty arrival. Hugging her son to her breast, Shannon closed her eyes, ready to slide into a well-deserved rest. Elizabeth's soft voice pulled her abruptly back from the edge.

"Shannon, Mr. Bright would like a few words with you if you're not too tired."

"Is it about Blade?" Shannon asked eagerly, her weariness slipping away.

"Why don't I let him tell you. May I send him in?"

"Oh yes, please."

William Bright tiptoed into the room, stopping beside the bed and smiling down on Shannon and the babe. "Blade will be surprised and pleased with his son. I'm glad Elizabeth and I arrived in time—although I'm certain you could have handled everything with your usual competence."

"You've heard from Blade?" Shannon asked anxiously.

"Not directly," Bright admitted, "but our spies reported just today that the Indians have dismantled their camp and left for the reservation. We owe your husband a debt of gratitude, young lady. I don't know what he said to convince Red Cloud, but the entire populace of Wyoming is grateful. Incidentally, the food and provisions we promised are on their way to the reservation."

"Then Blade should be on his way home!" Shannon exclaimed happily.

"I would think so," Bright concurred. "Get some rest now, my dear. I'm looking forward to congratulating Blade in person."

Elizabeth Davis arranged to stay with Shannon during her recuperation, or until Blade returned. As it turned out, Shannon was on her feet and caring for herself and little Grady long before Blade arrived. Since her delivery was uncomplicated, she regained her strength quickly and Elizabeth was able to return to her own family at the end of two weeks. Shannon was so certain Blade would show up momentarily that she refused Elizabeth's offer to remain longer.

Two weeks slipped into three, then four. Grady was a month old, and a terrible fear seized Shannon; intuition warned her that something unexpected and dreadful had happened to Blade to keep him from returning to her. December had arrived and no one had heard a word from Blade. Shannon was afraid—so afraid.

It wasn't as if she wanted for anything. Between the Brights and her other friends, Shannon was well provided for. What truly amazed Shannon was the change in the attitude of the townspeople. Those same people who had treated her and Blade with contempt had abruptly reversed their thinking since word spread about the great service Blade had performed in their behalf. Some of the neighbors and others who had once snubbed her on the street stopped by with kind words and gifts of food, apologizing profusely for their despicable behavior. But nothing or no one could heal the ache in Shannon's breast caused by Blade's prolonged and mysterious absence.

At first Shannon blamed Blade's continued absence on the bad weather. But as time passed an unexplained forboding replaced all logic. She knew that nothing, absolutely nothing save death or imprisonment, would prevent Blade from returning in time for his child's birth. A feeling beyond mere intuition told Shannon that something beyond Blade's control was preventing his return.

Two days later a break in the weather brought a visitor to Shannon's door. Hope leaped in her breast as she invited William Bright into her cozy parlor.

"You've heard from Blade! Is he all right?" Small talk was unnecessary as Shannon went directly to the crux of her concern.

"The secretary's office just received word from our Indian agent that Red Cloud and his people reached the reservation. Blade is with them."

"What!" Shannon was stunned. Why would Blade accompany Red Cloud to the reservation when he knew she was close to giving birth? It just didn't make sense. "Why would he do that?"

"It wasn't by choice," Bright said as gently as possible. "According to information we received, Blade is being held hostage until the provisions promised to Red Cloud arrive at the reservation."

"But you sent them long ago!" Shannon cried, her voice shrill with alarm. "Or did you lie about that?"

"We didn't lie, my dear. They were sent."

"Then where is Blade?"

"The supplies never reached the reservation. We think they were stolen by renegades. The men driving the supply wagons were found dead on the prairie half-way between here and the Black Hills."

"What are you going to do about it? Surely you'll not sacrifice Blade—not after he did the territory so great a service."

"No, my dear," Bright assured her. "We're grateful to Blade, very grateful. The governor has ordered more provisions to be sent. It's rather difficult buying cattle in mid-winter, but it's not impossible. It may take some time, however."

"What if Red Cloud won't wait?" Shannon asked frantically. "What if he is angered by what he perceives as false promises? What will happen to Blade?"

"Shannon, I don't think Red Cloud will harm Blade."

"You don't know that!"

"True, but I think Red Cloud is only using Blade as a weapon to insure that his demands are met," Bright surmised. "Try not to worry."

"Not worry! You ask the impossible."

"I've brought cheerful news along with the bad," Bright said, his face suddenly aglow. "It's official. Women now have the right to vote and hold public office. It's a stride in the right direction for the great territory of Wyoming. The first in the entire nation. And you, my dear Shannon, can be proud of the work you did in behalf of women the world over."

"That *is* good news," Shannon said slowly, her enthusiasm dimmed by her concern over Blade. "I worked for the cause out of deep conviction, not for any glory it might bring me. But about Blade—is there nothing you or the governor can do to help him?"

"Nothing that isn't already being done. Our Indian agent has been instructed to inform Red Cloud that more provisions are on their way and to demand Blade's immediate release. We can only hope for the best."

It was bitter cold, so damn cold that Blade's teeth set up a constant chatter. They had reached the reservation in the midst of a violent snowstorm. Food was scarce, and the one thin blanket he'd been given was too threadbare to provide adequate warmth. If the governor's provisions didn't arrive soon, there would be no Sioux left to receive them. Red Cloud was in a fine rage and several times in the past weeks Blade genuinely feared for his life.

Blade had no inkling what had happened to the provisions that had been promised. He had trusted the governor to deliver them, had staked his life and reputation on the provisions arriving at the reservation. Meanwhile, there was nothing to do but sit and wait and hope Red Cloud didn't decide to kill him in retaliation.

Blade's primary concern was for Shannon and how she must have reacted when he failed to arrive in time for his child's birth. If she hadn't given birth by now, she was very close. He knew she was being adequately looked after, but the length of his absence surely must be hard for her to bear. He had promised to be with her during delivery of their child and hated it because he wasn't.

Blade thought about escape often but deliberately refrained from formulating a plan. If he escaped, Red Cloud would have one more reason to hate and distrust the whites. But if he remained a hostage Red Cloud would know that he was a man of his word and that he trusted the officials of Wyoming to keep their promise.

Blade huddled close to the fire, its meager warmth welcome in the cold tipi. Wood was scarce and buffalo chips even harder to come by; it was no wonder the Sioux fought against life on the reservation. Suddenly the tent flap flew opened and Red Cloud stepped inside, followed by a white man Blade didn't recognize. Red Cloud spoke in rapid Sioux, which the man seemed to follow easily.

"The white chief in Cheyenne has expressed concern for you, Swift Blade. He sends his agent to demand your release and make new promises."

"Blade Stryker, I'm Miles Holt, the Indian agent,"

the man said, holding out his hand to Blade. "When I heard you were being held hostage I immediately wired the governor."

Blade grasped the man's hand. "Have you word of my wife?"

"No, sorry. But I've come to tell Chief Red Cloud that more meat and provisions are being sent to replace those stolen by renegades."

"So that's what happened to them," Blade said slowly.

"More empty promises," scoffed Red Cloud.

"The governor and secretary of state are trustworthy and honorable men. You'll have your provisions," Holt promised. "Meanwhile, they ask that you allow Blade Stryker to return to his family."

"Swift Blade is not free to leave," Red Cloud said. His features were cold and threatening. "His white wife will never see him again if another excuse is given to explain why our provisions have not arrived. Tell that to your white chief."

"I'm sorry, Stryker," Holt said, shrugging his shoulders helplessly. "The weather is working against us, but the provisions *will* arrive. This time a patrol from Fort Laramie will make certain that delivery is made."

"In the meantime I sit and wait," Blade complained bitterly, "while my wife has our child without me there to offer comfort and support."

Once Holt was gone, Blade stewed for a long time in indecision. He knew he couldn't wait any longer, that he had to leave with or without Red Cloud's permission. The provisions would arrive soon and he no longer felt the need or obligation to stand hostage for their delivery. Sitting, waiting, doing nothing was a complete waste of time. He worried about Shannon despite Bright's promise to see to her welfare. According to Blade's calculations his child was due in a matter of days, or had already arrived, and he wanted to be with Shannon. He must have been out of his mind to agree to this crazy mission. He began immediately to plan his escape.

Shannon spent a lonely Christmas, even though she was not alone. She and the baby passed a pleasant day with Elizabeth and her family, but it wasn't Blade. Mr. Bright had assured her that Blade was in good health and that he'd be home soon, but words meant nothing compared to the ache in her heart caused by Blade's absence. He didn't even know he had a son.

In the first week of January, 1870, an unseasonable thaw occurred, and Blade rejoiced, for it provided the opportunity for escape he had been praying for. He knew he must plan carefully and do it before snow and blizzards once again swept across the prairie, making travel difficult. And if at all possible his escape had to include Warrior. They had been through too much together to part now.

Red Cloud's usual habit was to place a guard inside Blade's tipi each night, and tonight was no different. Yet Blade knew he would never find another night better suited for escape. There was no moon, the sky was overcast, and a black curtain settled over the land.

Later that night Eagle Feather entered Blade's tipi and hunkered down beside the fire. He had guarded Swift Blade before and knew from experience that the man was wily and bore watching. But since Blade had been the model prisoner, he expected nothing this night. That was his first mistake. His second was dozing off in the middle of the night. Before he could gather his wits, he was quickly overpowered and trussed up neatly.

Blade left the tent by crawling beneath the buffalo hide and out the back. So far so good, he thought as he flattened himself against the outside wall of the tent to get his bearings. The next step was to find Warrior. He located his horse amidst the Indian ponies staked nearby and led him quietly through the sleeping village. He didn't mount until he was far enough away

to ride without being heard. If he was lucky, his
absence wouldn't be noticed till morning.

At first light Red Cloud and his warriors were hard
on Blade's heels.

Meanwhile in Cheyenne, Shannon learned that the
provisions promised Red Cloud were ready to be sent.
The moment she heard that a patrol from Fort Laramie had arrived to provide safe escort, she called on
William Bright and begged him to allow her to
accompany the convoy.

"What about your child, my dear?" Bright asked,
appalled that she should even suggest such a bold
move. "Surely you wouldn't want to leave him behind. No one knows how long the weather will hold,
and the wagons could become bogged down if snow
begins to fall again. No, Shannon, Blade would have
my hide if I agreed to so foolhardy a notion."

"It's been three months since Blade left. He doesn't
even know he has a son," Shannon cried in obvious
distress.

"I'm sorry, Shannon, it is out of the question. "But
I am glad you came today to see me. I have something
to tell you. Something exciting that I hope will please
you as much as it pleases me."

Shannon frowned. "What is it? I certainly could use
some cheerful news. Is it about Blade?"

"I wish I could tell you it was about Blade, but
perhaps my news will make up for it. You have been
appointed one of the first women in the territory to
hold public office. You have just been appointed
Justice of the Peace."

"I—I don't understand," Shannon stuttered,
stunned. "Surely there are more deserving women
than I."

"Perhaps, but you're the woman who has been
selected. In a matter of weeks you will be hearing civil
cases, as soon as an office can be located and furnished. Does that please you?"

"I—yes, I am pleased, but that still doesn't stop me

from wanting to go to Blade." Actually, Shannon was immensely pleased and proud of the honor bestowed on her, but she couldn't allow herself to think about it yet.

"He'll be home soon, Shannon, I promise."

Bright's promise wasn't good enough to satisfy Shannon, so she decided to take matters in her own hands in her usual reckless manner. Leaving Grady in the very capable hands of the wet nurse she had hired earlier, Shannon rode out to Peaceful Valley to see Jumping Buffalo and Sweet Grass. They had fared well so far in their snug tipi, living off wild game and the supplies provided by Blade. Both were happy to see Shannon but disappointed that she hadn't brought the baby, whom they had yet to see.

"What brings you to Peaceful Valley?" Sweet Grass asked as they hunkered down before the fire. "Do you bring us word of Swift Blade?"

"Blade is still being held by Red Cloud," Shannon confided, "but more provisions are being sent to the reservation to replace those stolen by renegades. A patrol from Fort Laramie will accompany them. I asked to go along but was denied."

Jumping Buffalo and Sweet Grass knew all about Blade's mission, for Blade himself had told them before he left.

Jumping Buffalo searched Shannon's face. His keen perception told him exactly why Shannon had come to Pleasant Valley, and he didn't like it.

"What do you seek from me, Little Firebird?"

"Take me to Red Cloud. I must see for myself that Blade is all right. Perhaps I can convince him to release Blade."

"Red Cloud isn't easily persuaded," Jumping Buffalo said, hoping to discourage Shannon. "It is a bad time to travel. This lull in the weather is deceptive. It is bound to change."

"I've considered all that, and I still intend to go. Will you take me?"

Jumping Buffalo hesitated for so long that Shannon threatened stubbornly, "If you don't take me, I'll go by myself."

"What of your child, Little Firebird?" This from Sweet Grass who followed the conversation as best she could. "How can you leave him, when he is so young?"

"I don't want to leave him, but I must," Shannon said fervently. "I've hired a wet nurse, a responsible woman with good references who will look after him. She recently lost her husband and has a child a few months older than Grady. She needs the work and can bring her own baby with her. My son will be well cared for in my absence."

Sweet Grass leveled a speaking glance at her husband. "I would do the same were I Little Firebird."

Jumping Buffalo grunted in obvious acknowledgement of Sweet Grass's words, and after a long thoughtful pause seemed to come to a decision.

"Meet me at the north edge of town. Bring supplies to last two weeks."

"What about Sweet Grass?" Shannon wondered aloud. "Will she remain at Peaceful Valley alone?"

"She will come with us."

It was settled. At least she wouldn't be sitting home wondering about Blade, Shannon reasoned. She'd be doing something positive. Right or wrong she had to find out what happened to Blade. Being selected Justice of the Peace had certainly thrilled her, but nothing was as important as her husband's life.

Chapter Twenty-Six

*B*lade's skill might have impressed whites, but it was extremely difficult to trick Indians, especially one as canny as Red Cloud. Blade knew they were close on his heels, and the winter-stripped hills and plains provided little cover in which to hide. He could only press forward and hope Warrior had the stamina to outrun the Indian ponies. When it grew too dark to ride safely, he found a gully on a hillside large enough to conceal both himself and his mount. Rolling into a ball to conserve warmth, Blade went to sleep hungry, having neither food to sustain him nor weapons to hunt his own dinner.

Shannon, Jumping Buffalo, and Sweet Grass passed the slower moving supply train headed toward the reservation two days out of Cheyenne. Sargeant O'Brien was in charge of the patrol. He was shocked to the core to see Shannon riding in the company of Indians and said so when he rode out to intercept them.

"Miss Branigan—I mean Mrs. Stryker—what are you doing out here? Who are these two Indians?"

"Jumping Buffalo and his wife are giving me escort to Red Cloud's village," Shannon said. Her chin rose defiantly, daring him to object or interfere. "I'm worried about Blade."

"Begging your pardon, ma'am, but Red Cloud's village is no place for a woman," O'Brien warned. "According to our instructions, your husband will be released as soon as the provisions are delivered to Red Cloud. We're along to see that nothing happens this time. I suggest you turn around and go back home."

"I can't do that, Sargeant. For weeks I've sat home wondering and waiting and I can no longer bear the agony of not knowing what happened to my husband."

"Then ride along with us," O'Brien said. "We have tents and provisions enough to make travel comfortable for you and your—er, friends."

"I will consult with Jumping Buffalo and do what he thinks best," Shannon decided. "He is Blade's friend and I trust his judgment."

After giving the matter considerable thought, Jumping Buffalo recommended that they continue on alone. Joining the supply train would only slow them down to a snail's pace and the unsettled weather could change at any minute. At this time of year, it could start snowing again or blow up a blizzard in a matter of hours. Sargeant O'Brien didn't like their decision, but he had no authority to stop them, so he allowed them to pass, wishing them well.

"Tell Red Cloud his provisions are on the way," he called after them, "and good luck."

Shannon offered a prayer of thanks when the weather held for yet another day. They were within a day's ride of the reservation now and her excitement over seeing Blade again was enormous. Only one more night on the trail, sleeping in a tent, she thought happily, before she'd be in Blade's arms. She couldn't wait to tell him he had a son, and that the townspeople had come to accept him after he had convinced Red Cloud to return to the reservation. It was good to know they no longer had anything to fear from the citizens of Cheyenne.

That night, luck deserted Shannon and her companions. In a matter of hours temperatures plummeted and the weather abruptly turned bitter. After a hastily prepared supper, they retired to their tents and Shannon fell asleep immediately—only to awaken a few hours later to the unmistakable sound of howling wind. Peering through the tent flap, she saw that a dusting of new snow already lay on the ground and more fell from the inky sky at a furious pace. It was bound to slow them down the next day, but unfortunately it couldn't be helped.

The same snowfall Shannon was lamenting, Blade blessed. Not only would the fresh snow cover his tracks, but it would slow down Red Cloud and his warriors. He hoped it would also persuade them to abandon their pursuit.

Blade's pressing need now was for shelter and food. He had no bedroll and the clothing he wore on his back provided meager warmth. He hadn't eaten a decent meal in days, and before that he had shared the Indians' scant rations. He had quenched his thirst by breaking ice and drinking from streams, but his stomach rumbled hungrily.

Blade shivered inside his coat, wishing he had a thick buffalo robe to protect him from the swirling snow and penetrating wind. It gave him small comfort to know that Red Cloud and his men had to endure the same conditions he did. Then, through the dense white curtain Blade saw a copse of bare-branched trees. Since it offered the only shelter for miles, he reined Warrior in that direction. He was shocked to see two small tents staked side-by-side and horses huddled together nearby. What would travelers be doing on the prairie at this time of year? No matter who they were, Blade was determined to awaken them and ask to share their food and shelter.

The cushion of snow muffled his approach and his footsteps were nearly noiseless as he dismounted, yet someone inside the tent had heard him. Blade froze, then turned slowly when he heard the unmistakable sound of a gun being cocked.

"Don't shoot, I'm unarmed," Blade said quietly. "I wish only to share your food and shelter for the night."

He dared to breath when the arm holding the gun slowly lowered. "Swift Blade, is it you, my friend?" Jumping Buffalo recognized Blade's voice immediately.

"Jumping Buffalo! My God, what are you doing out here in the wilderness at this time of year? Who is with you?" Blade asked, glancing toward the second tent. A terrible suspicion grew in his mind and refused to let go.

"Your woman."

"My—you're joking. Shannon wouldn't be crazy enough to—" His sentence trailed off. He knew damn well that Shannon was headstrong enough and rash enough to dare anything. But what about their babe? Surely she wasn't so reckless as to endanger a newborn child's life by exposing it to the elements? Suddenly a horrible thought chilled his blood.

"Jumping Buffalo, what of my child?"

"Little Firebird will tell you. Go to her. She insisted on making this journey to convince Red Cloud to release you."

"The little fool," Blade bit out tightly, appalled by Shannon's recklessness, yet loving her all the more for her desire to help him. "I'm being followed. I escaped from Red Cloud's custody. He wasn't prepared yet to let me go."

"Go to Little Firebird. I will keep watch. But you no longer need fear Red Cloud. His provisions are but a few miles behind us."

"Thank God. I was beginning to doubt the governor's word and my own foolish wisdom." He looked longingly toward Shannon's tent, needing her now more than he needed food and drink. A force stronger than life drove him to her. "Call me if I'm needed."

It was pitch black inside the small tent. Dropping to his knees, Blade crawled through the flap, his hands easily locating Shannon's bedroll. With an efficiency of movement he pulled off his jacket, shirt, pants and boots, lifted an edge of the blanket and slid down beside her.

Shannon sighed, drawn deeper into her dream. It was always the same. Blade was in bed beside her, leading her to that place where she was all response and pure sensation. He did it so well, she recalled, his hands and mouth playing her with the skill of a fine musician. Shannon reveled in her dream, her body responding instinctively to his unspoken commands. She no longer felt the cold; it was as if someone had built a fire inside her, warming her, heating her blood.

She wanted to open her eyes but knew that if she did her dream would evaporate and Blade would disappear, just as he had done dozens of other times. His hands on her flesh felt so real, his kiss more than mere imagination.

"Blade—" His name slipped easily from between her lips. "Love me."

"Forever," Blade whispered, his hands finding their way inside her clothing to caress the full curve of her breast.

This can't be a dream! Shannon's mind screamed. In her previous dreams Blade had never spoken. Nor had he felt so alive and vital. Jolted by reality, Shannon's eyes flew open. Her hands reached for him, finding his face, tracing his beloved features. "You're real—oh God, you're real!"

"Damn right I'm real and I know just how to prove it," Blade chuckled with slow relish.

"How—I expected you to be with Red Cloud," Shannon stammered, thoroughly shaken to find Blade in her bed in the middle of this frozen wilderness.

"I left," Blade explained tersely. Then he placed a hand on her flat stomach. "Not another word until you tell me about our child. Is—is it all right? Surely you didn't bring our child with you?"

"Your son is just fine, Blade," Shannon revealed. "He's in good hands."

"I have a son? Should you be traveling so soon? Dammit, Little Firebird, I ought to beat you for this."

"Don't fret so, Blade. Our son came into the world over two months ago. He was a few weeks early, weighing only five pounds, but healthy. He's as lusty as his father. I left him with a woman who came highly recommended. She has a child of her own and is a capable wet nurse. I had to come, Blade. Sitting at home, waiting and wondering, was driving me crazy."

"What did you expect to accomplish?"

"I'm not certain," Shannon admitted sheepishly. "I just knew I had to do something. Are you angry?"

"Damn right," he said fiercely. Then his voice gentled. "But with you here in my arms, there is room for no emotion but love. Oh, God, Little Firebird, I want to love you. I've been without you so long."

With trembling hands he peeled away the layers of her clothes. Both wore long underwear, but even those joined the growing pile of clothing beside the bedroll.

"I'm sorry I wasn't with you when our son was born. Was it very bad?"

"No. Grady Farrell was small, the birth fairly uncomplicated." Deliberately she oversimplified, leaving much unsaid. She didn't want to anger him again by telling him about Claire and how she was almost forced to deliver her child alone.

"Grady Farrell. It's perfect. You're perfect. I love you, Shannon. Thank you for giving me my son."

He kissed her then, his mouth claiming hers with all the pent-up longing in his heart. He had missed her—Lord, how he had missed her. His breath was warm on her lips as his hands slid along her body, worshipping her with his fingertips. Shannon's eyes fluttered shut and her arms around his neck held him close.

"Like a fire, you ignite a flame in my heart." He

murmured the words as he kissed the corners of her mouth. "I am consumed by you. You are as much a part of me as the heart that pumps blood through my body."

Shannon shivered with frenzied delight. His words were as much an aphrodisiac as his hands and lips. "You always know the right things to say," she giggled giddily.

Then his arms slid around her waist, pulling her tight against him, letting her feel the strength of his arousal as his head descended to hers. His kiss was anything but gentle. His mouth slanted over hers, parted her lips. His tongue slid inside, exploring the contours of palate and cheeks, running over her teeth and stroking her tongue. Instinctively she responded, stroking his tongue with her own.

His hands cupped her bottom, and Shannon could feel the heat and urgency of his need. Instinctively she rubbed herself against it, seeking to ease the ache between her legs.

"Jesus, Shannon!" It came out as a groan as Blade slid his mouth from her lips to her neck, then lower, to find and claim the tip of her breast.

Pure fire shot through her nerve endings as her body responded to the moist heat of his mouth. Then he was between her legs, spreading them apart. She quivered and arched and cried out against his throat.

"Not yet, my love," Blade whispered in a strangled voice.

His hand was between them now, resting atop the soft nest of fair curls. Her aching intensified until she shuddered with it, her thighs trembling. Holding himself from her with his elbow, he explored the quivering, burning softness of her, probing, withdrawing, his fingers driving her to the edge of madness. When he felt her control slipping, he arched his buttocks and pushed inside her heated warmth. Shannon cried out, clutching at his back to keep from falling too soon into the bottomless pit of ecstasy.

In eager response, Blade moaned deep in his throat,

driving himself deeper—deeper still, until Shannon felt him touch her womb, her very soul. Then she knew no more as her world shattered into blinding rapture. Hearing her soft moans sparked Blade's stampeding passion as he exploded again and again into the receptive heat of her body.

Twice more during the night Blade reached for her, and Shannon responded eagerly, her ardor still as strong as it was during their first coming together. Each time she made love with Blade was unique, an experience like none other; he was so good at it, she felt sorry for all the women in the world who would never know his special brand of love. A weak dawn colored the sky when they finally fell asleep in each other's arms, vowing never to part again.

Three inches of new snow covered the ground when Blade and Shannon awoke the next morning. The sky was clear and it had stopped snowing. Famished, Blade dressed quickly, urging Shannon to hurry. He was eager to reach Cheyenne and see his son. When Blade stepped from the tent, he let loose a curse that brought Shannon rushing to his side.

She looked around, stunned. "My God, Blade, what does this mean?"

Her eyes moved nervously around the circle of Indians surrounding their campsite. Jumping Buffalo offered an apologetic smile and shrugged his shoulders.

Blade walked slowly to where Red Cloud sat his horse, his face dark with anger. Blade spoke in Sioux, which Shannon tried to follow. "You no longer have reason to hold me, Red Cloud. The governor of Wyoming has kept his promise. Even as we speak, your provisions are on their way to the reservation."

"How do you know this, Swift Blade?"

"I would not dishonor my grandfather by lying to you. Jumping Buffalo and my wife passed them on the trail."

Red Cloud's penetrating gaze slid to Shannon, scrutinizing her thoroughly, finally settling on Jumping Buffalo. "You have seen this with your own eyes?"

"Swift Blade speaks the truth. Pony soldiers from Fort Laramie ride along to protect the provisions from renegades."

Obviously satisfied, the chief turned his gaze back to Blade. "Your woman does not look heavy with child."

"I have a son," Blade boasted proudly, placing an arm around Shannon's shoulders and pulling her close.

"What is she doing here? Why did she not stay in your lodge and wait for you to return?"

Blade smiled indulgently. "Little Firebird is a stubborn woman. She does as she pleases. She persuaded Jumping Buffalo to escort her to the reservation so she might plead for my life."

Red Cloud's thick brows angled upwards as he impaled Shannon with his dark gaze. Though his features remained unreadable, Shannon thought she recognized a grudging respect in his eyes. "Were Little Firebird mine, I would beat her," he declared haughtily.

"Perhaps I will," Blade agreed, a smile tugging at the corners of his mouth.

Suddenly Red Cloud raised an arm high in the air, wheeled his horse, and shouted a command that reverberated like thunder in the stillness of the snow-shrouded prairie. Then he rode off, his dozen or so warriors following close behind. Not until they were out of sight did Shannon allow herself to breathe normally.

"Where are they going?"

"To meet the supply train, I would imagine," Blade said. "Heaven help us if he doesn't find them."

Fortunately for them, Red Cloud did find the supply train. The next day Blade and his party encountered them, their ranks swelled by Red Cloud and his warriors. Blade assumed Red Cloud was taking no chances on the supplies reaching the reservation and remained with the supply train to provide escort.

Two days later Shannon and Blade rode into Cheyenne while Jumping Buffalo and Sweet Grass returned to Peaceful Valley. When they reached home, Shannon suddenly realized she hadn't told Blade yet about her appointment to the office of Justice of the Peace. But first things first. After he had greeted his son was time enough.

Grady Farrell was a tiny replica of his father, except for his eyes, which were a deep blue like Shannon's. He gurgled happily as Blade cuddled him in his arms; it was almost as if he knew immediately that this was his sire.

"He's a handsome little lad," Blade admired, ruffling the soft fringe of black hair covering his head.

"He's the picture of his father," Shannon returned, smiling impishly.

"I want to provide him with the best of everything, my love. We'll build the ranch into something our children can be proud of. I don't ever want them to be ashamed of their Indian blood, but neither do I want them to suffer for it. You should have married someone people respect instead of a half-breed."

"It was you I loved," Shannon said with quiet dignity, "you I wanted. Besides," she added with a twinkle, "things have changed for us." Shannon decided she couldn't find a better time to tell Blade about her appointment.

Blade slanted her an oblique look. "What in the hell have you been up to in my absence?"

"Oh, Blade, I have some wonderful news," Shannon gushed. "So much has happened I don't know where to begin. First, the women's rights amendment was passed in December. Women can now vote and hold office. Isn't that wonderful?"

"I agree, love, it is wonderful. It's no more than women deserve."

"Are you ready now for the really extraordinary news?"

"You mean it gets better than this?" he teased.

"Much better," she beamed. "I've been appointed Justice of the Peace. I'm to start hearing cases shortly."

Blade was stunned. He knew Shannon was greatly respected for her work with the suffrage movement, but he never expected so great a reward. His chest swelled with pride, and transferring the baby to one arm he hugged Shannon with the other.

"I always knew you were special. I'm happy someone besides me recognized your worth. But—well, frankly, I'm worried," he admitted. "How will the townspeople take this?"

"You're going to find this difficult to believe, Blade, but feelings about us have altered ever since you convinced Red Cloud to return to the reservation. Even Ezra Samms came by to apologize, as did others who had spoken out against you."

"Apologies won't bring back our cattle or rebuild our house," Blade said. He was still bitter over the loss of his home and livelihood. His losses would be nearly impossible to replace given his reduced finances.

"We'll start over," Shannon vowed earnestly. "Nothing will stop us this time."

"We have barely enough cash to live on," Blade admitted with brutal honesty.

"We'll have my fees," Shannon contended eagerly. "Spring is almost here. You can hire men and start rebuilding. It will work out, darling, you'll see."

Blade hated to dash Shannon's hopes, but he was a realist who knew it might take years of working for others before they could replace what they had lost. Prejudice and people's unwarranted fear had made their lives hell. It wasn't easy to forget or forgive. He revealed none of his thoughts to Shannon as she rambled on about Peaceful Valley and all her grand plans for their future.

February was a dismal month, winter's hold not yet broken. To Blade's surprise, Shannon's words about being accepted by the townspeople proved correct.

When he ventured out now, everyone he met on the street was eager to greet him. Where formerly he was shunned and feared, now people rushed over to shake his hand and express their gratitude for his help in persuading Red Cloud to return to the reservation.

By mid-February, Shannon was settled in her office hearing civil cases almost daily. She found the work stimulating and interesting despite the fact that it kept her from her child too many hours during the day. Thank God for Meg Ryan, who was still with her to care for Grady.

By the end of March, Blade was forced into a decision he dreaded making. The hills and valleys were turning green with new grass and streams ran high with winter run-off. He knew Shannon expected him to start rebuilding their cabin, but a careful tally of their savings told him the money just wasn't available. He might be able to erect a frame with Jumping Buffalo to help him, but what purpose would it serve? He deliberately postponed the decision until far into April, hoping for a miracle.

Blade was totally unprepared when the miracle he had been praying for arrived unexpectedly.

It was Saturday and Shannon had no cases to hear that day. She and Blade lingered over breakfast, discussing the adorable antics of their six-month-old son. Blade seemed distracted, his conversation stilted and remote. Elizabeth Davis had informed him yesterday that her son and his bride were returning from abroad and would need their house. He had yet to tell Shannon.

Suddenly he looked at Shannon squarely and said, "Shannon, I've postponed a decision long enough. It's time now to decide—"

A terrible racket at the door brought his words to a skidding halt.

"Swift Blade, open, it is Jumping Buffalo!"

Blade and Shannon exchanged alarmed glances, then Blade leaped to his feet, rushing to the door.

"Something is wrong!" Shannon was close behind him.

Jumping Buffalo seldom if ever came to town and both knew something serious must have happened to bring him there now. Blade flung open the door and the look on Jumping Buffalo's usually stoic features sent his heart plummeting.

"What is it, Jumping Buffalo? Has something happened to Sweet Grass?"

"No, my friend," Jumping Buffalo answered in rapid Sioux. "But a strange thing has occurred at Peaceful Valley. Something you will find difficult to believe."

"Come in and tell us what troubles you."

"There is no time. You must come to Peaceful Valley—now, to see for yourself."

"See what?"

"Cattle, my friend. All the cattle that were stolen months ago have mysteriously reappeared. Even as I speak, they gaze contentedly on the rich grass that grows in the valley."

"What is it, Blade? You're speaking too rapidly for me to follow. Is Sweet Grass all right?"

Blade quickly explained. Shannon's mouth flew open in dismay. "What does it mean?"

"I don't know, but I intend to find out. I'm going to Peaceful Valley."

"I'm coming with you," Shannon insisted, allowing him no time to protest. "Just give me a few minutes to dress the baby."

Blade stopped the wagon on a ridge behind the burnt shell of their cabin. The view was breathtaking, allowing them a panoramic view of the land Blade had aptly named Peaceful Valley. Shannon drew her breath in sharply, unable to believe what her eyes beheld. Grazing on the verdant hillsides, just as Jumping Buffalo had described, were cattle—over a hundred head.

"My God," Blade whispered reverently.

"Is it not as I said?" Jumping Buffalo told them sweeping his arm in a wide arc.

"Whose brand do they carry?" Blade asked, stil unconvinced. "That should tell us who they belong to."

"It is your brand," Jumping Buffalo said. "I have seen this with my own eyes."

"My cattle," Blade said softly, turning to Shannon. His eyes widened in wonder and disbelief. "Our cattle, Little Firebird—do you know what that means?"

Shannon nodded, too awed to speak. She did indeed know what it meant. It meant their dream of rebuilding their ranch and making it into something their children could be proud of was no longer beyond the horizon, but lay within their reach. Their future in the territory that had just become the first in the entire nation to give women the freedom they deserved was suddenly bright.

Shannon was proud to be counted as a citizen of the great Territory of Wyoming. Nowhere else in the world was she free to vote and make decisions nor mally restricted to men. The country was wild and untamed, just like Blade, but she liked it that way. Wyoming was her destiny.

"Shall we ride down?" Blade asked at length. " want to have a closer look at those cows."

"Oh, yes," Shannon agreed with alacrity. "Swee Grass will be anxious to see Grady."

Shannon was surprised and pleased to learn tha Sweet Grass was expecting a child, and the two women settled down together for a pleasant chat while Blade and Jumping Buffalo rode off to inspect the cattle.

"After our cabin is built, we will build one for you and Jumping Buffalo," Shannon promised. "You'l want something more permanent than a tipi for you family. And Blade certainly couldn't get along with out your husband's help. It will be good having another woman out here for company. Our children will grow up together."

Sweet Grass smiled shyly. "I would like that, if I can convince Jumping Buffalo to live within wooden walls. My people are no longer free to roam where they will. I don't want my children to grow up knowing only fear and hunger."

"They won't, Blade will—" Her words ground to a halt as she gazed over Sweet Grass's shoulder, fear turning her eyes dark.

"What is it, Little Firebird?"

"Wagons, lots of them. And people. My God! Blade! Where is Blade?"

Shannon jumped to her feet, relieved to note that Blade had already seen the intruders and was riding toward them hell for leather. Jumping Buffalo was hard pressed to keep up with him. She waited until he reined in beside her before asking, "What do they want? It looks like the whole town is riding out to Peaceful Valley."

"I don't know, love, but I'm not taking any chances," Blade replied, checking his weapons. "Take Sweet Grass and the baby inside the tipi. Don't come out until I tell you."

"Surely you don't think—"

"I don't know what to think," Blade said tightly. "Just do as I say."

Shannon hugged Grady protectively as she and Sweet Grass huddled together inside the tipi. Both recalled with vivid clarity what happened the last time visitors came to Peaceful Valley. Judging from the deafening roar of wagon wheels, Shannon had been right when she said earlier that it appeared as if all of Cheyenne was coming to Peaceful Valley. What chance would Blade and Jumping Buffalo have against so many? she wondered bleakly.

"Do you have a gun?" she asked Sweet Grass in sudden determination.

"Jumping Buffalo keeps a rifle here for my use."

"Give it to me."

Sweet Grass obeyed instantly. "What will you do with it?"

"Here, take the baby, I'm going to help Blade."

Sweet Grass scowled disapprovingly, but it did little to dissuade Shannon as she dumped Grady in the Indian woman's arms, picked up the rifle, and slipped outside. She was astounded to see at least twenty wagons and more people than she could count grinding to a halt before Blade and Jumping Buffalo. She had the presence of mind to note that not only men, but women and children were climbing down from the wagons. Many people she recognized, including Ezra Samms, who was the cause of much of their trouble. It was Samms who approached them now, and Shannon stepped to Blade's side in open defiance.

Seeing Shannon beside him, Blade scowled fiercely. "What in the hell are you doing here? I told you to stay with Sweet Grass."

"I want to help," Shannon said stubbornly.

"We don't mean no harm, Mrs. Stryker." Samms was close enough to hear Shannon's words.

"Why have you come?" Blade asked curiously. Though his voice was low, it was filled with quiet menace.

"Me and the townspeople, we—uh—" Samms shifted uncomfortably. "Well, dammit, we want to make it up to you for all the trouble we caused you."

"You are responsible for the return of my cattle?" Blade asked, comprehension dawning.

"A man does what he has to do," Samms muttered. "We want you to know how grateful we are for what you did for the Territory. We want to show our appreciation."

Blade's dark gaze left Samms and swept over the crowd of men, women, and children, and a puzzled frown wrinkled his brow. He still didn't understand what all these people were doing here.

"In what way?" Shannon wanted to know.

"We going to rebuild your house, Mrs. Stryker," Samms said, twisting his hat in his hands.

"That's right," agreed another, separating from the crowd. "We brought lumber, nails, everything needed to build as good a cabin as the one that got burnt. And our women brought food aplenty. We'll come back as many days as necessary to complete the job."

"I—I don't understand," Shannon gasped, thinking it all a wonderful dream.

All the values she had learned at her mother's knee, all her belief in the basic goodness of mankind had never been demonstrated so forcefully or dramatically as it was today. She and Blade no longer had to reach beyond the horizon to fulfill their dreams. Everything they desired in life was right here in Peaceful Valley.

Blade reached for Shannon, hugging her close as the men started unloading the wagons and the women saw to the food.

"If this is a dream, I never want to awaken," he said, his voice taut with emotion. "And to think I almost considered leaving Wyoming and settling someplace where we might live in peace."

"It's no dream, Blade," Shannon sniffed, close to tears. "I knew one day people would come to their senses where you are concerned."

"It is you they respect," Blade suggested.

"No, my love, you earned their respect. You may be part Sioux, but I've never known a more honorable man. I'm proud of what you are and who you are. I love you, Blade Stryker. I wish my family could meet you."

"You miss them very much, don't you?"

"I'd be lying if I denied it."

"We'll visit them one day, I promise. Didn't you say both your mother and brother had married?"

"Yes, and I'm truly happy for them. Mama married David Foster, the wagon master, and Tucker is wed to Maggie. I understand Maggie led Tuck quite a chase, but it all ended well. According to Tuck's last letter, he is quite anxious to meet you."

"We'll meet one day," Blade promised. "Shall we join the builders? Our new cabin can't be built soon enough to suit me. I'm anxious to make love to you in our own home. And just in time, too. Elizabeth Davis informed me just yesterday that her son will be returning from abroad with his bride and will need his house. If Grady doesn't have a brother or sister soon, he's going to be one spoiled little boy," Blade said with a twinkle.

"It's unlikely Grady will be an only child," Shannon returned tartly, "for you were well named, Blade Stryker."

Laughing uproariously, Blade grasped her hand and together they walked out to greet a bold new tomorrow.

Epilogue

July 1870

The heat was thick and oppressive this July day; a sere wind blew across the valley in hot, dry gusts, bringing Blade in early from the range. Pearly drops of water glistened wetly on his black hair, for he had come directly from his bath in the stream.

"Next week we drive the cattle to Cheyenne to sell to the army," he said after he greeted Shannon with a hug. In addition to Jumping Buffalo, Blade had re-hired the two hands, Slim and Milo. Fortunately, they were eager to return to work. "Is the baby sleeping?"

"Grady is napping," Shannon answered, stepping easily into Blade's arms.

It had taken two weeks for the townspeople to rebuild a cabin every bit as big and sturdy as the one Blade built originally. Someone had worked every day, though not always the same ones each day. They usually were accompanied by their wives, who brought food and made a picnic out of each meal. When the house was completed, enough lumber had

remained to build a sturdy cabin for Jumping Buffalo
and Sweet Grass. The money Shannon had saved
from her fees as Justice of the Peace were used
primarily to replace the furnishings lost to the fire.

Shannon had continued to function as Justice of the
Peace for a short time, but when they moved out to
Peaceful Valley she had resigned, citing her need to be
with her family. She was grateful for the honor
accorded her and relished her role in shaping the
future of women in Wyoming politics. But her family's needs came first. Blade had left the decision to
Shannon but seemed pleased with her choice, though
his pride in her accomplishments was boundless.

"Are you hungry?" Shannon asked.

"Famished—but not for food."

He kissed her hungrily, thoroughly, his hands roaming freely over her lush curves.

"It's the middle of the day," Shannon chided with
mock horror, loving how Blade smelled after his bath,
the way his hair curled wetly at his nape, the feel of his
ropy muscles beneath her fingertips.

"Making love with you is a pleasure any time of the
day or night," Blade asserted, grinning roguishly as he
edged her toward the bedroom. "And as long as our
son is cooperating . . ."

"Blade, wait, I hear something," Shannon stalled as
the distinct creak of wagon wheels reached her ears.
"Are you expecting company?"

"No, are you?"

"I don't think so."

Blade grasped her hand and together they stepped
through the front door onto the porch to await their
guests, who approached in a horse-drawn wagon.

"I wonder who it is?" Shannon mused thoughtfully.
"Perhaps Elizabeth . . ." Her words ground to an halt
when a man jumped to the ground then turned to help
the woman and child who accompanied him. "My
God!"

Shannon paled, then broke out in a wide grin.
"Tuck! It's my brother Tucker!" She took off at a run

throwing herself into her brother's open arms.

Blade stood where Shannon had left him, unwilling to intrude on so private a moment between brother and sister. Besides, he was more than a little doubtful of the greeting he would receive from Tucker Branigan.

"I can't believe you are really here," Shannon exclaimed happily, shifting her gaze from her brother to the lovely, slim woman standing at his side. "This must be Maggie. I can see right off you are perfect for one another. I'm so happy you brought your son." Shannon was so excited she couldn't seem to stop babbling.

Tucker's warm brown eyes crinkled with amusement. "You haven't changed, Shannon—still as impetuous as ever, I see. If you quit talking long enough, I'll introduce you to my wife." He placed an arm around the woman at his side and drew her close. "This is Maggie, and the little lad is our son Kevin. Maggie, meet my sister Shannon."

Maggie Branigan stepped forward, her smile warm and friendly as she gave Shannon an exuberant hug. Shannon liked her immediately, from her curly mop of honey-brown curls to her dancing gray eyes. She'd bet her last dollar that her stubborn sister-in-law led Tucker a merry chase. It was easy to see why Tuck loved Maggie. And it was just as obvious that Maggie loved Tucker. Shannon was glad Tucker had never married that flighty Charmaine Pinkham.

"You are everything Tuck said you were," Maggie said admiringly. "I'm so happy we've met at last. We received your letter announcing the birth of your son and just had to come."

"Yes, Grady Farrell is quite a boy," Shannon beamed proudly.

"Are you happy, Shannon?" Tucker asked, turning serious. "Mama has been terribly worried, especially after we learned you married a—a man with Indian blood."

"You are the last person in the world I'd expect to

harbor prejudices," Shannon chided. "Wait until you meet Blade before you make rash judgments. Blade and I are extremely happy. I couldn't ask for a better husband. Come along now," she said, taking his hand, "it's time you two met."

Tucker glanced over at Blade, who hadn't moved from his position on the porch since Shannon left his side. His expression was unreadable, the planes and hollows of his proud features mute testimony to his Indian heritage. But knowing Shannon as he did, Tucker felt reasonably certain she would not have married a man unless he lived up to her high standards.

Blade regarded Tucker Branigan with unaccustomed nervousness. What if Shannon's brother didn't like him? he wondered dismally. What if his Sioux blood lost him her family's regard? Not that it made any difference, he told himself. Shannon was his wife and no one could change that. Blade's expression remained proud and remote as introductions were made, both men wary and somewhat reticent until lasting impressions could be formed.

"Come inside," Shannon invited them. "I'll bet you're exhausted after your trip—and hungry." She couldn't help but chatter nervously, wanting so desperately for Blade and Tuck to like one another.

"Tell me about Mama," Shannon urged once they were all settled in the comfortable parlor that felt at least ten degrees cooler than outside. "And the children."

By the time Tucker finished, Shannon's eyes were misty. "I miss them all," she sighed wistfully. Then, thinking how it must sound to Blade, she added, "But I am truly content here with Blade. Wyoming is my home now, I wouldn't want to be anywhere but here with Blade and our son."

"Where is my nephew?"

"Napping, but it is past time he woke up. I can't wait for Kevin and Grady to meet." Shannon rose to leave the room.

"Wait, Shannon, I'll go with you," Maggie offered, taking Kevin by the hand. She was astute enough to realize that unless the two men opened up to one another, the tension between them would mount. She hurried after Shannon, intending to keep her away as long as possible in order to give Tucker and Blade time to get acquainted.

"I'm impressed with your ranch," Tucker said when the silence grew impossibly long. "Seems like a good place to raise cattle."

Blade allowed a smile to lift his dark features. "That's what I thought the first time I saw Peaceful Valley."

After that short exchange the tension increased, as if neither man knew what to say next. Suddenly Blade blurted out, "I love her, you know."

"What!"

"Shannon. She and our son are more important to me than the air I breathe. They are my life. Without them I am nothing."

Tucker's mouth flew open. Blade Stryker hardly seemed the type to utter flowery phrases. He looked hard and tough and dangerous. But obviously Shannon had tamed the beast in him. He smiled a secret smile. The Shannon he knew was badly in need of taming herself. She had always been a headstrong termagant, but now she appeared every inch the devoted wife and mother. She and Blade seemed a perfect match, though Tucker hadn't a doubt in his mind that when they clashed, explosions could be heard for miles around.

"I must admit I was worried when Shannon wrote that she was remaining in Wyoming and marrying a—"

"—half-breed," Blade finished tightly.

"A man with Indian blood," Tucker corrected. "I don't hold that against you, not if you are half the man Shannon said you were. We heard all about you in town, Blade. And Shannon, too. You can't imagine how proud I am of my little sister. But I'm not sorry I came to Wyoming. I had to prove to myself that Shannon is content with her life."

"And if she weren't?"

"I'd take her and Grady to Boise where she has a family who loves her," Tucker said without a moment's hesitation. "But I can see now that won't be necessary. I read my sister very well. Shannon is happy with you, Blade, and with your life together. I'll not interfere with that."

"You would have had one helluva fight if you had tried to take Little Firebird and our son from me," Blade said, his face set in hard lines.

"Little Firebird?"

"An Indian name I gave Shannon long ago. But don't get me wrong, I respect the love Shannon shares with her family. I wouldn't change it for the world."

"Then we understand one another perfectly," Tucker smiled, "for I'd never interfere with your lives as long as you and Shannon love one another and are happy together."

Tucker extended his hand. Blade hesitated only a moment before grasping it. That is how Shannon and Maggie found them when they reentered the room.

"I'm glad you and Tuck got on so well," Shannon said later, sighing contentedly as she snuggled against Blade in their wide bed. "I'm so excited about his visit and meeting Maggie and Kevin, I don't think I can sleep.

"Isn't it strange how values change as one matures?" she mused thoughtfully. "At one time I thought nothing existed outside of Twin Willows. I was unable to look beyond the horizon to the future that awaited me with the man I love. No matter how special my family is, they can't compare to you or the love we share."

"A woman as special as you has to come from a special family. I look forward to meeting the whole clan."

"Did you really mean what you said earlier about taking me to Boise soon?"

"If Tucker and Maggie wait until our cattle are sold next week, we can make the trip together. Would you like that?"

"Oh, Blade, you know just what to say to make me the happiest!" Shannon exclaimed joyously. "Now if you only knew how to make me sleepy," she hinted coyly.

A wolfish grin spread over Blade's face as he rolled over, pinning Shannon beneath him. "I know exactly how to make you sleepy."

Later, much later, Shannon wholeheartedly agreed as she sighed in contented exhaustion and drifted off to sleep.

A LETTER FROM
THE AUTHOR

Dear Readers:

BEYOND THE HORIZON is a tribute to women. I firmly believe it wasn't men who conquered the West, it was women. But first they had to conquer the men. Frontier women convinced Saturday-night men to stick around until Tuesday, so to speak. They would not be ruled by convention, but demanded their own way, and fought for it fiercely.

I chose Wyoming as the setting for Shannon Branigan's story because of the state's liberal treatment of women. Wyoming was the first in the nation to allow women to vote and hold office. The Territory in 1869 was wild, untamed, and still beset by Indians, but women braved these hazards in true pioneer spirit. Shannon's story is a tribute to the pioneer spirit of women the world over and to the great state of Wyoming.

I know you enjoyed Tucker Branigan's story, PROMISED SUNRISE, by Robin Lee Hatcher, and hope you liked my continuation of the Branigan saga.

I would love to hear from you. Write to me in care of my publisher. I answer every letter I receive and will send bookmark and newsletter. SASE is appreciated.

All My Romantic Best,

Connie Mason

Connie Mason

DON'T MISS THE STUNNING BEGINNING . . .

PROMISED SUNRISE

Robin Lee Hatcher

Bestselling Author of *THE WAGER* and *DREAM TIDE*

A Leisure Book

AN EXCERPT FROM ...

PROMISED SUNRISE
Robin Lee Hatcher

The luxuriant grass of the Kansas prairies in mid-May spread before the Foster wagon train like a rolling green sea. Wild flowers bloomed amid the grass like colorful banners, proclaiming the beauty of this untamed land. The spring climate was mild, the plains bucolic.

By their third week on the trail, the emigrants had become more proficient at handling their livestock and wagons, the routine a part of them now. Though the days were long and filled with hard work, their mood was light. By evening, the wagons circled and their camps made, they still had the energy for games and dancing.

Night had fallen. The May evening was balmy. The sky was dotted with a thousand tiny lights. Beyond the wagon at her back, Maggie could hear the fiddle playing, the hands clapping as couples danced and sang. It was a merry sound, and she was tempted to join the others. She felt lonely, yet stubbornly kept herself at arm's length from everyone on the train, reminding herself again and again that she couldn't trust anyone but herself to take care of Rachel, to insure the security of their future.

But her determination didn't lessen her loneliness, a feeling exacerbated by Rachel's defection.

Her shy, little sister had become fast friends with Fiona. Rachel now slept every night in the wagon, and as much as Maggie sometimes wanted to stop her, she couldn't allow herself to force Rachel to sleep on the hard, lumpy ground when she could share a bed with Fiona.

But worse that the friendship with Fiona, in Maggie's opinion, was Rachel's affection for Tucker. It had begun that first night when he'd told Rachel the story about his dog to distract her thoughts from a dead rabbit. Each day, she'd grown a little more at ease with him, until last night, Maggie had actually seen her climb into Tucker's lap and ask him to tell her another story about his hound.

Was Maggie destined to be all alone in this world?

"Why don't you join us, Maggie?"

Tucker's softly spoken words, coming in the wake of her own silent question, brought a startled gasp to her lips. She turned her head and saw him leaning against the end of the wagon, hidden in shadows, only his outline and the red glow of this thin cigar indicating his presence.

"I'm fine where I am." she replied. Even she could hear the lie in her words.

He dropped the cigarillo to the earth and ground it under the heel of his boot, then stepped toward her. "You know, the Branigans aren't really such a bad lot."

"I know." She looked back up at the night sky.

He came closer. "Come on. You might make some friends if you let yourself."

Maggie shook her head and felt a funny thudding in her chest.

"Maggie . . ."

She refused to look at him, her thoughts a mass of confusion.

"Dance with me, Maggie Harris."

She hugged herself with her arms, suddenly chilled, her pulse quickening even more. "I . . . I don't know how to dance."

He reached out and took hold of her hand, pulling her to her feet. "It's easy," he whispered somewhere near her ear. "I'll show you."

Don't do this. Don't do this. Don't do this.

He was right. It was easy. His hand at the small of her back guided her effortlessly in slow, easy circles. Her small, callused hand had disappeared within his much larger, more callused one. There was a strange buzzing in her head. She could barely hear the music now.

Maggie had never been held in a man's arms like this. She was aware of his scent. He'd washed in the stream. She knew because it wasn't the smell of sweat and dust. It was . . . It was Tucker. Her nostrils flared slightly. Her head felt light, and she was scarcely aware when he drew her closer to him.

Suddenly, he stopped dancing, yet the music played on. Questioningly, she lifted her face so she could look up at him, her mouth opening to speak. She was silenced by his descending lips. Heat spread through her, searing but slow, like red lava flowing from a volcano. She couldn't move, couldn't think. She could only feel.

Tucker still held her head between his hands as he drew back. She didn't move. She didn't seem to be breathing. He stared at her, unable to see her face in the darkness, yet knowing exactly how she must look. Like she'd been kissed for the first time.

Why had he done it? What was it about her that made her so desirable, so unforgettable?

It was more than her beauty. There was an innocence about her, as if she'd spent her life closed off from everything in the world. And, despite her strength, her stubbornness, her determination, he sensed fear was very much a part of Maggie. He wanted to drive that fear out of her. He wanted to make her feel safe and secure. He wanted . . .

What did he want from her? To find relief for the building fire within him? No, that wouldn't be fair to Maggie. He couldn't use her lightly. But he hadn't anything to offer her. He'd learned his lesson with Charmaine. He wasn't about to make a fool of himself again with a woman. Besides, he was virtually penniless, bound for who knew what in a scarcely settled territory, armed only with dreams for a better future but no guarantees he would find it. He had a mother and two small children to look after. Tucker had nothing to offer Maggie Harris.

Tucker dropped his hands. "I'm sorry, Maggie. I shouldn't have done that."

He turned and walked into the night shadows.

Maggie stood still for what seemed an eternity, letting the foreign sensations sweep over her again and again. Then, at last, she realized what he'd said.

I'm sorry, Maggie. I shouldn't have done that. Shouldn't have done that . . . Shouldn't have done that. . . .

Tears filling her eyes, she crawled beneath the wagon, feeling more alone than ever, and wept.

It was late afternoon when the train approached the Big Blue, a tributary of the Kansas River. Tucker sat on his black gelding, waiting while David's eyes surveyed the river.

Tucker had spent the day riding point with the wagon master, and he'd done it for one reason only— to avoid Maggie. Every time he thought of her, he was reminded of the way she'd felt in his arms as they'd danced the night before. He could almost smell the fragrance of her hair, taste the sweetness of her lips.

Branigan . . . he warned himself silently, cutting off his train of thought.

". . . should be able to ford it."

Tucker realized David was speaking. "What?"

"I said, looks like we'll be able to ford it." David looked toward Tucker with a puzzled expression, then glanced up at the sky. "It'll be another hour 'fore the wagons get here. Soon as they do, we'll start 'em across."

Tucker surveyed the green oasis before them. "Why not stay on this side of the river tonight? Looks like a good place to rest to me. We've made camp in worse."

David chuckled. "You're right about it being the perfect place to stop. This is Alcove Springs. Wait'll you drink the water. You've never tasted anything so good." The wagon master's smile vanished. "But our luck's held just about as long as it's going to. It's going to rain tonight, and we'd better be on the other side when it does or we could be stuck here a long time."

Tucker glanced up at the sky. Only a pale blue expanse met his gaze, not even a whiff of clouds on the horizon. Rain?

Reading his thoughts, David said, "I can feel it in my bones, son. Trust me."

Tucker nodded. He knew it must be important or David wouldn't push the day into evening. He suspected there would be some grumbling, though, when people saw they weren't going to make camp in this idyllic little spot on the trail.

By the time the Branigan wagon reached the bank of the Big Blue and was ready for crossing, black clouds were rolling across the sky, ominously heavy with rain. The wind had risen, whipping words away as men shouted at mules and oxen.

After tying Blue Boy to the rear of the wagon, Tucker climbed up beside Maggie on the wagon seat. He didn't speak to her. He hadn't spoken to her all day. Maggie kept her eyes averted as Tucker took up the reins, aware of his quick glance inside the wagon at his mother and the children before he said, "Hold on, everyone."

She gripped the side of the seat. Was it Tucker's

closeness that frazzled her nerves or the darkenin
storm clouds overhead? Would they get all the wagon
across before the rain came? The clouds had alread
made it nearly as dark as night. Would they be able t
see? She peered across the river, her fingers tightenin
their hold as the wagon jerked into motion.

No, it wasn't Tucker who was making her feel th
way. This was more than just nervousness. She wa
afraid. There were lots of emotions Tucker stirred i
her, but fear wasn't one of them. It couldn't be th
river crossing either. They'd crossed rivers an
streams before this. She'd even driven the team
across one or two herself this past week. Still, as th
wagon rocked from side to side, the wind whipping a
the canvas cover behind her, she had a terrible sens
of doom.

It came true midway across the river. But it wasn
the Branigan wagon that disaster struck. Maggi
heard the sound, like a tree splitting before it topple
to earth, then the Baker wagon in front of them tippe
sideways into the water.

"Tucker!" She grabbed hold of his arm. "The chi
dren."

She could see the two Baker boys bobbing in th
current as the river swept them away while thei
mother clung to the side of the wagon. Mr. Baker wa
nowhere to be seen. Without hesitation or fore
thought, Maggie jumped into the river and swam afte
them. Wind-whipped waves washed over her, hidin
the young boys from her sight. Her skirts, heavy wit
water, dragged at her ankles; the sturdy shoe
Maureen had given her threatened to pull her unde
She gasped and choked as the choppy water smote he
face.

Where were they?

She caught a glimpse of blond hair off to her left an
pulled herself in that direction. "Hang on!" she calle
but it was useless. Nothing could be heard above th
roar of the wind and river.

Just as she neared him, the boy was swallowed i

another wave. Panicky, Maggie groped beneath the surface. Her fingers touched something. His shirt. The collar of his shirt. With every ounce of her waning strength, she pulled upward. He fought against her, his arms flailing. She almost lost him but held tight as she sank with him into the darkness of the river. Together, they returned to the surface, and from somewhere deep within, she found the strength to help her pull the drowning boy to the edge of the river.

She pushed him onto the muddy bank, then dragged herself up beside him. She lay face down, drawing ragged breaths into her aching lungs and coughing up the water she'd swallowed moments before. Finally, her head clearing, she pushed herself onto her hands and knees and crawled over to the youngster. He was whimpering in fear, but he was alive.

"Miss Harris!" The voice was muffled, but she heard it all the same. "Maggie!"

She lifted her head. "Over here, Mr. Foster. We're over here."

The wagon master's big buckskin burst through the underbrush. David jumped down and hurried over to them. "Wills," he said as he picked up the boy.

Wills began to cry in full volume. David held him close against his burly chest. "What about Timmy?"

Maggie stared at him blankly, not understanding.

"What about his brother?"

Maggie shook her head. "I lost sight of him."

A pained expression passed across his weathered face before he said, "Come on. I'll get you back to the wagons." He pulled her to her feet. "It was a brave thing you did," he added.

She didn't feel brave, just tired.

With a hand under her elbow, David helped her into the saddle, then passed Wills Baker into her arms. The four-year-old child snuggled close against her as she wrapped her arms around him. She tried not to think about Timmy.

* * *

Tucker reached out to stop Maggie, but he was too late. She was swept away in the current, never hearing him call her name.

A moment later, a gust of wind shook the Branigan wagon. It rocked, then righted itself. The canvas top blew free from one corner and flapped noisily overhead.

Behind him, Fiona and Rachel were crying with fear. He glanced back to see Maureen, her own face registering horror as she held the two girls against her. Neal stood close by, his hand on their mother's shoulder, offering what boyish courage he could.

Tucker raised the whip and cracked it over the mule teams. He had to get his wagon out of the river. He had to get the rest of the family to safety before he could search for Maggie.

They skirted the Baker wagon as several men fought to right it against the river's current. He saw Mrs. Baker being carried to shore by a man on horseback but he didn't see Maggie.

God, don't let her drown, he prayed silently.

The moment the wagon wheels rolled up the bank, Tucker jumped to the ground and started running down river, hardly aware it had started to rain. He came upon them all of a sudden, Maggie and the boy astride David's enormous mount.

He stopped and stared at her in the growing gloom. Her hair was plastered against her scalp. Her dress was muddy and torn. She resembled a drowned rat.

She looked beautiful.

He moved slowly forward, reaching up to take Wills from her arms, then passing the boy to David. Turning once again toward Maggie, he took hold of her waist and lifted her to the ground. He was only vaguely aware of David walking on, leaving them alone.

"That was a crazy thing to do." He pushed her straggling hair back from her face.

She didn't answer, only looked up at him with wide gray eyes.

"Don't you ever do anything so foolish again." His hand slipped to her nape.

Rain water streamed down her face. Such a pale face, her skin almost pearl-white.

"Do you understand me, Maggie?" he said, so softly he could barely hear himself.

She just kept staring up at him with those blasted big eyes of hers, pools of gray he could almost drown in.

"Maggie . . ."

"I hear you, Tucker."

Heaven help him. He *was* drowning in her eyes.

The rain streamed down her face and into her eyes. She blinked to clear them, wanting to see him clearly, needing to understand the play of emotions she saw there. She ached for him to draw her closer. Ached for his mouth to touch hers once again.

What was happening to her?

She shivered as gooseflesh rose on her arms.

"You're cold. We'd better get you back to the wagons.

Not yet, her heart protested.

"Come on." His hand took hold of her elbow as he turned her around.

Was it rain or tears that blinded her? She stumbled as she took a step and suddenly found herself cradled in his arms. She pressed her face against his chest as her hands clasped behind his neck. She wished the wagons were farther away.

Connie Mason

The Laird of Stonehaven

He appears nightly in her dreams—magnificently, blatantly naked. A man whose body is sheer perfection, whose face is hardened by desire, whose voice makes it plain he will have her and no other.

Blair MacArthur is a Faery Woman, and healing is her life. But legend foretells she will lose her powers if she gives her heart to the wrong man. So the last thing she wants is an arranged marriage. Especially to the Highland laird who already haunts her midnight hours with images too tempting for any woman to resist.

- -

Viking!

CONNIE MASON

The first time he sees her she is clad in nothing but moonlight and mist, and from that moment, Thorne the Relentless knows he is bewitched by the maiden bathing in the forest pool. How else to explain the torrid dreams, the fierce longing that keeps his warrior's body in a constant state of arousal? Perhaps Fiona is speaking the truth when she claims it is not sorcery that binds him to her, but the powerful yearning of his viking heart.

___4402-1 $5.99 US/$6.99 CAN

Dorchester Publishing Co., Inc.
P.O. Box 6640
Wayne, PA 19087-8640

Please add $1.75 for shipping and handling for the first book and $.50 for each book thereafter. NY, NYC, and PA residents, please add appropriate sales tax. No cash, stamps, or C.O.D.s. All orders shipped within 6 weeks via postal service book rate. Canadian orders require $2.00 extra postage and must be paid in U.S. dollars through a U.S. banking facility.

Name_____
Address_____
City_____ State_____ Zip_____
I have enclosed $_____ in payment for the checked book(s).
Payment <u>must</u> accompany all orders. ❏ Please send a free catalog.
CHECK OUT OUR WEBSITE! www.dorchesterpub.com

CONNIE MASON

BOLD LAND BOLD LOVE

New South Wales in 1807 is a vast land of wild beauty and wilder passions: a frontier as yet untamed by man; a place where women have few rights and fewer pleasures. For a female convict like flame-haired Casey O'Cain, it is a living nightmare. And from the first, arrogant, handsome Dare Penrod makes it clear what he wants of her. Casey knows she should fight him with every breath in her body, but her heart tells her he can make a paradise of this wilderness for her.

___52274-8 $5.99 US/$6.99 CAN

The Rogue and the Hellion
CONNIE MASON

When an audacious highwayman holds up his coach and points a pistol at a rather crucial part of his anatomy, the Marquis of Bathurst has a critical choice to make—give up his dead brother's ring or lose the family jewels. Gabriel decides to part with the memento, but he will track down the green-eyed thief if it is the last thing he does.

When the most infamous member of the Rogues of London takes her in his arms, Olivia Fairfax knows his intentions are far from honorable. Gabriel's hot pursuit makes her pulse race, but is he after a lover or the hellion who dared to rob him at gunpoint? Either way, Olivia knows it is her turn to hand over the goods, and she is ready to give him both her body and her heart.